THE ROAD

John Ehle

Books by John Ehle

Fiction

The Road
The Land Breakers
Lion on the Hearth
Kingstree Island
Move Over, Mountain

Nonfiction

The Free Men
Shepherd of the Streets
The Survivor

THE ROAD

Harper & Row, Publishers

NEW YORK, EVANSTON,

AND LONDON

FIRST EDITION

LIBRARY OF CONGRESS CATALOG CARD NUMBER: 67-11334

L-Q

to M. S. Wyeth, Jr.

PART I

You can see it curled there on the mountain even now,
and hear the songs they sang at night—
   Lo, lo, baby, baby;
hear them moan way down buried in the very clay
they moved in order to put it there,
the Road, the iron road to Eden.

CHAPTER ONE

THE MOUNTAIN on whose body they were to work was set on the lowlands at Henry Station, which was a work camp being built by the Western North Carolina Railroad Company. It rose from that point, which was about 1,500 feet above sea level, to its peak, which was almost 5,000 feet. The mountain itself, in other words, was about two thirds of a mile tall. It was called Sow Mountain and was a massive monolith of earth, rock, vegetation and water, an elaborate series of ridges which built on one another to the top. From the base a man could see what he assumed was the top of the mountain and could walk there, only to find that he stood on the crest of a ridge which rested against the side of the mountain; he could walk to the top of the mountain as he had seen it from that ridge and find it also was the crest of a ridge and nothing more, and above lay the summit. So it went that by layers the mountain unfolded itself. Climbing to the top, Weatherby Wright once declared, was like ascending to some altitude of oneself.

The railroad they were to build was to scale the lower part of the mountain, turning and twisting about to take advantage of the most gradual ways until it reached the Swannanoa Gap, which was set into Sow Mountain and was the historic entryway to the mountain country, had served as such since the first settlers went up there about a hundred years earlier. The dome—topped heathland of the

3

mountain stood as sentinel over the Gap and those who passed that way.

In September, 1876, Weatherby Wright, the president, superintendent and chief engineer of the railroad company, moved his office to Henry Station and prepared to start the two-year operation authorized by the state government. He was forty-eight years of age, a big, deeply weathered man who had grown up in the mountains and at eighteen had left them to go to college. His main experience in life was roadmaking, and that had been got in the North, where he had lived for over twenty years, and where he had married a woman who was shy then and had remained shy, and who had borne him one son. She and the boy now lived in a large house he had rented for them on a park in the main residential area in Morganton, which was thirty-three miles from the mountain and was the place of the main yards of the company. She had wanted to move to Henry Station with him, but he had not agreed. "The workers will mostly be prisoners, Mildred," he told her. "It's no place for you to be."

"I'm afraid we'll grow apart," she said.

"No, no," he said. "No, Mildred. It's only for a little while, until the Road gets made to the Gap. Others can take it west from there."

"We've never been apart for long," she said. She was a pretty woman of forty-six, graying slightly, an infinitely patient and attentive person. She had always said the most fortunate thing she had ever done was marry Mr. Wright. "Do you have to use slaves? You've always been so much opposed to slavery of any sort."

"These aren't slaves. Convicts aren't slaves."

"Is there really a difference?" she said.

He looked at her for a long while, then nodded slowly and sighed. "I think so, Mildred."

All the buildings at Henry Station were of hand-hewn oak logs, barked and chinked. The two barracks buildings had two windows and one door each, the door made of double-thickness oak pegged nine times. There was one open fireplace inside each barracks, and a water trough located outside the main door; the water came from springs on the mountain and flowed through hollow split logs to the trough, then out into the ground.

Each of the barracks had a yard surrounded by a stockade made of foot-width, fifteen-foot high logs, buried four feet in the ground and pointed at the top.

On September 5, even as the final rails were laid from Old Fort to the Henry Station yard, Weatherby moved into his new quarters and began operations from there. He at once sent his chief foreman, Louis Babcock, out to rent mules and oxen from the neighborhood farmers; Babcock returned with word that not many farmers would rent stock unless money was in hand. Since the State Assembly had restricted its $70,000 annual appropriation to the purchase of iron and a few other materials, there was only the small profit from operating the Road—maybe a thousand dollars a month—to barter with. Weatherby bought twenty mules and six oxen himself and leased them to the Road, and Babcock rented such others as he could on credit.

About forty men were to be hired by the Road. Beyond that, there was an understanding with the state that as many as 600 convicts would be supplied. One hundred fifty were to be sent soon, along with fifteen guards. They would be housed at Henry Station, while about half the hired workers would move on up the mountain to construct a second camp. When that was completed, 150 more convicts would be dispatched to the Road. Finally the carpenters would build a major camp near the Gap, to be used by the convicts who were to make the tunnels, and 300 convicts would be sent there. It was agreed with the Prison Department that each convict was to receive one and one-third pounds of cornmeal per day, half a pound of fatback, and a serving of cabbage, potatoes or beans, and that injuries and sickness were the responsibility of the Prison Department, not the Road. Even the doctor's salary was to be paid by the Prison Department.

All this was contracted in writing.

On September 7 Weatherby wrote the Prison Department, asking for the first shipment of convict labor. One hundred fifty convicts were dispatched by train on September 13, 1876, and at once excitement swept the station. Word went quickly across the mountains that the work was about to begin; curious mountain men and boys, and a "scattering" of women began to arrive on the morning of the 30th, in wagons, on horseback, and on foot, mostly tall, lean blond people of Scotch-Irish and German ancestry. They stood waiting about Henry Station, visiting with each other and with Weatherby, who walked among them, asking how the farming had been and asking how his own people were. The men traded saddles, knives, bridles, whisky and brandy, and even horses.

At noon they were waiting still, though not as patiently. Some of them had had no food all day, so Weatherby ordered that cornbread be baked and cabbage be cooked with bacon. The mountain people ate it greedily. Somewhat full and better composed, they began to argue about religion, which introduced politics. This resulted in fist fights in which one young man was badly bitten on the shoulder by his opponent. He was helped to his horse and sent off in the direction of Old Fort, in hopes that he could find a doctor there.

A train was sighted soon after that and a shout went up, but Weatherby said it wasn't the convicts' train, for it had no boxcars. "I expect it's an excursion train from Morganton," he said. The engine was black, there was no gleam to it at all, even to its square metal lantern; there was no gleam to its wheels either. It was an odd piece of machinery, built before the Civil War, with a huge funnel set at the very front of it, threatening the balance of the whole, and with a boxlike open cab behind the horizontal boiler. There were eight wheels of equal size, and since it had been so constructed that the main and side rods moved in opposite directions, by reason of interposed gearing, the engine as it approached appeared to be trying to go in two directions at once, and, perhaps also as a consequence, it churned up dust and loose dirt from the track, which fanned out in waves at the sides and struck the bottom of the boiler with a big racket.

The cab had been enclosed with rough boards and canvas to help protect the engineer and fireman from the weather, but it had broken free at many places, adding a tattered, woebegone appearance to the whole, and sticking out of the canvas was the head of the grubby-faced engineer, a snuff stick jauntily poking out of one corner of his mouth.

"Morning," he called to Weatherby.

"Mornin'," Weatherby said. "How long did it take you?"

"Oh, an hour and a half. A Mr. Cumberland is on board."

"Who?"

"That college man who's bookkeeping for you."

The Mud Digger belched and shuddered to a stop. Two sweaty hired men tapped her cocks and she disgorged herself, enveloping herself and them in steam. As if in sympathetic action with their engine, Bolton and his fireman climbed down, unbuttoned their pants, and urinated on the ground.

A Negro picked up an oilcan with a long nozzle and began poking about among the boiler tubes. Another Negro climbed up on the engine, directing a water spout toward the orifice of the tender.

Two passenger cars were attached to the tender, and their occupants dismounted, talking boisterously about the speed with which they had arrived. Among them were several women, but Weatherby noticed with relief that Mildred was not one of them. Today's was simply not the sort of show he thought a woman ought to go out of her way to witness.

About three o'clock a shout went up that another smoke plume was in sight. At once several men put their ears to the rails and reported that a train was indeed near. The multitude, now numbering over two hundred fifty people, gathered on the station side of the track, and sent up a welcoming chant for the train and its human cargo. The engine, named the "Pioneer," appeared and with gasps and rumbles bore down on them, dragging five old cars, all tightly closed and securely locked. Its bell clanged for the track to be cleared, but the spectators crowded close by anyway, and the pressure from the back of the crowd was such that those up front were forced forward to meet the oncoming locomotive. The engineer and fireman responded with angry, insulting shouts, and Babcock fired shots in the air, warning the crowd, but the people pressed in close to both sides of the engine and cars. The train crept forward, steamy and creaking, its bell sounding ominously.

It stopped. The engineer spat onto the ground and looked out over the waves of faces until he saw Weatherby. "I brung all 150," he said.

Weatherby came forward. "Where are the guards?"

"In the last car playing cards," the engineer said.

Weatherby walked to the last car, a second-class mail and passenger car, and called to them. The guards were seated inside; he could see them in there, but they paid no attention to him. One of them, a big black-haired man, won the pot and laughed uproariously. Another picked up the cards and began to shuffle. Weatherby knocked on the door, but got no response. He nodded to Lou Babcock who took hold of a small log, came close to the door, and gave it such a blow that he tore the door loose. That brought the guards to their feet at once.

"You're at Henry Station," Weatherby told them. "Stand down." Behind him were several other railroad men, and behind them were many mountain men, so the guards left their cards where they were and did as they were told.

The first of the boxcar doors had been locked so securely that initial efforts to unlock them were futile. Weatherby told Babcock to shoot the lock off the door. The noise served further to impress the guards and quiet the onlookers. Warily four guards came forward to help roll the door open.

The opening door revealed a black room filled with forty chained convicts, whose eyes scowled out of their bruised faces at the watching congregation. All were Negroes except three, all were cut and battered, either from fights within the car or from the rough ride itself; all were filthy and smelly. They had lived inside the crowded car for two full days.

The chief guard, who was the big black-haired man, told them to get down.

They didn't move.

A bullwhip cracked. A big guard approached the door with it. It slashed out and two convicts, chained together, leaped to the ground and stood, catlike, watching. Others jumped. They were all chained two by two, so two jumped at a time. One pair fell when they struck the ground, and both tried to roll out of the way of the whip, which cut through the air near their heads.

The second car's door was shot open, revealing another forty filthy, resentful men, and these also jumped down, two by two.

The third doorway was shot open, and an even more angry, resentful group of forty white and Negro men stood there, all stripped to their waists, all naked except for striped britches. They were high-security prisoners, ankle-chained by a single long chain. The order was given for them to jump from the car, but they didn't move. The bullwhip slashed the air. Not one moved. The whip slashed against their bodies. The front line of men, unflinching, accepted the pain, thin lines of blood appearing on their bodies as the red gashes grew. The whip struck until a man finally leaped, dragging with him another; both men fell, and other men leaped and fell on top of them, dragging others, too, until the mass of men was on the ground below the train door, the bullwhip beating at them while the guards shouted at them to "get to your damn feet and get into ranks."

All of this the mountain people watched, stunned to silence and made wary by it. The convicts dragged themselves erect, some of them glaring at the others, cuffing or kicking them. "Get on!" the guards said, striking at them, and they untangled themselves and walked, a limping company, to form ranks.

When the fourth door was shot open, the spectators gasped, for thirty women stood there, all Negro except four. They were not chained, and when they were told to jump down, they did, young and old, some of them falling. They were dressed in gray prison dresses, which were filthy. They apparently had been fighting, for some of their dresses were torn and the dress of one elderly woman was little more than a rag. They were a bruised and smelly lot, and the mountain men drew back, their teeth showing, chuckling at suggestions of seductions.

Babcock bellowed out: "Where the hell did them women come from? We wanted 150 men."

The guards shrugged. They didn't care what he wanted.

"What the hell are we going to do with them?" Babcock demanded, pointing vaguely toward where the women stood, glaring at him.

"I brought what they sent," the chief guard, Blackie, said resentfully. "They can cook and wash, can't they?"

"We've been building this road all the way from Morganton to this mountain without women help." Babcock moved to face the women, frowning at them as if accusing them of some indiscretion. Abruptly he turned away from them, cursing, and shouted at his own men to count the convict men and parcel them out to the three foremen, each taking forty men as they came, nobody selecting the best ones for his own gang. "Everybody gets his share of the old and lame ones," he said. "And keep them women close to their boxcar. They'll have to live in there."

The men were counted out, the foremen watching apprehensively, each hoping not to get all the poorest men, nor the most rebellious. One convict limped to his place in line, and a guard shouted at him, "Stop that there limping, damn you," and the convict did so at once.

Babcock shouted out, "Get them to work. Get them mules and oxen and men to work! It's not much past three o'clock." The foremen gave instructions to their gangs, and the hired laborers ran to get the mules and carts and tools. The camp swirled with activity, and the crowd watched appreciatively, anxious to see the great long-promised enterprise begun. Their own wagons and horses were in the way, of course, and they were in the way, too, and the children kept trying to touch the convicts, to be able to say they had touched a convict, but all the confusion merely added to the spirit of festivity. The Road was about to begin; the men were going now to cut open the flank of the mountain.

The first gang set to work felling trees. Three small trees were downed, each one the cause for shouting of convicts and crowd, and for drinking among the men who had brought brandy or whisky. Babcock told the people they must stand back a ways or there would be no more work done. "There's never been a railroad built this-a-way," he announced. "It's unsightly what's going on here with this crowd." But Weatherby walked among the people and talked with them, pleased with them and the events, and the convicts, too.

The convict women were cooking supper in the outdoor kitchen, and they had stacks of cornbread and black pots full of beans stewing with bacon. They had made twenty gallons of coffee, using one part of coffee to four parts of rye. The excursionists and the mountain people made fires for cooking what they had or were able to forage. A few men went off into the forest and were heard shooting at game, and one man came back with a hog he had shot. The men brought in everything they could find and skinned it and put it on spits over the fire; men, women and boys squatted before the fires, talking about the start of the Road and wondering about the convicts, who surely were as rare and marvelous a sight as they had ever seen. Even men who had been in the Civil War and had seen prisoners said they had never seen anyone tougher and meaner looking than the convicts. The brutal faces of the men and the haggard appearance of the women moved the mountain men to make up stories to scare the children with. "That woman with the stringy hair, that old white woman there, once killed her husband with his own knife, cut him up, and put his parts under the stones of her own hearth. She cooked on him for a month."

"That there nigger once grabbed a pig out of his pen, bit a piece off and ate it raw, while the pig squealed."

"That man with the red eyes, he got them eyes from looking at the sun all day long, claiming he was Jesus come back to earth."

All this was most seriously explained, and the children were awed by it. The campfires became centers of storytelling.

"That there nigger woman by the cook pot, she bore a baby white as your hand and killed it with her own teeth."

"That man there by the fire dug up his father from a new grave, took the body home to his house and put it in a cradle. A week later it was found by his own neighbors, who smelled it two mile away and come to find him setting indoors a-rocking hit."

One singer remembered about a murder:

> He opened her bosom that was whiter than snow,
> And out of her eyes the tears they did flow.
> He pierced her to the heart, which caused blood to flow,
> And down in her grave her pale body he throwed.
>
> On to hell Sweet Willie did go,
> On to hell Sweet Willie did go,
> To pay to the Devil the debt he did owe.

As the convicts ate, the visitors drew near to watch them. One man, snickering, asked, "Does a nigger eat through his mouth or his nose?"

"Which end does he eat through?" somebody else said. There had never been many Negroes in the mountains, or even in Morganton, and the people were wary of them and curious about them.

The two groups, the convicts and the curious, moved about the pots, serving and eating and talking. Tin plates were provided the convicts, but one man dug his hand into the steaming pot itself, and came out with a big piece of bacon. A woman convict pinned his hand to the pot with a fork. "Let that go!" she said. "Drop it."

"You old hag," he said angrily. "You saving it for somebody else?"

"Let it go!" she screamed, stabbing him harder.

He tore his hand loose and swallowed the meat in a gulp.

Babcock shouted that he wouldn't abide the mixing and mingling of the visitors and the convicts, but the mixing went on anyway, and the eating and spitting and swallowing and talking and yelling. The visitors got some of the tin plates and the food, too, so the place was a bedlam of belching bodies moving about seeking acquaintances and strange sights, everybody heralding the start of the Road. Now and then Babcock would cast a worried look toward Blackie, the chief guard, but there was no way to stop the celebration.

Babcock told Weatherby that a riot might develop, but Weatherby rather enjoyed the excitement and did nothing to discourage it.

By the time the food was gone, which was before the women convicts were served anything they didn't grab for themselves from the bottoms of the pots, the sunlight was gone, too. There was no moon, for the sky was overcast and ugly, so the women, by the light of the fires, began to wash the black iron pots, rolling them down to the creek, guards keeping a close watch on them. The excursion train tooted its whistle, announcing that it was ready to start back to Morganton, and the weary, satiated excursionists wandered toward it, talking excitedly as they went, recalling the marvels of the day, turning to look one more time at the place where they had watched the convicts start the mountain road. But when they were all aboard and the engine had at last got up steam enough to leave, the mountain men took hold of the engine and announced their intention to detain it. A blacksmith from Swannanoa stationed himself on the track itself, facing it. The engineer swore they'd all be ground under or sucked through the funnel when he "opened her up," but they braced to hold the engine anyway. He told them to stand aside, but they would not. He let out a big expulsion of steam to startle and frighten them, but to no avail, so he opened the throttle.

The train wheels threshed on the tracks; the engine spun its wheels, that was all. It spun its wheels and made a loud noise. There it stood, skidding on its own small piece of track, the mountain men and boys shouting out in triumph. Babcock told the hired railroad men to push. "Help it start, damn them," he said. They pushed for all they were worth and the train began to creep forward. The blacksmith backed down the track, until he was actually running backward. He leaped aside, to escape being taken to Morganton on the cowcatcher, and he joined in as the men cheered him, and cheered the train and their own exploits, and prepared now at last to go on up the turnpike to their homes.

They were well pleased. They had had a good time at the new station. If the Road prospered as well as this day promised, it would win out over the challenges and arrive at the Gap in the two years allotted to the builders. Then the mountain people, instead of having every October to drive their hogs and sheep and cattle and geese and horses down the mountain trails to the Gap, and down the turnpike to Old Fort and Morganton, where they had to take what money they could get for them or drive them home again—instead of that, they could drive their stock to the railroad and sell them for a fair price and have them shipped out of the mountains to many markets. This was an old dream, twenty years discussed, and now, after the delays of the Civil War and other frailties, it was coming about, was being realized by a mountaineer named Zeb Vance, who was an ex-governor and the governor-elect, and by an engineer from the mountains whom the state had put in charge.

The Road had been born there at Henry Station today.

There were many fires left to put out. There were two horses still tied to trees; nobody in the camp knew whose they were. There was the sound of lonesome singing from the boxcar where the women were locked up for the night and from the two stockades.

Weatherby came out of the office building and walked to the main fire and said good night to the guards, who stood about drinking coffee. A few hired workers stood there, too, speculating about the work of the next day and wondering if any convicts would try to escape. It was idle talk, mostly.

Weatherby walked past the stockades, to the place where the trees had been felled, where a cut had been made in the hill. The night was quiet as death here now; this place of celebration but two hours before was a place of darkness only. He turned to look up at the side of the mountain and wondered, feeling strange at the thought, if the mountain was as lonely and forlorn as he, and felt as humble as he, here at the beginning of the enterprise. Old, old woman, he thought, we are ready to begin.

Could a mountain feel pain? he wondered. When men came with axes and cut at her, did she know it? When men bled her with picks and shovels, did she know it? When men severed the old arteries of her body and gouged out new ones, did she feel the sharp pain, did her huge body respond with fever or anguish? When men came and blasted on her shoulders and cut tunnels through her muscles, did she not know it, and did she know it in a single mind, or in many minds—in the way that a man also has many minds, as well as one mind? For the hand can think; it knows heat from cold and responds instantly. The heart can think, for it senses longing. How many hands has a mountain? he asked himself; how many different minds, how many hundred minds, and does it accumulate in one mind ever all that it thinks, and does it accumulate in one heart ever all that it feels? Does it not know heat from cold or light from darkness, or that today we received convicts to dig and cut and blast a road upon its back and through its flesh, cutting muscles and breaking bones?

He had grown up on the side of a mountain, one known to resent people. It had tangles of laurel and rhododendron to trap them; it had nests of snakes that haunted the caves and paths; it had more wolves than it could feed and accommodate. Over beyond the river, across the valley, was another mountain which never seemed to harbor animosity, which had no wolves; on its sides a man encountered no dangers at all, nobody ever got lost on its shoulders.

The moon appeared. It shone on the aged and wrinkled mass of rock above him, wrapped in night secrets, cloaked with major trees and massive bushes, all of them softened and tamed by the moonlight. Cloud wisps were now clinging to its ridges, and a cloud lay solemnly attentive at the Gap. "Old woman," he whispered, "I mean you no harm."

He went down to the creek, which made a rushing noise as it swept swiftly through this place, and he sat down there on a rock that was in the mist of the cascades. He got to thinking about himself, forty-eight, ready to start the big effort of his life. His father had been the same age when he died. He had taken cold one January, and in a few days he complained of headaches and a pain in his side. Weatherby's mother told the boy to fetch the gourd that contained pennyroyal, the only treatment she knew for pneumonia, which was a cold-weather scourge in the mountain country.

His father's fever soared, and by the fourth day he was so hot that he began to babble in his speech and say words that made no sense at all, and to talk to his own father, Mooney Wright, who had been dead for years. He even talked about the mountains and how they trapped a man in, how they were cruel and could chew a man to death—all of this Weatherby was hearing, but he realized his father was delirious.

"Does it kill always?" he asked his mother. He was standing at the foot of his father's bed, listening to his hoarse, hollow breathing.

"No, no," she said.

"If it kills, how does it kill?" he said.

"It smothers to death."

"That's an awful thing."

"Yes. He's preached many a funeral sermon following after it."

That was so; he was a preacher as well as a farmer and a miller. He did all three by natural right; he had a memory that never forgot anything, and any man in that valley, if he forgot something himself, such as the date he was married or the day his son was born, could always ask Mr. Wright for the information. Whenever Mr. Wright preached a funeral, he was able to recall all sorts of facts, and name the day a certain incident had taken place or a kindly word had been spoken. He would stand there in the cemetery by the river and talk at length of earthly incidents and recite Bible verses by the score, tears welling in his eyes and rolling down his cheeks and falling on his leather vest.

"Pneumonia fills your lungs," Weatherby's mother said. "Your grandfather King had it and when he died his chest when thumped didn't even sound hollow."

For four more days Weatherby watched his father's wrestle with the grippe that was inside him. The crisis came, and for a while it appeared that he would survive, for he could talk plain again. "Weatherby, you leave, you hear me?" he said, speaking as if every word brought him closer to the edge of suffocation. "Leave. God damn this place."

He loved this place, the boy knew. He had always loved this place, as he loved the family.

"We are cut off here," he whispered. "No help, no help, no help."

There was no doctor anywhere about, that was true, and no medicine, except the herbs the women had collected from the woods.

"My father came up for land and we stay for hunger," he whispered, his illness smothering even his words.

People came from everywhere and stood around in the yard, waiting, and when Mr. Wright died, a number of preachers were on hand to bury him. His funeral lasted more than three hours, and when the preachers were done talking, suddenly Weatherby, who more deeply than his brothers and sisters felt the loss of his father, began speaking, almost as if to his father there before him in the coffin. He had no Bible in his hand, but he was saying verses from the Bible; he was reciting in his father's voice, and from memory, as his father had done, and they were his father's verses. His blond hair, like his father's, was moving gently in the breeze, and he stood with bowed head and looked down at the dead face and recited for half an hour the biblical messages of poetry and promise.

"He's got his pa's mind," somebody said.

He did have, too.

"He's got his pa's heart," somebody said.

And that was true, too, for even as he stood there, tears were rolling down his face and falling on his vest and his big hands.

He had traveled out a long way since that burial time, off to learn in college and off to work in the North, and he had mastered a storehouse of facts and methods. He was as large and muscular as his father had been; his face had weathered brown like his father's, and his hands were big, with long, thick fingers. His eyes were as blue as his father's and his mouth was as ready to smile. His mind was keen as ever, but now it was filled not only with Bible verses, but with data about engineering and machinery and the Road. He stood at the cobbly creek, at the foot of the ten-square-mile place in which he would lay the Road, curve the Road, twist the Road, blast and cut and fill and drive through the Road, tunnel the Road, to open up that whole territory, one as large as some states. He would open it up at last, and others later could take what he had done and go on with a new way to the West. "Old woman," he whispered, "are you ready to begin?"

CHAPTER TWO

THE NEW MAN, Hal Cumberland, who was treasurer of the company, heard Weatherby approaching across the yard, stopping now and again to talk with a guard, asking each man how he was and where he was from and what his father did for a living. Cumberland was impressed with Weatherby, with his unassuming brilliance of mind and friendly nature, and with the way he had of finding ways to identify with a person. They had talked only for a few minutes that afternoon, but in that time Weatherby had found out about Cumberland's family and his work at the college and why he had left. Cumberland had taught mathematics for three years, in the same college Weatherby had attended, at Chapel Hill. They had even had two of the same teachers. Cumberland had taken this job in order to gain practical experience that might make his teaching more effective once he returned to it, and make his life more his own. Now his life was too much one his family and various institutions had arranged for him. He was the only son of a wealthy man, a planter in the central part of the state near Pittsboro, and he realized he needed to be out working on his own for a while, wrestling with some challenge that could be met only by a total commitment on his part.

Weatherby came into the office, hung his coat on a horseshoe nail that had been driven into the wall, and sat down at one of the three clerks' desks. He was more rugged of feature than Cumberland,

and much more deeply tanned from outdoor work. "Working late?" Weatherby asked.

"Going over papers. Did you see the crucibles that arrived from James Henry Company?"

"Yes. Tomorrow you'll want to pay for them, and send a clerk to Newton to see if Virble has the lace leather I ordered a month ago and if Pomroy has the black lead."

Cumberland wrote a note on a slip of paper.

"And we need about $300 worth of nails, which might as well be bought nearby at Old Fort."

Cumberland asked about three bills, one from Richardson and Company for coach trimmings, a sum of $328.79, and two from J. R. Anderson and Company, one for $6,570.95 for car wheels, and the other for $7,910 for wrought locomotive tires.

Weatherby authorized payment for all three, then he put his feet up on the desk and began to talk, telling the younger man how the Road had been built as far as the mountain's base. Every bridge and tangent and curve seemed to matter to him and was introductory to the great work that was now about to commence. He said the Road had been authorized long before the war, but no work west of Morganton had been done until 1868. In 1870 the carpetbagger president of the Road had got Weatherby to return to the state and accept the post of chief engineer, but Weatherby couldn't work for him and returned to Pennsylvania. A year or so later the president absconded with $4,000,000 in state bonds, bankrupting the Road. It had taken seven years and the efforts of an ex-governor from the mountain section to get work resumed, this time with Weatherby in charge, responsible only to a board appointed by the state.

Weatherby, sitting there in the clerks' office, explained to Cumberland the order of railroad construction. First the culverts and bridges and viaducts were started. Second, cuts were made in the ridges and the earth was used to fill in nearby valleys. When the grading was finished, a foundation for the rails was laid of gravel or stone. Stone ballast ought to be small enough to pass through a ring three inches in diameter, and even this was too big, he said. The ballast was spread along a portion of the line and sleepers, called ties, were half buried in the ballast. The distance between the ties was 2½ feet, center to center. The rails were secured to the ties by chairs, which were cast-iron pins.

"How long has it been known that a road could be put up the mountain?" Cumberland asked.

"Nobody knows that it can be," Weatherby said, smiling briefly.

"You aren't certain?"

"Oh, yes, I'm certain; I surveyed it several years ago. But sometimes I'm wrong."

"If you're wrong, all the work of bringing the Road to the mountain will have been wasted."

"Not entirely. But it has been a gamble, amounting to millions of dollars; it has bled this poor state. But now the rails are poking at the mountain's base, are ready to start up. I'm going up there as soon as the leaves fall and mark the route more clearly and set it once and for all."

"I'd like to go," Cumberland said.

"Would you? Then you come. And my son is coming in on a train and will go, too, for I promised to let him. Sunday at home we were breaking black walnut hulls with carriage wheels, sneaking out into the road and putting the walnuts in the wagon ruts, so that the next wagon or two would break the hulls off. It made for hard carriage riding, but it helped us a great deal; we would gather up the hulled ones and retreat to the living room, where I keep a nut rock by the fire. He and I cracked them and picked them, and I got to listening to him beg to come."

"How old is he?"

"Eleven. I don't know what I'd do without that boy. He's mine, you see, and I don't even see his faults when Mildred points them out to me."

Cumberland had to laugh. "I'd like to meet him."

"He won't help us much, I'm afraid. What we have to do is be sure the route has a maximum grade of 105 feet per thousand, and a maximum curvature of 9 degrees. Think of that."

"I don't believe it can be done."

"Oh, it can be, but to build it will cost us, you and me and those other men out there, cost us dearly." He got up and went into his private office, which was set back between the two bedrooms, one of which was Cumberland's. He sat down at his desk and through the open door studied the younger man. "You ever sacrifice for anything?" he said to him.

Cumberland looked up, startled. "No," he said.

"That's why you're here, is it?"

Cumberland thought about it. "Yes," he said.

"Not because you feel guilty, I take it."

"I don't feel guilty."

"You feel cut off from your right to believe in something and give yourself over to it?"

"That's what I think."

"So do I," Weatherby said, studying him thoughtfully. "And I think you've come to the right location to find it."

Lou Babcock was going on the trip with Weatherby, too. He was fifty-five, a craggy small-statured man, scarred from working around picks and mules for thirty years building roads in North Carolina. He was not well schooled, but he had accumulated a world of experience about handling work gangs, making trestles, figuring out where to drag the earth for fills and how to blast rock with black powder. Except for a one-year period when he had served in General Johnston's Confederate Army, where he had been one of the officers responsible for food supplies, he had rarely been away from working the roads. He had become very much like the ballast and the ties and the iron; there was not any more imagination to him, either, and this was one reason Weatherby chose him. Babcock did what he was told to do, exactly, perfunctorily, working day and night. One didn't have to explain anything to him. He was willing to be part of the machinery that responded to orders that were given. He was a man of the Road, not of administration, just as the new officer, Cumberland, was a man of administration and not of the Road. Each offered a segment of the total need, and each was chosen by Weatherby to complement himself and serve as a willing assistant, each knowing his own work and being able to carry it on, but neither being able to interfere with the pattern he established for the whole.

On Wednesday morning, the fourth week in October, Weatherby unpacked his surveying instruments and asked Babcock to get an ax, a bucket, a bag of lime for whitewash, a supply of fatback and corn meal, and two guns, with enough shot and powder to last for four days, then he went down to the rail end of the Road and waited impatiently for the train plume off to the east that would indicate Troy's arrival. He picked up a dried piece of pine and whittled a small rabbit, using a knife borrowed from a guard. "I'm not much on making things that are smaller than my hands," he told the guard.

"What is it?"

"You can't tell? You see his tail here, and this ear laid back on his shoulder?"

The guard scratched at a bug bite on his face and sucked at a tooth that needed to be "jumped." "Is it a cat?"

Weatherby considered the matter. "Might be," he said agreeably.

The train arrived with much noise and smoke. It had struck a hog on the way and blood was on the face of it, Weatherby noticed. "Where's my boy?" he called to the engineer, and at once Troy's face appeared over the edge of the cab. He was a grinning, blond-headed, handsome boy who was smoke-coated except for his eyes, which glistened happily, and his white teeth.

Weatherby helped him down; Troy didn't need any help, but Weatherby wanted to touch him and hold him. "You're not tired, are you?" he asked him.

"No," Troy said, noticing the carved animal in his father's hand. "I like to ride it," he said.

"Here, I carved you a cat, or something like that."

They walked together to where Babcock, Cumberland, and

a Negro helper named Ham were waiting. Together, loaded down with goods and accompanied by a dog, they walked out of Henry Station toward the north, past the gangs of sweating convicts and their mules, through an ancient forest to a large tulip poplar tree. Weatherby marked it, then looked along the valley to the north-west, a tree-cloaked valley dampened by Mill Creek which flowed on down past Henry Station. They were sixty feet above the bottomland of the creek valley, on Dendron Ridge, a mountain spur which separated the valley of Mill Creek from Jarrett's Creek to the east. It was a rocky, thickly shaded, snake-infested territory.

Cumberland reflected that at this moment none of the five men, save Weatherby, had the slightest idea which direction the Road would take or how it was to unwind above them. They waited silently as he turned toward the northwest, along the side of the ridge where they were standing. "It goes through there," he said.

All day they marked the route on the lower shoulders of the mountain, through the watery, virgin land. When they camped that night, sweaty and weary and hungry, Weatherby mixed meal and water in his hand, patted it into dough and laid it on hot rocks. The smell of cooking trout soon was in the air, and the dog began to sniff at the fire. The men ate greedily, using the rocks for dishes, using their fingers and knives, washing the food down with cold water. It was dark when they finished, and at once Babcock took the fish bones and what was left of the fish and put them in the creek. "I don't want bears called to them," he said. He came back to the fire and stretched out on the ground. "Does a railroad kill fish?" he asked Weatherby.

"Not that I ever heard," Weatherby said.

"I heard it did. And made cows not milk and chickens not egg."

"I don't think so," Weatherby said. "Some who don't want the Road say that."

"Be a shame to kill off the fish in that creek," Babcock said. "What's its name?"

"It has no name," Weatherby said, lying back on the ground. "What do you want to name it?"

"Fish Creek."

"Babcock's Fish Creek. What of that?" He repeated the name slowly, ignoring Babcock's embarrassed protestations. "I know this creek pretty well. It rises steep and branches in three ways about a quarter mile up the gorge. We'll cross all three of its branches tomorrow. One leads up to a graphite stand, the prettiest I ever saw. Another goes right to the top of that northwest gap, where there's tulip poplars so tall they can't ever be cut down and got out. The third branch washes down from the west, from Birch Ridge, up there behind us."

"We going across that?" Babcock said.

"We're going up on it to gain elevation." He shaped another meal pone and laid it on a fire rock; that one was for the dog. "You can sit here at Babcock Creek, and consider the road all around you, down here at this level and far up on the ridge as it swings around. You see those rocks standing out, 200 yards up there? We'll be there tomorrow."

Cumberland said very little. He was content to watch as Weatherby's mind unraveled the problem which encircled him and wrapped him with its trees and creeks and rocks and wonders; he was a visitor on the mountain's side even as he sought a way to conquer it.

Next day they curved the Road around on Sow Mountain, coming at last to a place only 200 feet from where, the day before at midday, they had been. They could look down at the other camping place, and Weatherby wondered aloud if the lower road would be covered by the fill from the higher road. He made notations on the face of a rock, writing with the tip of his knife, and decided there would be 10 to 30 feet to spare.

The Road moved to the north for a ways, curving over a major cut; then it moved to the west, toward round Knob, and turned northwest where the route had been surveyed before them, and this time came to a cliff below which they could see a spot where, earlier in the morning, they had surveyed. They ate dinner, then moved northwest, along the mountainside, to the second branch of

Babcock Fish Creek, where a culvert was to be made. Lying between this branch and the third branch of Babcock was a ridge called Birch Ridge, and it was possible to cut through it, but Weatherby decided to gain as much elevation as he could by going around the spur of it.

They reached the third branch about evening and crossed it and camped there. They had marked off two or three miles that day.

They camped on Horse Ridge, where chestnuts abounded, so they roasted enough for breakfast, and to eat as they worked.

They moved to the east. Now they were above the camp of two nights before and could look far down at it.

They turned the Road to the southwest, through what was to be a long, deep cut. They came to a bubbly creek, merely a branch, and directly before them was the spit of a ridge, an outcropping of rock. Weatherby stopped beneath it and said this was the site of the first tunnel. The men must blast through the rock, he said. He and Babcock climbed to the precipice, and an hour later came back, talking, studying. It was the work of another hour to determine that First Tunnel would be about 125 feet long.

The party ate smoked pork while sitting in the shadow of the spur, then moved around it to the next little spur, which Weatherby and Babcock clambered over; they decided Second Tunnel would be 200 feet long, maybe 225.

They surveyed now to the southwest, gaining elevation. They came to a spur which Weatherby named Lick Log, for he found there a forked log which once had been used by men "salting" cattle or deer. He surveyed a tunnel through that spur and estimated it would be 760 feet long, and he named it Lick Log tunnel.

In late afternoon he moved on a ways to another outcropping of rock, and clambered over that. A tunnel would be blasted out here, he said, a small one, 150 feet in length.

The camp that night was facing the southeast and was high on the mountain. They were about a mile from the turnpike, so they could hear the drovers' music being played, could hear men yelling and singing, for the wind was from the south. A lost sheep came into camp, and Weatherby let it stay. It lay down in the campfire light and panted like a dog, so scared it was, so fast it had run, so close it had come to wolves. The next morning the sheep followed along as they marked the Road, which was to go along the side of the mountain for about 4,000 feet, until it crossed the turnpike at the middle of a straight tangent. The men reached the turnpike at three o'clock and it was a welcome sight to see people again after three days. Weatherby gave the sheep to a farm boy, who reminded him of himself at a young age, and he rested for an hour or so before he led the way across the turnpike into the deep woods on the other side, where he marked the route through a great forest of hardwood trees, to the site of the last tunnel.

The men sprawled on the ground, rested almost within sight of the turnpike. Babcock bought a goose and cooked it. Also he traded a knife for a jug of whisky, which the four men drank, all from the same jug. Troy got none, and he complained about it.

At dawn Weatherby left the camp. An hour later he was standing on the rocks above Swannanoa Gap, which had been named by the Cherokee Indians. On the west side of the Gap, set at one end of a vast field, was the Praying Rock, which perhaps the Indians had used for religious services and which now Protestant preachers used as the gathering place for camp meetings in the summertime.

Beneath where he stood a tunnel would go, connecting at last the outlands and the mountain country. It would be the new river, the new road, the new narrow channel that would make possible the rising of cities, the growth of commerce, the increase in wealth and health and stability of the region which extended 50 miles westward from where he stood.

When he came back to camp, he began to survey the tunnel. He spent all day doing it and found it to be about 2,000 feet in length, and he named it the Swannanoa tunnel.

They camped at its eastern portal. To one side of them were the lowlands. On the other side of them was the jagged face of the mountain, hiding from their sight the mountain plateau, which had a river flowing through it and mountains rising around it. The river flowed on westward through other valleys, accepting water from many tributaries until it merged with the French Broad River at Asheville, a little town of 2,400 people. Once the Road got through the Gap, it could follow the bed of that river on into Tennessee.

Troy crept close to Weatherby and asked if they were about done walking. "I'm tired," he said.

"You're a little boy and are tired? I never heard anything like that before," Weatherby said, smiling at him.

"My knees are tired."

"About to fold up on you?"

"I think so," Troy said.

"You tell them we're through, except for walking down the turnpike to Henry Station tomorrow." He took the boy's hand and cupped it, with the palm up. "Henry Station is at the tip of your little finger. We went along the finger and had to make a long bridge onto your palm, and we had to curve around your palm in many different ways to gain elevation gradually. We made a tunnel onto your thumb, and other tunnels in your thumb and we're now near the end of your thumb, where we'll build the big Swannanoa Tunnel."

Troy turned his father's hand palm upward and studied it. "Your hand would be harder to build on than mine," he said.

"Neither one's as hard as the hand we'll be using. Nor as old."

Troy lay back on the ground and studied his palm and listened to the men talk. He heard Babcock lower his voice and say to Weatherby, "A nigger can breathe up here, can't he?"

"Yes," Weatherby said.

"I knowed within reason he could. A nigger is made like a white man, when it comes to air?"

"I think so."

"He won't suffocate or strangle?"

"No, no," Weatherby said.

HenryAnna came down to the overlook to see how the day was going to be, and she found them camping there. They were all asleep, except for the big Negro, who had his head leaning forward on his chest and was breathing raspily through his mouth. Even their dog was asleep.

She was eighteen and pretty, with blonde hair tied with a thong, and she wore a dress made of cloth she hadn't yet dyed any color. It was light tan, and it was tied at the waist. She was of medium height, thin, and her expression was mildly infused with curiosity, for nothing in the world seemed to her to be without a note of humor in it, and without a note of sadness in it. "Law, I never saw such tired and sleepy people," she suddenly declared aloud, bringing the men to their feet and waking the dog.

Babcock was irritated to be awakened so abruptly. "You are a soft-walking creature, ain't ye?" he said.

"I'll hurry home to get a bell to wear," she said, enjoying his consternation. "I've been many times to this place, and I never saw you here before. You come out of the sky?"

Babcock moved closer to her, staring at her suspiciously. "You drop by men's camps ever chance you get?"

The remark stung her, and rather defensively she declared she came to this place to get away from men, "But looks like the world is getting smaller ever day. If it goes on like this, it's going to be too small for a woman at all. It'll be filled up with men and mules and their kind."

Weatherby smiled at Babcock. "Sounds like we've met our equal," he said.

"In terms of words, anyway," Babcock said.

"If you're going to come through here ever spring and fall with your stock, the least you can do is stay on the turnpike and off'n other people's property." She sniffed and scratched one leg with the foot of the other one, and frowned at the boy, who was glaring at her with wonder, holding as best he could to the dog, keeping it quiet.

"We're sorry to come on your property, but I thought I was on land I own myself," Weatherby said.

"What do ye mean own?" she said. "I've been here so much, it's the place I come to to get off to myself, and I'm the only living person I ever saw here before."

"But do you own it?" he said.

"I own the right to be where I've always been," she said. "How can you own a place you've never been to before?"

Weatherby was puzzled by the comment, though impressed by the soundness of her argument. "But do you own it?" he said.

"I never heard so much talk about who owns something which has been mine for years. If you mean did I ask somebody in an outland office if I could have a paper on it, I haven't had a paper on a woods in my life. I don't see how you can own a tree any more than you can make one, or how you can own land you didn't make the dirt for, or how you can be so proud as to say you buy what's nobody's to sell."

Weatherby nodded kindly. "Yes, but we do own the land and we're marking a road on it."

She scowled at him, studying that silently, squinting under the pressure of her own intense concentration.

"I found out in the North that it's better to own the land one works through, rather than merely have a right-of-way, for there's always need for timbers and firewood and the like, so I bought all this lower part of the mountain personally. We're making a road for the train," he said.

Not a whisper of response was seen in her expression. Slowly she looked around at the massive tree trunks and huge rocks, at the small branch which washed from a spring. She looked off at the lowlands. "I never heard that said afore," she said.

"A tunnel will go here," Weatherby said.

A smile crept over her face. "You're joking with me, are you?"

"Going to be a tunnel through that rock. It will come out in the far valley." Weatherby spoke gently to her, trying not to frighten her, respecting the natural, plaintive way she had of asking and wondering about things.

She stared at the rock, then down at the ground beneath her, then suspiciously at Weatherby. "Did you lose your stock last night?"

Weatherby had to laugh, for she was so utterly pretty and innocent, yet wise and quick. "No, no," he said.

She did believe him, he realized, but didn't know how to cope with what he said. She knew the ways of nature very well; there was nothing in this place which she had not been able to understand before today. "I'm going home," she said simply, and at once turned and started off.

"Wait now, don't worry, don't worry," Weatherby said quickly, afraid he had hurt something gentle in her.

She turned and stared at him.

"We can explain it," he said.

She considered that for a moment only, then turned and walked through a thicket of the woods.

He followed as far as the path. "Wait," he called to her. But there was no reply.

He returned to the fire, the others watching, all of them wondering at his anxiety. Babcock said, "She's just a witch-child. They have them up here."

"She left no footprints," Ham said, looking about for them on the path.

"Nature's children grow up like the lions," Babcock said. "They usually stay away from people. Eat berries, I reckon, and breed all the time."

Cumberland commented on how pretty the girl was. "A girl-woman," he said.

Ham groaned about her maybe being a witch-child. He began to breathe deeply, trying to fill his lungs with enough of the mountain air to save himself from suffocation.

The talk about HenryAnna was soon lost in the fuss of getting breakfast, but each man had thoughts about her lingering with him. Weatherby had known her at some other time, he told himself, in these same mountains, before he had ever gone away—not her but a girl like her. He was not strongly attracted to new women usually, but this woman he had known years ago, before he had met Mildred; all of a sudden she had appeared to him again, a reminder of youth and youthful notions.

Cumberland also was thinking about her. In the girl he saw one who viewed the real world in terms of her own experiences, who was natural and free as life itself, and who was, therefore, his own opposite, not only in that she was from a different culture but also that she had experienced, not simply considered and discussed, her own world.

Ham complained about the dangers of the place and wanted to start home, and there was no reason not to, for the marking was done to this last tunnel, but Weatherby instead went off into the forest to the south, along the ridge. Once he was out of sight of the camp, he turned to the west, the direction the young woman had taken, and soon he came upon a trail. He walked in the shadow of the tree trunks for a long way, and finally, where the path crossed a creek, in the mud he saw the prints of her bare feet.

Apparently she had just now been here, for the water was still muddy where the footprints were.

The trail led to a hacked-out clearing where cornstalks stood in awkward, untended rows. Beyond them was a cabin and crib, a wagon which was broken down, and an old horse. Just now a woman, hefty and ill-kempt, came from the cabin, shooing children before her. "If I hear another sound of fussing from any of you young'uns, I'll take you to the woodpile." They scattered in the yard, laughing and mocking her, calling out defiantly that they were grown up already.

Weatherby saw the girl. She was sitting on a fence, her arms crossed casually, watching the other members of the family, saying nothing. The mother called to her. "Well, are ye a princess or are ye going to help me cook and clean? There's clothes to boil and beat."

The girl said nothing, and the woman went back into the cabin, which, so far as Weatherby could tell, had no door.

She lived in a natural state indeed, he thought, like the Plover family up near home, tucked back amid the weeds and cornstalks and the snake fence. No wonder she wandered down along the path to the clean creek, and to the faraway view of the lowlands.

The girl began to sing. He couldn't quite hear the words, for she was singing to keep herself company, but he was impressed by the lilting quality of her voice, the sadness in it, and in the way she tilted her head. As he watched she walked from the fence to the chopping block, picked up an ax, and with a whop brought it down on a kindling log, splitting the log.

She drove the ax into the log again, then left it there. Disconsolately she came back to the fence and with an easy, graceful motion stepped onto a stump and leaped the fence. She started off across the cornfield, not toward Weatherby or the trail he had used, but toward the big woods back of her house.

She even walked like a Plover, he saw.

On impulse, he skirted the field and moved along just inside the woods until he came to the trail she was on.

He heard a waterfall ahead. He saw an opening in the laurel, nearby to his right, and he moved toward it, pulled a limb of a bush aside and looked out. The waterfall was just below him, so close he could touch the slick water as it began its leap into the air. It cascaded some twenty feet to a rock, washed over that in a gradual slide, the water sunlighted brightly, and fell ten feet or so into a pool. As he watched, he saw the girl, naked, dive into the pool.

She rose to the surface, blew water from her nose and mouth. The thong had been removed from her hair, and her hair was lying along her back, and some of it was on her chest and breasts, which were full and firm. To Weatherby she appeared to be the most beautiful woman he had seen, and it was fitting in that place to see her. He scarcely dared take a breath, lest she disappear.

He started down the side of the ridge, toward the pool, hoping she would think he had merely stumbled onto her, that he had been out surveying the country. Let her think he was as surprised as she— He stopped suddenly, for appearing at the pool was another man, who went directly to the edge of the pool and spoke to the girl. It was Cumberland.

"I never heard a person make so much noise coming through a woods," HenryAnna said, crouching in the water. "Couldn't you find any trail except one you made for yourself?"

Cumberland was staring at her, and apparently had no power of speech just now.

"If you lived in this woods for a year, it would be so torn up we'd have to patch its bushes in order to grow berries," she declared.

Cumberland, staring at her silently, intently, began to unbutton his coat.

"What'd you do with your railroad train?" she asked him. "You planning for the engine to come through this woods here, too?"

"I'm—to be honest with you, I'm surprised to find you here," he said, dropping his coat to one side.

"I'm surprised you found me here, too," she said frankly.

"I mean, to see you without your clothes on."

"I never bathe with my clothes on."

"No, but at home we have bathtubs we set in the kitchen." He unbuttoned his shirt.

She was standing now. He could see her clearly from the waist up. She didn't care, apparently. "If I had a tub and if I had a kitchen, I'd still rather bathe here."

"That may be," he said, dropping his shirt.

Once more she crouched down slightly in the water, as if modesty required it, and threw water on her face and shoulders. "A mountain man with courtesy wouldn't watch a woman bathe," she said.

"I'm tired of being known for my courtesy," he said, slipping off his boots. He pulled off his pants and waded into the water, approached her step by step, watching her.

"You're like the others, are you?" she said.

"You stand there and we'll see," he said, walking forward until he was close to her. She darted away. He dove for her, his hands touching her, but her wet body slipped through his hands, and she came up at the far end of the pool.

"Want to try again?" she said bluntly, angry with him, but confident.

He started toward her. Step by step he approached her and was almost at arm's reach before again she darted away. He dove for her, caught hold of her leg, held to it. Like a wildcat, angrily, with her nails she raked his back and opened the skin. He let go of her, startled, and rolled over painfully in the water, which turned red all around him, and when he got to his feet again and fully recovered his senses, he saw her standing on the warming rock, her clothes in her hand.

"I could take your clothes, too, but I'll not," she said, "and don't you come near me again, for I've had enough trouble with you and your kind already. It's a pity when a lady can't take a bath in her own pool of water."

She walked up the path toward where Weatherby was, almost blinded by her own tears of frustration and anger. He stepped behind a bush, and she didn't see him as she went by, nor did Cumberland see him as, cursing, he crawled painfully onto the warming rock, where he tried to dry off with his shirt. His back was still bleeding. Weatherby could see big red streaks, five or six of them, where the girl had cut him. She's a Plover, he thought, must be a Plover. There never had been a woman any more playful in a bed, or more likely to bite or scratch a man than a Plover.

In the weeks following their return to Henry Station after the trip up the mountain, Weatherby and Cumberland spent considerable time together in his office. Weatherby couldn't resist the urge to recall stories out of his youth, often about the Plover girls, and each time he talked about them Cumberland would become uneasy. With his secret knowledge of the incident at the pool, he could effectively spoof the young man, referring to cold water's effect on romantic notions, talking about physical courage in the face of violent women. "When those Plover girls got old enough to be courted," he said, "church attendance went up immensely. All the young men, myself among them, were always at worship. The trouble was, the Plover girls weren't deeply religious, and they didn't come to church every time, and then they came late. Plovers are always late for everything. So here was this pack of suitors singing hymns, each one keeping a wary eye on the church doorway, wondering if little Pearl would come to church or not, or Annie, or a little blonde thing called Soozie, who was as pretty as a picture. There were several of them, and every one about the same in appearance. When they did arrive, all us young men got up and took one to sit with, and the congregation was completely disrupted while we reseated ourselves."

He told a few stories that took place near a pool of water, too, exaggerating, of course, and watching Cumberland's face. He told how the Plover girls could scratch a man, and implied they would bite on occasion, too. All of this he told in the flattest voice, never intimating that it could possibly have anything to do with Cumberland.

"You're an amazing man," Cumberland said. "You not only know what you know, but you sense what you couldn't know."

"You remember, by any chance, that pretty little girl we met up at the lookout near the Gap?" Weatherby said. "I knew she might be one of that same Plover family, and she is, for I asked a worker about the Gap community. He said there is the one Plover family. The Plovers bear few boys, but a Plover man married into the Matthew family, and there are four girls and two boys born to them, he said, and they live at Swannanoa Gap—all blonde girls with long thin legs and pretty faces."

CHAPTER THREE

THROUGH AUTUMN and into winter the work unfolded. One could stand on the mountainside and look down at Henry Station, could watch the camp movements, which were as intricate and intermeshed and controlled as a big machine's. They had been carefully designed by Weatherby.

The main activity began in the morning, an hour before dawn, when the women were awakened by the guards. They came from the boxcar, wiping the sleep from their eyes, trying to get the soreness out of their muscles, stretching and yawning and cursing each other, finding their way in the dark to the creek, where they were required to bathe, shouting out in anguish at the burning coldness of the water.

The guard who watched over them, Tommy Goodman, had a lookout above the washing spot; he could see the women in the water and on the path coming to it and going back to the boxcar. He carried no rifle. It was Tommy's claim that he could outrun any woman in the camp, which was doubtless so. There wasn't any running away from Tommy and there wasn't any privacy from him, either. Even when the women went to the slit trench, they squatted in plain view of him and, of course, of anybody else who happened to be watching.

The women built big wood fires in the open area that came to be called "the kitchen." They made mush from corn meal, salt and water. They made coffee, too. While the black pots were steaming, the men were called out of the stockades and were trooped to the slit trenches, then to the creek, where they were ordered to wash; some of them did. One guard stood at the water's edge with a rifle; another guard stood on the same ledge Tommy Goodman had used. The men were chained together, two to a chain. Sometimes a man was chained to a metal ball; this was a form of punishment, as well as a deterrent to escape. If a man did decide to try to escape, the guard wouldn't try to catch him; one man tried to escape on the second morning and a guard shot him in the back between the shoulder blades.

When the men had washed, they were led up the creek bank to the camp, where the mush was served in tin plates and the coffee in clay mugs. The older women ladled out the mush, a wooden spoonful to each man, and dipped up the coffee. The younger women stood back a ways; they never went close enough to the men to be grabbed by one of them. Instinctively a man might tear a woman's clothes or hurt her in some way, out of meanness or affection, nobody could tell which; the offender would be flogged, but he would accept the punishment for a chance to grab hold of a woman, even if he could only hold her until the guards began beating him.

The mush was not any good. Nobody liked it, but the men were hungry, so they shoveled it from the plates into their mouths, using their spoons or thumbs; they stuck their faces close to it and sucked it into their mouths, making loud noises, swallowing it down and letting its heat burn their mouths and throats, feeling its heat in their bellies, liking that better than the taste.

When they were through eating, they were put into crews and were marched away to work, and five of the women began to wash the plates, mugs and pots. Fifteen of the women went to the men's barracks and cleaned up there. Weatherby had decided that every morning the floor of the barracks, and every square inch of the stockaded yards, had to be swept and limed. The mattresses and bedding had to be hauled into the barracks yard and laid in the sun; each man was given a muslin sheet and one blanket, and these were hung on the stockade walls to air.

When they finished this, the women sat in the stockade yard near the closed gate and talked for a while, until Tommy Goodman came along and unlocked the gate; they walked with him to the cooking place, where they helped cook dinner, which was beans or cabbage cooked with pork. Some of them helped do this, while others went down to the clothes-washing yard, where five or ten women had spent the morning. The men changed clothes once each week, so the clothes for 120 men had, in the course of each week, to be washed. Also there were clothes of the regular laborers and foremen to be washed. The clothes were boiled in black pots, then were beaten on stumps, the beaters using wooden paddles. Beating the clothes was the only way to get the dirt and grime out of them. They were rinsed in the creek and put on bushes to dry. Looking down from above, one would see each morning a streak of cloth appear on the creekbank, and begin to creep along the creek, along the edge of the water. One morning the women would wash shirts, another morning they would wash pants.

The afternoon set in languidly; the women were more tired then. The women could wash plates or cook, or they could go down to the creek and turn the clothes over on the bushes, or they could go over to the stockade and help drag the tick mattresses indoors and make up the beds. About an hour before sundown, they assembled at the kitchen again and began to cook. Supper was corn bread, bacon and coffee. The men would come into camp roaring hungry, aggrieved and exhausted. They would eat all they were given, then would be ordered into the stockades and locked up.

The women would wash the black pots and let the fires die down for the night. They would sit by the lowering fires for a little while, listening to the music that came from the stockades. There was a guitar in each barracks, provided by the Road. Some of the men sang, mostly work songs, mostly Negro songs. The white men in each barracks stayed to themselves and didn't sing much, or even talk much.

Two of the women each night took coals from one of the cookfires and carried them in a bucket to a site thirty feet from the office building. They made a bonfire, so that the camp would have a night light to see by. They set a pot of coffee on it, for the guards to drink, then they went down to their boxcar and were locked up.

On Saturday night there was always music to be heard, and a party for those convicts who were trusted. The party was held in a big field to the east of the camp. One main attraction was a white convict named Tom Burlington, who could sing and play the fiddle. He would press the fiddle against his chest, lean far back and play and sing old songs about hunting and loving and killings and hangings. He had been sentenced for murder, for shooting his cousin from a laurel patch near Asheville; often he would sing the long ballad he had composed about the murder and his trial.

The best Negro singer was a woman named Beulah. She could sing the music of the plantation Negroes from the East. Her voice was so clear that one night it was answered from high on the mountain by a panther. She and the beast sang that night, she claimed. Whereas Tom sang with little emphasis on the words, with more emphasis on rhythm and the swift forward movement of the simple story of the song, Beulah lingered on the sounds of the words, on the roundness and bigness of them; that was more important to her, apparently, than the story she was telling, which often was nothing more than a fragment of an idea, anyway.

In addition to Tom and Beulah, there was a group which called itself the Convict Quartet. It had a guitar, two fiddles and a banjo. The banjo picker was from near Hillsborough and was said to be the fastest and best in the prison system. One night he agreed to a competition with a mountain picker; each decided on his own tunes, and the contest waxed and waned for about an hour, the victor being the Hillsborough man, for he continued after the mountain man had collapsed.

The women convicts were allowed to come to the party, but they had to stay pretty much to themselves. A few mountain people came, most of them men, and they were allowed to mingle with the convict men, but at their own risk. If there was a fight between mountain men, that was all right, and a fight between convict males was all right; but a fight between a convict and a mountain man brought the guards swiftly and, unless the fight stopped at once, ended the party. As a consequence, a mountain man might insult his peers, but he was polite to the convicts and treated them with studied respect.

It was agreed that, if the party went well, and if the week's work had gone well, there would be a period toward the close of the evening, after the mountain men had been sent home, when the guards would permit the more trustworthy Negro convict men and women to go together into the patch of woods at the east side of the field, and the white trusties to go together into the woods at the west side. It was purely voluntary, and it was understood that any convict who used this privilege to effect an escape would abolish the system itself, with consequent retribution to himself once he was caught.

After the woods orgy, all the women who had taken part were

herded to the creek, where they were told to wash with soap. "Let that cold water run inside ye," Tommy Goodman told them. He insisted that they stand in the water for at least ten minutes. They yelled and cursed and shoved and fought. The women had plenty of jealousies which were aggravated by the sex play each week; some woman seemed always to have taken another one's lover, and then, too, there were women who were jealous of each other.

When the women were allowed to come out of the water, they were made to jump up and down. This helped dry them off; also, as Tommy Goodman said, it interfered with pregnancy. He liked a lot of jumping. The old women had to jump along with the others. Then they all went up to the boxcar and went to bed. The boxcar on Saturday night was noisy far into the night, with hairpulling and fussing. Tommy said he didn't know what went on in there and was afraid to ask.

Tommy's interest in all his women remained clinical. If a woman got sick, he would sympathetically diagnose her condition himself and decide if she needed to rest; if a woman got scratched or bitten or otherwise injured in a fight, or in the woods on Saturday night, he would worry over the injury as much as the woman did, often more. He would spend hours discussing the condition of his women with Babcock and Weatherby whenever he got a chance.

If one of the male convicts was particularly rough with his women on Saturday night, he would report the man to Babcock and ask that he not be allowed in the woods again. One of the convicts bit two women, both on their shoulders; Tommy warned him to behave. The next Saturday night the convict conducted himself acceptably, but on the Saturday night following, one of the Negro girls suffered a nasty wound; she said she couldn't see the man's face who had done it to her, but Tommy matched her wound with the scars of the wounds on the other women and had the male convict deprived of further contact with his women.

"I tell you, Mr. Babcock," he said, "I get laughed at by some of the other guards because I'm particular about my women, but I feel about them like I would my own sisters or daughters. If one of them gets hurt, I'm hurt. If one of them gets a time-of-the-month and don't want to work, I don't want her to have to go cramping around changing beds. I let her set and cook, or go down to the water's edge and wash shirts. When one of them gets bigged, I can feel the knitting needle as much as if she was poking it up me rather than her ownself. If one of them gets bit—there was a convict named Raymond who tried to bite the nipples off of one of my women. Now you know that's not right. It seems like some of these men want to hurt 'em. The way I figure it, we just got the one life, Mr. Babcock, and we got to watch out fer the womenfolks."

It was not permitted that a guard beat a prisoner; only the overseer of the convicts, Blackie Sullivan, had authority to do that. Any guard with a complaint against a prisoner could make it to Blackie, and could, if he chose, bring the prisoner along to be punished at once. The punishment was given with a split hickory rod, which would bring blood with each blow. There were convicts, however, who were so tough of body that they would as soon take the blows as work the Road, and apparently punishment only hardened them all the more. Two such men, one white and one Negro, were sent back to Raleigh the second week, along with one woman who appeared to be addled.

The purpose of the camp, of this social machine which was always in motion, was labor, not in the camp itself, but on the Road. Babcock and Weatherby were rarely in the camp, except each night. They could be found out where the mules and oxen and men were cutting through the forest and earth. The average laborer could load three cubic yards of common earth in a day, so two workers, one with a pick and the other with a shovel, could load six cubic yards of earth into mule carts.

One gang worked ahead of the digging crews, clearing the trees out of the way. This was dangerous work, for the trees were sometimes so large that four men couldn't reach around them, and not infrequently a man would have to stand inside the cut itself to enlarge the wound of the tree. Only one such tree could be felled by the crew in a day's time, and its weakening in late afternoon was the occasion for a gathering at the scene. In falling, the tree made a cracking sound, often loud enough to be heard half a mile away. The first branch spread out from its trunks 50 to 70 feet above the ground and the trunk rose for 200 feet in all, so it appeared to fall slowly. Far off one would see the fan of the top branches moving, rotating slightly as the tree began to tilt; far down the cove one could see the branches strike other trees and break, making splintering sounds, like rain striking a roof. That sound continued for several seconds, until the trunk struck the ground with a thud.

Bits of branches kept falling; it was quite a while before there was quiet again. Not a bird chirped, of course; not a beast cried nor a man spoke. Then the foreman of the tree gang would give a rebel yell and shake his hat in the air; he always was gleeful whenever a big one fell. And the other men would yell and jump up and down in excitement. "Did ye see that one? Did ye see that one?" the foreman would shout.

The tree gang would use oxen to pull the trunk out of the roadbed. They would often cut it to use later in a trestle. Sometimes they would cut the branches into firewood either for the camp or for the engine. The camp at Henry Station required 2½ cords of wood a day to keep its fires going; soon the camp at Babcock Fish Creek would be activated, too, so that meant five cords a day must be cut and left to dry, for the camps alone.

To move the bigger logs, six or eight oxen were yoked together. The brutes would struggle in the yokes as the whips cracked above them, and the men sometimes put their shoulders against the great logs, too, and pushed as the oxen pulled. It was work enough to make muscles bulge in men and brutes both and sweat stream off their bodies.

Behind the tree gang came the diggers and the sweaty, smelly mules, and behind the diggers came the track gang, laying ballast and ties, setting work track and clearing out rocks and sticks, making ditches so that surface drainage would not erode the roadbed. Generally, they put things in order, raking the road and burning the stumps and roots. They also carried messages back to camp, when needed, and if a mule got sick or an ox wouldn't work, it was turned over to them to take care of. Or if a man in a forward gang got injured or sick, he was left for them to take care of. A trusty was left sitting by the road; a convict who was not a trusty was chained to a tree.

It was this gang, also, that served dinner to the other men. Two of the men would return to Henry Station with two ox sleds and bring the black pots forward to where the men were working.

After noonday dinner the men would rest for half an hour, flopping on the ground, tending to their wounds, washing them and rubbing pork grease into them. All the crews had their chief sources of danger. The digging gang was thought to be the safest, but it was the one least preferred by the men, for there was no excitement to it. Usually the least cooperative of the convicts ended up as diggers. The favored crew was the track gang, because the men had a variety of functions to perform and each man was given more freedom, as a consequence, in carrying out orders.

Some of the men were floaters; that is, they were moved from one crew to another as needed. One of the best floaters was a Negro named Moses. He was the biggest of the convicts, and appeared to be the strongest one in the camp. He was broad and heavy; his fists were six inches wide. The edge of his hand was so hard he could break limbs with it by striking them sharply. His skin was coal black and weathered tough. When a member of the digging gang, he could upturn a mule cart by himself, and often did. When the other men couldn't make a mule work, they only had to call Moses; as soon as he appeared, the mule moved smartly. There was always something dangerous about his appearance, even when he sat at rest. There was something angry about him, even as his big head rested forward on his chest. He never talked much. He never asked for anything from anybody. He never touched anybody and nobody ever touched him. If a man stumbled and fell against him, he backed away quickly, apologizing. It was believed that, with any motivation at all, he wouldn't hesitate to kill a guard or prisoner, a mule or ox.

One day at noon the digging gang came upon a rock that wouldn't yield. They had tried black powder to break it. They had built fires on it and had doused the heated rock with cold water; this normally would split a rock, but it hadn't done so this time. They called Moses. He took the sledge hammer and stood for a moment considering the rock. As far as anybody could tell, he was idly wondering where to strike the rock or how best to strike it; he was accepting the rock. After a while he moved to the rock and climbed onto the side of it. The ten-pound sledge hammer in his hand merely dangled there, as if he had forgotten it, but suddenly it swished through the air, not with any sign of effort on his part; it simply moved in an arc from behind him and swept over him and smashed down on the rock before him. The hickory handle of the sledge vibrated, trembled from the blow. The sledge bounded up and was once more arced high. He struck along the center of the rock, without seeming to move except that his arms swept the sledge up and around, but moving a few inches at a time until he got to the bottom of the rock. And the rock split.

He stood there alone, the sledge dangling from one hand, staring at the split rock without any show of feeling; he stepped off the rock without looking to right or left, and went back to where the mule carts were. He had won out over the rock, but more than that, he had won out over the digging gang; he had bested them all, but he didn't seem to care.

The tree gang used him sometimes. Six oxen and all the men sometimes couldn't move a log, so they would send for Moses. He would be the margin of difference every time. As the log would crash down into the creek valley below, he would turn and without a word go back to the mule carts.

During the first few weeks, the three gangs worked close together, but during the second month the distance between them increased, which made it easier for everybody. The tree gang didn't need to worry so much about crushing a member of the chopping gang, and the digging gang didn't have to worry about black powder explosions hurting the others. Progress was everywhere apparent, and the men began to take pride in what they did, and to work harder. Weatherby often would visit with them, would sit down with them when they were resting and tell them about the Road and where it was to go and how nothing like it had ever been attempted before anywhere. He would tell them that another camp was soon to be opened, another 150 convicts were to arrive, and those other men would have rocky country to work in and trestles to build. "I'll move some of you men on up there," he said one evening, "if you like." He said this, glancing at Moses, and no doubt Moses realized he had been challenged, but he said nothing.

Because of Weatherby, the men began to respect the Road, to talk about the forested marvels of it, to stand in awe beneath the cliffs and wonder if ever they could reach the Gap. They had begun to move in sympathy with the labor they were doing, like a woman drugged by pain during childbirth. Weatherby moved among them, sat down and talked with them, listening sympathetically to each complaint and to every story of personal history. Almost all the men had been wrongly accused, to hear them tell it, and few of them admitted guilt of any crime at all. They told him what they thought about the work, the camp, and each other, so a communion was created between him and them, one different from their relationship with the guards or the foremen or the free laborers. They trusted him. They were honored that he took time to know them and that he, more than any other, took time to listen to them. And never did he violate any trust, or embarrass any one of them, or misuse any confidences.

One of the convicts Weatherby liked best was a Negro named Esau, a handsome man of twenty-seven. Esau two years before had escaped from the Raleigh prison; a month later he had been found near his home, in the woods, and he had surrendered without endangering anybody and without protest. Soon he escaped again and was caught a month later in the same woods. He surrendered again willingly. Now he didn't seem to object to the work on the Road, for he was so powerful and agile that nothing asked of him was beyond his power to do, but it was believed he would try to escape most any time he could.

He was, by reason of his two escapes, respected by the other prisoners. If one of them contemplated an escape, he would ask Esau about it, and might ask him to help plan it. On one occasion Weatherby watched a young Negro boy crawl over to where Esau was sitting. "What time of day would be best?" Weatherby heard the boy whisper.

Esau smiled at him. "What you dreaming in your mind, boy? You can't do nothing."

"Sundown?"

"Sundown they have you locked in that stockade wall. Can you leap an eleven-foot wall?"

"I can do what I has to."

"They can shoot you down, too, even if you fail," Esau said.

"Dig a way out?"

"Those posts go into the ground, are set on the hard pan. You better stay and work, boy."

"I could run now this minute. They couldn't catch me."

"Which way you go?"

The boy stared at him, begging with his eyes for the answers. "I go home."

"Which way is home?"

The boy looked upward at the sun, which was in the southwest now. "I follow the sun," he said.

"The sun don't mean to be followed. It moves and ever day makes its own escape. The sun is a daytime thing, anyway, and you need a nighttime thing, a star to see by."

"Which star, Esau?"

"Ah, boy, there's no star for you." He knew the boy couldn't get home. He might get away from the camp, but he would falter soon unless he knew which road to follow, which river to go down, where to find food to eat, how to silence dogs. Escape was demanding and cruel and painful. The question of a man's escaping had to do with the man's mind, how much he knew; and with his heart, how much he wanted to succeed. The boy might have the heart, Esau didn't know, but he didn't have the mind. He didn't know the woods, how to eat roots and berries and greens; he would too soon reach the point where he would want to be found because he was so tired of trying to live and get to where he wanted to go.

Weatherby's daytime was spent on the road with the men, but he had office work to do at night. In the office the chief problem was money. He needed to save money at every opportunity, but he was already down to the bare necessities, the lowest salaries, and was a month behind in pay. His hope was to anticipate his coming needs and make his own supplies. Rather than pay 20 cents each for ties, the crews cut their own. Pigs were being raised, and corn and sorghum and oats were to be planted soon. Beans could be planted with the corn, and patches of onions and cabbage would be set out. He and Cumberland made plans for a planting, had the fields cleared in bottomland and big cribs made, and the Negroes plowed and harrowed with oxen and mules, much as they had done on the plantations from which they came.

CHAPTER FOUR

WHEN HENRYANNA came to the camp for her first visit, a paralysis struck in the kitchen where the convict women were washing the breakfast pans and pots. Tommy Goodman saw her first and knew what to expect. "All right, keep working," he told the convict women, but they saw her and stared angrily at her.

HenryAnna was young and pretty. Beyond that, she was unlined and unmarked, uncontaminated and untormented. Even beyond that, she was free, not only in the sense that she could go and come when and where she chose, but she carried with her the breath of the mountain air; she was free in the sense that she was natural, and in her own place.

"God damn it, you women keep working," Tommy yelled at the

women convicts, but one of them began at once to beat with a wooden spoon on a metal pan, and another woman began to cry out hoarse obscenities.

"Damn you, Maim, I'll wring your neck if you don't shet up!"

He meant it, too, and the women got quiet, but they were watchful, and it was obvious that they hated HenryAnna, who was not conscious of them at all, not really.

"Just keep washing pots," Tommy said sympathetically, glancing at HenryAnna himself as she walked up the path toward where two guards were transfixed on the office steps, both of them having interrupted their talking when she came into sight. Tommy murmured, "Trouble walks there, all right." He grunted sharply and mopped sweat off his face. "I'm glad she ain't to be tucked in no boxcar of mine overnight."

A few male convicts, who claimed they were sick, were squatting near the office. They saw her and began whistling and catcalling and carrying on. But HenryAnna didn't have the slightest idea, apparently, that all the noise was because of her idly walking along the path, looking at the sights here in the valley.

She saw Cumberland and stopped in her tracks, frowning. He was sitting behind a desk, just beyond the open doorway of the building, busily working, and beyond him were two clerks.

She saw Cumberland and stopped in her tracks, frowning. He was glanced at her, then looked up, appraising her frankly. Cumberland saw her and fairly leaped to his feet. He appeared to be more awkward than he needed to be. "Can we help you?" he said.

She scratched at her shoulder and looked around idly at the clerks. There was the heavy smell left by an oil lantern, and she didn't much like that, or him. She saw Weatherby and another man bent over a desk in the back room, studying a map and talking, so she moved past Cumberland and stopped in the doorway to Weatherby's office. He came forward at once and welcomed her, fetched a chair for her even while he sent the other visitor away.

Cumberland, outside, stared at her uncomfortably. She saw him and stretched out one long, graceful leg and nudged the door closed in his face.

"I've come for no special purpose," she said to Weatherby, folding her hands in her lap and smiling at him. "I was wondering about you and the other men."

He asked her about the Plovers, and she was perfectly at ease as she talked with him, explaining that originally the Plovers had come into the mountains to make their fortune, "and those that ain't starved to death are here yet." She bubbled along at length about her family, especially her father, "who can talk at length on any subject," and about her mother, "who should be put in charge of an army that really wants to win." She got Weatherby laughing at what she said, so he sat in there for an hour past dinnertime, with foremen and guards, and even Babcock, waiting for him on the Road.

He talked with her about the mountains and the people, and about this mountain particularly and what its personality was. "Each has its own, I decided as a boy," he said. "Some are peaceful more than others, some are mean, some are noble."

"This one has been tramped over so much by every drover in the country that it's mean," she said. The stock has been so risky of a fall that wolves have gathered on it more than any other, and panthers and wildcats. It can't never rest for long before a drive starts, and now you come with a road."

"So it has to adapt itself to outside changes, season to season, does it?"

"It's had to learn to protect itself, in spite of all odds," she said simply.

He smiled at her. "Have you?" he said.

"I've had some trouble around laurel bushes in my time," she said.

"How old are you?"

"Eighteen."

"A child is all you are."

She groaned over that. "Not for a while, now." She said she

wanted to watch the men work, and Weatherby said that was all right, but to stay far back from them. She went out of the office, walked past Cumberland without so much as a glance, though she smiled brightly at Babcock, who was impatiently waiting for Weatherby.

Weatherby followed after her to the office porch. Two guards were there and he said, "One of you better trail along behind her."

"You want us to stop her?"

"No, no. Let her alone, if you can manage it." When one of them had gone hurrying after her, Weatherby told the other one, "I once knew a girl she reminds me of."

"I wish I had." The guard was a freckled fellow with floppy hair that fell over his forehead. It was more red than brown. He was a pleasant man, though none too smart of mind; he wasn't mean, though, as several of the guards had proved to be. "I'd like to get that one alone for a spell."

"No, leave her be," Weatherby said simply, and he went on to his office and sat there behind the desk, thinking about Loren Plover, whom he had once made love to. That was years ago. They had been special to one another. They never argued; they never seemed to disagree about anything. They were close to each other in an adolescent sweetness that knew no sin—or acknowledged none, anyway. If he hadn't gone off to school, no doubt he and Loren would have been married and would by now have a valleyful of sons and daughters, and be hoping to get a little bit ahead on the next drive.

But after college, when he went back to see her, he was aware of the world of differences that separated them.

Weatherby hoped HenryAnna would return through camp, but when next he saw the guard who had gone to watch her, the guard said she had stood near a maple tree and looked at the work for half an hour or so, then had gone up the side of the mountain, toward the Gap. A frustrating sensation of loss came over Weatherby. "Mountain women have a nice way about them, you know it," he said to the guard. "There's no pretense about them, and there's not much fear either, and they move close to life without forgetting to be both sad and playful." He noticed that Cumberland hung on what he said about the girl. "Does she stir you up, and you a college man?" Weatherby asked him.

"I wouldn't let a college train me out of that," Cumberland said.

Both of them got to laughing about that, and about life generally, and the work went easier that evening for Weatherby, though Cumberland made a few mistakes, the first he had made since signing on with the Road.

HenryAnna came back in about a week. Again Weatherby dropped his work and spent as much time talking with her, and joking with her, as she liked. The fact that she was attractive to Weatherby made her all the more attractive to Cumberland, who could hear them in there talking about the people of the mountains and joking about themselves. "You'll have these convicts breaking their chains and chasing you in the woods, young lady," he heard Weatherby tell her. "What you ought to do, Anna, is wear a sackcloth over yourself."

"That's all I have to wear now," she said. She would bubble on for half an hour about anything—what she wore or should wear, or what she ate or would like to eat, or where she lived and what sort of house she wanted for herself, and what sort of children. "I want no more than five," she told him that afternoon, with Cumberland sitting beyond the door. "I don't want a big crowd gnashing at each other. We have so many children at home you have to wade through them to go to and from your bed, and then you find all the beds full. They have to soup together out of the pot, because they've stepped on all the bowls."

"Can your father work?"

She studied about that and sniffed and rubbed her nose. "He might work for a minute or two," she said, and winked at Weatherby, who laughed out loud in a booming voice. "I tell you the truth though, it would be a pleasure to us if he did have a job working, for it's a pity to be in a family that hasn't got nothing at all." She was now talking so softly that Cumberland could scarcely hear her. "My mama has one pot. She milks the cow in it, then she mixes dough in it, then she cooks in it, then she washes the dishes in it. Finally she washes it."

He laughed again, but she was serious as could be. "It has to be something fine, though; the job has to have some name put to it, like engineer, for my papa is proud. He won't work like other men. He's got to be a general or he won't go to war. He's got nothing in this world at all, except that batch of children and my mama and me, but he won't bend to nobody. If somebody ordered him what to do, he'd stomp off."

"I don't know that we can use him, Anna," Weatherby said, "the way you list his qualifications."

"I'm only telling the truth."

"What did he accomplish in the war, or did he even hear about it?"

"You think we've not in my family heard about somethin' as big as a war, with men going and coming and horses trodding through the night? Raiders even come to our place and asked where my pa was, as if he was an enemy volunteer. Mama said he was off in the woods some'ers. They said she lied, that he was off fighting. She said he was in the woods fishing and philosophizing, and if they found him to send him home to supper. They said she lied and ordered her to produce evidence of 'your man.' My mama is a big woman; when she stomps, the ground shakes. She stomped and told them she'd produce him if they would make him take a job and work, and short of that to get off our place. They got so brave they burned down a chicken coop and rode away heroes. When my papa come home to eat, my mama told him we had suffered our first casualties in the war: 'You lost three hens,' she said. He went to see, and there wasn't nothing left of the battlefield but a charred piece of wood on the yard and some feathers. He commenced to moan so sad, and when she called him to supper, she called him general, and whenever after that he sat down by the fire at night, she'd start to croon a soldiers' song."

Weatherby laughed uproariously.

"I do make you smile, I see," she said.

She had a winning way, all right. All this she had said with the most wistful, serious look on her face. Her words had come tripping out, each chasing the others, as if her mind was moving ever so much faster than she could reckon with it.

As she left, Weatherby walked with her to the turnpike road and embraced her. "I'll try to find your papa a job," he said.

"I've thought about it myself until I'm almost sick," she said.

"Could he string wire?" he said.

"If it can be strung close the ground," she said, winking at him.

"I do need to get a telegraph line run from Henry to Babcock Station, and on up to the Gap."

"He might be willing to head up a telegraph company."

Weatherby said gently, "It's not much different from fishing, in a way."

She came to see him often in March and April, and the visits were rejuvenating to him. He could be heard to start chuckling even as he sat at his desk to begin a conversation with her. He told Cumberland that she represented the people he was trying to help; she reassured him of their inherent value. And he needed that assurance, because working for them was the purpose which night and day occupied him, and troubled him except when she was there and except for those times, almost every week, when he sneaked away on the engine leaving for Morganton Friday and crossed the yard and walked up the hill. Sometimes it was nine o'clock, sometimes it was after midnight, but invariably the light would be there in the window of his house, which was hers more than his now, and he would run the last little way. Mildred would hear him coming and would manage to get the door unbolted and open and to take him into her arms even as he reached it.

Cumberland got so he couldn't work as well as he wanted to because of his thoughts about HenryAnna. It was, he told himself, completely unreasonable of him, a well-educated person, once a college instructor, to be interested to a point of distraction in an untamed, uneducated female. But he was.

"She comes in here," he told Babcock, "with those pretty eyelashes bobbing, and not a sign of a smile for me."

"She smiles at me," Babcock said. "I try to smile back, but I don't know how well I do with it, or what I'd do at my age with her."

"I'd go see her, but I don't know that she has any place to entertain in, unless a person likes to swim."

Cumberland wouldn't explain what he meant by that, and on Friday when he saw Babcock talking with HenryAnna, he suspected she was being asked about the comment and what it might mean. Even at a distance of fifty yards, Cumberland could tell she got huffy all of a sudden.

He decided, once the weekend came, he would go see her come what may. He couldn't lose anything, after all. Rejection wouldn't embarrass him further, and as for the work, the clerks could take care of it, or simply delay matters until Monday.

He said nothing to Weatherby, of course. A few weeks before, he might have mentioned it to him, but Weatherby of late, rather than talk about the Plover girls as provocative symbols, had begun talking about HenryAnna as a personal friend. It was as if Weatherby were the girl's father, or even the girl's suitor. When Weatherby on Friday asked what his plans were for the weekend, Cumberland said he would stay at the camp, unless he took a notion to go hunting with Babcock. But as soon as Weatherby left for Morganton, Cumberland hauled two buckets of hot water into his bedroom and poured them into a tin tub. He brought in two more bucketfuls and dumped in one of them, got out a bar of flowered soap he had bought the year before in Raleigh, and lathered his body well. Babcock came by and they talked through the closed door. One convict had injured another one in the eye, Babcock said, and he didn't know whether to send the injured man to Old Fort or not. "That doctor in Old Fort drinks more than he heals," he said.

Cumberland began humming as he bathed. "Hell, I don't know."

Babcock said, "I went up to Babcock Station this morning and it's nigh built, so we'll get them other 150 prisoners in directly, to fight and gouge one another."

Cumberland rinsed off, pouring the full bucket of water over himself, then dried off. He climbed into bed naked and covered up. His mother had always told him to take a bath of a morning, never of a night, for the hot water opened the pores to diseases, which were more spirited in the night air. He pulled two quilts up close around his chin.

Babcock was droning on about his problems. Cumberland closed his eyes and thought of HenryAnna as he had seen her in the pool.

He slept well, and at dawn he dressed in clean clothes, ate a big breakfast, and waited impatiently for the stage. Once aboard, the bouncing of the coach only intensified his desires to be with the girl, and he chided himself for his thoughts, they became so flagrant. There was another theory of his mother's, God bless her, that there were three levels of sin: (1) a sin committed; (2) the appearance of sin; (3) a thought of committing a sin. These were apparently of equal importance, or at least all three were damnable, and the three working in tandem had placed her under considerable strain before she died; she was burdened down with the guilt for sins she had not even had the pleasure of committing. Cumberland much preferred his grandfather's theory, which held that any sin of the Christian was forgiven before it was done. "If God forgives us, why not forgive ourselves?" he said. He would wag his finger threateningly before young Cumberland's nose and in his mystic, fine voice say, "Beware the man or woman who does not forgive himself. It's ungodly."

The driver stopped at the Gap and Cumberland thanked him for the ride, as the man flicked his whip again and the horses moved on toward Asheville.

There was stillness everywhere about him now. The birds were quiet; no doubt they were watching him, they and the squirrels and the coons and the chipmunks, and maybe, he thought, the bears and mountain lions, and maybe HenryAnna. He felt uneasy, even standing on the turnpike itself, but he forced himself to enter the forest to the left, where the big tunnel someday was to be. Beyond there, somewhere in the woods, was her house and the pond.

He located the lookout by following the line he had helped Weatherby mark a few months ago. He had hoped she would be there, and he even managed to call her name a few times—but not loud; he didn't doubt he would sometimes be made a fool of by her, but he didn't want to make a fool of himself, standing out in the middle of a wilderness calling to somebody who wasn't even present, who hadn't even known he was to be there.

He sat down on the rock and wondered what to do, and at once noticed on the rock floor before him a single wild flower, one so newly picked that dew remained on its petals.

"HenryAnna," he said, turning expecting to see her there. "HenryAnna!"

Another flower was on the rocky floor not far away. Beyond that, where a path reached the rocks and led off into the woods, was a third.

He wiped sweat from his face, his hands trembling. He was close to her, he realized. She knew he was here, too, and perhaps was watching him from a hiding place. How could he outthink her, induce her to show herself or come to join him; how did one ever know what was in the mind of such a wood nymph, anyway?

He entered the woods and saw on the soft earth her naked footprint.

He walked deep into the woods until he heard the waterfall, and as quietly as he could he approached it and the pool. He peeked out. There on the drying rock was the outline of her damp body, and on the stepping rock was the outline of her damp feet. "Anna," he called, looking about desperately.

She was nowhere to be seen, and on the path across the stream, on the ground, he saw a flower.

He crossed the pebbly creek, stepping from one rock to another while the water swirled near his feet. Holding to laurel bushes, he pulled himself up the far bank.

He saw her footprints there.

After a ways a path crossed this one, but he saw her footprints going on up the mountain, so he followed. Soon he could look down at the Swannanoa Gap village, which was a church and a few buildings at a mill pond. It was all quite beautiful. He could see men on the turnpike and a wagon as it made its way toward the Gap, a boy walking behind it. Far below he could see Henry Station.

"Anna," he said softly, questioning where she was. There was no answer, and he went on up toward the bald.

Soon the path opened onto a field, which was blossom-covered with wild flowers. There were many acres of flowers. Maybe this was where she had been leading him, he thought.

"Anna," he said.

There was no answer, but on the path to his right, which moved along the edge of the wild garden, was a single flower.

For a long way along the garden's border, he hurried on. The sun touched him warmly, so that he perspired freely. He came to another high lookout, and he could see the lookout he had rested at earlier, over 500 feet below him.

Wearily he sat down on a rock and swatted at his pants legs to get the pollen off them. He smelled like a flower, and he laughed at the spectacle of himself, being led by fallen blooms into this wild, festooned country. Below him the wind was rustling the leaves of the trees, turning them this way and that, so that the light green of the leaves was changed as the wind moved.

"Anna!" he called.

There was no reply.

He was disappointed in her, he decided. He could accept a game as well as anybody, but a game ought to end sometime. He was tired from the climb, and the smells and sun warmth were making him doze. He could imagine himself getting lost up here, misled by this nymph, drugged by the garden; it was exasperating, and the more he considered the extent of his humiliation the more angry he became.

He moved along the path, looking for a promising route down to the Gap community, which, as he could see, was directly below him. Let her come find him, he thought. He saw an inviting trail which entered the laurel patch, the "slick," as mountain people called such places, and he chose that one. He supposed any path that went downhill would sooner or later lead to the village.

Let her follow him if he wanted to, and she would, he suspected.

The trail grew narrower as it went along. Also it closed in from the top, so that there was not quite room enough to walk erect. He bent over and pushed on through the branches. Certainly he wasn't going to turn back and let her see him come up the mountain again, more harried than before.

At one place he had to crawl, but the trail opened out soon. When he went around a bend he saw he would have to crawl again, and this time the laurel trunks were so close he would need literally to snake his way along. Well, that was all right, too, he decided.

He got through at some expense to his clothing and further expense to his dignity. The trail opened out on the other side, and he hurried on. But at the next curve it narrowed and soon was almost gone.

He talked to himself aloud about this whole damn day, which had begun so hopefully, and was approaching the ragged edge of his patience. He had suggested to Babcock that HenryAnna didn't have a place to entertain a gentleman; well, he had reason to change his view, for she had many places, some more favored than others. This particular place was not one he liked, and the fact that he had led himself into it only added to his aggravation.

He got down on his hands and knees and crawled down the mountainside, pushing his way through, come what may, taking whatever route offered itself at any turn. His clothes were snagged repeatedly, but he supposed they could be mended. All he wanted now was to be free of here and of her, to reach that little village and go at once to Henry Station. He pushed forward furiously until abruptly the path ended. Before him were laurel trunks growing so close that he couldn't hope to get through.

He tried to turn around and found he couldn't do so.

He tried to stand, but the branches were close to his back; they were so thick he couldn't push them upward, not even a foot.

Terrified, he lay there trying to silence his own breathing. He began to wriggle backwards, forcing his way along, the effort exhausting him. He was lathered with sweat when he found at last that he could kneel. He tried to turn around. He could do so if he could get a laurel trunk out of the way.

He tried to push it over, but that did no good. It was limber enough, but its limbs had intertwined with other bushes overhead.

He stretched out on his belly and wriggled backwards again, gasping for breath, telling himself not to panic. When he could turn around, he began to crawl, and when at last he could stand and was free of the bushes' hold on him, he began to run up the mountain, so anxious was he to be safe. Only when he got back to the main trail did he turn to survey the place he had been, and he was amazed to see how inviting the path appeared to be.

The path was a trap, he realized. So was the garden. So was the girl. They were all kith and kin and had been leading him here. Now in the middle of the day he was in this remote place, his shirt and pants ripped to shreds, his back and arms cut deeply by the bushes.

And there on the path before him was a single flower.

By midafternoon he had retraced his steps past the waterfall and the lookout to the Gap. He walked down the turnpike, a torn, sore and embittered figure of a man who has been entertained for a morning by a mountain girl. For a short way, toward the end of the journey, he got a ride in a hay wagon driven by an old fellow who belched a great deal and didn't think there would be a railroad coming up this way. "I tell you," he confided to Cumberland, "the mountains have a habit of staying set in their own dear ways."

CHAPTER FIVE

THE WORKERS and mules went out each sweaty, spring morning of this year, 1877, and moved more earth than even Weatherby had expected them to, and the Road began to take shape in among the trees, along the creek, with an even, steady grade as it began to climb. There was no rock to move, except here and there a major boulder, which could be blasted through if it didn't yield to fire and water.

Mountain people came by to inquire about the progress. This Road was their hope and diversion, and often Weatherby would walk with them to where the men were working to show them the convicts and would describe with sweeping gestures how the Road would wind about to make its grade, all of this in prospect, of course, and predict when it would reach a certain point on the mountain. He assumed delays would occur, but there had been none; there had not even been a fatal accident.

Sometimes visitors would stay overnight, camping in the field below the station or stacking a shelter of boughs against the stockade wall. There were always visitors about.

One night in May Cumberland and Weatherby were in the outer office, working together on a large map they were making, when they heard somebody outside the door. They turned as the latch on the door was lifted and the door opened from its own weight. The light from the office lantern flooded onto the porch, and they could see the smiling man who stood there. He was unbelievably ragged, his clothes holding at the seams but having worn out between and having been draped over him, so that here and there his bare skin showed plain. His shoes were ribbons of leather which had been hand-laced. His face and hands were wrinkled and dried like the leather, but he wasn't old, and his blue eyes were youthful and glimmered with kindness. "Air ye the ones?" he said. He advanced to the threshold of the door, more fully to share the lanternlight with them. "I need to see ye," he said, stepping into the room, bringing with him the sweet smell of snuff. Receiving no reply, he closed the door and latched it, then set a leather case and leather pouch against the door, as if to forbid any further use of that way. "Air ye the one with the Road?" he said.

"We are," Weatherby said.

"I wasn't sure, for I saw no scars on you, nor even deep lines in your face, nor even a frown there yet."

There was something eerie about him, and his voice, which had been holding to a tune as he spoke, seemed to linger in the room.

"You come for a drink?" Weatherby said.

"No. But I'll take a sip to keep company."

Weatherby got a jug from his office and took a sip himself, on the way back. He handed the jug to the visitor, who sat down in a chair, adjusted his body to it comfortably, and lifted the jug to his lips. He drank until his Adam's apple had bobbed four times. "I'm a four-bob man," he said, plopping the jug down nearby, where Cumberland or Weatherby could get it. He sat there with his mouth open and his eyes watering. "It burns good," he said. "Lord knows that's pure stuff. My, my." He was trying to get his breath. "When I was young I could down a jug without stopping. I was an eight-bob man. Ye ever see one?"

Weatherby nodded.

"Have ye done it?"

"No."

"I done it regular until once I was tricked by a distiller who had only took the first of a run, so it was strong as lightning. Of course, I supposed it was like other whisky, maybe half alcohol, but it was almost entirely pure fire. I was playing at a barn dance, I remember, and I downed eight bobs of that stuff and, God knows, it done reamed me. I never was so het up over nothing in my life, and I went out of doors and walked around the barn four times trying to get my vision clear, them boys alaughing at me like asylum guards. I could barely walk and couldn't talk, but when I got back into that barn, God, man, could I play!"

"Could ye?" Weatherby said, laughing.

"Man, I was strung to my own bow, and when I come to my banjo, I was inside the skin, one with it all." He cackled, delighted with the memory. He took up the jug and drained it, set it on the floor and studied the two men before him, his eyes bleary, watering, and his lips pursed in a silent whistle as the steam from inside his stomach came through. Suddenly he wiped his nose with his hand and said, "I come for to ask for work on this infernal Road."

"No money to hire with," Weatherby said simply.

"I'm by profession not a doctor nor a lawyer nor any other such damn liar and thief. I'm not a teacher, for I'm still trying to learn what my own life is about; them that knows that should teach, and others should keep their mouths shut. I'm not a miller, cause I don't care much fer sneezing near flour. I'm not a smith cause the noise is jarring to my ears. I'm not a tinsmith, for I never—I never—what the hell did I never do with tin? Well, hit don't matter. And I'm not a farmer, for I don't care that much for manure." He belched and tottered a bit on his chair, then cleared his throat to continue, but his mind faltered on him.

"What is your line of work?" Weatherby asked kindly.

"Huh?"

"What is it you do for a living?"

"A living ye say?"

"Well, tell us what you do."

"Why, sir," he said, gripping his hands together, "I'm a music man." He sat on the chair most solemnly, reverent before the name of his own profession. "I bow to no man for that."

"I wouldn't think you needed to," Weatherby said gently, "but we don't need one here."

"A tinsmith sells a dipper. I have no dipper. A dipper is worth something to a man or woman. We all need one. But I have a song to sell, and what's a song worth? How do you measure its worth? You can't measure it, so it's worth nothing. It's worth nothing, but it's worth it all."

His fingers, as if alive with their own thoughts, began to open the leather case, unbuckling it while he looked straight ahead, involved with the thoughts and visions of his own. His hands fastened on the instrument, a three-stringed dulcimer, made of walnut and inlaid tastefully; there was no dent or scar to be seen on it. It was most beautiful as he held it, not looking down as he took it from the case and put the case on the floor beside his chair. At last he leaned over the dulcimer, which was laid on his knees; his right hand gently stroked the side of it as if to awaken it, his thumb stroked the strings as he tuned it, all the while leaning over it.

He sat back in his chair and sighed longingly. "I bow to no man. I bow not to any statesman, for they took us into war. I bow to no soldier, for they build shaky edifices. I bow to no preacher, for they are my natural enemies, except if I want to sing their hymns fer them, and I don't most often, for I'd rather sing about people I know, or people long ago dead I wish I'd knowed, and about love and life and the gallows we're all dangling from." He waved one hand warningly before his face, then began to sing, moving from speech to song easily, naturally:

> I wish I was a little sparrow,
> One of them that could fly so high.
> I'd fly and sit on my true love's dwelling,
> And when she talked I'd be close by.

His fingers moved slowly on the strings, only sad sounds coming out of them, accompanying him. His voice was sad, too, and he sang in the minor key of the folk people. The song had a tinsel quality to it, so that Weatherby feared to breathe lest he break the texture of it.

> Neither am I a little sparrow
> And neither do I have wings to fly;
> So I'll sit down and weep in sorrow,
> I'll sing and lay my troubles by.

He remained leaning over the dulcimer. Slowly he straightened, and a smile came over his face. "Now wasn't that pretty?"

"I tell you it was," Weatherby said.

"Why was it? I've not got a pretty voice. Once I had, but I lost it a few years ago. Is it because I have such a fine dulcimer? Why, others have ones as grand. Is it because this is such a great concert hall?" He was murmuring more than talking, as if talking to himself.

Weatherby watched him intently. "Why?"

The old man smiled. "It's because I love it so." He nodded and winked. "I can sing all night." He suddenly smiled. "Yes, Lord. But I can't clog. My legs wobble. I can't do a lot of things I once thought were such vitalities. Not long ago I found myself in bed with a woman and was limp and never seemed to change one damn bit. I wish I had control over such as that."

Weatherby laughed. "Age lowers a man, does it?"

"It limps me something bad at forty-five years. But a boy don't know how to make love with any skill, so it evens out. Oh, my God," he said, as if in pain, "think on that and fret fer a change." He cackled a broken laugh, then picked up the jug and put it to his lips. His mind slowly focused on the fact that it was empty. "That's what I mean," he said.

Weatherby leaned back in his chair. "You come on business, is that it?"

"I come because I arrived here. I don't have a lot of places to be tonight." He belched.

"What's your offer?"

"I make no certain one. I couldn't bind myself to any work, or any time, or any schedule, as you can tell. The best of ever day I spend thinking. With some of the poorer time I make instruments for music, as I made this dulcimer here. I make fiddles out of sourwood as pretty as you ever saw. I made one out of curly maple, with the front of white pine. I used to make one fiddle a month, but I'm not so swift now. I can make banjos, if I can get the skins, but cat or groundhog skins are the best and the good ones are hard to find. Quality is what you're talking about; quality is what the thing is. Music is nothing, except in the air, which is why it pays so little and I'm so hungry all the time." He smiled, his toothless gums showing; then he said, "I ought to make me a banjo again, cause I know many a dance song. Could you find me the skin of a mountain cat?"

Weatherby stared at him for a long while, then breathed deeply into his chest. "I'll certainly try," he said.

"I'll play for you, if I want to. I won't play for you if I don't. I don't bargain myself off."

"You offer nothing even for the skin?"

"I offer all I have."

"And that's what?"

He smiled plaintively and quietly said, "It's in the air."

Weatherby laughed softly as he got up. "Well, you are a strange one." He went into his office and came back a minute later with a chart. "We have no listing here for a music man, no opening at all."

"I preach some," the music man said.

"After what you said about preachers?"

"I said nothing unkind about God, did I? Not that I haven't, mind you." Again he wagged his hand before his face. "Life to me is a puzzle with more arms than heads to it, so I can't grapple it down before it rises again."

Cumberland said, "I'd like to hear you preach sometime."

"The other preachers are as alike as if they come from the same womb; but I have my own mind to think matters through."

Weatherby was still looking over the list of jobs he might be able to justify filling.

"I'd want a title. I'm particular about what I admit I'm doing."

" 'Music man' is a good title," Weatherby said. "We could switch this title of warehouse laborer to music man, and put you down for his salary."

"How much is it?"

"Twenty-five dollars a month."

The music man grumbled and grunted depreciatingly, his mouth flopping open in agony. "Ohhh, you don't pay well here."

Cumberland laughed out loud, which made it all the harder for Weatherby to keep a straight face.

"You hire cheap on this Road, for something so ambitious, challenging a mountain. You'll meet rock afore you're done, you'll meet pain to yourself, too, each of you. Which of ye is the one called Weatherby?"

"I am."

"I thought you was. And you're Cumberland, the college-bred?"

"How do you know me?" Cumberland said.

"HenryAnna told me all about you."

Weatherby stared at him intently. "You know her?"

"For many years, in good times and bad. I'm one of the few who has ever seen HenryAnna cry."

"You her father?" Weatherby said.

"Yes." The two men stared at each other for a long moment, then Weatherby looked back at his chart and picked out the salary for the telegraph foreman, which was five dollars a month higher than the salary of the warehouse laborer. He mentioned that title and figure, and the music man nodded, accepting it. "I can do that work," he said, "though I don't know anything of consequence that can be said on a wire." He put the dulcimer away, then squinted at Weatherby, and his little face poked up close to his. "I ought to go now, though I don't know why." He turned to Cumberland and stuck his face up close to his, too. "She's fond of you, ain't she?"

"Who?"

"I don't know just why, but she is, or she wouldn't cuss and discuss you so much." He turned and went out as quickly as he had come.

Cumberland stood staring at the doorway, the last words of the visitor in his mind. He saw that Weatherby was looking at the empty doorway. Suddenly Weatherby shrugged and cleared his throat, "We've been needing a man like that."

"For what?"

"Lord knows," Weatherby said.

The days were hot and steamy, but the nights were cool and the work went well on the lower stretches of the mountain.

In June the digging crew reported an unusual occurrence at a cut in the mountain. The earth, when dug away, revealed soft rock, which, when torn away, revealed a bed of white mud. This was easy to shovel into the carts and haul off. However, there seemed to be no bottom to it.

Originally Weatherby had estimated that 80,000 cubic yards of earth would need to be removed here; over 80,000 cubic yards had been moved, and still the foamy mud obstructed the Road.

Weatherby noticed that, for some reason, the mules and oxen didn't want to wade into it, and he sensed a clammy chill, himself, on seeing the white, bubbly bath. Babcock ordered the men to force a mule to go into the cut. They could not, so he told them to throw one in, which a group of convicts did. The mule sank down to his belly and waded desperately toward hard land, which it reached finally amid the shouts and laughter of the convicts. It came up out of the mud, kicking at everything around, and kept kicking until it was out of sight.

The men waited about for Weatherby to tell them what to do. He talked with them about the mud and said he didn't know what to do, except to dig it out. They went back to digging, making a great show of slopping mud over each other. "You a white boy now, Curtis."

"Let you harden for a statue, Milt."

They dug it out one day, only to have it rise again overnight.

One morning Weatherby awakened earlier than usual. He realized he had been dreaming about this mud cut, and he dressed, left without waking Cumberland in the nearby room, and walked the mile's distance to it. The mud had risen in the night, like a yeasty dough, had returned to its former level.

He picked up a handful of it. It was moist, smooth, thin-grained white kaolin clay. He studied the mountainside above it to the west, and the side of the range opposite. No doubt the weight of the two were putting pressure on the opened wound, forcing up this mud bath.

He waded into the mud. He sank in it to his knees. He waded on farther and sank to his thighs. He told himself it was foolish to go on, but he was bound to do so, even when the mud came up around his waist and sucked at his body. It was as if the cut would take him in, if it could, would swallow him.

As he waded farther, his legs grew tired, but he went on, the mud encompassing the trunk of his body. He reached the middle of the cut and stood there, resting, supported by his own weight against the mud, which was under and around him up to his chest. When he moved on, the mud came up to his armpits. He waded into it, walked through it and against it, feeling his clothes and boots heavy with it, angry at it. Then the clay was only at his waist, and later only at his knees. He reached the other side and could look back and see outlined in the mud the path he had made.

The mud was now slowly filling it in.

All that day men worked at the mud cut, clearing a swath wide enough for the carts to pass through. Working knee-deep and sometimes waist-deep, they worked the mud out, chopping it and slopping about in it.

The Mud-Digger engine reached the cut by midafternoon. Track was laid into the cut, and the engine and three flatcars were rolled into it. Sixty men were sent into the cut to shovel mud onto the flatcars, then they rode the cars out of the cut and shoveled the mud off the sides. By this method much faster progress was made.

As night came the men built fires at each end of the cut, and they worked in the firelight, Weatherby with them, not tiring, keeping with them as they cleared the mud away. At last they rolled the Mud-Digger and its car through the cut.

All the men were dead-tired by then. Weatherby told them to return to camp and wash themselves and their clothing. He admitted to Babcock he needed sleep himself. He said he hadn't realized, until the cut was clear, how deeply he had feared failing here.

The two men walked back to camp, and Babcock came into the office with him and helped him take off his boots, which were caked with dried clay. He helped him get out of his clothes, too, and

Weatherby in his underclothing lay down on the bed. Babcock threw a blanket over him. "I never saw it done before," he said.

"That's potter's clay," Weatherby said.

"How did clay get under that mountain?"

"It was captured there, somehow, centuries ago. We're dealing with the body of an old, old woman here. Some say these are the oldest mountains in the world."

"A mountain has surprises," Babcock said respectfully. "Nothing like that ever happens down East."

When Weatherby awoke he thought he had been asleep for only a few minutes. However, there was light flooding through the window and outside he could hear the convicts talking and yelling and beating their tin breakfast plates. Babcock came into the office and approached the bedroom door. Weatherby sat on the edge of his bed scratching his chest and looking about, sleepily wondering why Babcock was there.

Babcock said, "It's the same as it was before."

"What is?" Weatherby said.

"The mud. It's not different."

"We laid track through it," Weatherby said.

"It's all gone. The mud ate it up, track and ties. It's like it was yesterday morning."

Weatherby pulled on his clothes, which were damp from the night's washing, and went outdoors. The three foremen were standing there, waiting for instructions. "Better put all three gangs in there," Weatherby said. "We'll take the Mud-Digger through again."

All that day the gangs worked with the help of the engine and cars; they moved 600 cubic yards of white clay. Ties were laid, the old iron was washed off. The mud had twisted some of it cruelly; it was as if giant hands had taken the pieces and twisted them. So some new iron was laid, some old. Weatherby ordered the engine to pull four flatcars into the cut. The cars were loaded with mud, and this time Weatherby ordered that the engine and the cars be left there, to hold the track in place.

The convicts were taken to camp, but Babcock and Weatherby stayed at the mud cut, as did Bolton, the engineer. A dinner pail was brought to them, then Bolton curled up in the cab and buried his head in his arm; he always slept in the cab of his engine. Weatherby, Babcock and Ham found a soft place near the lip of the cut.

A moon was out well enough to see by. They could see the trees high on the ridge across from them, and the black engine below them, with the white clay below it. A wolf howled, then another. One was on the ridge and the other was on the mountain. Other wolves began howling, too, and Babcock said a pack of 100 wolves had visited the new Babcock Station, had looked at the camp, then had gone away without much noise. Weatherby said that he doubted if the workmen had counted accurately.

"That's what Tom Lawrence said. Tom can count to a hundred."

"What are the wolves congregating here for?"

"I asked Tom and he said he don't know what wolves think."

There was no other sound from the mountain, except a few wolf calls, and the whispery breeze as it went past them and over them, where the trees were leafy.

A drizzly rain started, not enough to bother them. They curled up under laurel limbs and went to sleep and slept well until sometime during the night a snap sounded, a shot, an explosion. The three men were on their feet at once, turning to the woods to meet whatever enemy was attacking, but there was no threat from the woods. They turned to the engine and saw that the engine, on its side, was rising. It was rising as if it were breathing. It was pulsating on the white mud. The track, even as they watched, was being twisted and sucked into the clay. The clay was undulating and the engine was rising as the clay breathed and heaved.

"My God," Babcock said. "Bolton, you awake in that engine?"

The terrified face of Bolton appeared at the cab window. He cried a lonely sound without words, begging for instructions. The mud was bubbling, oozing around the engine. The engine was sinking into the mud even as Bolton crawled onto the side of it. He cried as a child would cry for his parent. The world was white mud rising, taking in the black Mud-Digger, snapping and taking in the iron track, taking in the heavy wooden ties, taking in the flatcars, lifting them even as it took them in.

"Hey!" Weatherby shouted, throwing a piece of wood so that it fell near Bolton. "Grab that and it might float you!"

Bolton clung to the writhing engine, which was now being turned onto its back.

"Call the men," Babcock said, even though the men were far away and couldn't help. "Call the men! Get the convicts out!"

Bolton was crying like a baby. Weatherby waded into the mud, but the mud was breathing all around him and he couldn't keep on his feet. He caught hold of a bush and pulled himself back to the bank. "Bolton," he shouted, then to Babcock he said, "What in hell is happening here?"

The mountain moved. He looked up to see the hillside sliding toward him, hurling trees and rocks. Desperately he fled, and behind him Babcock was shouting and Bolton was screaming, and trees were breaking and rocks crashing as the earth rolled down.

When the gangs arrived soon after dawn, they found Weatherby standing before the 450-foot-long mound of earth and rock in which his engine and engineer lay buried. His own clothes were covered with the white mud, but there was no more white mud in sight now. Down in the womb of that mound of earth, rock and tree trunks, where the engine lay, was the mud. Under it all was where Bolton lay, too.

Weatherby had tried to work out an explanation for all of it. He knew Mud Cut lay at a sharp point of the mountain where the talus at the bottom of a cliff, as well as soft rock, overlaid hard rock. Apparently the removal of some of the hard rock had opened up the white mud bath; also it had taken the props from under the mass of material above, so it had come down in a grade slide. All this could be explained. Perhaps, Weatherby told himself, much of it could have been predicted. It was all rooted in natural causes. But, at the same time, he attributed it to the personality of the mountain itself, to the harshness of her attitude.

The convicts waited back a ways from where he stood. Finally one of them said, "What you want us to do, Mr. Weatherby?"

One mouth of the mountain was white mud, Weatherby thought, and through that mouth it had taken the engine and the cars and the track and the engineer. It was clear enough what the personality of this mountain was and what sort of methods she would choose.

"Mr. Weatherby?" the man said. All the men were waiting for instructions now.

"Put it back like it was yesterday," Weatherby said.

PART II

When I get to heaven I'm going to ride on a train,
Not going to build one, I'm going to ride on one,
A golden train.

CHAPTER SIX

ILL CREEK TURNED MUDDY all the way to the Catawba River, and the story of Mud Cut was told around the countryside. People shook their heads and sighed, and some of them said God wouldn't abide the making of a road. "He put that mountain there to block off such as they're doing, ain't that so?" they said.

In time the convicts uncovered the engine. They got the earth and rock pulled off of it, but the mud kept reclaiming it every night, and they couldn't find Bolton's body anywhere. They wrestled with Mud Cut day after day, and a depression fell on Weatherby, which he tried as best he could to hide, even from Cumberland and HenryAnna's father. The old man had taken to stopping by each night and talking expansively about how much line his men had run that day for the Western North Carolina Telegraph Company.

Weatherby kept the men at work in the Cut, even though they hated and feared it. If a man was too afraid to work in the Cut itself he would be assigned to some other duty, or if a man was sick he would be given light work to do, but Weatherby tried patiently to persuade most of the men to overcome their fears and illnesses and help deliver the engine and the dead body of the engineer, and he worked in the mud with them.

One day about noon it appeared that maybe they could get one of the flatcars out. At twilight the car was clear of mud on all sides, and Weatherby called for the logging chains, oxen and mules.

The men attached the chains in such a way that they could right the car, for it lay on its side. Then they drove poles under it, to break the suction of the mud. When all that was done, Babcock ordered the mules and oxen hooked up, and he told the men to get a handhold wherever they could, and he called on his Negro friend Ham, who sent up a chant, something for the men to strain and release by, a monotonous, rhythmic song.

The men and beasts, sloshing and sweating in the mud bath, righted the flatcar and in the dark pulled it free.

Each day after that a car was pulled free. By Thursday night only the engine was left. Weatherby had planned to go home on Friday, but he decided to use all day for engine hauling, to do the work once and for all, so he helped get the workers up and he went with them to the Cut, where, of course, the mud had covered up the engine. They dug the mud out all right, and got the engine exposed. In midafternoon the oxen and mules were taken to their hitching places along the chains, were driven into place with loud cursing and fierce whipping, for they were tired of hauling. There was tremendous pulling done that day, the drivers shouting and urging and coaxing. The men, well over a hundred of them, strained with the brutes, but all to no effect, for the black engine stayed in the mud.

When darkness came on, Babcock wanted to keep the men at work. "If we let it alone, by tomorrow it'll be mud-covered again."

But Weatherby said the men were tired out; and so was he. When the men had made a final search for the body of Bolton, they wearily went back to Henry Station, even as the mud began to ooze around the Mud-Digger.

On Saturday morning Weatherby did take the stage to Morganton. Cumberland stayed at the office, but with Weatherby gone the generating force was missing, and nobody was able to do much work. Babcock came by and wondered when the 150 new convicts would arrive. "They could help with that engine," he said. "I'm making a try today again, but it's only spraining backs, I'm afraid." He said he had sent the carpenters on up to start building the tunnel station. "Want to walk up there?" he asked.

It was about three miles, all of it uphill, but Cumberland went with him. There wasn't much to see when they arrived, either, except where trees had been felled for a clearing. The site was about a mile from the turnpike, near Lick Log tunnel, and it was perhaps half a mile through the woods from the Gap. Four barracks were to be built here, as well as an office, a flophouse, and a few other smaller buildings.

Babcock got to talking with the carpenters about where the buildings were to be put, and Cumberland got to thinking about being near enough to the Gap so that he could walk to the village, could be there in ten minutes. He didn't plan to see HenryAnna, not if he could help it, but he wouldn't mind talking with her father for a little while and seeing if he had got him the cabin to lease, the potter's cabin which he had said could be rented reasonably for weekend use.

Cumberland didn't say where he was going, for he didn't much want Babcock to follow him. He wandered off alone, then walked along a trail to the turnpike, and up the turnpike to the Gap.

It was a cloudy day, but it took kindly to him, for just as he reached the Gap the clouds let the sun peek through. From where he stood he could see twenty or more cabins surrounding the valley, and on the valley floor was the cluster of buildings. The new sunlight was being broken by the moving clouds, so that it swept across some of the roofs and fields, even as it disappeared on others, making the houses and fences sparkle and seem to breathe. The millwheel was turning and beyond it the millpond was no bigger than a corn patch and had a gray rail fence around it. There were a few sheep on the lower reaches of the mountain, which he realized was the same mountain, rising above the Gap, on which the Road was being built.

It was a quaint, appealing place, and Cumberland was drawn at once along its raggedy road.

He was greeted warmly by three men standing at the smithy. The smith himself was the one who had once pitted his strength against the train engine. He could wield a hammer in each hand, and did so now, one of the other men holding a shoe in place on the anvil. Ringing sounds vibrated against the far-off ridge and bounded back again. As he worked he talked in a loud voice, telling Cumberland that this was the Gap community, if it could be called a town at all, and had existed for sixty years "as time is measured elsewhere." What he meant by "as time is measured elsewhere" Cumberland didn't know. Perhaps time was not measured that way here, or was not measured here at all. The smith said his name was Gordon Snow, but that he was called Smith or Smithy by everybody because of the work he did. He wore a suede leather shirt, leather pants, and a horsehide apron which had often been burned and scorched and was now a deep brown, almost black. He wore hard-leather shoes which were so large that Cumberland commented on them. "I made 'em out of iron," he said, "leastwise, they have iron in them. It's so when I drop metal on them it doesn't break my toes."

He stopped his infernal hammering and dipped the horseshoe in water; it hissed and sizzled there, steam gushing up from the barrel.

The men didn't ask Cumberland who he was or what he did for a living; it was indiscreet to express curiosity about personal matters. They did, however, begin to volunteer information about themselves, about their work and hunting, about how many children they had and how their crops had been growing. All of this Cumberland came to realize was meant to assure him that such information about himself would interest them, so he proceeded in much the same way as they to tell about himself. He said he had been born in eastern North Carolina on a farm, or plantation, of about 2,000 acres of flatland. He had no wife or children, and had gone to school "somewhat overlong," as he put it, and now had a job working for the Road.

The men showed instant surprise and interest. One of them from his pocket took out a folded piece of paper, torn and stained, on which was marked the outline of the route the Road was to use. "Air this nigh accurate?" he asked.

"It seems to be perfectly in order," Cumberland said.

"A parson made it," the man said. "Made three of them by following the markings."

"He sold Jim Henry that one for a high price," Smith said, "and went on to Asheville and sold the others."

"He said he'd walked the roadway that was surveyed. He said he had walked other roads laid that-a-way, though never in so wild a place."

Smith leaned close to Cumberland and confidentially said, "Can it be done?"

"What?"

"The Road. Can it come past my shop?"

"Why, I see no reason why not. Where do you want it to pass?"

"Where does it appear from out the belly of the mountain?"

"At a tunnel, near that far rock."

"Near Praying Rock? Then if it could wander on down this way, I'd be pleased to see it."

The smith had the enthusiasm of a boy. He had always worked with metal, and now he was near the greatest metal creation of all, one made by master smithies faraway, one nobody in the mountains had a forge big enough to shape. "If I had time enough," he said, wiping sweat from his face, "I'd like to try me an engine. You show me a train out there in that field, and I'll make one in here," he said, proudly waving his arm at his tiny shop. "I'll make it or it'll break me."

Cumberland caught a vision of the man, working for the rest of his life on his masterwork, not a painting or a church steeple or a great building on a town square, but an engine.

"I'd ride it out there," Smith said, waving his arm in a vast motion which included the entire valley. "Round and round," he said happily. Suddenly he leaped into the air, caught up by his own energy, and made quite a racket when his heavy shoes struck the ground. "Ay, God, bring me a train!" he said. "Ay, God, bring me one of them engines!"

Across the street was a rickety store, big enough for a small amount of merchandise and six or eight men to gather in and talk over the matters of the day. Cumberland thought he might find the music man there, but as he approached it he caught a glimpse of an empty house nearby, half hidden in a grove of small trees at the headwaters of the millpond. He moved along the edge of the pond toward it and came to a marker set in the soil, much like a tombstone. The marker appeared to be a piece of wood, but when he ran his hand over it and some of the dirt fell away, he saw that it wasn't wood at all. He used a piece of bark to scrape the mud from the sign, and he used his handkerchief, which he sopped in the millpond, to wash it clean.

At last he stood back and looked down on a brilliantly shiny, salt-glazed pottery tablet, inscribed with the words: Ben Barnes, Master Potter.

"I've brought you back to life, I see, Ben," Cumberland said.

He approached the house through a work area. A brick ground-hog kiln, about twelve feet long, was set into the gound. At eight-foot intervals around it were eight brick columns, each eight feet high. Large wooden beams rested on them. The roof had caved in around them, and some of the rived oak boards were scattered on the ground. Here and there, lying with them on the ground, or jutting out of the ground, were fragments of clay pots, jugs, crocks, dishes, cups, bowls. . . .

Before the house were two large willow trees. Behind it, shading its back yard, was a grove of maples. The house itself faced south and was made of logs, chinked with clay. The walls, as he could tell by looking at the edge of the front window, were a foot thick. It was a husky, one-story house with a large roof overhang, and a massive wooden door, deeply carved and now deeply encrusted.

He approached it with caution, almost afraid the house would sink from sight. It was as idyllic as the pond and the mill which could be seen across the pond—and could be heard clattering across the pond, too, he noticed.

On the west side of the house was a chimney made of such large rocks that he could not imagine how they had been lifted into place, and so closely fitted that only a little clay chinking had been used around them. There were loft windows on each side of the chimney. A kitchen wing jutted out from the house behind; the wing was made of planks and was weathered a deep gray. The back door was ajar, and he pushed it open.

The walls were paneled in poplar; some of the panels were two feet wide. They were clean and sound. The floor was made of wide planks of oak and was neatly swept and mopped, so that the grain of the oak was clearly marked. And on the floor, just before the open doorway, was a single flower.

He found HenryAnna in the main room of the house, sitting on the raised front ledge of the fireplace. She had a small broom in her hand, one she had lashed together for herself, and with which she had been cleaning the hearth. "You arrived early this morning," she said, putting the broom aside.

"Are you the potter?" he said, impressed to realize anew how refined she was in feature and how considerate in the way she approached sound and movement.

"Did you see his kiln?"

"Yes."

"My papa knew him well, and they would talk part of every day away, and sometimes I would come over here and visit with him, especially at firing times when the fire would rise out of the kiln as big as the treetops and the kiln would roar and the earth would shake. He would sit out there under that willow tree and nod and tremble with it, reading a book all the while, turning the pages with only a glance now and then toward the kiln, and an occasional order to the man who helped him at such times: 'more wood,' or maybe it would be 'put on the light wood now and let it rumble,' or maybe it would be 'let it cool for a day.'"

"Where is he now?"

"Out back," she said.

"Buried, you mean?"

"There's a patch of white clay out there, and he wanted to be buried naked in it. When he died papa and my brothers and me come up here with shovels to dig him a spot, and we had to send for axes to cut that wet stuff. It was all day we chopped it. The miller wouldn't help none. He never liked the potter. The Presbyterian preacher who farms down the road come and dug, or axed or cut or whatever it was we had to do, until about sundown we had enough depth to bury him. He had told papa once he didn't want a box for himself; he said he would let the clay fill him in. The preacher said we had to have a box, he said it wasn't right what we was doing, but when he tried to get a Bible verse to prove it, he couldn't find one. Then the preacher claimed he couldn't preach over a naked man, but my papa said the potter had a right to go as he had come. He was skinny, and his skin was dried out and his veins stood out blue on him. He looked like a map of a river valley. Papa set him in the hole and put beside him a selection of his choice pots. The preacher didn't like that, either, said it was heathen, and he refused to pray. I remember begging him to pray, to get it done, so we could cover over that poor old naked man who sat in that cold, clay place. At last papa prayed, and we began to throw clay in, but by that time the water had seeped in. The clay splashed in water and floated on top of it. Nobody knew what to do. The preacher told papa it was justice rained from the sky on us. My father said it seemed to have come from the ground. My brothers kept pouring in clay, and it got soggy and mounded up. We couldn't push enough clay into the hole to fill it. We was all sweating, and three or four women drew nigh to see us, and they started singing about beautiful Zion."

She smiled wistfully, as if she appreciated very well the irony of it all.

"Finally papa said it was done, and the next day he went back out there and put a fence around it, for the grave was no more'n a clay top to a water well with a dead man at the bottom of it."

"It's there yet?" he said.

"Yes. Nobody will move it," she said, suddenly smiling.

There were chips of pottery in the fireplace. Beside the fireplace was the iron door of a bake-oven. Across the room was a steep, enclosed stairs, which led to the loft.

"I'll look upstairs," he said, "if I may."

On the loft floor he found the feathers of two birds that had got inside sometime before and, unable to find a way out, had died there. Hulls of nuts, which squirrels had left, were neatly stacked in three piles.

When he came downstairs, HenryAnna was still sitting on the hearth.

"Do you like it?" she said.

"Yes," he said. "I want it."

"Let me show you something." She went into the kitchen, a square bare room with a pottery sink. There was a wooden trap door in the floor which she opened; exposing a small storage bin, rock-enclosed with a clay floor, one large enough for the storing of apples, potatoes and canned goods.

"How much would it cost to rent this house?" he asked.

"Oh, it's leased already," she said in a hushed voice.

"Is it?" he said, surprised. "It wasn't leased last week."

"No, that's so," she said.

"Who leased it then?"

She sniffed and wiped her forehead with the back of her hand, almost as if she were feeling her own temperature. "I leased it myself," she said.

He controlled his temper, but it required much effort, and only because he had learned that anger didn't achieve anything with her, or with any of these mountain people. "Now no doubt you'll sublet it to me, at a profit?" He did want the place, was quite bound to the hope of having it, reclaiming it from the thicketed woods, and he could even imagine himself setting a fire in the kiln again and feeling the earth tremble, as in times past. "If I were to rent it by the month, how much would the rent be?"

"I'd hate to part with it, now that I have it at last."

"But you didn't have it last week, did you?"

"And I wouldn't want to charge you much for a little house like this, when you'd have to pay to cut down all the thickets and pay to mend the roof, and pay to put window glass in the windows where it's broke out, all when you're only renting it, you understand, by the month."

"I'll do it all, damn you," he said. Money was not his problem, but having the house certainly was. He knew that rented houses could be found in the lowlands for $5 a month, and he knew Weatherby rented his house in Morganton for $7 and it was much larger than this, and finer, too, in its way. "How much? Four dollars a month?"

"I'd hate to see you get yourself involved in such an old place." She really seemed to be worried on his behalf, but suddenly she smiled, and it was like the sun coming out on a stormy day. "But if you want to repair it, and if you don't mind my using it when you're away, I'll arrange for you to have it for $8 a month."

Waves of relief and anger simultaneously swept over him. He had been so afraid of losing it entirely that he was, even by such a rough-hewn compromise, elated. Yet he knew she was cheating him.

He went through the house a second time, seeing everything on his own, looking out the windows on every side of it to judge the view he would have once he had paid to have the thickets thinned out properly and had got the windows cleaned. It was a perfect place, he realized. A perfect place!

He took a roll of money from his pocket and counted out the first month's rent.

Later the same morning, she helped him buy a bed. It happened that a furniture maker was passing with a wagon on which a bed was placed, one he had made, and he happened to see that there was smoke coming out of the potter's house, so he stopped to inquire. It was a walnut bed. Cumberland did need it, of course. He asked its value and the old man said he would sell it for $18, at which point HenryAnna started a fierce argument about the price. She found scratches that the eye could scarcely see; she objected to the grain of the wood on one post and wondered aloud if the bedstead was wobbly. Finally the furniture maker agreed to a price only half of what he had initially asked, and Cumberland was quick to comply.

The furniture maker appeared to be furious with HenryAnna; he did, however, return within the hour with a chest of drawers on his wagon. He said since he had sold the bedstead for so little he hoped to get more for the chest. It matched the bed and Cumberland needed it, and he was rather surprised to hear HenryAnna tell the man to take it away, that it was an inferior chest, that it was so much out of balance that "it's going to fall over on the floor." The furniture maker was furious with her, and he and she almost got into a fight about the worth of the chest of drawers, he finally agreeing to a price so low that he said he was losing the value of his labor and half the value of the wood, too.

A quilt woman, a smithy with a poker and a few big black pots, a chairmaker, and finally a potter appeared that day, each in turn. Each got into a fierce argument with her about the worth, if any, of his products.

"A man comes to live among us and you try to sell poor goods to him. We ought to be pleased he's come here," she told a poor old lady who had come to sell a pair of curtains which, by chance, exactly fitted the parlor windows.

It was late in the afternoon, after Cumberland had bought four chairs, a down mattress, two quilts, a table, a poker, two pots, eight dishes, and the curtains, that he focused on the strangeness of it all: one craftsman arriving almost as another left, all of them being dealt with by HenryAnna. He mentioned to her that it was strange that the curtains fitted the windows so well.

"Why, she knows the size of ever window in this valley."

He tried to think the matter through. "The tinsmith hasn't arrived."

"He's in Asheville today," she said.

"Are you sure?" he said, watching her carefully.

The faintest look of guilt crept into her eyes, and suddenly she sniffed and rubbed her nose. "Don't you trust me?"

"God, no," he said.

There was a knock at the front door, and at once HenryAnna

admitted an old lady who carried a pot in which there was a beef
stew; the woman also had two spoons. She set all this down on the
ledge at the hearth, poured the stew, then took a small pone of corn
bread from her apron pocket and broke it in two pieces. She picked
up the pot and went to the door, curtsied and went outside, where
she waited on the path.

"What in the world?" Cumberland said.

"It's a bite to eat," HenryAnna said.

The stew smelled good. "A gift? That's kind of her, isn't it?"

"Oh, she's kind. She's a widow woman who lives next to the river
ford, and she cooks for people who needs it done for them. She's
got nothing to live on herself except what little she can sneak out of
the pot, and what people give her."

"You mean she expects money?"

"Something to show your appreciation," HenryAnna said.

He felt in his pocket and brought out a single coin—all he had
left. She took it to the woman.

When she got back, Cumberland said, "Is she kin to you?"

"First cousin," HenryAnna said, as she tasted the corn bread.

"And the quilt woman, is she kin?"

HenryAnna nodded. "My uncle Charlie's wife." She began eating her bowl of stew.

"And the bedmaker?"

HenryAnna nodded. "That was Uncle Charlie," she said.

He considered all of it and said, "I'm not quite sure how you got
it to come out even, HenryAnna."

She frowned up at him questioningly.

"I don't have a penny left on me. How did you figure exactly
enough to take it all?"

She went on eating, glancing at him now and then, simply to
judge if he was angry with her yet.

Cumberland began a journal, so that he could record the day-by-
day experiences of the Road. Also, he put down a few words about
HenryAnna, recording that "she came by my potter's house on

Saturday last and dropped by again on Sunday morning. A tinsmith, her Uncle Henry, came by and we bought a bucket from him and several spoons, Anna doing the fiercest bargaining I've yet seen, at one time ordering him off the property. Later a potter came by to show his wares, and he spent much time apologizing for appearing on Sunday. Anna condemned him for a criminal for bringing such pottery to the house, 'which had been a potter's house its own self,' and the man sold us what he had for very little, as a consequence, and went away downcast. These mountain people can never prosper so long as they condemn each other's labor out of hand; a little praise is good for the spirit. I thought well enough of Anna's help to praise her for it, which sent her into a spasm of house cleaning and singing."

He did not set down in the journal that he had tried on Saturday to induce her to come to bed with him, without any success at all, or that he had tossed and turned all night for want of her, and had moaned aloud he felt so lonely and was so sorry for himself. To fall in love was bad enough, but this girl was such a shyster.

A few days later he had occasion to record his observations on the unloading of the second group of 150 convicts; he described how they had leaped from the cars and had fallen in their chains, and how the boxcars smelled of human excrement. "We'll never get the odor out of those cars," he wrote. "Weatherby was furious about it and sent another letter to the Prison Department, urging that the next load of convicts be given rest stops on the way, at least twice a day. 'This is not only humane,' he wrote them, 'also it is practical recognition of the value of a boxcar.' "

At another place Cumberland wrote: "I admire Weatherby completely. It is difficult for me to believe it in myself, for I've usually been guilty of adopting a mildly sarcastic view of people and events. I find nothing in him which should not be admired in a man. He is strong, yet compassionate. There is no convict so humble that he cannot gain his ear, and for whom he will not go out of his way. He is in command of every detail of the construction of this vast undertaking, which has been listed in the Northern press as one of the most difficult earth-moving projects thus far begun in America, yet he is calm before the undertaking, is confident."

At another place Cumberland recorded what he recalled of a conversation he overheard in July between the guard, Tommy Goodman, and a new woman convict, "the prettiest of the lot, a Negro girl of about twenty whose name is Lola."

"What's the rest of your name?" Goodman asked her.

"Lola's all I recall of it."

"What you sent to prison for?"

"I don't recall."

"You a murderer?"

"They say I committed a crime."

"On Saturday night, since you're pretty, you better stay out of the woods, lest you get yourself tore. Them other girls'll tell you about it, but don't listen to their saying it's not wearing on a woman, for some of them would want you tore because you're prettier than they are. Pretty women gets preyed on by women and men both here. On Saturday you better walk back to the boxcar with that old woman over there, Mrs. Almer, for she don't lay men at all because of an internal condition. And when you're serving, stand back from the men, for you might start them fighting over you."

"I ain't here to fight."

"No, you're here to suffer, like them others, for your sins and crimes."

"I never said I was sorry for what I done."

"No? What did you do? I can write Raleigh and find out. Did you murder? Did you kill a child?"

"I'm not going to say."

"You kill your own child?"

"God damn you, mister."

"Your flesh and blood? Did you?"

"No, mister. Please, let me be."

"I've seen women afore that done it. I've saw the same look in their eyes. Well, was it your lover then?"

"I killed a man, they said."

"Your lover?"

"Yes. They said he was."

"You the one I heard about that knifed the man while he was making love to her in her own bed?"

"God damn you, mister. Please."

"Knifed him while he was on top of her, they said. That you?"

"Let me alone, I'm not going to remember."

"You can cry, I see that. Well, you're not completely hardened by it yet, anyway. I'll say that for you."

CHAPTER SEVEN

WEATHERBY SOON FOUND a creek high on the mountain above Mud Cut, and he told Cumberland he thought he would borrow it for a while. The next day he took fifty diggers up on the mountain, and fifty other men who could fit wood together in a sluice, and nobody except him had any idea what they were making, but that evening, when he had them cut away the creek bank at a certain place, the stream flowed into this new channel, rushed along the raceway provided for it, gathering speed until it flowed off the end of the sluice, falling a hundred feet directly onto Mud Cut. The water landed with such force that it churned the mud almost at once into an ooze. It carried some of the mud with it as it flowed out the end of the Cut and rolled on down the mountain, regaining after a few hundred yards its old creek bed.

The sluice was a miracle to the workers. They had been digging mud for weeks, and here came this water out of the sky and did the work for them. They splashed about under it, roaring their approval. Not only was it a relief to have such help, but the device said something to them about whether the Road could be built or not. Any number of them had been wondering up to now, had been asking if the power of a mountain wasn't greater than the power of men, even 300 men. But here came an answer out of the sky itself, that said the power of the mountain could be used to win as well as lose, for it was the mountain's water falling down the mountain's heights that melted the mountain's clay and flowed it off toward the Catawba, without a man touching it.

The next morning every one of the convicts and free laborers gathered at the Cut. The logging chains were fastened to the engine and the oxen and mules were harnessed. The poles were driven under the engine, and about 300 men gathered along the chains or stood in the mud near the engine itself, got wherever they could grab hold, and Ham stationed himself at the lip of the Cut and began to sing out:

> White mud give it up!
> White mud give it up!
> Give that engine up!

The men answered him each time.

> White man standing by the Road,
> Black man standing by the Road,
> Ox teams standing by the Road,
> Mule teams standing by the Road,
> Give that engine up!

The mighty force strained at the chains and pushed at the poles, and the muscles of the men and teams tightened under the load.

> Heave it, boy, heave!
> Heave it, man, heave!
> Heave it, mules, heave!
> Heave it, ox, heave!
> Heave!
> Heave!

The engine broke with the mud with a loud sucking sound, as if the engine had broken the gums of the mountain's mouth.

> Stop them mules!
> Stop them mules!
> Stop them damn mules!

They got them stopped, and the oxen too, and put the chains on the engine so that they could drag her out of the Cut. Weatherby told them first to move the sluice so that the water would fall on the engine. That was done, and they bathed her well. "Just let it flow on her," he said. They did, then they hitched all their power to the chains and the wheels, and Ham called out a chant again.

> That engine's going to rooooo–llllllllll
> That engine's going to roooooo–llllllllll!

As he elongated the last word, the might of the men and beasts increased, and each time the engine crept forward.

> That engine's going to roooooo–llllllllllllllll!

So, by this means, they rolled her out of there.

Under the place the engine had been, they found, spread-eagled, the body of the engineer, Bolton, perfectly preserved by the mud. When Moses picked the body up in his great black arms, Bolton looked like a statue, and Moses waded with him to the falling water of the sluice, moved into the water itself, and with his arms locked under Bolton's armpits, held him erect and let the water beat on him, let the water strip the clay from his hair and face and clothes, even as the men watched. It was almost as if Bolton were coming to life again.

They buried him near Babcock Station, and Cumberland said the Road ought to have a clay tablet made. Weatherby didn't understand why it should be clay, but Cumberland said he would pay for it himself, and he had it made by a potter, one of HenryAnna's cousins. It took a week to get it delivered, and by then the burial had taken place. Even so, Cumberland delivered it to the grave on an ox sled, and he and Weatherby wrestled it into place. It was glazed a brown color—the potter said it was tobacco-spit brown—and it had Bolton's name on it. Nobody knew his full name, so it said "Bolton, an engineer," on it, and under that was the year, 1877, and under that were the words:

> Killed at Mud Cut, North Carolina,
> Making the Road

In order to find a replacement engineer, Weatherby put a notice in the Morganton and Raleigh newspapers. Two men applied. One had driven trains for the Union and the other for the Confederacy, and Weatherby had them both try out the Mud-Digger. The man who had been with the Union was the better engineer, that was obvious from the start. Also, he had been born in the West Virginia mountains, which Weatherby liked about him. The man said he had worked for ten years after the war in the North, helping with roadmaking.

His name was Red Tuttle, a raw-cut man with a big nose, red hair and freckles all over his face and the backs of his hands. He talked with clipped words and an irritating haste to be on with what he had to say, so that he tripped over his own language, even when he didn't change his mind often about what he wanted to say. "I was up there in Grover and had a train, an engine—was a rainy season like a monsoon so that the track was about washed out like a drain board, had a trestle slide that caught the wheels of the train in itself as it went sliding down, and down we went, held erect as pretty as you please. Was up there four year fighting weather and riding trains . . ."

Weatherby had Red Tuttle get aboard to show what he could do. Several of the guards and foremen stood around to watch, and Tuttle leaned out the window and waved his hand at them. He spat tobacco juice on the ground and hauled back on the throttle, let the Mud-Digger dust her wheels for a couple of hundred revolutions while standing in place. Dirt was flying all over the men and the train, and Tuttle was politely grinning at them. He eased up on the throttle and the train bolted forward; he pulled down on the whistle cord to let the engine clear her throat, and he gave a highball signal to clear the track. He settled down at the window as the engine pulled out of Henry Station, a roaring, whistling threat to the countryside.

About halfway down the straightaway he eased back on the throttle a couple of notches and let her take her steam. The last that the onlookers saw, the engine was thundering and roaring, careening on the track at the far curve, and Tuttle was yanking on the whistle cord while, calm and cool as you please, he was leaning out the cab window, the wind almost blowing his head off, waving at them.

He went to Old Fort and returned in fifteen minutes. Weatherby couldn't get a contract written out fast enough, and Tuttle signed on for the rest of Bolton's two-year term, murmuring about being embarrassed to work for a road that still was using an old Mud-Digger engine.

He did awfully well with it. First chance he got he took it through Mud Cut with the sluice canal running; the water battered down on the engine, spewed into his boiler fire. He went on through, his whistle blowing, the convicts roaring with fear and then with laughter. He got hold of a huge bearskin, which he lashed to the front of the engine, and he set the antlers of a five-point buck on his lantern. To Tuttle an engine was his own marvel; he treated it respectfully but made it do tricks and move quick. He did well by the men, too, moving his engine and cars close after them, running on track that was laid over rough land. The men got to saying that Tuttle could drive the engine where there wasn't any track.

At night the men of both camps would go home dead-weary, their faces covered with grime which had dug into their skins, their eyes black from the shock of blows from axes, shovels, earth, trees, rock, from hard contact with tools and mules and each other and chains. They would be half-deaf from the sounds; they would have to shout at each other to be heard. They were easy to anger, too, for the work and danger had intensified them to the point where each man was capped for an explosion. The guards and foremen stayed away from them.

Sometimes two of them would start fighting, would find a physical release for their emotional stresses that way, would stand facing each other and would try to beat each other to the ground with full, shocking blows. The other men would shout angrily, and call for harder blows, harder, harder. "Come on here, man, you playing? Hit him!"

"Knock him down. Hell, hit him!"

"Jesus, what sissy boys we got to work with."

"Hit him in the face, man!"

"Hit him with your elbow!"

They would shout the fighters on until one of them was down and couldn't get up, and if they hadn't liked the way he had stood his ground, they would spit on him and kick him and even urinate on him. No guard said a word to them, either.

The women began to complain about the way they were treated in the woods, and Tommy Goodman swore the guards would have to keep most of the men out of the woods, "or I'll not stand responsible." The women claimed they were afraid not only because of what was done to them, but because of what men said as they got their food served each day, what they murmured to them.

Some of the guards wanted to be sent back to Raleigh. They said the black powder had got into the blood of the men. "You can't use whisky around an Indian or black powder around a convict." Two of the guards walked out of Henry Station one night and weren't seen again; they paid their own train passage from Old Fort to Raleigh. "We want to live a full lifetime," they said. Weatherby decided that a subsidy would be given each guard, 25 cents a day, to be paid whenever money was available. A guard made only 45 cents a day from the state, so this was a major increase, and the guards didn't talk of leaving after that. But the added cost to the Road was $7.50 a day, and already the Road was two months behind in meeting its bills.

The convicts also talked incessantly about the dangers they faced. "He was working under that hill and it give way and buried him. He's under there now."

They talked in the barracks at Henry or Babcock, often argued the night through.

"How do you know?"

"I heard him cry from under there."

"Did ye?"

"Crying like a baby from under them rocks. Jesus!"

"Oh, my God, did ye?"

"Who was it, Henry?"

"That little runt man that was sleeping over there."

"Hell, he ain't dead."

"Where is he then?"

"He was sent back to Henry Station."

"How you know?"

"I saw him being sent."

"Then who—who is under them rocks?"

"How you know somebody under them rocks, Henry?"

"I heard 'em cry. Don't you look at me like you don't believe me."

"Oh, man, listen, Henry, I believe you like I do myself."

"You don't believe me. God damn your soul, get up."

"Hit him, Henry."

"Get up, I say. Call me a liar."

"I didn't say nothing to you."

"You call me a liar again right now? Listen, I heard him cry, God damn you. That runt, or somebody else like him, under there, where you goin' to be, damn ye. Get up, I say. I'm goin' to show you what it's like down there under them rocks."

"Hit him, Henry."

"Let me be, Henry. Jesus, man, don't you fool with me."

"You threatening me?"

"Henry, you get angry over nothin' any longer. Hey, don't kick me, Henry. God damn, my back—"

Henry was a tough man and nobody wanted to fight him. Most every night he beat up somebody.

Within the barracks, groups were formed for protection, but entire groups would sometimes get to fighting. The guards would stand outside the locked doors and finger the triggers of their guns and look off at the lighted office where Babcock or Weatherby was.

Mules and men, men and mules; one got to be like another after a while. Hauling dirt, cutting mud, splitting oak, breaking rock until their bodies were only muscle and bone and they were too tired to think.

What was there to think about anyway, except breaking, hauling, cutting, shoveling, pushing, heaving? "That fill's beginning to creep, ain't it?"

More earth needed.

"You men get down there and stack them rocks in a wall. Stop that creeping."

"What if it come down on us while we there?"

"Get down there, damn ye!"

"Build a wall while a fill is creeping, stand under it?"

"Get down that hill, by God. Move!"

So they would.

Stack rock. Make a wall.

Somebody would sing, making up the words, and somebody would reply:

> This hill ain't gonna stand here.
> Going to fall on me.
> Going to fall and bury us down.
> Hear us cry from out of the ground.

Somebody would call out:

> Beasts don't have no brain,
> Beasts don't have no song,
> But beasts don't have no burden, neither,
> All day long.

Men remembered songs from the past, bits and pieces of songs. They had songs about women; every part of a woman's body was mentioned in music. A woman was dissected, bisected, loved, torn, cut, beaten, sucked, cut, licked, crushed, scratched, twisted, bent. . . .

The men would listen to the songs, their lips thinly smiling, their teeth showing, their fists clenched, their eyes glassy, their tongues moist.

"Weatherby, we've got 300 convicts here," Babcock said. "Thirty guards can't shoot them all, if they start after us." He began to worry night and day about it. Whenever he saw Weatherby on the road, he thought to mention the danger to him.

"We'll have 300 more soon," Weatherby said gently.

"God knows. You'd be better off to hire men and pay them."

"No money to pay them."

"How we going to hold these 300 we got?"

"Nobody's escaped yet."

"See their cuts. Look at their faces; see the meanness in there. How we going to hold them?"

"Work them hard."

"That's not going to hold them."

"Work them." That was his solution for it. Let them get to be like the Road itself.

He got with Esau, the smartest of the convicts, and said, "You let me know what I need to know."

Esau understood what he meant, all right. "If they find out I'm spying for you, they'll kill me."

"Don't tell them," Weatherby said. "I'll help you with your needs."

"They'd kill me so slow that all night long it would go on. They don't allow spies."

"Nobody said anything about spying."

"If they suspect—"

"They're not that smart."

"Smart? They're smart as any other animal. They know how to survive. Each man of them is smart enough to live."

Weatherby let him think the matter over. As for all these other dangers, he accepted them as inevitable. He rather welcomed the fierceness and strength, for he suspected they would be needed before the Road was done, directed not against each other but against the mountain herself. He wanted to double the convict force and get on with it. He was anxious to hear blasts from the belly of the mountain. He had already seen enough to know the men could cut through a clay ridge, but he didn't know what they would do to a rock ridge yet, or when they were told to go into the belly of the ground.

One day later in July a gang was working on an abutment of a bridge, lifting stones about 4 feet long and 2 feet wide and 1 foot thick, using grabs and a hand-operated windlass crane. The grabs were tempered poorly and the points kept breaking. In midmorning a foreman sent the grabs to the blacksmith at Henry Station, and they were returned that afternoon.

The crew began lowering a rock into place, and a grab gave way. The stone pitched down at a sharp angle, striking a young convict's leg below the knee, pinning it against another stone. He was blinded by pain and began to pray, yelling in a shrill voice. He was not much older than a boy.

Four workmen carried him to camp and the doctor in Old Fort was sent for. The boy lay in the sun the remainder of the day, swarms of flies, like disturbed yellow jackets, lighting upon him as he lay on his back.

The doctor didn't arrive that day or night, either. The convict was in less pain by morning, and he asked that his leg be put into splints and bandaged. This was done by the guards, one of whom began at once to carve a pair of crutches from a stout limb. He said to the convict, whose name was Happy, "If that doctor arrives, you might not need these, but if he don't arrive, you will, so it won't hurt to make 'em, cause if you don't need 'em, somebody else will."

Weatherby was deeply grieved about the doctor's not responding, and that second night he went into the stockade to see how Happy was. Nobody except convicts had ever gone in there, but Weatherby knew the men would treat him respectfully. They did, too, in this hot, damp, thickly odored place, and he let them tell him what was on their minds. They said they wouldn't work any longer in dangerous places without doctor care. He told them he would see that a doctor was hired and stationed at the Road. "I'll post one at Babcock or Henry," he told them.

All this was welcome news, of course, though it didn't help Happy.

Another convict was injured that week, and the Old Fort doctor didn't arrive to see him, either, until the next morning. He excused the delay by explaining that he had a practice in Old Fort and had calls all the time from out in the country, and he sometimes couldn't get around to everybody. That was all there was to it, he said.

Happy wouldn't let him set his leg now. He said it was all right. He was trying to avoid all the pain that resetting would bring. The doctor said he might end up with an extra joint, if he didn't reset it, or might lose it. Happy said it felt all right. As long as he felt all right at the moment, he was satisfied. "I'm not one to think ahead about trouble," he said.

The next week Happy was back at work. He used the crutches. He didn't do hard labor, as before; most of the time he tended the fires at Babcock, which was about all he could do. Some of the men told him he had improved his position on the Road. They joked with him about how maybe they would get a chance to bust their leg before long. "We out there cutting logs to 43-foot lengths, and you here burning sticks and shavings."

"We haul logs and you carry two crutches."

Actually they didn't haul logs, either. A pair of wheels had been made and the big logs were chained to them and were snaked through the woods, oxen doing the brute work. What the men did was cut them for the mortise and tenon joints.

"We haul by the ton and you by the pound," they told Happy, but they were only joking with him.

August arrived with sweltering weather. Flies were a big nuisance. Dysentery went through both camps, and the new doctor arrived as the disease was at its worst, and he stayed up night and day treating patients, turning half of one barracks in each camp into an emergency dispensary. Four men and one woman died, and almost everybody was sick for a time. Weatherby relaxed the work loads, so the schedule of the Road again suffered severe delay, but at last the danger was past.

August also brought to Weatherby the first shipment of nitroglycerin, an explosive which had proved useful to Northern and Western railroads in their construction work, but which had never been used in the Southeast before. Finished nitroglycerin was a liquid, and would explode if drops of it fell even two feet, or received a blow; so Weatherby asked that the ingredients, glycerin and nitric and sulphuric acids, to be shipped separately, and one afternoon he and Cumberland sneaked off alone and mixed a quantity of nitroglycerin in four vials. It was an oily transparent liquid that looked like water.

Nobody knew about the nitroglycerin except the two of them, and neither of them had any idea of its power or how best to use it—whether in liquid form or mixed with corn meal or some other ingredient. Weatherby wanted to start experimenting with it himself and have a formula ready by the time the gangs got to the tunnels. To move earth or shale, which was about all the men were doing now, wasn't as difficult as moving solid rock. "If it'll shoot rock better than black powder, we need a major supply of it," he said.

Only the cost was a problem. The existing part of the Road made a profit of $1,000 a month. Finished nitroglycerin was about 90 cents a pound; in large quantities he hoped to mix his own for 50 cents a pound, but even so, it was more costly than black powder. "If it proves out, we'll need to make a manufactory up on the mountain, near that new camp we're raising," he said. "We'll get the money somehow, if that doctor will stop ordering so much medicine, even if we have to lay off a few hired men."

"They'll leave anyway, come harvesttime," Cumberland said.

"Is that music man doing anything?"

"He's stringing line. He goes here and there, from one tree to another."

"I saw some line the other day out in the woods, and only the

Lord knows where it was supposed to be going. It was so low it'd choke a rabbit, if one came by unawares."

Cumberland laughed, just as many times before he had laughed to himself about that telegraph line. "He seems to string line wherever he's going, rather than where the line needs to go."

"How many years will it be before he gets it done?"

"I don't know. But don't fire him. I like to talk with him. We sat out in the woods one afternoon and talked for three hours about life. He's a devout believer in it."

CHAPTER EIGHT

HENRYANNA BROUGHT THE WORD to Weatherby that a child evangelist had been giving sermons against the Road and had decided to use the summer camp meeting at the Gap to issue a declaration against its construction. Each summer there were three days of meetings at the Praying Rock, and a number of sermons were preached by different men. The sermons often had a political cast, but this was the first time the Road had come in for criticism.

The child evangelist didn't know anything about the Road; he had simply chosen this as a means of attracting attention. He was an eleven-year-old boy with long white hair and pink eyes, and a clear speaking and singing voice.

Troy had come to Henry Station to spend the summer with Weatherby, so the two of them and Cumberland went to Swannanoa Gap, arriving the day the meetings were to get under way. Already in the field along the river were hundreds of wagons and tents, brought in by mountain families. There were many children about and even more dogs. The dogs were of every conceivable size, color and shape, and were busy noticing each other and barking at the horses. Most of them were hunting dogs and were snarling, unhappy creatures, scarred from combat. One of them had a fresh gash along his side, where a bear had slashed him with his paw.

The first meeting on this first day was to start at sundown, but one preacher already was standing on a stump, proclaiming a message to the children and to a few adults who were standing nearby, their arms folded, their faces masking their emotions and opinions. He was not coherent at the moment; he had been carried away by his convictions and was speaking in tongues. The spit from his mouth spewed on a few of the children and on the open Bible in his hand.

HenryAnna said the camp meeting would have a thousand people present this year, and that the child evangelist was the main attraction because he had done several miracles of healing in the valleys north of Asheville. Some claimed he had saved and healed entire families. Weatherby nodded to all she said, as he went about seeking friends.

He stopped when he encountered the oldest of the evangelists, whose name was Malachia Johnston. Weatherby knew him as a friend of his father's. He was a good person, caught between the hidebound ways of the world, on the one side, and of the mountain churches, on the other, hampered by the poverty and ignorance dominating both. Many of his colleagues were against change unless it worked to strengthen their position in the communities. They were, for that reason, opposed to medical doctors, believing that a minister could administer healing; they were opposed to schools, except for the teaching of basic reading, writing and arithmetic, because the preacher was available to advise the individual or community on matters of ethics, justice, logic and politics. Malachia Johnston, however, respected knowledge; he had a thirst for learning and encouraged it in others, though there were few ways to satisfy it in these isolated hills.

He was elderly and had a long white beard and blue eyes that seemed to survey all before him without noticing any detail. He was handsome and bold, and there was an entourage of followers with him. Even the children and dogs got out of his way and stood respectful while he passed; several of the women curtsied, and the men stopped whittling and nodded to him.

His eyes focused on Weatherby, much as a marksman might spot a target, and he came forward slowly, close enough to put his face near Weatherby's. Satisfied that it was indeed he, he fumbled in his pocket, took out his handkerchief and blew his nose; he got his pipe out of his pocket and stuck its stem between his teeth. He puffed on the unlighted pipe diligently, studying Weatherby all the while, and at last smiled. "Well, have you come home at last?"

"I'm this far home," Weatherby said. "I'm taking a heavy weight up the mountain with me."

Malachia took firm hold on each of Weatherby's shoulders and shook them, as if testing his health. "Your father had your build, or you have his, whichever way it goes."

"I wish I had his mind."

"Some say you do."

"No, I forget things now and then."

The preacher laughed gently. "Your sisters will want to see you soon, your brothers, too." He smiled slightly, briefly, a flicker, that relieved any suggestion of criticism. "What do you want of me?"

"To take care of a little boy for me."

"Which boy?"

"The child evangelist."

Anger flashed into the old man's eyes, but one had to be quick to see it, and had to be meant to be allowed to see it. "He has done ever so much good for the Lord," Malachia said simply.

"Why would he oppose what we're doing?"

"Oh, it's hard to say. What the Lord tells one man clearly, he might not even whisper to another." People were standing about, of course, and those who were most interested in the matter had drawn so close that the two men were encircled by them. "But I've known it to happen that the Lord's message was misunderstood," Malachia said.

"This boy is predicting calamity, not only to us but to the people up here."

"The people are in favor of the Road. Without the Road they're going to get so lean and poor and broke that they can't survive." A flush of anger went through him. "Why would God want them to starve?" He was deathly serious and waited patiently, as if somebody might want to supply an answer. Suddenly he tilted his head back and sniffed the light mountain air. "But if God leads that little holy child, who has done so much healing and so much good, if God, I say, leads him to that view, the child will need to take his stand on it. He will tonight?"

"Yes."

"My, my."

"If the people are in favor of the Road, will they pay attention to him?"

The old man smiled. "I suppose God will lead him to find a way to reach around their minds on the matter. Do you follow?"

"Not entirely," Weatherby said, conscious of the many listeners.

"For example, we all get weary of those in the lowlands who believe we here don't have modern ways, and that they ought to bring their contrivances to civilize us." He winked at Weatherby ever so slightly and quickly. "I might even claim that we here are closer to God than they are. Yet here they come, ripping apart the hills with their belching machine spewing forth smoke and fire, cutting the land so that it bleeds as far east as the rivers."

The people who were listening nodded. He had struck a response in them, all right. Deep in the center of their insecurity, he had located the seed of their pride.

"Oh, he could make some sort of case like that," the old preacher said to Weatherby. "He could turn the people against the Road, some of them, the ones who could be counted on to cause the most trouble later on, those that go where emotion leads them. It's an old story, sir. It's an old tune, and it can be sung by a child."

"Can it be answered by an old man?"

"Stomp out emotion with reason? Didn't you know the wind can't be deterred by throwing grain at it?"

"Will you come with me to see him?"

"No, no. He's got his own station and following."

"You're the oldest of the preachers, and by all odds the best—"

"He has his own—"

"You're the leader of the evangelists. I can ask anybody on this field who the greatest man of the Church is and you'll most often be named."

"No one man has the only word from God."

"But you have a word from God."

"I can't fight a child."

"Can't you go and talk with him," Weatherby said, "if not for me, at least for all the time you spent with my father?"

The eyes were watery now and once more didn't seem to focus well, and Weatherby regretted what he had asked, for he saw that the strength of the old preacher had worn so thin it could be pierced.

"I'll go with you, of course," he said.

The little boy evangelist had his wagons and house tent at the west end of the field, close to the river, and to get there Malachia and Weatherby had to make their way past the campfires and wagons of a multitude of people. Here and there an ill person was laid out by the road, in hopes that one of the preachers would cure him. Even to touch Malachia would be enough, one ill man said, and his relatives cried out to Malachia to stop. He did so, and to many others he made gestures of concern and blessing as he walked by.

They passed a place where a youthful evangelist was kneeling on the ground with a sick woman, his head thrown back, as was hers, the sun beating down on their closed eyes as the man prayed. They passed a snake worshiper who was preaching to a cautious group of onlookers, two copperhead snakes curling themselves about his body. Malachia murmured, "Ignorance, ignorance," as he moved on. And he said, "Here among all this beauty that God made."

The little boy evangelist was inside his tent, his advisers disdainfully watching the approach of Malachia. Normally when one evangelist approached the quarters of another, the host would rise at once and come forth to greet him, but the boy evangelist didn't appear. His father was sitting on an oxcart out front of the tent, smoking a pipe and acting as if he didn't even see the entourage approaching. He was none too courteous a man, anyway. He had been a poor farmer, whose wife had borne this albino boy. There were many neighbors who said the boy was possessed of evil spirits. The boy wasn't allowed in school or church, but he did come to a camp meeting near Asheville when he was nine years old, and on his second day there he apparently got a call from God. He jumped up on a stump and began to talk so wonderfully well, with such clarity of tone and beauty of spirit, that every listener was moved. The women particularly were made to weep. Even though young, he had suffered, one could tell, and he knew the Bible, could quote long passages out of it. Where he could have learned it all, nobody knew, for his father was no-count. Maybe his mother had taught him some of it, but the easiest explanation was that the boy, what he knew and the beauty of what he said, was a miracle. He was a miracle sent by the Lord, possessed not of devils but of the Holy Spirit.

The news went out into the hidden coves and far reaches of the mountains, and sick people were brought to the little farmhouse of his father. Many were healed: the lame walked, the deaf heard, the blind saw. It was true that not all were helped, but the father said that their faith was not enough or that God did not favor them for some reason. Who questioned God?

The boy could be seen now sitting on the cot inside his house tent, grooming his white hair with a long-handled brush.

Weatherby was known to many of the mountain people; Malachia was known to everybody standing there that day, as the great preacher of the mountain country. Both were important men, and they had come to call on the white-haired boy. Two leaders of the church and world were standing there, waiting.

"Is the boy here?" one of Malachia's attendants asked an attendant at the tent.

"He's busy now," the attendant said, suddenly grinning. "He'll be along."

The sun beat down on the field, and on the dignified white head of Malachia, who waited, expressionless, motionless, as if God had stationed him at this spot, as if he represented God, which was only what he had claimed over the years. No one watching him could have known what lay in his mind, whether love or hate, or what he thought of the child evangelist, whether respect or aversion. He waited, saying not a word, making no sound.

Inside the tent the little boy combed his long white hair.

Somebody in the crowd said, "He's in there. I can see him moving inside there."

Several minutes passed, Malachia not moving. Weatherby could sense that the authority of the old man was faltering, was melting away in the sunrays, his followers now wondering if perhaps they should not listen more attentively in the future to the boy, or to one of the younger preachers, and if they should make their contributions to the boy rather than Malachia, and if they should ask the boy's opinion rather than Malachia's, for even Malachia waited on the boy at the boy's tent.

The boy stopped combing his hair. He was standing now. He began to move about from time to time. The idea came to Weatherby to go into the tent, drag the boy out, turn him over his knee and flail him, and he had to force himself to think of something else, to keep from doing so. Now and then somebody in the crowd said something about the boy, or Malachia, or the Road. "Why is the Road man here?" they asked.

Being here was a blunder, Weatherby realized. He had been so utterly confident that he could talk this child out of his error that he had come to the arena the boy controlled. He should be down at the place where the tunnels were to go, testing the nitroglycerin he had received, seeing if—

His mind caught on that idea. That would have attracted the people, all right. He would have taken them away from the field and the preachers entirely.

An attendant came quickly out of the tent and stood, anxious, to one side. The flaps were pushed open and the boy stood there. How brilliant was his appearance! His eyes were closed, the sun beat down on his fair skin; his white hair shone like spun white silver. He stood there, so gently held by sunrays, framed by darkness behind him, dressed in black leather jacket and pants, with sandals made of deerskin. His hands holding the tent flaps were as white as paper and his nails were long and neatly clipped.

He opened his eyes and their pink color was the only spot of color to be seen near him. "Mr. Malachia," he said and bowed, as if humbled by the old man.

"This is Weatherby of the Road," Malachia said.

"Yes," the boy said.

The father stared off at the Praying Rock, slowly shaking his head, as if to warn the boy to be wary.

Weatherby said, "We want to talk with you in private."

The boy said, "Have we secrets from the Lord?"

The father smiled, and the people supported the rightness of that, for they didn't want to miss out on the conversation.

"You can say to all these people whatever you want known to me," the boy said in the pure, clear voice which seemed to carry without any effort on his part to every ear of that multitude.

How vicious the system is, Weatherby thought, scarcely knowing where to begin or how to defend the Road.

He heard the old preacher speak. "You don't like the Road, I hear. Let me say what I see in the Road," Malachia said firmly. "I see God's hand in the way the Road is planned to link the chosen country of God with the rest of God's world."

"God didn't make the Road," the boy said. "He could have made it, if he wanted it there."

"He didn't make the turnpike, either," Malachia said.

The boy flinched. "If he had wanted a road he would have put it there," the boy said, repeating himself.

"He didn't make that wagon. No, nor the tent you're holding onto."

The boy took his hands off the tent, as if they were burned.

"Nor did he clothe you, nor shoe you, nor comb your hair, but he gave you and each man sense enough to know how to care for himself and make improvements."

The crowd agreed. There was a flurry of comment that rustled through them.

The boy smiled kindly toward the old man. "It was because of sin we clothe ourselves. What is the sin that makes us build the Road?"

Weatherby felt Malachia start, and he heard a murmur of astonishment go through the crowd, and he saw several old men nod, as if what the boy had said was worth considering.

"The sin that made us clothe ourselves also gave us birth," Malachia said.

"Do you favor sin?" the boy asked.

"No, but I don't fear it, either. If we were fearful of sinning, we would all sit home by the fire all day long, but that's a sin in itself, one of waste. We must move on, must grow somehow. We have all sinned and come short of the glory of God. The question is now not how we can reverse the sin that gave us life but how we can make something worthy of the lives we have. To deny life is not to deny the sin; it is only to deny all that is worthy which survived the sin."

The boy stood quiet. Perhaps he had not been able to follow the argument. His father stared critically at him, and his attendants were unsettled. One of them whispered, "You'd best go in out of the sun."

But the boy said to Malachia, "What is sinful should not be done; we start with that."

"No, we only end with that. We start with this: he who says he is without sin, lies, and virtue is not in him."

The boy panicked, and to save himself further loss, he suddenly began to preach. He could do that, even if he couldn't debate. "They came out of the lowlands with their fire and smoke; the outlanders try to save us from our ways, but we are closer to God here than they are there. Stand on that mountain and the clouds touch you." He was merely reciting his sermon. "From down there they come, tearing apart the earth, changing the streams, filling the beds with rock and clay, blasting, cutting so that the mountain bleeds . . ." His voice vibrated, seeking to touch the emotions of the people.

Malachia raised his hand to stop the surge of words, but the boy continued, his eyes closed now, his clenched right hand cutting through the air before him to add emphasis as he denounced outlanders and new ways and machines; he denounced the sciences of the lowlands, the colleges of the lowlands, and when he was done, in a crescendo of emotion, he cried out: "God save your people, God protect us from the outlanders' ways!"

He was quiet then, and the people in the field were quiet, and Malachia gently, so that only a few people heard, said to the boy, "He who calls his brother a fool, young fellow, is damned already." He turned and angrily led the way across the field, the people parting to let him and Weatherby through, rolling back from them in waves, pulling their children back. Malachia walked swiftly away, leaving the white-skinned boy standing at the door of his black tent.

Malachia had been preached to, and he didn't like it. The boy had not confounded him in argument; he had merely been presumptuous. He could not have impressed any thoughtful person with his evasion of the issue in favor of a tide of emotionalism. Furious, Malachia wanted to get off to himself and rest and review the matter for the few hours before the evening session began.

But Weatherby followed him into his tent.

"A little child shall lead them," Malachia said, throwing his coat on his cot and plopping himself full length on top of it. "Ay, why did the Bible open the door to such as him?"

"I'm sorry, Malachia," Weatherby said.

"Oh, I've been involved in worse," Malachia said. "What a damnable region. How infernal it is to work forever with ignorance." He swung his legs over the edge of the cot. "People have an image of Jesus confounding the elders at the age of twelve. Mark my word, that little bastard's followers are out there reminding the multitude of that now, this minute."

"But he didn't confound you."

"Of course not. He has only one tune, and it can be played by those who wind him up of a morning. In every camp meeting there's likely to be one of those infernal children preachers, and behind the child is his tutor, who collects the money from the lame, the sick, the dying, the poor in spirit, as well as those who get political gain over some issue or another, such as this."

"Such as what?"

"The Road. There are moneyed people who don't want it, and they can easily buy a song from this baby. He'll sing for them tonight. We only made his voice a bit more hoarse from overuse, that's all."

"The people shouldn't listen to a child."

"The people are trying to listen to God. They think God speaks through willing instruments, and the less likely the instrument the more likely people believe God has chosen it. One can't blame the people, or even blame the boy. He gets nothing much for it, except a new hairbrush when he wants one." He snorted. "The Bible's got a thousand verses in there about respecting one's elders, but it's that one verse about a child leading them." He was obsessed with that verse. "I know God spoke it all, or inspired it all, and I don't question one jot or tittle of that Holy Book. Without it, where would we be in coming to know Jesus, and through him to know God? I love that book," he said, trembling even as he spoke. But his gaze fell and his shoulders slumped and he murmured, "Every camp meeting might nigh for ten years, I've had one of them children evangelists, and they are every one the same, except this is the first one with pink eyes. They are every one so angelic in face, so pretty of hair, slender of form, pretty of voice that the women swoon and the other children all grip themselves with wonder and wet their pants. I can get up there and tell those people the truth, and I have to put up with children swarming all over the grounds and dogs howling at pet coons. But let that little boy start to talk, and every child sits down in awe, and every dog. How he does it to the dogs I'm damned if I know."

By the time Weatherby got outside, HenryAnna and Cumberland had gone down to the potter's house. Troy walked with him. When they got to the house, he was still worrying about the preacher's problems, and he scarcely paid attention to the house itself, or to the food he ate, which some old woman brought to the door in a pail, the bread in her apron pocket. That had attracted his attention but not his concern, and all that he saw that did concern him was the way HenryAnna seemed to be making herself at home in Cumberland's house.

Cumberland sensed that Weatherby was worried. "We can run a few tests of that nitroglycerin this afternoon. We have time," he said.

"I'd like to run a test under that boy's father," Weatherby said. He picked up a glass jar of the liquid, and a sense of its power swept through him. He went outdoors and walked along the edge of the pond. He walked around the pond until he could look across at the water wheel. It spun water in soft, white, foamy rings. There's power, he thought. There's power in the wheel, power in the pond, power in the streams that feed the pond. That's what has to be harnessed. There's power in the men of Henry and Babcock Stations, and that power has been harnessed and can now be directed against the earth itself, be made to move the earth. There's power in a locomotive. There's power in my own hand right now, in this vial of experimental water never before exploded in the Southeast.

He knew there was power enough in one jar of nitroglycerin to blow up part of that great mountain. He could blow up that Praying Rock across the field, send it into heaven. There was more power here than that child held or could comprehend.

He set the jar on a stone in front of him and knelt before it. "You're a strange-looking little god," he whispered. He took off the cap and smelled it. There was no odor. "Can you lift part of a mountain?" He wet his finger in the millpond and let a drop of water fall from his finger into the vial. It lay, a single droplet, on top of the liquid. He shook the vial. The drop of water sank to the bottom, then rose to the top again; it would not mix, yet both water and nitroglycerin appeared to be the same. "Can you do God's work?" he asked.

He believed it could. "Very well," he whispered to it.

With nitroglycerin it was conceivable to him that he had power enough either to embarrass the Church, or to make the Church strong. He asked himself: Should the Road defeat the Church, or use its strength to strengthen it? It was the same power, either way. Which was more honest? he wondered.

HenryAnna found her father, as Weatherby instructed her to do, and brought him to the cottage. He came in smelling of snuff and fish and whisky, all at the same time. Weatherby saw at once that he was in no condition for work or discussion, so he asked him to help him in only one aspect of his plan. He explained it to him.

"You want me to tell them that there's to be a sign at sundown?"

"As the sun drops beyond the peak."

"What sign?"

"Tell them to watch the Praying Rock."

"What's it to do?"

"It's to move, if God wants it to."

"Oh, how can it be that a rock can move? It's been there all along."

"It's God's way to show displeasure with that little boy," he said.

Plover couldn't follow all of it, but he was willing to tell others about it. He was ideally suited for starting rumors, Weatherby decided, for he was confused easily and was a mystic, anyway.

Weatherby sent a written message by HenryAnna to Malachia, then he and Troy, carrying the four jars of nitroglycerin, walked over to the Praying Rock. Below them and before them was the field, made smoky from a hundred cookfires scattered across it. A crowd had gathered and was gathering still. The Praying Rock was behind the speaker's platform, about fifty yards up on the hill, and the people faced the Rock now as they took seats on the ground. Behind them the campfires were smoking, like sacrificial altars. Cows and horses were tied to shrubs and wagon wheels.

The people began to sing "We Are On Our Journey Home."

Just before sunset Malachia arose and went to the platform. "Let us pray," he said. Some members of the crowd bowed their heads, but others stood looking at the Rock.

Weatherby set the vials to one side. He removed the dirt and leaves from around the base of the Rock and found several holes which seemed to be deep and were full of water. He selected four of them close together and into each poured a quantity of the nitroglycerin, holding the lip of the jars close to the water in the hole, letting the nitroglycerin fall into the water and not onto the rock.

> We can see that distant home,
>   Though clouds rise dark between,
> Faith views the radiant dome,
>   And a luster flashes keen
> From the new Jerusalem . . .

He took out a detonation cap and with his teeth crimped the end of a fuse into it. He covered the cap with soap and placed it in one of the holes. His hand was trembling, but he told Troy he was almost done. He covered the capped hole with damp mud, tamped it down tightly but gently, then mounded mud over it.

> O! our hearts are breaking now
>   Heavenly mansions, fair to see;
> Blessed Lord! thy heavens bow,
>   Raise, Oh raise us up to thee,
> To the new Jerusalem . . .

He covered the other holes with sticks and mud. "You ready, boy?" Weatherby whispered to Troy. He heard Malachia begin to speak as the last words of the hymn faded away. He was calling on God to "speak in your own time and to your own people in a loud voice."

Weatherby lit the fuse and started running down the hill, Troy beside him. They ran across a small trail. "Down," Weatherby said, and he and the boy fell face down in a gully.

The sun was setting, and a thousand people were watching the Rock. "God, speak to your people," Malachia pleaded, and as if in answer the Praying Rock moved.

The multitudes saw the Rock rise. The trees around it also rose, and much of the earth beneath it rose into the air before them and above them. A wind and a roar swept across the field. Horses broke free and stampeded toward the river, dragging tents and wagons; men fell to their knees, women lay prostrate on their faces and wept.

Rock and earth and bark and wood began to fall to the ground all around them, and the sky filled itself with ashes and smoke.

On their knees, humbly, the people rent their clothing, and those who were ill begged aloud for healing, and the sinners asked forgiveness, as the dust from the Praying Rock swept across the field.

CHAPTER NINE

LITTLE OF THE BALLAST had as yet been put on the roadbed, but, where it had not been spread, ties had been laid on the surface of the ground itself, and track had been laid so that the work engine could bring in flatcars. Such a track was open from Henry Station to the long bridge just below Babcock Station.

Beyond Babcock Station the men had managed to cut through one ridge and to work the road up the mountain toward the place where the tunnel would someday be started. In order to get the engine up to the tunnel places, it would be necessary to build the long bridge over Babcock Creek, a trestle 164 feet in length.

That summer the bridge ought to be put together, Weatherby believed, so that in the fall when 300 more men were due to arrive, work could begin on the tunnels.

The sills for the bridges had been cut by the tree gang of Henry Station, but the long bridge was located near Babcock Station; both stations had a right to raise the first bridge, and both wanted to do so. Weatherby conferred with the foremen and convicts, and he concluded that any decision would aggravate half his men, unless he could, by some means, use the bridge to improve the competitive instinct and team spirit of them all.

He asked the Negro convict Esau to plant the idea at Henry Station that there should be a contest waged between the two camps, the contest to consist of various measurements of strength and agility. There were to be boxing matches, wrestling, horse-throwing, races, rock hammering, jumping, and other contests of individual achievement; also there were to be team contests, among them rope pulling, relay racing, and a mass free-for-all. The camp that won would be chosen to assemble Long Bridge.

The challenge was, of course, immediately accepted by Babcock Station, and Moses was named captain of their team.

Weatherby was approached by Esau, Moses, and four other convicts from Henry and Babcock Stations with news of the proposed event and a request that a day be provided for it. He assigned the approaching Friday; on that day, he said, no work would be required of the men, although there would be more work than usual for the women, for there should be better food served than was the customary ration.

Nothing that had happened up to now had caught the men's interest so completely. The contest was a constant subject of speculation as new events were conceived of. A committee of convicts was invited to meet with Weatherby and Babcock to set a schedule that would be acceptable to everybody, and this committee decided that there would be no second places; the winner of each contest was the sole winner and got one point if an individual and two points if a team. There were to be twelve individual contests and four team contests, making a total possible score of 20.

There was some discussion about a possible tie, but the only solution was to add or delete an individual effort. To add one would yield the number 13, which the men said was unlucky, and nobody wanted to delete anything.

The contests were to begin at breakfast time and to end at the close of day with a party. The women were invited to everything.

That Friday morning the new doctor, Frederick Chester, came early to the field. He was a scholarly-looking fellow with two big black suitcases, both made of excellent leather; one was full of medicines and the other of surgical tools and bandages. He had spent most of his time since his college training either working for the Union Army or working for the roads in the North. He had left there because he had heard that this North Carolina effort was the most dangerous one being undertaken in the country. He was not himself one who sought danger, but he was attracted to places where others were in danger, much as a moth is to light.

Red Tuttle knew him. That very Friday morning at the gaming field when they encountered each other, each stopped in place and Tuttle spat on the ground and said, "You figure you'll interfere with this work down here, too, will ye?"

"I'll do what I have to do," Chester said, his voice trembling noticeably. "I tend the sick; that's my job."

Tuttle turned from him and went on off toward where Babcock was waiting for the games to begin. "That damn doctor is an interferer," he told Babcock. "He's known for it in Pennsylvania."

Chester heard that, and it hurt him. Shaking his head, unnerved by the crudeness of the Road men, he went off alone, sat down on a log and waited patiently for the contests to begin.

At ten o'clock the boxing, racing and throwing contests started, and the pent-up enthusiasm of the men released itself. There was a shuddering knocking together of heads and bodies, and by noon some 250 men from the camps were battered with bruises and sprains and another 250 mountain people had gathered to observe. At the time of the noon meal, when biscuits were served in place of corn bread, the score for the individual contests stood 7 for Henry and 6 for Babcock.

After the meal there was a four-mile relay race, started by a gunshot Weatherby fired, and accompanied by constant shouts of encouragement and despair. The Henry Station team won the 2 points, due to the fleet-footedness of a man named Crowbar, who "weren't even visible partway," as one mountain man commented. The next effort was a team rope pull, and for this a logging chain was provided. The teams were twenty men each. Again the starting signal resulted in a tremendous effort, not only on the field but among the onlookers, some of whom had to be thrown from the playing area bodily. The effort was fierce, with the captains of the teams shouting, urging still greater effort. The Babcock team pulled Henry Station's across the line, though the Henry men doggedly were still clinging to the chain.

The score was now 9 for Henry and 8 for Babcock, and the next effort was the goose pull, which was worth 1 point. Few of the convicts knew much about the sport, but several of the mountain men present said they knew how to do it and would demonstrate. "You keep back out the way," they were told.

Only horses that had never pulled a plow were saddled. A goose was provided. Its head and neck were coated in grease, and it was raised on a rope to dangle ten or twelve feet above the ground. The first try at the goose was to be made by a Babcock Station man, and the first rider was Esau, who earlier in the day had won the foot race. He mounted and at once a whip slashed out and the horse bolted forward. The goose began to complain mightily as Esau rode down on her, reaching high as he approached. He threw himself upward at the goose, but missed so completely and surprisingly that he tottered from the horse and fell heavily to the ground.

He got up stunned, strangely enlightened about this new-found sport, and limped toward the starting line.

Henry Station's first rider, a white man named Carson, thundered toward the goose and missed, too, but at least didn't fall to the field. He came riding back, grinning broadly and claiming to have "almost done it."

There were several other riders for both camps, and some of the men tried a second time, but only a few could grab hold of the goose's head and nobody could hold on to it.

Esau said he would try again, so he was tossed up to a saddle.

"You ready, Esau?" Weatherby asked him.

"You going to fall off again?" a Babcock man called.

"You break the ground, Esau, should you want to. How much he get if he break the ground?"

"Let him have a quarter of a point if he break the ground."

"Why don't you Henrys put Esau on a rocking horse and carry him down there."

"You kill that damn goose, Esau. Bring its greasy head back here."

The whip cracked, the horse bolted forward, the hooves thumping the torn ground of the field, a dust plume curling up behind, while the people tried to see through the dust.

The goose squawked and began to weave her head. Esau bore down, standing in the stirrups. With a windmill swipe of his hand, he gambled for the head and fastened his fingers around it. He heard the squawk of the goose stop in mid-sound.

He swept past the tree and lowered himself into the saddle and looked down at the head.

There was a lot of complaining and cheering as he came back. The score was tied, 9 to 9, with only one more effort to go.

That was a team effort, worth 2 points, and it consisted of nothing in the world but one team trying to beat members of the other to the ground with fists.

"Nobody can beat Moses," the Henry men said sadly. "Not even Esau can do that."

"I'll tell you what we do," a Henry man said, "we'll have to get Moses first."

"How you plan to get Moses?"

"We'll set six men on Moses."

"No, we'll all fall on Moses; we'll worry about the others later."

"What they going be doing to us while we're falling on Moses?"

"Don't worry about us. The first thing to do is get Moses."

There were no restrictions on what could be done in the fight, so men were assigned to do just about everything to Moses. "Kick his balls, Jim. And you, Curt, bite his damn ears off. Henry, you kick his balls, too."

Each station's full complement of men was its team. Many of the men stripped off their shirts and pants. Since there were a few women present, they agreed to leave on their underpants. Some men left on their pants but discarded their belts. A few of the men painted their faces with berry dyes, which made them look like Indians; indeed, some of them were part or full Indian.

Dr. Chester took a position near Weatherby. He had eight stretcher-bearers, all of them guards.

The day was getting worn out now; the men were weary and angry at each other, and were gutsy in talk and manners. Each team had gone through a lot of pain thus far and didn't mean for any of it to be wasted. The sun was only a finger's width above the mountain when Weatherby gave the signal and the two mighty groups moved toward each other. There was a roaring encounter, an immediate tangling of bodies. Men stood toe to toe, slugged each other, kicked each other and fell on top of each other—struggling, flailing men. The onlookers, which included convict women, squealed and screamed, as if the blows were being received by them, as if the shock of the blows was reverberating through them. A fit struck one mountain man, and he fell to the ground, saliva dripping from his mouth; a seizure struck a boy and he fell to the ground and began to wriggle, moaning. Several mountain men began to speak in unknown tongues.

A quarter of an hour after the fight began, the field was strewn with 250 bodies of men who had had enough of it. Only two men remained on their feet: Moses and a young slight Negro named Raspy Turner. Raspy was from Henry Station. He had lagged during the early part, had found a spot near the back of the crowd.

Nobody on the Babcock team had taken the trouble to seek him out. He had been getting along easy, while Moses was being battered and beaten by the Henry men.

Now Raspy moved around the giant, his lips drawn back from his teeth, as if he were fierce. His face was smeared with red dye and sweat. He spat suddenly at Moses, who was as blood-covered and deathly tired as a bear at the end of a hunt.

The boundaries which had held the crowd back out of the way were ignored now. Men came close; they formed a tight circle, and their bodies swayed with those of the fighters.

Raspy darted forward, kicked Moses in the groin, and darted out of reach before Moses could lay a hand on him.

He darted in again, landed a blow to Moses' head and darted back.

A third time Raspy moved in, kicked him swiftly and got away in time, and the encouragement of the Henry men increased as it became clear that they had a chance to win.

Raspy moved to one side of the big man. Moses turned to face him. Raspy's foot kicked him in the groin. Raspy came in closer and began to hammer blows to Moses' head. The crowd's swaying and shouting rose, carried almost beyond the point of endurance. Moses staggered. Raspy pressed in close.

All in a moment Moses' big arms swept out and encircled him. The cry of the crowd stopped in a gasp, astonished as the giant closed his arms tighter around the battling man.

The flailing stopped and they heard a single sound, as lonely as any they had ever heard. It said, "Mama, Mama." It came from the open mouth of the little man, who was not now standing on the ground but was held in the giant's arms. They heard a snapping noise, something cracking; a rib had cracked. They stood in silence, stunned, as Dr. Chester ran forward and began to pull at Moses' arms. "Enough, damn it," Chester said, "enough."

Moses couldn't hear anything.

"He said enough," a man yelled into Moses' ear.

"Mama," Raspy said.

Another of his bones broke, and Dr. Chester with the edge of his hand struck Moses at the back of the head. The giant staggered, then fell to his knees and crumpled to the ground, Raspy still clutched in his arms. He fell on top of Raspy, unconscious, as a cheer went up from the winning Babcock team.

Assembling Long Bridge was a strangely unrewarding prize, the Babcock men had to admit, and they got to laughing about it that night in their barracks. One of the men asked who in hell wanted to put a bridge together. They laughed about it and fussed, and somebody said to let Henry Station do it.

Moses sat silent in the corner of the barracks. Dr. Chester had given him medicine and whisky, which had helped relieve his head and body pains, but his soul remained morose. He had won a victory, but he had no way to sense or acknowledge pleasure. In his life he often won, but never was he elated because of winning. He never took part in celebrations.

A convict named Collingsworth crawled over to him and asked him how he felt.

Moses didn't answer.

"The guards agreed you could go into the woods tomorrow night with the trusties."

Moses sniffed and wiped his flabby nose with the back of one cut and swollen hand.

"You can have any woman you want. We'll give you first choice and all the time you want."

Moses sniffed and his fat tongue came out and moistened his lips.

"Annie likes you, I hear." It wasn't so, but he said it. "Maybe the woods ain't the best place for love-making, with everybody rushing about, but you could be a allowed a private place for the whole time." He could tell that Moses was interested, though wary. Moses wasn't afraid of a fight, but maybe he was afraid of a woman.

"You tell me which one you want, and I'll pass the word on to the men and will tell the woman, and you can take whatever place you want." All of this he said softly so that nobody else heard them talking. "After all, you won for us."

Moses was nervous, was strangely aggravated. Collingsworth moved a foot or so away from him. "What say?"

"I'll take Lola," Moses said, so softly he could hardly be heard.

"Who?"

"Lola," he said again.

"But she's one of the ones that don't go in the woods."

"Lola," Moses said again.

Lola, when she was told about the choice, said she didn't want to be made love to again. She said she wouldn't meet Moses. The other women heard about it, though, and said she shouldn't act so aloof and superior. "He chose you. You're not better'n any of the rest of us. Who you think you are?" they demanded.

"It ain't as if you was a virgin, after all, for we know you killed one man while he was having you."

Lola began to weep; she was that upset about it. She pleaded with Tommy Goodman not to let them make her do it, and Tommy, who didn't want to stir up trouble on either side, sought a compromise, but none appeared.

"Use that laurel place that you have to crawl under a bush to get to," a big hefty woman named Clara advised her. "You can lie on laurel branches and keep your mind roaming."

Another woman agreed that that was the best place.

"There's a cliff to one side, so nobody comes at you from that direction, or any other except through the place they crawl through, so it's never been crowded in there."

"I can't, I can't. Don't make me," Lola said.

But the women said she had to, and Tommy Goodman wanted to keep peace in the family, so he said she better consider it, anyway.

That night at the party she was frightened all the time. She stood near the singers and stared at the ground, her lips moving as if she were saying a prayer. Clara said she was talking to the man she had killed. When the party was about ended and certain of the women were ready to sneak off into the woods, two old women came close to her and whispered for her to follow them. She walked with them, past where Goodman stood; he was still debating in his own mind whether it was right for him to intercede. She could grab hold of him and persuade him to protect her, and, of course, he would; but he couldn't protect her in the boxcar later or help her win back the friendship of the other women.

All the men were watching her and she felt naked as she walked past them. In a way she welcomed the protection of the woods.

Her escort stopped. The women waited a little while, until four men came toward them. One of them was Moses. He came close to her, reached out a trembling hand and touched her hair, pulled at a strand of it, and smiled. He was awkward even in smiling. He put his arm around her and held her for a moment, and as the others watched his hand went to her breast and he felt of her breast, and a wave of longing seemed to sway him, and made him moan, even while aversion and anguish made her tremble. He took her hand in his and led her away from the others to the place where he had to drop to his knees. Directing her to follow, he crawled along a path, grunting as he moved against the stiff laurel branches. His shirt caught once in the branches and he pulled it free. He came at last to the private place and lay on his back there, panting from his long-ing, and she could see the stars up above them, and the moonlight was strong enough for her to see the cliff above them, too.

He was lying there and he said, "I want you."

She stood before him. With a single languid gesture as if she were drugged by her mind's pain, she took hold of the hem of her dress and pulled the dress over her head and dropped it to the ground. She knelt naked in the moonlight, trembling.

"Come here," he said. "Unbutton it." She unbuttoned his clothes. She took off his shoes and pulled off his pants, and all this time his breathing grew deeper. She lay down beside him, and he abruptly lifted her body in his hands and rolled on top of her. He entered her and was large over and inside her, and she tightly, in horror and pain, shuddering, closed her eyes against him.

Long after the other men and women had gone back to the camps, he lay there running his hands over her body and kissing her body and face. "Huh," he grunted, his big round face smiling, and he kissed her nose, then laughed quietly, his body shaking with pleasure. "You come here next Saturday night."

She said nothing.

"To me?" he said, his hands tightening.

"Yes," she quickly said.

"You're the one," he said. "You come to me?" he said.

"Yes," she said.

He grunted and laid her on her back on the laurel and leaned on his elbow over her. He looked at the body before him and ran his fingers over her body as if it were a possession of his own. "You come to me?" he said again.

It was a two-tiered bridge. The men set the first tier so that it was 25 feet above the pit of the valley floor. They raised the other tier 25 feet on top of it. Great strength was required to handle the logs and fit them, and the work took as much time on the second layer as the first, for they had to raise the logs aloft and work high in the air.

On Wednesday one man was accidentally knocked off the bridge. He was carted off dead. On Thursday a man was snagged by his clothes; a log caught in them and pulled him off the bridge and hurled him out into space. He also died.

Friday noon, as the bridge neared completion, the men from Henry Station were allowed to come and watch. Moses and seven other men, all of them working naked now because of yesterday's accident, put the last few timbers into place. It was a mighty work, and when it was done a great cheer went up from the men of both stations.

The bridge was the yellow color of new timbers, and was pieced together in an intricate maze. It fitted together well, like a puzzle; each piece had fallen into place, and the men who had done it were proud of it, even though it was well beyond their power of mind, of comprehension. They saw it standing there and couldn't deny they had made it. They had cut the logs and notched them; they had assembled them. But they didn't know how it had been made.

Somehow they and Weatherby had done it. Without their labor it wouldn't have been done; without him it wouldn't have been done. With him they could perform miracles; it was often surprising what they could achieve when they worked with him, and when they worked with each other.

The men in both stations had been brought closer together by the very creation which had caused their controversy, and they were stronger now, as men of separate stations and as men working together to build the Road. The Road could be built; they had evidence from this bridge that they could achieve more than they could reason out. Together they could do it all. They together, and Weatherby.

On Saturday they celebrated with a party. They went into the woods that night, almost all the women and most of the men. There was a great deal of commotion in there, of course, and the life-spirit did seem to move everybody. Several small trees were broken and a clay creekbank was disheveled by the wriggling bodies. Only one place was not literally writhing with forms, and that was in the laurel slick, up the narrow path that one must crawl to get through. On the ground where one could lie and look up at the cliff and the stars, in the private place, Lola again bore the weight of the man, and he again sensed in her pleasure for all he had done.

CHAPTER TEN

HERE AT THE TOP in a heathland—or a bald, as it was called by the mountain people—deer grazed. There were perhaps a thousand cleared acres, unfenced, untended. Nobody knew for sure how it came to be here, but another mountain close by also had a bald top and deer grazing. These balds were the footprints of a giant who had once walked through, some of the mountain people said.

"You could put cattle up here," Cumberland told HenryAnna.

They were sitting on the ground and he had been wondering if he could build a cabin near where they sat.

"You're always trying to tame everything," she said.

"I did try to tame you once or twice, and failed," he said.

She tossed her long hair back from her face and smiled, more in self-satisfaction than at him.

"I could put a cabin up here and put a fence on part of this land."

"It's not yours to do to," she said.

"I could buy it."

"You can't own what's not yours to own," she said. "What would the deer do?"

"I wouldn't take all of it." He wouldn't take a bit of it, was the truth of the matter, for it would be colder up here than he liked, and more windy than a house could stand. It was a proper place to come and see the world from, but not the best place to live. "Does it give you a feeling of power to be up here this high?"

"I like the valleys better for living," she said, "and this for climbing to."

"But doesn't it give you a feeling of power?"

"No more than it does that woody vine on the rock."

He supposed she was telling him she was part of the place and he was not, that even yet he could come here and think he owned or possessed or dominated it, but he didn't even know it. Maybe, he thought, this was one other difference between them, in terms not only of the place but of the people, too. She found it easy to be natural around almost anyone, but he was more aloof, selective. Being with her had helped him overcome this somewhat, he felt. He needed her, the warm intuitive responsiveness and naturalness of her, and he might be of help to her in introducing the world of the lowlands, which was now about to arrive at her own community. Each of them was a transitional means serving the other, and now and then they would draw close to one another. Each remained apart, even so; they were inherently so different that even in companionship they were separate. Never, certainly, did they come as close as he wanted them to.

They had sought to write down the different species of trees on the mountain. She had not been enthusiastic about this, even when he explained that scientists could systematize such a list and use it. To her the list was starkly removed from the substance of the mountain itself; she didn't much want to help him, but as he worked at the process of identification, she was an accompanying witness.

"You see this leaf has evenly placed stems, and that one is uneven," he would say.

"I've known that since a girl," she said, though it wasn't quite so. She hadn't noticed all the details he found significant, and before long she became interested in spite of herself and helped him gather leaves and carry them to the valley house, where together they pressed and dried them. They identified over 100 different species of tree and over 125 species of shrubs. Evergreens they listed in two categories: those with needles, of which there were several different pines and two handsome hemlocks, which HenryAnna said were called "spruce pines"; and the broad-leaved evergreens, most of which were shrubs or understory trees, rhododendron and laurel being chief among them.

The hardwoods, which dominated the forests, were listed by

species: the wild plums, chinquapin, buckeye, oak, poplar, sour-wood. . . .

Some of the tulip poplars, Cumberland noted, stood like a column, with scarcely a perceptible taper, and with the first limb jutting out about a hundred feet from the ground. The girth of one such tree they measured to be 32 feet at head height. The tree they estimated to be 200 feet to its crown. Buckeye and horse chestnut trees grew 125 feet high. One chestnut was 11 feet thick. They measured a yellow birch that was over 7 feet thick. They measured the pool of shade at noon that was cast by a single white oak, and found it to be 133 feet across. This oak was part of an oak woods in which each member stood in its own dignity, with no underbrush except rhododendron bushes, and here they also grew singly and immaculately.

The northern slope of the mountain was shaded entirely from the sun, and the earth was damp. The trees were more twisted and were not so tall as on the western slope, which had sun in the afternoon and also caught the moisture-laden winds of the prevailing westerlies. The eastern slope was the driest of all, for the sun reached it each morning, and the southern slope was the warmest, for it had sun almost all day, and it had the southern winds.

Sometimes they would see thin puffs of clouds scurrying through the trees. Maybe the night before there had been a rain in the valley, and the vapors were rising, so that the cloud rose in bits of fleece which first courted and later enfolded the trees. If HenryAnna and Cumberland sat long enough, they would be embraced by clouds, too, and later would be released and see the valley below and the clouds above. Later still they might see the cloud cover break up and the sunlight fall through to them. All the while there was the sound of the mountain, of rushing water, and of wind—the sound wind makes when it blows the mist off trees.

At one place they could look down perhaps a thousand feet into a single gorge, and one late-morning they reached that place and gasped to see a thin, windy mist below which made the valley appear to be veiled. Breezes were moving through the veil and under and over it. The mist moved through the pines, too; it moved gently against the face of the opposite mountain, feeling along the cliff there. It rose slowly, playing and rolling, until the floor of the valley was free, and the valley trees and the river were free and dark; the mist rose about HenryAnna's feet and wisps of mist came up to moisten her hand and face, even as Cumberland watched her.

Later in the day they came back to this spot. They saw that the mist had clustered on the summit of the next peak. Below them the valley was clear of clouds, and the leaves glistened in the dusky light.

Such trees as fell in the forest decomposed quickly, except for the mature pines that for many years lay forming "fat pine," or "lightwood," as HenryAnna called it, a piece of which would kindle at the touch of a match. They made a fire out of a small pile of it one day and cooked a piece of beef that Cumberland had brought. It was beef from a steer that had been killed the day before, so it was not aged at all and required much smoking. The odor of the burning pine was heavy and resinous, and the smoke was like lampblack. The meat was pine-tasting when they ate it, but they pulled it apart and enjoyed it, anyway, holding the dripping pieces with their fingers, arguing with each other about the merits of their experiment.

What he liked most was being with her. He liked being among the vines and bushes and trees and in the sky and on the ground with her, listening to her prattle on about some subject or other.

"There was a storm here one day that drenched the world to muddy water," she told him. "The memory of the old folks recalls it. Two old men even remember it, and one of them has a book where ever day he writes notes on what he does that day. He has had six wives and sixty-one young'uns. He's got three wives to this day, and they all go to preachin' together, cook together, quilt using the same frame. His book says it rained so much one week that it filled all the springs, and that the creeks rumbled when they were filled to overflowing, exactly like a stomach rumbles when it's full.

The water was coming down off everything so much that he says the water was damming itself up in places. The flood took the logs in the forests and rode them down to the creeks, and rode them down to the lowlands and left them in that flat near Henry Station. It piled them along the valley, near Mill Creek, so that there were logs there house-high and hundreds of feet long. He said there were deer and bears carried down in the waters. He said you could stand at your cabin door and see the little spring branch that you drank from become a river washing your own chickens away."

"Oh, listen now, Anna—"

"Little babies were torn from their mamas' arms and were carried off."

"Oh my, Anna, I don't think so."

"The sky was like a black pillow, and the trees on the mountains were bending. The vines, like that one, were snapping and breaking tree limbs, and the roots of the trees were uncovered. The rocks broke free and fell into the valleys, so that you could hear a sound like thunder and see part of a mountain crumble."

"Come along, you can't believe that. That tree must be two hundred years old. And that vine has been here for a hundred years or more."

"The air got to boiling with clouds and rain, so you couldn't breathe. There was nothing in the world but water, unless you stayed indoors, where the air was so damp the fires went out and the people were left to shiver and blanket-warm themselves. The babies were squalling because there was nobody to feed them anything but water. The mother's milk was nothing that day but water—"

"Oh, God—"

"The bears tried to come indoors with the people."

"Anna, for heaven's sake, hush. Now tell me where this old man is."

"Up a draw a ways, in a cove, setting and studying his women and young'uns, trying to remember their names. He comes to meetings."

"Are all his children as honest as he is?"

"They're all honest as the day is long. He's got all this in a book."

"A book doesn't make it so."

She stared at him in astonishment. "You don't think the Bible is so?"

"Is it in the Bible?" he said.

"He writes in the Bible some of the birth dates and other matters, like the dates of storms, and he writes the rest of it in another book."

"What the Bible says and what he writes are not from the same authority."

She frowned at him critically. "Why would he write it down if it wasn't so?"

"Maybe he believes it."

"Would you write down something that's not so?"

"Would I? No."

She shrugged. "Mr. Thompson is fully as proper a man."

"I don't even know that everthing in the Bible is so."

She turned on him. "God will strike you down if you talk like that. There's not a preacher in this country won't admit it to you."

"Anna, it's not likely those preachers know any—"

"Why, that rock will fall on you." She crawled away from him to sit in a safer place. "You'll be going home some night and a bolt of lightning will fall and strike you down at a ford. A bird will come to your window and peck your eye out."

"Oh, hush," he said, but not unkindly. The superstitions of these people did trouble him sometimes, though. "I'm not saying the Bible isn't so; I'm saying I don't know. I would almost prefer for it to have errors and contradictions, as one would expect in a series of books written over many decades, dealing with life and man and God. That might be a sign of honesty in it."

She was not won over by any argument she couldn't understand. It was difficult enough to follow what he was saying when he talked about something she agreed with, but at times like these he got to using such ideas that she would have to have angel wings to flip in and out among them.

On their way back down the mountain they came to a spot where a bear had dug for the soft whitish larvae in the ground nest of yellow jackets. They passed wide around that place. The vines were everywhere twining and climbing and festooning and overlaying and tying: the clematis, the woodbine, the trumpet vine, the smilax, the grapevine. The insects were darting here and there; a cicada sprang with a rattle and whir past their faces. The little downy owls were irritably fretting in the late-light.

They walked along the river to a place where her uncle Charlie was raking hay. Nearby his wife and two of his daughters were walking among the corn hills, picking beans from the vines which had been allowed to climb the cornstalks. Charlie willingly stopped work long enough to pass the time of day and mention how warm it had been. He said he had made application for a job on the Road but he didn't know whether he wanted it or not, if the weather held so healthy. "I like natural things better than the Road," he said. He was a tall, willowy man with kind eyes captured in a narrow, bony face. "Is my bed aholding up," he said to Cumberland, "the bed I made?" He was Anna's mother's oldest brother and was best known locally for his irritation with politics, which had become so aggravated by the Civil War that he had stood his ground against both Confederate and Union raiders, refusing to admit obedience to any authority, and reportedly had broken one officer's rifle over his head when he had threatened him with it.

Cumberland and HenryAnna walked on together. Along the edges of the field the butterflies were working the last bit of moisture from the goldenrods and joe-pye weed and from the few white Indian pipes at the branch. At the pond they came upon meadow rue and black cohosh and white snakeroot.

They sat near the pond and listened to the bells of the cows coming home from across the field. A dog was barking after them. The daytime moon was turning from silver to gold, as the sun went down, and the pond was sparkling in those places where shadows fell. They heard the most lonely sound, the first cry of the whippoorwill.

"I hope a preacher don't ever hear what you said up there."

"I hope not," he said. There was no argument between them now. They watched as the miller's house was lighted by a lantern. Three boys went walking along the road, talking and laughing. They threw stones into the pond and the ripples washed out evenly and ended at the shore near Cumberland's feet. The boys stopped near the kiln, which Cumberland was having repaired, then they went on toward the river, and Cumberland wondered about himself, how it was he worked all week in a world of harshness and physical challenge, and all weekend in this other world, one he could retreat to permanently if he only dared to do so.

The first September frost withered the ferns on the higher reaches of the mountain. The hobblebush, which HenryAnna called "witch hobble," turned to brilliant colors, its leaves covering it generously and graciously, its orange-red fruit clusters almost unnoticed against their rich hues. The strawberry bush, which Henry-Anna called "hearts abustin' with love," dangled its glossy crimson fruit from pink husks. The fiddling of the katydids and crickets and grasshoppers increased, and the first of the winter birds arrived, the white-throated sparrows and ruby-crowned kinglets, and some of the Northern birds on their way south stopped for a day at the pond, to rest and clear their throats. They were warblers mostly.

By the end of October the fields were cut and the granaries were full. Children took pears out to sun and helped their mamas string red peppers and green beans. Apples were stored in cool places. So were sweet potatoes. Corn was in the cribs, tobacco in the curing barns. The trees were turning to bright colors.

During October the annual torrent of stock and men poured out of the mountains along the turnpike in the drive to the lowlands. Soon after it began, men were trudging home with dour expressions on their faces. It was another lean year, they said. Not a few of them wanted a job on the Road. They stood outside the Henry Station office by the hour, and all Weatherby or Cumberland could say was that there was no money to pay them anything.

"I ain't asking for much. I drove my stock to sale and I've got nothing for my land payments, so I'll chance what land I got. I'll likely lose it come New Year plus a day if I can't pay. God knows, how can I pay?"

Hundreds of them had the same story to tell, but Weatherby had little money to pay men with and he knew mountain men were poor hired laborers. They wouldn't accept instruction or orders; if somebody told one of them what to do, he would throw down his shovel: "Who you talking to, damn you?" he would likely say. Also, they wouldn't live in camps; they preferred to camp out on the hillside. With winter coming, they would be unhappy with the cold, and be unhappy knowing they were not home.

Now and then Weatherby would hire a likely-looking mountain boy, one who might be able to help around one of the stations, and he would offer to pay him a boy's wages: room and board and 15 cents a day. He hired forty-one boys that way. He would rather have them than their fathers, for they would be less likely to kick up their heels and leave, and they had less reason to be home.

The boys, if given individual tasks to do and if given time to hunt, proved to be able workers. Each of them had brought a dog or two with him and most of them had brought rifles. They shot a lot of game, and the meat as often as not ended up in the cook pots at the stations. If one of the boys, after a week or so, did decide to go home, he wouldn't report that he was leaving. He would simply go walking up the turnpike toward home, and in time he would be missed. He figured it this way: When he was missed they would know he was gone, and if he wasn't missed it didn't matter that he was gone. He didn't need to waste time discussing it with them, either way.

Nobody ever shouted at the boys, or paid less than full attention to what they were saying. Although they talked softly, if they didn't get what they felt was their due, they would leave and there would be no way to find them.

"They won't dig or haul, but they can do some other things well," Babcock said about them respectfully.

"You going to try to keep them out of the woods on Saturday nights?" Weatherby asked.

"I'll do it or die, one," Babcock said.

As it turned out, he had no problem; the boys had nothing to do with the convicts, even in passing. They were particularly aloof to the Negroes, were superstitious about them and wary of them.

Most of the boys slept out in the yards at Henry or Babcock Station, rolled in blankets, or they stretched out under a shelter made of boughs. A few of them found that the Tunnel Station was about completed and moved in there, since nobody else was using it.

Just who would use it was a problem in itself, for Weatherby didn't know whether to house new convicts there or move the old convicts on up the mountain. "The hardest work is going to be done up there," he old Babcock.

"Yes, but the new men will harden, and if you move the old men now, they'll get nervous. They like the places they've come to know."

"The new men won't be as ambitious for the Road," Weatherby said.

"Nobody was at first."

"The next big challenge is up there, the tunnels."

Babcock soon relented, and together they selected the best men from both Henry and Babcock; they agreed that when the new shipments of convicts arrived, some 300 of them in all, they would take the healthiest of those men and women, too, and send them to the Tunnel Station.

The act of moving the experienced workers proved that Babcock had been right about the convicts. There was much uneasiness, expressed in shouting and hollering along the route of march. A few of the men had been chained, and they began to curse most vilely, to proclaim their innocence from any crime, and to condemn the mountains for smothering them and chilling them. "We'll all die up here. We'll be smothered in this here light air."

"Look there off there at that valley. See there, Ernie?"

"God, God, we fall off here won't stop rolling till we hear the trumpet."

"I'm going home first chance I get, how 'bout you?"

"You'll more likely fall into a field and they'll run the train over you."

"I don't care. I can't hear it rumble with that clay in my ears."

"We had us a nice camp down there, and what we going to now?"

"Heaven, Ernie."

"Air too thin to breathe."

"Cold winds, Ernie."

By the time the men reached the Tunnel Station, they were furious. They beat their mattresses with their hands until the stuffing fell out, and generally felt destructive, protesting the land and air and buildings and cold water and everything. The Tunnel Station, though twice the size, was almost identical to the stations they had left, but they didn't like it.

"I ain't goin' to live here, even overnight."

"I can't breathe up this high, can you, Ernie?"

Women began weeping. The mules began to bray. All of this was going on in the main yard of the camp. The women wouldn't even unlash their iron pots or start fires. "We have no bake-oven in this place," they said. "We have no tables, no lean-tos, no cover-ups, nothing here." They hadn't had much at Henry or Babcock either, but they had made a few improvements, month by month, and this new place lacked facilities.

"The water's cold. God, man, taste that water! It won't do to drink cold water that freezes your hands. Look at that hand: it froze from my touching that there water." Of course, it wasn't frozen at all, but Ernie said it was and everybody agreed that it was. He went around showing his frozen hand.

Babcock told the men to get into the stockades, but he was shouted down and told to go to hell. The chief guard, Blackie, fired a rifle into the air and a tremendous shout of defiance went up from the men. The other guards drew near to Babcock, and the mountain boys fingered their rifles apprehensively. When Weatherby arrived, he evaluated the situation as quickly as he could. "Most too wet to plow here," he said to one guard, and began to move among the men, talking quietly, so that everybody got quiet to hear him. "Who put chains on these men?" he asked. "You ought to take the chains off these men. They don't need chains put on them. They have worked as loyally as men can work for months now, and somebody chains them." He spoke gently, softly, shook his head as if he couldn't understand what he was seeing.

The guards were frightened and hesitated to do as Weatherby directed. Blackie objected, but Weatherby insisted that the chains be removed, which caused the convicts to send up a big shout. Now the convicts and Weatherby were on the same side, against the others. That more or less evened things out, they felt.

"And where's the bake-oven for the women?" Weatherby asked quietly. "These women aren't common; they don't have to make bread on rocks. How about you men gathering enough rocks to make an oven." Convicts jumped at once to do so, and an oven began going into place.

"And where's the new shucks for the mattresses?" Weatherby asked, noticing that many men had destroyed their mattresses. "You guards get back to Henry Station and bring six mule loads of shucks, will you?"

Not a word of criticism did he make of the convicts. He had a mild word of criticism for everybody else, though, and well before sunset the convicts were contentedly in their stockades, the doors locked, filling their mattresses with new shucks, and the women were happy with their new oven.

In November the Tunnel Station reached full strength; there

were 300 convicts, and 150 were at each of the other two stations. In addition to the convicts, the Road had 60 guards, 15 foremen and lesser supervisors, about 20 other employees who worked as clerks or carpenters or smiths or in the mills, 50 mountain boys, more or less—some 750 people in all.

There was considerable anticipation among them, in the three camps now, for the work on the tunnels brought the men against their toughest challenge of all. There were hundreds of rumors about the proposed length of the tunnels and the dangers one would encounter underground. Some were terrifying stories that the convicts created to scare one another with.

HenryAnna heard these stories from her father, who tended to believe them, and she asked Weatherby about them. "Well, I doubt if we have that much trouble, Anna," he said kindly, but he never told her the stories weren't possibly so, and he even let her glimpse his own worry. "A tunnel is a dangerous matter," he admitted to her.

But he had confidence in the men, and confidence in the nitro-glycerin. He had made the nitroglycerin manufactory, merely a shed and a wooden mixing trough, and he had devised a formula for the mixture, using six parts of "blasting oil" to one part corn meal and one part sawdust. The three substances were put together in the trough, and small boys were assigned the task of mixing them thoroughly into a mash, which wasn't as dangerous to handle as the liquid.

"It has to be mixed entirely even, or we'll have uneven use from it," he told the boys.

"We stirred all morning."

"Stir all afternoon, too."

They complained of fierce headaches. "That stuff gives me head-aches, too, and other body pains as well, but once you get used to it, the headache goes away," he told them.

"Is it much better than black powder, Mr. Weatherby?" the foreman asked.

"We'll see how it does," he said simply.

As time approached for starting the tunnels, he began to show tension. HenryAnna noticed this, and so did others. He spent most all his time at the Tunnel Station, and even moved his clothes and papers up there. Cumberland suggested he move his own things up there, too, but Weatherby told him the main office ought to remain at a place where railroad traffic was possible, that the Tunnel Station was merely an outpost until the iron reached it. There was truth in this, but his main reason was that he had noticed Cumberland and HenryAnna had been seeing each other often. Every weekend Cumberland left the office and went to visit her, and apparently she spent much of her time during the week staying at the cottage. Weatherby didn't intend to encourage that by stationing Cumberland close by. Sometimes opposites attracted; that was a well-established adage in love and life. But rarely did the relationship result in a lasting union.

There was no jealousy of Cumberland involved, he told himself. He was certainly committed personally to Cumberland and had much respect and regard for him; there was, he admitted, a twinge of annoyance once Cumberland became the one at Henry Station whom HenryAnna came most of all to see, and the one she had rather be with, but jealousy was not the major consideration, he decided.

He felt awkward about leaving Cumberland stationed at Henry Station, so he tried to make it up to him by being attentive to every suggestion he made. And he made it up to HenryAnna by finding odd jobs for her to do, for which he paid her. He wanted her to be near him, now more than ever. He had come to depend on her, and as the tensions increased, as he came closer to the day when the blasting of the tunnels could begin, he had need for humor and the attention a woman could give easily and naturally.

On the weekend before the first blastings he stayed at the Tunnel Station rather than go home to Morganton. He worked all day Saturday at the nitroglycerin manufactory, making different mixtures of mash and experimenting with small quantities of them. When night came he put a small amount of the mash in his shirt; he had found that he got a headache when he was going to be away from the mash for a while, but as long as he kept some of the mash with him, he had no trouble.

He ate supper at the kitchen alone, and he got to wondering how Cumberland was. He missed him. No doubt he was at the cottage at the Gap, which wasn't far to walk. Weatherby decided to go on up there and see him.

The walk along the path and the turnpike was gently lighted by the moon. There was a deep tranquility in the night air and sounds. He came to the wagon road that led to the millpond and the village, and as he drew close he saw that the cottage had its candles lighted in the main room. Some of the light splashed out on the path that led to the door, and he could see that the kiln and the work area of the pottery had been repaired, and that a quantity of clay had been delivered to the place and was damp and glistening in one corner. He stopped at the cottage door and knocked, and called Cumberland's name.

There was no answer, but he heard him moving about inside. "Cumberland?" he said again.

When he touched the door latch, it yielded. He pushed the door gently, and it swung open slowly on its hinges, revealing the room. Standing by the bed was the girl, HenryAnna, dressed in a nightgown. She was staring at him, her mouth open as if she were wondering if she ought to speak; her eyes were wide and shiny in the lanternlight, and she was nervous, even afraid. Her hair had been let down and it was hanging to her waist, where a thin ribbon was tied, holding her gown close over her breasts.

Without taking his eyes off her, he closed the door behind him. He tried to find his voice and heard himself ask about Cumberland.

She tried to speak, too, but the words caught in her throat.

"You stay here when he's away?" he said.

She nodded.

He knew he must stop looking at her. He moved abruptly to the hearth and stared down at the embers of the fire. "Do you stay here of a night with him?"

She was still standing by the bed. "No," she said.

He was hateful within himself for asking, knowing he was seeking to find a flaw in them or their relationship which would excuse the feeling he had inside himself.

He looked up and she was standing near him, barefooted, the firelight reflecting on her body. She was watching him questioningly. Her tongue came out and dampened her lips.

"You're beautiful," he said. She was quite close and he could touch her. The bed was there, the fire, the woman. It was all arranged as if by some devil or other to plague him. "I'm going to walk to the door, Anna, and I'm going to open it and go through it and close it, and I don't know why I'm doing it this way, for I remember as a young man that sometimes interesting nights could be discovered if a man took advantage of a meeting arranged beyond his power, or a girl's power."

She was standing there yet, looking at him.

"Oh, God, Anna," he said deeply, and he turned and held out his arms and she came into them, but tenderly, not passionately, and he held her comfortingly and kissed her face, her forehead and cheeks, and touched her face with his fingers gently. "He'll be a difficult man for you to win, Anna. He's a bit unbending and stiff for you. I don't want you hurt, by him or me."

"I know that," she said.

He held her gently until abruptly she stepped away from him and said, "A potter is coming tomorrow to help us learn to make clay things. He sent his clay ahead, and he's bringing us a wheel that we'll put in this room."

"Dishes and bowls and such as that?" he said.

"And cups. Whatever we think we can make."

They were standing so close he could sense each breath she took, yet they were not seeking each other. This was a new sensation for him, not immature, not unnatural, but certainly different from any feeling he had had toward a woman before. "Here you are, half naked and standing so close I can feel you breathe, and we talk about pottery, and about you and Cumberland."

She pressed his hand. "I think of you different from the way I think of him."

"Do you?"

"But I love you, too. I love you because of so many different reasons that I love you in different ways. It's like a spring or a place in the creek where children have dropped colored stones, and as the water ripples, you don't know, you can't say what color it is."

"I've seen springs done that way."

"It's nice when I'm with you, that's all."

"And it's nice to be with Cumberland, too."

"Yes. But I trust you more."

"You've been lonely for someone, haven't you?"

"Yes."

"So was I once." He kissed her forehead and stepped back and said, "Be careful of him, for both your sakes." He touched her chin, then suddenly turned to the door and went to it and stopped there. "Good night, Anna," he said, hoping she would ask him to stay, and hoping she would not.

"Good night," she said.

He went out, but even as he closed the door he saw she was still standing by the fire, watching him, waiting as a woman would wait for the decision of a man, unprotestingly, as if she were listening for a decision, as if she had no power to change the decision he would make.

CHAPTER ELEVEN

THERE WERE NOT NEARLY enough mules for all three stations, and the foremen at Henry and Babcock resented releasing any to the Tunnel Station, especially any of the better ones. This was one of the problems that faced Weatherby that weekend—trying to work out cooperative arrangements among the twelve gang foremen.

"Ever week I've got to move mud out of Mud Cut, Mr. Weatherby, and I can't do it without mules to pull carts," one of the three gang foremen at Henry told him.

Of course, the Henry foremen had flatcars and an engine to pull them, and he had a sluice canal to help him, but there was no benefit in outright defiance of the man and his authority.

Finally he released four mules to the Tunnel Station, and the other Henry Station foremen released a total of five, and on Sunday afternoon Weatherby went down himself to pick them out, to be sure they weren't sick ones, and again he had to argue mildly and kindly over each one.

The same problem occurred at Babcock, though with better reason on the part of the three Babcock foremen, because they did have much earth moving to do, and rock moving, too, including the deep, long cut that Weatherby wanted done as soon as possible at what was called Bloody Ridge. The convicts had named it that; they said it was going to cost the blood of several men before it was finished. Weatherby selected eight mules at Babcock Station. So by Sunday night he had seventeen, which was not half enough, and he told Lou Babcock, "Those downhill foremen are already peeved because they weren't put in charge up here, and they're making it tough on us."

Babcock didn't seem to care. He sat on the edge of his chair, breathing deeply and moaning to himself, complaining.

"You sound like one of the convicts," Weatherby told him.

"Four men are gone," he said.

"Escaped?"

"They were here last night, and they're not here nowheres now."

"Did you send guards after them?"

"I sent mountain boys."

"Were they black convicts or white?"

"Black."

"The mountain boys won't bring them back."

"You can get replacements."

Weatherby was struck by the callousness of the comment. He stared at Babcock for a long while, wondering how tough and cruel he was, and to what extent he had the capacity for deep feeling. "I respect the men," he said, "don't you?"

Babcock felt keenly the criticism. There had never been, before now, a word of complaint pass between him and Weatherby. "I don't respect them if they escape."

"We don't know why they escaped. In any event I don't think we ought to sentence them to death for trying to leave here."

"I didn't sentence them."

"They've been sentenced, though," Weatherby said. "You wouldn't send mountain boys after Ham if he left, would you?"

Babcock thought about it. Finally he said, "This nigger business gets so full of starch sometimes I don't know what to make of it, Weatherby. I've always liked Ham well enough, I'll say that, but when a man escapes, if you want him found you better use mountain boys, for the guards ain't so swift themselves. If you don't catch the first ones that escape, you'll have a swarm leaving here soon, do you know it?"

The two men sat staring at one another. "It's too late to call the boys back, is it?" Weatherby said.

"Hell, yes."

"Did you give them any special instructions?"

"If you send mountain boys, it don't do to tell them not to shoot their guns, if that's what you mean. When they go hunting, they always shoot, you know that, too."

"All right, all right," Weatherby said.

"It's just as well to mistreat four men," Babcock said, "if we aim to save six hundred."

But Weatherby didn't agree, and Babcock was hurt by his show of resentment.

A mountain boy came by to say the nitroglycerin mash had been put in five-pound lard buckets, as Weatherby had ordered, and was waiting for the tunnel blasting work to start the next morning. Weatherby asked him to sit down for a while, and the boy did. He said he came from the valley where Weatherby's own people lived; the boy knew Weatherby's sisters and brothers well and told about their health and farming, but Weatherby asked nothing more about them. When his father had died, his brothers and sisters didn't have him buried before they were arguing about how to divide the land, and he never had cared for them since and had let them alone. "How old are you?" he asked the boy.

"Ten plus four, or more."

"You ever go to school?" Weatherby said.

"No, sir."

"Can you read and write?"

"I can write."

"Can you write your name?"

"Yes, sir."

"Can you write anything else?"

"I can write figures."

"How high can you count?"

"Easy to ten, then I can go by ten-plus to twenty and can count from twenty to ninety-nine, for I've done it."

"It's that figuring between ten and twenty that gets you down, is it?"

"Yes, sir. It's confusing. I generally say ten plus one or ten plus four, and it does all right. When I get to twenty it straightens out."

"Uh-huh. I'll teach you to count those other figures if you want me to."

The boy studied about it. "How much would I owe ye?"

Weatherby supposed the boy would need to pay, for mountain people were too proud to accept a gift. "I'll dock your pay five cents," he said.

The boy considered that. "What if I don't learn?"

"I'll still dock it the five cents. I'll tell you the way the numbers go as many times as you like, but if you don't learn it's your fault, not mine. You're buying knowledge and I'm supplying it, but I can't sell learning."

The boy thought it over. "I'll tell you later on," he said. "I'd hate to buy what I can't make use of no time soon."

"You won't forget it, once learned, and you're likely to need it often from here on out."

The boy didn't appear to be convinced. "I ain't so sure," he said.

Cumberland came in, blowing his breath on his hand and trying to get warm. "I planned to walk down home to Henry Station," he said, "but it's too cold out."

"You stay here," Weatherby said, glad to see him. "We have a cot in that other bedroom."

Cumberland had been throwing pots on the wheel, he said, and he was full of information and ideas about it. The potter had shown him and HenryAnna how to ball the clay, to clean it and make it ready for use; he had taught them how to throw a pot, or had tried to, but Cumberland said he was poor at it, himself.

"I like to see it done," Weatherby said. "I used to spend hours at a time at the potter's back home."

"Anna made a pitcher. You ought to see it. It won't set even. It has a lip on it as big as a sow's ear, and a huge handle. She says when a pitcher is full, it takes a firm grip to lift it easily, so she made a handle big enough for all of one hand and part of the other." He was proud of what she had done, and his fondness for her was evident. "When we get ready to fire that kiln, maybe we'll bake enough of those crazy, flap-eared pitchers of Anna's for everybody in the county to have one."

They sat up late, talking, and the next morning they awoke expectantly, thinking about the work that must begin on the tunnels; they washed in cold water at dawn, ate breakfast, then the three men—Weatherby, Cumberland and Babcock—walked nearby to where Lick Log tunnel was to be made, each man carrying a pail of mash.

Weatherby studied the face of the rock, then called on Esau to advise him about where the holes ought to be drilled. Esau and another Negro, named Adam, discussed the texture of the rock and the veins in it and speculated about whether there were hidden crevices that the drill would get stuck in. They decided six three-foot holes would be enough "to shoot" the face of the wall, but Weatherby said he thought half that many would do well enough with this new mash.

Adam held the star drill and Esau swung the hammer. He swung it with his hands held tight, without either hand sliding up the handle after a swing; he swung the hammer in an arc that landed each time at the very same place, at the end of the steel drill, which Adam turned an eighth of a turn each time. Another Negro came up with a steel hammer and began to hit the same drill, alternating with Esau. They stopped once to pour water into the hole, to keep the steel of the bit cooler.

When the hole was two feet deep, Adam changed to a smaller drill while Esau mopped the hole out with a wet rag wound around a stick. He and the other man swung at the smaller drill until it had gone into the rock about a foot and a half, then they swabbed out the hole and began another one, Adam keeping his head down, of course, turning the drill and moaning to himself.

Weatherby crimped the fuse into the percussion cap, and when the three holes were drilled and swabbed, he funneled mash into them, being careful not to drop it from a height, gently tamping it in with a stick to get it laid in the hole tight; otherwise he would lose compression in the blast. He put the cap well down in the center hole, then stobbed it with a stick. He daubed all three of the holes, using stiff mud. "You want to take on this work sometime?" he asked Esau.

"I'm not anxious to," Esau said. "I don't like anything that's always about to explode."

They had trouble getting the caps in place and the fuses set, but when that was done Weatherby waved the men back. "Esau, you want to join them?"

Esau said he would stay with Weatherby.

"You better go back with the men, Cumberland," Weatherby said.

"No, I'll stay," Cumberland said.

"Very well," Weatherby said. He lighted the fuse, and the three of them hurried to a big rock they could get behind. They crouched there, waiting. All the convicts were watching, some from behind rocks and others from behind trees, and quite a few of them were merely lying on the ground in the open, a fair distance away.

Weatherby silently counted to thirty. He sat with his back to the rock and counted to sixty and there was no explosion.

Esau whispered, "Is it time yet?"

Weatherby counted to a hundred. "We're in trouble with that thing, gentlemen."

"Why?" Cumberland said.

"That's the trouble; I don't know why."

"Is it going to explode?"

"I don't know."

Cumberland whistled softly, then mildly, calmly said, "You won't want to find out anytime soon, will you?"

Weatherby took out his tobacco and lighted his pipe. "Something was wrong with that fuse, maybe." He puffed at the pipe and wondered if he shouldn't go out there now and see what was the matter. "I meant to get a man to come in here, a detonation man, but nobody around here has ever used this stuff before, so we'd be paying for experience the man wouldn't have."

"It's not worth it for you to risk your life," Cumberland said.

"I agree with you entirely," Weatherby said.

"You got a wife and family?" Esau asked.

"Yes."

"I do, too," Esau said.

Weatherby puffed at his pipe and wished the nitroglycerin would blow. He would give a lot to have that stuff blow and not have to inspect the fuse. "The men are getting anxious," he said.

"My wife is probably give up on me by now," Esau said. "I wouldn't blame her, either, for I got twenty years and then I tried two times to escape and that doubles the time."

"Wouldn't be surprised if she has."

"Once I counted up and decided I'd have to live to be a hundred five years old to get out of here, and that's too long for a woman to wait."

"Even if she's fond of you," Cumberland said.

"I'd like to see her," Esau said solemnly, "if all I find out is who's with her."

Several of the convicts were getting up from the ground and walking about. Weatherby knew he had to take some action, so he got to his feet and put his pipe away. "You men stay here," he said.

"Might get lonely here," Esau said.

"You stay put." He took a deep breath and stepped out into the open and faced the rock wall. He faced its sunlighted side. Blankly, it was before him. "My, my, Mildred," he murmured, as he started walking toward it.

He wasn't aware of anything except the rock and the danger. If the explosion came now, there would be no warning; the first sight of light would be the fire that killed him; he wouldn't even live long enough to hear the roar.

The convicts were watching silently. There was no sound at all, except of his boots on the gravel. He went past two tree stumps and stopped before the rock, within reach of the fuse and the cap. A premonition came to him to turn and flee. He turned and saw standing before him Esau and Cumberland, and on Cumberland's face was a small smile, as if he held the danger in mild contempt.

"It's all right. Ain't it all right?" Esau said nervously.

"I think so," Weatherby said, regaining his composure.

Gently he knocked the mud off the center hole. He pulled out the stob. When he reached into the hole and lifted out the cap, relief came over him so strong he sank down to his knees.

Esau knelt, too. Weatherby said, "Your knees weaken on you?"

"Sometimes I like to be near the ground," Esau said.

It took a few minutes to set another cap and fuse. Again Weatherby lit the fuse and ran for cover. "Fire in the heading," he shouted and dove behind the rock. This time, almost at once, the blast came, and it shook that rock and shook the ground on which they lay. It was a terrifying sound, and debris filled the air; rocks fell around them.

Then there was quiet, broken by a shout from the men, who surged forward, dragging mule carts and shovels behind them.

Weatherby, Cumberland and Esau stayed where they were, there behind the rock, and after a while Weatherby said, "Don't you want this job, Esau?"

"Oh, I tell you, Mr. Weatherby, I want to live my full hundred five years and see my wife."

"I might be able to get you a pardon sooner than that."

Esau glanced up. He thought about it. "How many years you have in mind?"

"I can write to Raleigh and see."

Esau stared ahead, his body tense now. "She might be missing me, like I miss her. I'd do anything to see her again, and I wouldn't blame her for any match she's made, for she couldn't wait her lifetime out."

"I'll write them. I'll see if they'll agree to let you go when the Road is open to the Gap."

"Only one more year?" Esau said.

"More than that," Weatherby said. "About seven weeks more than a year."

Cumberland said, "One year might be a lifetime."

Esau nodded to that, but he was anxious to make the deal.

They walked together to the tunnel's face, and it did have a face now; it had jagged teeth in the face, and even pockmarked eyes and a nose. "She's looking at us," Weatherby said.

The convicts were moving the blasting out of the way, and Esau began to drill for the next blast. "We need that much mash this time, too," Weatherby said. "And we'll keep it higher from the floor, or we'll dig holes we can't fill in. They'll only collect water."

"One year and seven weeks," Esau murmured, as he brought the steel hammer down on the drill.

They worked that day through, and that night Esau went to the barracks and Weatherby went to his office where he wrote the letter to Raleigh. Babcock came into the room and said the four escapees had been caught beyond Mill Creek.

"Captured?" Weatherby said.

"No," Babcock said. "Dead."

"Could they have been captured?"

"I wasn't there," Babcock said.

Most of each day Weatherby spent on the Road, watching the men work. He never tired watching them, as they led the mules up to the rock wall and loaded the mule carts with rock, using shovels sometimes and using their bare hands more often, using sledges to break the biggest stones, singing; leading the mules away to the fill, dumping the carts.

> Black man make a way
> For the train
> Riding the iron track
> Far from home . . .
>
> Not a soul in iron
> Not a soul in a train
> Not a soul in a black man
> Far from home.

One Friday morning in November Weatherby stopped near a convict who had got lame. A guard had ordered him to get back to work, but the convict lay on the ground whimpering. The guard cursed him, but he lay there, so the guard went off, murmuring and cursing, threatening him. Weatherby sat down beside him and felt of his forehead. The man jerked his head away; he never had been touched by a white man before. "It's all right," Weatherby told him. He felt his head once more. "You have a temperature," he said.

"No, suh. I'm all right."

Weatherby called to a mountain boy. "Will you do something for me?" he asked him.

The boy was listening; he didn't say yes or no.

"When you get a minute, fetch me a blanket out of the office."

The boy continued working on a whip he was plaiting, but soon he got up and went along toward the camp, walking in the loose stride of the mountain people, a relaxed, unhurried, seemingly effortless walk. He brought a blanket, and Weatherby covered up the convict. "How old are you?" he asked him.

"I lost count," the man said. He was embarrassed because of being shown all this attention. He knew it might go hard with him later in the barracks, but he was sick and felt helpless.

"You fifty years old?"

"Oh, I can't remember being as young as that."

"You from down east?"

"Flatlands. You can set down at home and not endanger yourself falling off a cliff, leastways." He winked at Weatherby. "It's so flat to home that the water won't flow."

"How do you keep it fresh?"

"I don't know. The fish drink it and keep it moving. Catfish mostly." He bobbed his head in pleasure, thinking about it all. "I wisht I was home."

"You married?"

"Oh, God, I been married off and on and here and there so often I don't know how to add and subtract it all, but I'm learning my lesson now, sure enough, in this chain gang." He sniffled, then spat onto the rock floor on which he lay. There was blood in his spit. He squinted his eyes at Weatherby. "Air we going to have a Christmas here?"

"I've not planned much of anything, except maybe an orange apiece."

"That's when Jesus was born, you know. That's the only day I care about, when that little fellow was born. He was a rooter and snorter, wasn't he?"

"He appears to have been."

"I expect he broke his share of rods and staffs. I wish he'd come and get me out of here."

At sunset the men were given a chance to wash under a waterfall; a stream from higher on the mountain had been diverted and fell from a wooden trough, fell about ten feet, then flowed on down the mountain. The water was icy cold and the men shouted in glee and pain as they went under it. Each man was supposed to stand under it for the count of five, holding his clothing outside the water in one hand. Not many men stood the pain any longer than that, then they dressed and were taken to the supper place, where the women served them. Some of them were shivering so much they could scarcely hold the plate of food, and their teeth chattered as they ate.

"Don't put the men through that again," Babcock told the guards. "We might lose some of them this winter, with such foolishness. Dirt don't hurt, never has," he said, walking on. "At least, it don't hurt them."

They were given corn bread, molasses and boiled fatback to eat, and they ate all they got. Weatherby went among them, talking with them in a relaxed way, alert for signs of dissension or hints of trouble. The men on sick call joined the other workers. "Hey, you men been playing with rocks?" one of them called.

"You men been blasting? Can't sleep here in camp for the noise you'ns make."

There was a good deal of laughter before the men grew quiet and began to move toward the big gates of the stockade. Soon the gates were locked with hickory poles and the night guards clustered around the cookfires, tried to get close enough to warm.

Weatherby went to his building, to the bedrooms off the office, where he stretched out. He lay there thinking about the Road and about himself. It seemed that success was within sight. Yet he was under pressure, he was raw inside, worn thin and worn down. He was getting to be more like the convicts and foremen. He was caught as they were in the mesh of the operation, which grew larger every month. Maybe he would break down before it was over, as might Moses, Esau, Babcock, Cumberland. If one of twenty men broke, each man in turn might break.

He thought of Mildred and wondered if he should go see her now. He could spend Sunday with her. He felt such warmth and comfort in her house, being with her, listening to Troy discuss his own many projects, eating at a table, washing before his meals, sleeping under a quilt comforter. If he didn't get away more often, the pressure on the Road could harden him like a rock. Yes, and crack him like the rocks.

Dr. Chester and Babcock came into the outer office beyond the bedroom door. It was cold and a light snow was falling, which was unusual for November. Chester was complaining about an old Negro with tuberculosis not being sent to him. He was angry about it. "He'll die for certain tonight," Chester said. "What cruelty these guards have."

"It's going to take time to soften the ways of a convict camp, doctor," Weatherby said, joining them. "We can expect mercy, but we're not likely to get it here." He found the old man's name on a list of convicts and wrote "tbc" in the margin by the name.

"Take him down the mountain before he dies," Babcock said.

"What?" the doctor said, surprised.

"They think high mountain air smothers the lungs. It won't do to encourage that idea."

Chester was incredulous. "He shouldn't be moved."

Babcock tapped his foot on the floor as he rocked in the rocker.

"It's a matter of one thing agin another," he said. "It's what's best for the man and what's best for the Road."

"I understand," Chester said bluntly, "but as a medical matter, the man cannot be moved."

"As a medical matter, the man is going to die," Babcock said. He glanced at Weatherby. "It won't do for him to die up here, I tell you that."

Chester was fiercely jealous of his authority, and normally he wouldn't have considered a request of this sort, but he had never been accepted as a friend by anybody here and he felt somewhat insecure. Also, he was paid his $75 a month salary by the Prison Department, but he had been hired by Weatherby; he wasn't certain what his authority was.

Weatherby wondered aloud if there was any coffee about. He went outside and got some, came back and sat down at his desk. Chester was still dejected. Babcock rocked back and forth, waiting.

"Want coffee?" Weatherby asked him, offering him his cup.

"I'll send a boy for some later," Babcock said.

Weatherby called to a mountain boy in the yard and said Babcock and the doctor wouldn't mind having coffee. Then he sat back and studied Chester, who was obviously waiting for him to say something. "It's your decision, doctor, either way," Weatherby said.

Chester smiled briefly. "I appreciate that," he said.

"We're up here on a mission," Weatherby said, "one we have prospects of winning, but its price is going to be dear. Nothing gets changed unless a high price is paid. We can pay much of it with ourselves, but some will need to be paid by others."

The mountain boy came in with a mug of coffee and set it down on the desk. He stood there waiting to be spoken to, and finally Babcock asked him if he had something to say. "The old man is calling for the doctor," he said.

Dr. Chester sat there, still unable to decide anything apparently, and Weatherby said finally, speaking softly to the boy, "Bundle him up in blankets and bring him to my porch in an ox sled."

"Sir?" the boy said.

Weatherby repeated what he had said. Chester sat there on a straight hickory-split chair, saying nothing.

The boy went out, and Weatherby said, "I'll walk down to Henry Station with you, doctor."

"That's not necessary. There's not much use in either of us going now. He's going to die either way; he'll die sooner now."

"I'm heading home, so I need to go to Henry anyway. Babcock, I'll have Cumberland move his own clothes up here, for if this is where such decisions as this are going to be made, we'll need him for advice."

"He thinks about things too long to suit me," Babcock said.

"Yes, he's inexperienced, but I'll talk to him about coming up here to stay. Such decisions as this weary me, you know it? But maybe that's part of the price we have to pay ourselves."

The next morning, Saturday, Cumberland left Henry Station and walked up the turnpike, carrying his suitcase and his bag of books. At the Tunnel Station he hung his clothes in the empty bedroom and put his books on his desk in the outer office. He went into Weatherby's office and imagined he could feel even now the sway and temper of the man himself, and he recalled the night before at Henry Station and the remarkable sight of the old convict in an ox sled, and the tortured look on Weatherby's face as he and the sled stopped in the pool of lanternlight at the Henry Station office. Cumberland had gone outside and asked what the convict was doing there, and Weatherby had said the man needed treatment. Cumberland spoke to the man, but the man said nothing. One of the mountain boys tried to wake him; he poked him slightly, then tilted his head back from his chest, and the head fell backward limp, dead, and Weatherby backed away from him so quickly he fell.

Later he would say nothing about it, except that he wanted to see Mildred and talk with her about it, and he told Cumberland to please move up to the Tunnel Station. Then he went off. Even though it was the dead of night, he went off down the Road toward Morganton. There was no train running and no stage for an hour.

Cumberland followed him, deeply concerned, but Weatherby sent him away. "I'm all right, I'm all right, let me be," and he hurried on, his head bent forward, his body bent against the wind.

"You going to work up here?" It was a clerk who spoke. He had just come in.

"Yes," Cumberland said.

The other clerk came into the office and began to work, and Cumberland, more interested in thinking about Weatherby and the old man's death, went outside and started up the trail toward the Gap.

The sun was melting the snow; he saw a rabbit sitting under a bush, a gray one with big eyes which watched him and the strange white lacy world, the erratic late-autumn world. Cumberland saw quail tracks, too. The sun was out and it fell against the leafless trees and shadowed the ground with trunks and intertwining limbs. The pine trees were sunny, and there was much else that was green, including burdens of mistletoe in the high branches of the oaks, where they lay pale green. There were holly trees spaced about in the woods, some of them with bright red berries, and stands of laurel were holding even to the steep places.

When he got to the Gap he stopped to consider the little twists of smoke rising from the cabins and houses that were in sight. The fields were dead and empty, except where cattle stood near the fenced haystacks. Now a farmer crossed untrampled snow toward one of them, a pitchfork in his hand, and began to throw out hay to them.

Cumberland started along the turnpike road, walking faster. His feet were almost frozen in his boots, and he began to run; the cold air burned his lungs, but he ran on until he came to his house. "Anna," he called, as he hurried toward it.

But she wasn't there. Even the hearth was cold, so he hurried over to the store to get warm.

The proprietor, Old Whitaker, was in there, of course, rummaging about looking for his goods. He had not much better idea about what he had to sell than had the customers. "I'm nigh out of everything," he said, talking to the stove more than to the six men who had assembled around it, "and here it is with snow on the ground and it not but November."

He had a pain in his back which he guessed was from the cold. He also had a pain in his left leg which he guessed was from a poor batch of whisky he had traded a man for. "With a head start on it, winter's going to be so cold you can't bury a man if'n he dies, unless you use an auger."

"Not likely to be cold like it was ten winter ago," one of the old men, whose name was Pinkny, said.

"You got a memory like a fox trap, have ye?" Whitaker said. He didn't like for other men to say anything in his store while he was in a talking mood himself. He put wood into the stove and belched. "I ain't never saw awful cold weather up here, not less'n ten below zero."

The miller came in. He was grumpy and slant-eyed, as usual, and Old Whitaker said, "Come in and shake the cold off'n your coat and set."

The miller drew close enough to examine each of the other men suspiciously. Satisfied that they were all right, he sat down on a stool and warmed his hands against the metal side of the stove.

"You got no fire yet, I reckon?" the old man, Pinkny, said to him.

The miller snorted depreciatingly. "You got no fire neither, have ye?"

"I got no mill neither," Pinkny said and spat. "You got the only mill I ever saw where a man could freeze his insides while waiting for his meal to grind."

"What miller keeps a fire?" the miller demanded.

"Ever miller I ever knowed has a little fire to warm his customers."

"Not so," the miller said. "Let them come when the weather is warm if they want meal. A man can't grind when ice is on the pond, nohow, or he'll bust his wheel."

HenryAnna came in, slamming the door behind her. "Well, I was awondering where the community was," she said, moving up to the fire and warming, shaking dampness over Pinkny, who began to fuss at her for it. "A band of Indians could move in here and take over all the settlement," she said, "and you wouldn't know it till closing time."

"Indians?" Pinkny said. "I ain't saw an Indian for law knows when."

"You ain't never saw one," Old Whitaker said bluntly.

"I saw and killed what I saw," Pinkny said.

"You ain't never," HenryAnna said, stooping low so that she could look him in his rheumy eyes. "You tell me you killed somebody?"

"Why, hell, yes, you biddy. I killed what was in my way, in my time. They used to camp not far from here. That was afore the war with England."

"You remember that?" she said, still staring at him.

"Lord, no. I ain't no hundred year old, am I?"

"You ain't?" she said quizzically, winking at Cumberland.

"I don't think so, and if I am, I weren't but a babe then." He grunted and spat. "My pa was the one who fit the Tories."

Nobody knew the truth from a lie when Pinkny talked. The miller asked if there was any lard in the place.

"I meant to order some lard, but my lard man ain't come through here yet," Old Whitaker said.

"I need lard bad," the miller said.

"Why, there's a plenty of it," Old Whitaker said. "It's everywhere abounding, now that hog killings are started. You can get it from ary soul in this valley."

"I can't get it from you, can I?" the miller said.

"No, I'm out, as I told ye."

"Well, if it's so much abounding, why are you out?"

"It ain't no use to have what everbody's got of his own."

"I ain't got any. Didn't you hear me say I ain't got ary bit."

"Cause you don't grow hogs. Name one other man that don't grow hogs."

"You."

"Huh? Well, name me another'n."

"HenryAnna's pa."

She flared up at that. "Why, he has fourteen hogs, if he has a one."

"Fourteen? Where air they?" the miller said.

"In the woods above the waterfall."

The miller grumbled. "That girl would lie any day to protect her pa from fair comment."

Old Whitaker cleared his throat. "When is he going to finish that telegraph he's the director of?"

"What you mean?" she said defensively.

"Where do I go to use the telegraph?"

"I tell you the truth, I don't know," she admitted. "I went onto the mountain one day last week and asked him when it was going to be used, and he said he was so pestered trying to get the wire strung that he hadn't had time to work out the scheme yet. I told him some of it looked to be so low to the ground that the moss would overgrow it."

"Is he home?" Cumberland asked her.

"Why, he's not been home in years, except now and then."

"Where is he?"

"Yes," the miller said, "where does he go when it snows and he can't fish or string the telegraph?"

"Why, he can fish, if he busts the ice pack."

"Then that's where he is," the miller said. "Down there on a cake of snow and him not knowing hit's cold."

They expected her to flare up angrily at that, but she said nothing for a while, then she said softly, "Listen."

They listened.

"Hear it?" she whispered.

"What?" the miller said.

"That there mill is grinding."

"Huh?" he said, looking up sharply. "Who's grinding hit?"

"Hear it going?" she said.

They listened, breathless.

"I hear it for a fact," Old Whitaker said, winking at her.

"Huh?" the miller said. He hurried to the door and dashed outside. When he got back everybody was laughing, and Henry-Anna had taken his chair at the stove.

"You give me back my place," he told her.

She wouldn't do it though. He began to rant and fuss, but she held up her hand and suddenly said, "Listen."

He stopped and stood there, listening. Then he saw the little smile appear on her face as the other men began to laugh.

CHAPTER TWELVE

LICK LOG TUNNEL appeared to Moses to weep, so he trusted it to do him no harm. Its tears would flow down its walls or drip from the ceiling to the floor. Whenever he went into Lick Log tunnel, once he got accustomed to the light, he would see the water dripping through the smoke left after each explosion; the tears were slipping through the air and through the smoke, falling in drops and then flowing in streams to be gathered in pools.

Candles were put here and there in the walls, and sometimes the drops of water would strike a candle and it would splutter and splatter wax and go out, but there were always candles burning in there, except during a blast.

Two boys named Closet and Penny, brothers of HenryAnna, were the afternoon candlelighters. About noon dinnertime a blast was usually ready to be set off; they would gather up the candles, blowing them out one by one, and would put them in the candle cart, which they pushed themselves. When they reached the portal, Esau and the other nitroglycerin men knew the tunnel was clear, clear of men and dark as a womb and waiting for the explosion.

Each time they blasted it seemed that the earth itself shook and shivered with pain. Moses could sense the pain the ground must feel. A doctor probing in a wound or a man with a hot wire burning out a bad tooth caused no more pain, he suspected, than a tunnel blast.

When the blastings had stopped flying and the dust was settled, the candle boys went back inside, one boy working each wall, and they quickly lighted candles from the master candle on the cart, keeping several candles in their hands at a time, setting them in amid the rocks on the tunnel wall. Behind them came men with sledge hammers and shovels, cursing always, vociferously claiming to be unafraid.

Each time the men went farther back, walked deeper into the ground, Moses in the lead. He never was sure what he would find inside; each blast was to him an adventure of its own, for any blast could open up an earthen room, could open a hole that led to other places. He always went at the lead because he wanted to be the first to see what was opened up. He urged the candle boys on and sometimes would take a candle for his own and would cup its blaze and move head of them, making his way over the strewn stones to stand at last at the far end. He was always disappointed, for never was there a door there, or a passageway, or any opening.

He would set his candle down and wait impatiently for the mule carts to arrive. The first few carts always had to pick up strewn rocks along the passageway, so it was a while to wait.

Then it was time to lift the rocks. Get the rocks in your hands. Heave the rocks. Break rocks with the sledge. Shovel them. Move the rocks with your hands and arms and the muscles of your legs and back, and feel the weight in your body, get rock dust under your nails and in your skin, and breathe the rock dust that was in the air and hovered near the quivering flames of the candles that now were burning on the wet rock walls.

All the while sloshing in water on the floor. Sometimes Esau would lay mash too low, and the blast would leave a hole in the floor that a pool of water would collect in, and once in a while an opening would be left in the floor that water would seep out of.

Sometimes an opening would be left in the floor that the water would shoot up from, too, in a little spout, as if an artery had been opened. Moses would wash his face in it, let the water spew over him, being careful not to splash it on the candles. One day it would gush up strong, another day, after a few more blasts, as the tunnel work would go on past it, it would dry up, maybe to start again on another morning.

Nobody could say what would happen when you cut a body open, be it flesh or stone, that was the point Moses made. One body was as alive as another, he thought, for they all had seams and veins and skin and fluids.

"You put too much mash in that wall." How many times had he heard somebody say that to Esau. "You going to open up the bottom of this place afore long and we'll fall through." Esau did it his own way, though, making pools on the floor. He would shake his head sadly when he saw what he had done, but he said nobody knew how to blast out such a place as this, in such hard rock, anyway, with the mixture of the mash being changed, as Weatherby experimented with it.

"Goin' to blast a hole into a pit, Esau, and we'll all fall through."

Moses thought that would do very well for Esau. He was always talking about escaping, anyway.

Only a few men worked there at the heading. Not room for many men. Moses was always at the heading. The others were often different men, but Moses never rested. Breathing was not easy at the heading. Not much air, if any air at all; the heading had been solid rock, and when it had been blasted out there was no air to fill the space, Moses thought, for there hadn't been much air in the tunnel to start with. That's how he figured it out. So there was no air and you had to breathe mist and dust. The dust got in your nose and mouth and throat, and you had to swallow it or spit it out. You got used to swallowing it because your throat got raw if you spit it out.

Working at the heading.

Most of the other men were working at benching, widening

the tunnel or heightening it, and they had air to breathe—not much, and they claimed they had less than enough, but they had more air to breathe than the men at the heading, who had none. Even the candles at the heading didn't burn brightly. They burned with a little flame that wouldn't light anything, except a totally dark place like this. There was not much that needed to be seen, anyway, Moses thought, until they came to one of those secret places. Any blast now might open one up to him. A big cavern would be there, maybe, and no blasting would need to be done inside it. It would be a room that led through the under regions of the mountain, and ties and iron could be laid in it easily. There would doubtless be a banquet hall for eating the midday dinner, where the ceiling would be so high it went up to the tree roots, which curled about each other and showed their age. There would be light filtering down here and there, and animals sitting on the topmost crests, each animal having its own tunnel for escaping to the world outside.

Seemed to Moses what was needed was for the foremen to seek such a cavern and run the Road through it, rather than blast a way through rock all the time.

There would be pits of snakes in one cavern, and scores of bears in another, and hundreds of nests where birds and bats bred and multiplied. Here would be the den where the mountain lions went years ago, and in one room wolves by hundreds would be asleep, the little blue wolves crawling over one another, biting at one another playfully. The skunks would have a room to waddle in, and the ground squirrels would chip-chip-cluck in their place, and the catamount in his, and the panthers at night would silence them all with a long, quivering womanlike wail, which seemed to come from nowhere and end up everywhere, and the elk and the wood bison and the otter would be there, and the red fox and the gray fox, and high up the ravens would be perched, watching over it all bleakly.

Where was the cavern? Moses wondered. Each time after a blast he took his candle inside to the heading, each time he came to solid rock. When would they come to the cavern? he wondered.

Break the rocks. Lift the rocks. Haul the rocks. Breathe the rocks in the candlelight washed with the tears from the mountain's eyes. Move away the rocks and walk on the rocks, into the rocks, toward the rock cavern. Arms heavy, muscles twisting, muscles growing bigger; no seams in clothes were made to last forever. Shovel rocks, haul rocks, dump rocks, blast the heading on, make the benching wide, all the while splashing in the water, bleeding your own cut blood into the mountain's tears and blood, while men drilled new holes for more mash.

Every sound was loud and troublesome, but the sound of voices troubled Moses the most. He had his own thoughts, and whatever he wanted to say he could say later, outside the ground. Let the only sound here be the noise of rock breaking.

In early December at Lick Log tunnel, a cave-in caught three men inside the tunnel, and by the time they were freed they were scared to death and had to be held to the ground to keep them from trying to flee, which might have got the dogs and mountain boys on them. "Lie down, man, don't chew at my hand. Here, stop that, man. You crazy?"

"Listen to him now, mister crazy man. You stop scratching at the ground. You're free now, don't you know?"

"He's telling you the truth. We got you out. You're free—except you're still on the chain gang."

"All right, men," the foreman said, "back inside. We got more work to do today than we had yesterday, cause of that there cave-in."

One convict said he wouldn't go back inside, so they chained him to a tree, and he lay there on his back all day staring at the sun, with his eyes open, as if he couldn't believe he could see the sky again.

> Break 'em up,
> Dump 'em down.
> Haul, man,
> Haul, mule.

They worked right along, in rhythm to their songs.

"Don't stop there, man. You stop and can't get started again. The hardest part is to start."

Break 'em up, haul 'em out.

Blast and get the blastings, fill in that valley with the blastings.

He lay with the sun in his open eyes, and Dr. Chester came along and knelt beside him, felt of his face, which was warm from the sun. "What you thinking about, boy?" he said.

The man looked at him. His eyes were so small in pupil that they scarcely saw him at all; the doctor was blurred before him. "I won't steal no more," he said.

"No, I know you won't. Nothing here to steal."

"Can I go home?"

"When your term is up. Here now, what you staring at the sun for?"

"I been in there."

"Yes, but you're safe now."

"Safe? Safe? Be safe if I was blind."

"Oh, is that it? You'd rather be blind than be a chain gang boy. But they'd use you blind."

"I don't want to be blind, mister," he said.

"You don't know what you want, do you?"

"Yes, God, I know," he said. "And I won't steal no more."

"Well, I have no power over what you do, but I can't set you free. You'll have to get your courage back and start to work again."

Babcock came to see the man and asked him what was the matter. The man didn't know how to tell him. Chester thought to put in a word, saying the man ought to be assigned only to work on the outside for a week or two; Babcock didn't take well to the doctor telling him how to assign the convicts. "You get on in there, boy, and help those other men," he said.

They had to drag the man into the tunnel. They hitched his chain to a mule cart and the mule dragged him in, the man yelling all the way, his voice getting more hollow as he was dragged deeper into the tunnel. Babcock and Chester stood on the outside and Babcock said, "It's a kindness to them to cure them. God knows, I've seen worse than to chain a man to a mule."

He looked about at the other men, all of them staring at the mouth of the cave where the sound of terror was. Then finally there was no sound at all.

"You see there," Babcock said to Chester, "he's cured now."

Break 'em down, load the carts, haul them out, mules and men, breathe the rock air, mix the blood from your hands with the water from the rock floor; be the stone you break, be the stone you lift, be the stone you carry; lie down with stone in your mouth and stone in your throat and stone in your belly, and sleep with dreams in your mind of the unfound cavern.

Where the little blue wolves lie down with the catamount.

Moses felt the man shake him. He was in the barracks. In the dark he couldn't see him, but he liked to look toward a man he was talking to, so he turned toward him.

"You was talking out loud in your sleep, Moses, talking about a cavern like heaven in the ground."

"Was I?" He didn't like to be awakened. "Shut up, then," he said.

"I wasn't complaining. But it's hell that's in the ground."

"Shut up."

Silence.

Years before his own papa had called him into the kitchen of their house one night and had said, "Moses, you stop talking in your sleep or I'm going to make you a cure, like your grandpa used to cure me. Now I'm warning you, Moses." Later he woke Moses up again and said, "Didn't you hear me a while ago? Now get up and come in here." So Moses did, and he could remember clearly walking into the room with his father but he couldn't remember anything after that. Four times in one week he was awakened and he walked into the kitchen with his father, and he couldn't remember what happened at any time, but whenever he was told he talked in his sleep, he got sick to his stomach for a spell, and sometimes he threw up.

The convict said nothing else, so Moses relaxed. What was it that man had said: "Hell is in the ground." Yes, Moses knew that was so. He had heard that all his life. It was down there, and heaven was in the sky.

The man was right about it. Maybe someday a blast would come and would open up not any cavern of great fine banquet halls, but hell, with brimstoned bodies writhing in the heat, trying to breathe where there was no air. Maybe sometime he would hear the blast and go hurrying into the tunnel, cupping his candle flame with his hand, stepping over the strewn blastings, until at last he came to hell.

Maybe what he would see was a hole in the floor with smoke rising from it, and he would hear screams.

White men screaming, as well as black.

Yes, white men screaming, and screaming louder, and screaming not knowing how to scream like a black man knew and had learned for years past, for a nigger never screamed out loud unless he also wept inside. A white man would scream from fear only.

White men screaming down in the ground, and a nigger foreman was walking on the ledge, and the fire was licking at the white men's feet. There the women come, their hair long to their waists and their eyes hollow where the fire had dried up their eyeballs, their teeth rotted from the brimstone and their breasts drooped to their waists, their own juices dripping down their thighs as they walked in hell, drying up, cooking.

Maybe hell would be the cavern that opened up, for it was more likely, since the tunnels were not in the sky at all.

He would see it first, whatever it was, whenever it appeared. He nestled his big head on his arm and thought about it, and thought about Lola and the time last Saturday night he had lain with her in the snow, and his mind went back to the sound of a blasting and he dreamed he caught a candle from the cart and lighted it and went inside, and there was a long corridor, like the tube of a woman; he walked the corridor through the moist skin to the end, where the womb opened out, and at the far side of the womb Lola waited beside his father in the kitchen room.

Now and then a man would be injured, even killed at Babcock or Henry Station, but the bloody camp was Tunnel Station, where five men died in a week's time, mostly from unpredicted explosions, and there were many sick men and women, and injured men, too.

"We better plan something to get their minds off of it," Babcock told Weatherby one Thursday night in early December. They were sitting in Weatherby's office.

"We can plan a Christmas for them," Weatherby said.

"Hell."

"We can plan a Christmas they'll like," Weatherby insisted.

"Have it in Lick Log Tunnel? We can stick a thousand candles on the walls."

"Sounds like Christmas all right."

Cumberland came into the office. "Cold out," he said. "These nights are killing."

Weatherby studied one of the papers on his desk. Abruptly he looked up at him. "What can we do for Christmas for them?"

"Give them presents," Cumberland said at once, a grin on his face. "We'll give away Anna's unbaked pitchers."

"Give them a gun to shoot a guard with," Babcock said. He got to chuckling at his wit. He sat on the edge of his chair, his body vibrating with mirth, his eyes glistening as he gazed at the other men. "Tinkle, tinkle, little chains," he said.

"We could put sleigh bells on the Mud-Digger," Cumberland said.

Weatherby moaned and began to grumble about their sense of humor.

"You think they could go caroling?" Cumberland said.

"Wouldn't you like to see the tunnel gang singing church songs?" Babcock said.

Weatherby couldn't help but laugh with them, but he tried to think seriously about it, too. "They'd probably like to get warm, for one thing," he said.

"Could we make Moses into a Santa Claus and teach him how to laugh?" Babcock said.

"I'm trying to be serious," Weatherby said.

"Could we hang mistletoe on their ankle chains?" Cumberland said.

Dr. Chester came into the room and stared about, uncomfortable. He glared critically at Babcock. When he had sat down, he said matter-of-factly, "It's started snowing again."

"Tell it to the bears," Babcock said.

"More'n twenty men are sick of the croup," Chester said. He saw an empty coffee mug. "Any coffee?"

"At the fire," Babcock said.

Chester waited for somebody to offer to order it. When nobody did, he went to the outside door. "Hey, boy, bring coffee in here." He shut the door and came back, complaining about the cold wind.

Of course, the boy didn't bring him any coffee. Finally he went to fetch it for himself, getting only one mug. He was not a selfish man, but he was not accepted by the others, so he didn't bring them coffee. He fretted over every patient and was considerate of those who needed him, but only if they acknowledged their need for him.

Weatherby asked again about Christmas. Cumberland wanted to have HenryAnna's father arrange a program. Babcock snorted at that.

Weatherby admitted all the better preachers were contracted for by now. "But he's not a preacher, any more than he's a telegraph man."

Chester suggested that the men be given better food and a day off from work in the tunnels.

Babcock said any change in the system brought trouble in the camps. "Once the men get the idea that things don't have to be done a set way they get to wanting to change everything."

"They're all weakened by labor and inadequate food," Chester said. "They need more rest, especially in the dangerous months here at winter."

Babcock snorted. "We going to build a road, doctor, or are we going to pick pansies? You want to see them tunnels blasted through?"

"I?" the doctor said, startled.

"The men ain't complaining about what we do. It's you that's complaining."

"Men are dying because of what you do."

Babcock got to his feet, furious, but Cumberland caught his arm and restrained him. "He didn't mean that," he said. "Forget it, Babcock, forget it."

Babcock sank back in his chair, murmuring threats, and Weatherby sat at his desk almost as if he were frozen there, staring at Chester, then at Babcock. He looked up at Cumberland.

"We start talking about Christmas and end up with this," he said.

"You think I don't know men are sick?" Babcock said to the doctor.

"I think you know it, yes."

"Well, I don't know what to say to you," Babcock said. He was hurt, and he was angry, too. "I don't know why you said what you did."

It was a tense moment, and Chester could have apologized and relieved the situation, but he didn't. Weatherby said, "I've made out a schedule here. I hope to find room for a more relaxed one later on, but, doctor, we have five tunnels to cut, and we're only working on one now, and I don't know how we stand for the year ahead. I fear we stand none too far along."

"Are men to be treated like mules?"

"Not by me," Weatherby said, his hands on the desktop, tensely looking down at them, letting his anger settle. Abruptly he relaxed and said he planned to go home for his own Christmas and hoped each man in the room would, too. "We need to keep perspective," he said. "We work with criminals, and we work against nature, so we're endangered by violence in two directions. I hope you'll try to gain sympathy for the tasks that face each one."

It was a criticism of both the doctor and Babcock, but gently made, and neither man had any animosity toward him for it.

"If you get any Christmas ideas for the men, any practical ones, I would like to have them," he said.

CHAPTER THIRTEEN

THE WINTER, which had started early this year, became warm in mid-December, the official start of winter itself. The crevices lost the pools of snow they had protected, and the earth released much of the water it had held and became soggy and treacherous to men working the fills and tunnel. A few small flowers began to bloom near the office at Henry Station.

Weatherby, on the second Friday in December, had hoped to awaken early. He wanted to go down to Henry Station with Cumberland and talk with an official from Raleigh who was coming in on the train, but he got delayed at the tunnel with one thing and another; then just as the two of them were ready to leave, word came from Babcock Station that the east fill on Long Bridge had started to creep. Weatherby told Cumberland to go ahead to Henry, that he would detour by way of Babcock and study that situation, and join him later.

He had gone about a mile or a mile and a half into the woods when a mountain boy came running after him. "They had a wounded man happen," he called as he approached. "Up at the tunnels they blasted a man."

"Not Moses?"

"No. I don't know just who, but they want you."

Weatherby found a dry rock and sat down. He put his elbows on his knees and leaned forward, frowning at the dripping, drooling earth. The mountain boy crouched nearby, staring at him quizzically.

"You put your shirt on backwards this morning, didn't you, boy?"Weatherby said kindly.

"It was dark when I come to wash and dress."

He saw three men down on the mountain a ways, walking along with a mule.

The boy said, "What do you aim to do?"

"I don't know yet," Weatherby said. "I have several critical things to do all at the same time." He took out his pipe and filled it. "Was the man bad hurt?"

"His back was busted."

"Is the doctor there?"

"No, sir, he's not found yet."

"What do they think I can do for him?"

The boy scrouged up his face. "Whenever anything happens, they allus send for you. The hurt man asked for you, too."

"Well, I'm glad he did. Did the other men stop work?"

"Yes, sir, while Esau mashed the holes at the heading."

"What are those three men doing down there, do you know?"

"That's them telegraph men aworking."

"They were working near the Gap yesterday. They have wire all over this mountain, and for what effect?"

"Yes, sir," the boy said. He crouched there, content to be near Weatherby, for he liked him and was honored to be with him. They sat there for a while, Weatherby smoking his pipe.

"Well, see here, boy," he said. "We have one fill creeping, and one wounded man, and one Raleigh official, each at a different station. Tell you what, you go on back to the tunnel and tell Babcock to handle the situation there and to keep the men at work."

"Yes, sir."

"I'd better go see about this fill. We could lose Long Bridge."

The boy left, and Weatherby went on down the trail.

As he approached a spot high over Mud Cut, his foot slipped and he fell. He grabbed a laurel trunk, but his hand failed to hold onto it, and he fell into a ten-foot ravine. It wasn't a dangerous fall, but he knew even as he landed that he had injured himself.

He lay there murmuring, exasperated with his poor fortune. He moved his right hand. It wasn't broken. He tried the other hand. That one was all right, too. He tried his right foot. He could move it. He tried his left foot. He couldn't move it at all.

He propped himself up on his elbows and saw with relief that there was no blood on his pants or on the ground. He looked around for pieces of wood that he might make leg splints from, and pulled himself across the ground toward a clump of laurel. He felt around under the laurel bushes, but found nothing usable there.

Of course, they would find him, he knew that. Those mountain boys were certain to find him. "Hey, you," he called suddenly. "Hey, up there," he called. Those three telegraph men might still be about somewhere. He cupped his hands to his mouth and shouted at the top of his voice. "Hey! Hey! Music man, come down here!"

He called many times, for well over an hour, before he began to admit to himself that nobody had sent out a search party to find him, that no one at the camp knew he was even lost. And they might not know for a day or so.

He looked down at his broken leg. There was blood there now, staining the snow.

He had matches in his pocket, but there were no dry twigs, so he was in for a cold night of it, he supposed, and he might as well do what he could to make the most of it. If he tried to walk, he would only rupture his leg all the more.

He began dragging himself to the edge of the ledge. Sometimes the mountain held pleasant surprises, as well as unpleasant ones. He pulled himself along, letting the left leg dangle behind him. He came to the edge of the ravine and saw below him a further drop of perhaps ten feet to another rock ledge; below that was yet another drop of ten feet to a place where the mountain's shoulder rolled more gradually downward.

He took hold of a laurel trunk and leaned over the edge of the ledge as far as he could. It appeared that there was a cave under there, or some indentation which would at least help protect him from the weather.

There was no way to get down there, except that one birch sapling might bend far enough to lower him to it. The maneuver was risky, but he did need to find shelter. He took hold of the sapling and began to inch out onto it. The sapling bent evenly as he lent his weight to it. He moved out a hand at a time.

He dropped, landing on his good leg and falling forward, cushioning the blow. He lay there, breathing deeply.

He looked behind him and saw the cave. At once he crawled toward it, inching his way along, his hands almost frozen by the snow. He could see beyond the dark mouth of the cave a dry spot where he could lie. The cave went quite a way into the ground beyond its narrow opening, and there was no beast inside, not that he could see. Everything was hospitable.

He pulled himself through the opening onto the dry floor and crept farther into the cave before he flopped on his belly and lay there listening to his heart and to his own breathing. The rock felt warm after the hours of lying on the wet ground. It was all right; he would be safe here until they found him.

The gang foremen at Babcock Station hadn't waited for Weatherby. When they saw that the embankment was still creeping, they put all their gangs to work throwing up a rock wall to hold it, and sent an emergency message to each of the other two stations, asking for convicts to help out. The messages left the impression that Weatherby was requesting the men, so each camp sent a gang of men under guard. About 250 men in all were put to work.

Everybody was worried about the Long Bridge, of course, and nobody had time to wonder where Weatherby was.

During the day the telegraph men walked their line and that night they began testing their signal. To everyone's surprise at the Tunnel Station, especially the director of the Western North Carolina

Telegraph Company, the signal worked very well. When the clerk tapped the key, there did come a response. He tapped the signal for Babcock Station and was answered immediately; he tapped the signal for Henry Station and was answered, though somewhat less clearly.

"Send a message to Weatherby at Babcock," Babcock suggested.

The message was tapped out slowly by the clerk, who was no better at telegraphy than he needed to be, and who was surrounded by talking spectators, all of them excited.

In response came a few random noises, then the steady beat of the machine. The clerk followed it all as best he could. "Weatherby's not there," he said.

"Ask them how Long Bridge is," one of the men said.

The clerk began tapping out that question, but was interrupted by the clacking keys. The clerk wrote something out, then studied over what he had written. "Says it's not creeping," he said. "I don't know what that means."

"I know what it means," Babcock said. "Ask him where Weatherby is."

The clerk prepared to do so, but others of the group were more concerned about the bridge and wanted more information about that, so the clerk tapped out questions they originated, and Babcock retreated from the stuffy room and stood in the yard, confident that at any moment Weatherby would appear.

A guard came out of the office. "They say they're getting tired at the bridge."

"Are they going to be able to hold it?" Babcock said.

"They're going to build the wall through the night."

The guard swaggered toward the flophouse. There was quiet in the camp, except for the sound of water falling on the mountain. A wolf howled, then another. The pack was roaming tonight. The hungry pack was no doubt following every track that promised food, every footprint, every drop of blood on the ground.

Where was Weatherby? Babcock wondered. There was no need to worry about him, because he never needed concern from others;

of all men, he was the most self-sufficient. Babcock didn't mean to worry about him, but he couldn't help wondering about not being able to locate him.

Men began pouring out of the office building. "The damn contraption broke," they said. Babcock went inside and watched the clerk fiddling with the instrument. Plover was helpless and despondent. He had known a few minutes of high exultation while the telegraph worked; he knew correspondingly low dejection now that it did not. "It's only the warm weather that bothers it," he said. "It's unseasonable to be so warm in December."

"You might check the line between here and Babcock. I'll walk part way with you," Babcock said.

"I'll wait till morning."

"Can you get Henry Station?" Babcock asked the clerk.

"The line goes first to Babcock, so if that's out, there's no way to go on down the mountain. Something's wrong between here and Babcock."

"Maybe the wolves are eating it," Babcock said.

"You work your tail off," Plover said, "and you keep having troubles along the way."

Abruptly the telegraph line began to crackle, and Plover jumped up in glee. "Ay, God, it works, it works agin!"

It was a message for Weatherby.

The clerk replied that Weatherby was not at the Tunnel Station. A second message began. "Where is he?" That was all it said before the signal stopped and the line went dead again.

Perhaps some misadventure had befallen Weatherby, but the very thought made Babcock feel inadequate. It was inconsiderate to think that Weatherby would need help at all. If Weatherby were ever to need help, Babcock thought, he would plan the occasion so carefully that the help would be on its way before he needed it.

The idea struck him as being funny and he had to laugh, and when a guard asked him what was the matter, he said, "I was only thinking something might have happened to Weatherby," which he realized didn't explain his laughter at all well.

He sat down at Cumberland's desk and began to fidget with the inkwell. A mountain boy came to the door with a cup of coffee. "Come and set," Babcock said.

The boy did so, and Babcock said, "In this soggy mush, you think it's too late to trail a man that went out of here this midmorning?"

"Might be."

"I think it might be, too."

He could send out a search party, but it was a mark against a man to be lost, or to have others say he was lost.

"Where's Mr. Weatherby at tonight?" the boy asked.

"I don't know yet," Babcock said. He didn't want to take charge, that was it. He didn't want the responsibility falling on him. He wanted to do what he was told to do; that was all he could confidently control, could maneuver through. He was not a man of new actions, but a repeater of old ones. He was making a road, which was innovative, but he was not himself an innovator, and he just didn't know what to do.

Cumberland got back to the Tunnel Station early next morning. He had been down at Henry, he said, waiting for Weatherby. When he found out that Weatherby wasn't at the Tunnel Station and had never reached Babcock, either, he immediately called in the mountain boys who stayed there, about fourteen of them, and told them Weatherby was missing. "Can you find him?" he asked.

"We'll find him," one of them said simply.

"We'll find him, if he's out there," one boy said.

Weatherby had slept fitfully, his dreams filled with throbbing and troubled with the touch of a hand which kept moving over his injured leg. At one time in his delirium he had caught the hand and pushed it away, and for a time there had been nothing touching him at all.

He lay on his belly on the floor, his body aching from the rock bed, and from the cold, and from the wound, and from his fears, which were more acute now than before, He had never before considered his own death, but he knew the mountain world well enough to know he was caught in one of its conspiracies. Just as a spiderweb traps an insect or a laurel slick traps a wanderer, there were nets and traps for the mountain man, too.

In his mind was the thought, cyclically recurring, that the mountain knew he was there and had planned all this. He was himself a maker of plans, and he could recognize a plan made by another; he could identify facets of the plan that had fallen into place, and he supposed other facets would fall into place, that the plan was not fully revealed yet. He knew this was not one of the uncomplicated sort of plans that Babcock would make, or the privately oriented plan Moses would make, or the adventure-conscious plan Esau would make; this was an impersonal, intricate, complete plan, founded on a natural sense of balance and justice. It was more like a plan he would make.

Lie still, he told himself, and save your strength. Lie still. If you struggle, you'll only be the silly insect in the web.

He saw the first sunlight filter into the cave. His teeth were chattering, and he suffered painful chills and streaks of fire in his body, but he lay still.

All night he had heard the hollow tone of the wolf howls, which had become closer and closer until they were nearby, even at the cave's entrance. Why had the wolves not come into the cave? he wondered. Wolves knew the mountain, every cranny of it. What did they know about the cave that had kept them out of it?

He concentrated on himself and asked if he should continue to lie on his belly or if he should try to turn onto his back or side. It was difficult through the pangs of pain to keep his mind on any one subject; an idea seemed to him to be slippery, like the hand he had grasped in the night. If he were to turn onto his back, he could see the entrance of the cave, and maybe, conceivably, there would be somebody pass that way. There was small likelihood of this, but it was a hope, anyway.

He took hold of his injured leg and moved it. A fierce pain went through him. He moved it again, turned it ever so slightly, watching the leg, trying to see where it was broken and how best to hold it. He turned it again, until he was lying on his back. His eyes were tightly closed now, and he let the pain course through him until at last the pain was only a throb. He realized there were tears on his face.

A man crying, he thought.

"You have my leg, don't you, woman?" he said to the mountain. "You have my leg in your jaw."

No, he thought, she has me, all of me in her open mouth, and she will eat me alive if she can.

Since Mud Cut she had waited so quietly, he thought, ignoring the work on bridges, tunnels, cuts, embankments, camps; then with one single move she crippled it all.

The light grew brighter. It was another clear day. He looked up at the ceiling of the cave and saw the light as it vibrated and was shadowed by the moving branches near the opening.

How strangely they move, he thought, not quite like shadows of branches at all.

He glanced toward the cave opening and saw the snakes, moving as if in rhythm to a tune. They were crawling on the rock entryway, and it was their shadows he had seen.

His gaze trailed along the ceiling and walls of the cave; here and there in the walls he saw other snakes, not moving now, merely lying asleep. They were the color of the rocks, and he could scarcely make them out. They were denned-in rattlers, lying in this cranny and that one, here and there, lying on the rocks all around, responding to the temperature changes around them.

He wanted to cry out, but he didn't dare utter a sound. If he was in the mouth of the mountain, he thought, then the tongue of the mouth was awakening now. The sun was rising and more and more light and warmth would come into this place; the snakes would awaken, the membrane of the walls would awaken, the threads of the web would awaken.

He lay there helpless and watched as the light increased, saw the membrane of the walls moving, first slowly as the light began filtering inside, then more actively.

He felt no pain in his leg now. His mind was clear. Nothing complicated the one idea he had at this time, the snakes and the necessity of survival. Even if he could move quickly, the snakes would strike him many times before he could reach the narrow lips of the cave opening.

Death would take him when the mountain decided, he thought grimly, when she was hungry for him. He couldn't even hope for mercy. There was no way to discuss anything with her or negotiate any compromise. What could he say to the walls of the mouth that would devour him?

Mildred, he thought. Please God, keep her away from even knowing of this. Anna, he thought; what if she were to find me? She would crawl through that narrow opening to me, and only then, looking back at the sunlight, would she see the snakes on the walls. Too late. Too late.

He saw her coming. "No," he told her. "Go away. Go away. Anna, go away."

Suddenly she was gone, and he realized she hadn't been there at all.

He saw a hand on the rock just outside the opening. "Mildred," he said, rising to his elbows, aware that the snakes were moving more vigorously, now that he was talking. "Go away, Mildred."

The hand on the stone was not a hand at all.

He lay back, gasping.

He saw Mildred in the stone ceiling of the cave, coming toward him, walking in a white dress down a dark road.

The mountain boys didn't work as a team. It was simply that now and then one or two of them would go out with a dog. They walked into the woods, and the woods seemed to absorb them. Soon after they had left the Tunnel Station, Cumberland would lose sight of them, then would notice a movement near a rock and realize a boy was there, standing, looking, listening, sensing. The boy would go on a ways, always appearing to be unconcerned, unhurried. He was asking more than he was saying; he was wondering more than he was deciding; he was waiting to be accepted into the natural way of things. When he was part of the way things were, the mountain would perhaps reveal to him the secrets it held.

Even though the mountain boys didn't go out together, by mid-afternoon five of them were crouching silently before the opening of the same cave. Their dogs were quiet, too. There was no sound, for the boys didn't talk to each other. They watched the entrance of the cave and listened to the man inside, who was talking. They didn't listen to what he said particularly. He was talking sometimes to his wife, at other times to other people. He was talking only in his delirium, they realized.

The boys didn't call for help. There was no need here for more people. Better for the guards and convicts, and others of unfeeling natures, to stay away now. Such men had their methods, which were to blast and dig. Those ways wouldn't do here. This wasn't a challenge of power, nor of mind, but of temperament. It required that one first know the feeling of what he was dealing with.

The boys could see the snakes. There was no way into the cave except to crawl by them. The opening of the cave was less than four feet high and four feet wide. The cave itself widened into a room, but not a large room, and even that was lined with snakes.

A sixth mountain boy arrived and, without a word, crouched nearby and waited.

The man inside the cave began to call. They could make out what he said. "Help," he said, over and over. Probably he didn't know they were there. It was as well he didn't know, for he might do something suddenly, might try to force the trap, which would only make it close on him all the more.

One boy—his name was Dozen, for he had been the twelfth child in his family—crept closer to the opening of the cave. He began to sway, so that his shadow moved against the floor and walls of the cave. Later he began to hum to himself. He was humming a hymn, as if to keep himself company.

The man inside the cave grew quiet. Maybe he saw the shadow or heard the hymn; maybe it simply penetrated his confusion and he was trying to determine what it was.

Dozen, swaying, humming, moved close to the mouth of the cave. Another boy crept close, too, and quietly, ever so quietly, began to sway and to hum the same tune. The music was soft and very slow.

A third boy began to whistle the tune, then the other began humming or whistling. Sometimes a boy would stop for a while, then he would start again. Nobody gave directions; they did as they felt like doing, all of them watching the mouth of the cave.

Not a sound inside the cave.

Crouching, Dozen moved to the very mouth of the cave. He swayed slowly and hummed more loudly, and as if in reply the snakes began to move, those near the cave entrance first, then the snakes farther back, swaying gently as they clung to the walls and ceiling of the cave, until all the snakes were moving, the walls were swaying to the movement of the boy.

Dozen crawled into the mouth of the cave, humming, the boys behind him swaying and humming and whistling gently, watching the mouth of the cave. Somebody far off in the woods shouted, but the boys didn't answer and not even one dog moved, as Dozen moved farther into the cave, humming.

Dozen touched Weatherby's foot. He moved forward until he was lying beside him. He waited until Weatherby saw him. Weatherby started to speak, but Dozen shook his head slightly, ever so slightly. Weatherby was trembling all over and his teeth were chattering, and Dozen motioned toward the entrance to the cave. He took Weatherby's hand and arm and began to turn him in the cave. His body contracted in pain, so Dozen waited until he saw the blood on the floor, then moved first the injured leg, then moved Weatherby around so that his head was closer to the entrance of the cave.

Dozen was on all fours now and was close to the top of the cave; the snakes were moving back and forth, brushing against him. He dragged Weatherby toward the entrance of the cave. He could see the mountain boys outside crouching, swaying, humming, and from far off he heard the bothersome noise of a man shouting. That could be the disaster to all this. More quickly he pulled the body toward the entrance of the cave, where the snakes were swaying across the entryway.

He reached the entryway and crept through, leaving the body just inside; he crept free of the cave and fell forward on his face on the ground and lay there, breathing deeply, gasping. Another boy reached past the snakes, grasped Weatherby's hand, and began to pull his shoulders through the hole in the rock. When Weatherby's head was outside the cave, his delirious eyes stared blankly at them. There was no sudden movement even yet, no abrupt sound, except of the stranger shouting as he came toward them through the woods, too close, too close. Hush, they thought; what sort of fool was it that shouted in the woods?

Weatherby's waist was through, the snakes weaved over his body. Slowly the boys pulled his legs through; they pulled him out onto the rock and two other mountain boys crept close to the entryway of the cave and hummed the tune, swaying more and more slowly, growing quieter, until finally the snakes stopped weaving on the walls and were still.

Dozen rose from the ground. "His leg is broke, is it?" he said.

"Splint two rifles," a boy said.

"That man that's shouting, go tell him to shut his damn mouth," Dozen said.

A boy left to find the man.

Weatherby dazedly looked up at them.

"Is he going to be crazy?" a boy asked.

"Likely to be," Dozen said.

"You shouldn't a gone in there, Dozen."

Dozen grinned. It was so, he knew.

"He don't appear to see us," a boy said. "When he comes to, he'll be as mean as old man Bentz was when he spent the night with snakes. He never got over it."

"Maybe, maybe," Dozen said.

The man who had been shouting was the guard Blackie, and he came to where they were and began to give them instructions. He said to make a litter. They said nothing to him, but they finished the splinting of the leg, then one of the boys picked Weatherby up by his sound leg and one of his arms and draped him over his own shoulders. He moved past Blackie and walked up the sloshy path past where the dogs were.

"I said make a litter," Blackie said.

The boys went on up the path, ignoring him.

The sun set beyond the mountain. The slope where the cave was shadowed early. There was no movement inside now, except that a snake crawled to the warm place on the rock where the man had been and coiled there.

The wolves began to howl. Their lonely sound came into the cave; the echo filled the cave as they came closer to the place. One wolf moved to the mouth of the cave.

There was a growl, then a yapping fierce challenge from the doorway, and a snake struck. The wolf backed away, showing his teeth, snarling.

The wolf turned and went back up the path by which he had come and disappeared quickly and silently. He had seen that the man was gone.

CHAPTER FOURTEEN

RAIN FELL ALL THAT DAY and night, on the new wall being built at the Long Bridge embankment, and along the gash at Mud Cut, and on the men who unloaded the carts at the tunnels. Yes, and on the roof of the room where he lay, Dr. Chester attending him, the leg set and splinted now.

But he didn't know the doctor or the room, or even Mildred when she came to help take him home.

A cot was put in the aisle of a passenger car. She sat in one of the seats beside him, Chester in the other. "He's all right; he's in shock, that's all," he told her over and over.

The train moved slowly, ringing its lonely bell. It stopped near Icard and she heard the engineer say, "Mister, drive yer sheep off the road. I'm carrying a man 'most dead."

A man 'most dead, she thought. She held his hand in her own. She felt that she was closer to him now than ever she had been of a daytime, for always he had been so able to care for himself. His need for her had been obscured, except sometimes in the darkness, and though this had been only for a night or part of a night, those occasions she remembered as the ones closest to her heart.

He was carried from the train station to the house, and it was her suggestion that he be placed in the parlor, that he not be taken upstairs. It would be easier to tend to him there, and it would be easier for friends to visit him. Whenever he was home, everything that happened in the house revolved around him, anyway.

Dr. Chester left instructions for every eventuality. Weatherby was not to be allowed to put any weight on his leg, and he was not to try to walk even with crutches until the leg had had time to mend. Both bones in the leg had been broken, he said. The small one, since it bore no weight, was of little consequence; he had not bothered even to set it. "Sometimes these mountain men get a break and call it a leg break, and it's nothing in the world but the little bone, but what Weatherby has is a break of the tibia, and it will have to take its time to heal. Perhaps a year."

"It's not likely Weatherby will wait a year," she told him.

"He can move about on crutches after three months. You listen to me now—he is not to walk until I tell him to."

"He has that road to build."

"His mind is more worrisome to me than his leg, to be honest about it, and that's where you can be of most help. Even now he doesn't know he's here."

She didn't want to believe that. "He knows where he is."

"He doesn't know you're here, either."

The words seemed cruel to her, and she wished the doctor would go and let her be. Affection was the medicine she had most confidence in. A sick person needed attention and care, and somebody to pat his pillow fluffy for him and pester the blankets and keep the fire high in the fireplace and cook food he liked.

"Have you got a bedpan?"

"Yes."

"You tend to his needs and feed him broth and whatever else he wants."

At last he left, and the railroad men who had brought Weatherby to Morganton left, too.

She boiled a chicken and mixed dumplings; she made coffee. Troy came to the door and watched her, sniffing the air appreciably. "Is papa going to stay with us?" he said.

"For a few months," she said. She dropped dumpling from a spoon into the broth and covered the pot with a lid.

"I hear him talking, mama."

She hurried to the front room. Weatherby was talking, that was true, and she and Troy stood at the foot of the bed, answering him, but he went on calling for them, anyway, and calling for others, not in a loud voice but quietly, as if afraid of being heard. It was eerie to stand there and listen to him talk like that, and she wrung her hands in her apron and almost wished the doctor was here again, for he might tell her how to talk to him when he couldn't hear what she was saying.

He ate nothing that she fixed. Never in her lifetime had he not eaten her food. She sat by his bed, a bowl of dumplings in one hand and the spoon in the other, and stared perplexedly at him.

Troy was also in misery. "What you going to do?"

"Why, I don't know," she said.

"Why does he cry?"

"Cry?"

"The tears."

"That's just water," she said.

"It looks like tears."

"Oh, I don't think your father would cry." She could see the water on his cheeks, but she knew him well enough to know he couldn't weep; what she knew was of more significance to her in a time of doubt and grief than what she saw.

She decided warm milk might attract him, and she went to get him some, but the milk was frozen.

She set the milk crock near the coal stove to let it warm.

Troy appeared in the kitchen. "He's talking again," he said.

She hurried into the parlor. The two of them stood there listening to him ask for help. She went close to him and said, "You're at home and safe now."

He was listening, seemed like.

"You are as safe as you've ever been, under three quilts, with a fire burning in the grate." She was deeply anxious for him not to remain any longer in fear, to be where she couldn't reach him. She didn't want to show pity in her voice, not for herself, but she guessed she did; she so much wanted him to talk to her. "The long ride on the train is over now. You were brought up the hill to this room, which you know so well."

His eyes moved as he gazed around the room.

"Troy, say something to your father."

"What do I say?" he said.

"Say something loving to him."

He moved close to the head of the bed and said, "Papa."

The eyes rested on him.

"Papa, I love you," he said. He didn't know how to say it any better.

"Do you, Troy?" he said.

People would come to talk with him about the Road, but he paid little attention to them. Often he didn't even reply to what they asked. When Dr. Chester came to examine him, Weatherby said little to him, either, even when Chester got to talking about influenza killing two of the workmen and how Cumberland had relaxed the schedule of the tunnel men as a consequence. He didn't ask about anything or seek further details; and that night he had a bad night, with the sweat breaking out on his face and with much talking in his sleep, so that Mildred and Troy came downstairs, knowing they might be needed to hold him on the bed.

Next day she spoke to Weatherby about the matter. "If the Road worries you, I'll keep the people out."

"No, I'll listen to them," he told her.

"You've got your window shade pulled down again." She went to raise it, but as she touched it his hand touched hers, gently restraining her. He held her hand, even now, and smiled at her. "I don't want to see it."

"See it? Why, there's nothing out there but the valley, and the mountains beyond."

He pressed her hand and kissed it lightly. "I appreciate all you've been doing for me, Mildred." He pulled her arm gently, and she sat down on the bed. He put his hand on her face and felt of her neck, then let his hand rest on her breast. She closed her eyes, and he put his hand behind her neck and pulled her forward so that she lay on his chest. "Don't you sleep, Mildred? Where do you sleep?"

"In my bed upstairs."

"Whenever I wake up, you're here, in this room, either standing by the bed or sitting in the rocker over there."

"It's not far to here," she said softly.

"Do I talk before I wake?"

"Sometimes you do."

"What do I say?"

"You ask for help most often."

He considered that. "Do I talk to anybody?"

"Now and then to Mr. Cumberland. Or to Mr. Babcock. Or to other men."

"To women, too?"

"Now and then."

"To what woman?"

"Your mother."

"Oh, my mother has been dead for years. She was a kindly woman, Mildred."

"You talk to her. And your sister Annie, the one who died."

"Do I talk to Annie? What do I say?"

"Old things from the past. It's as if you was reliving old days."

He rubbed her neck and back, and maybe he didn't know how warm it made her, how flustered inside, for she loved him so much she almost broke in two whenever he touched her.

"What other woman do I talk to?"

She said nothing.

"Do I talk to any others?"

"You talk to Anna," she said.

"Anna?"

"That's the best I can make out of it. That's part of the name, anyway. Often you talk to her and ask her to help you."

There was a long silence; his hand lay lifeless on her. "Do I talk to you, Mildred?"

"Yes."

He lifted her head and brought it close to his own and kissed her gently. "You and I can talk of a day, too," he said, and the idea was so fond to her that she felt almost like crying. His hand began to fumble with the fasteners of her dress. When his hand touched her breast, she pressed her head firmly against his shoulder and kissed him.

"You make me feel warm inside," she said.

"Don't you worry about HenryAnna," he said. "She's only a child. I think of her more as a daughter."

His hand was on her breast, tenderly on her breast. "I don't have will enough to worry, except about your health," she said.

He ate what he could and was kind to her and loved her, and he needed her to be there whenever he did awake, for his dreams troubled him. They always recalled the work he had been doing on the mountain, and they were always about death. The death was of his workers and his friends, and of the old man who had died of tuberculosis that night in the snow, and sometimes was his own. Before now the Road and life had been related; now the Road and death. He couldn't think of one without thinking of the other. So when men came to talk with him about the Road, he felt a heaviness kin to despair.

The Road was itself a snake, the track its backbone, its body stretched across the hills and rivers and ravines. It was now coiling on the mountain.

Babcock and Cumberland came to see him. They brought a wealth of information, but he couldn't force himself to think about men working inside a tunnel.

He had passed through death and was still dead enough to know he was not yet alive in the way he had been alive before.

"Now, you can begin to walk about with crutches," Dr. Chester told him. "The convicts at Babcock Station made these for you out of oak, and they'll see you a year's wear without difficulty. Here, you want to try to use them now?"

"No, not now, doctor."

"Well, as you choose. It wouldn't hurt to try them now, while I'm here."

"Later, later."

"You can't put weight on that leg, even though it has splints on it. You're too old to have a busted leg heal quickly. A child's leg heals faster than a man's.

And a child's thoughts, Weatherby thought.

"You came close to dying up there."

I did die in one respect, he thought.

"But now you appear to be mending all right, in leg and spirit both, though don't rush either one. And you can get around now, so come back to work when you like."

Come back to work, he thought. He peeked past the blind and saw Dr. Chester leave, saw him go across the yard outside, puffs of mist coming from his mouth in the cold afternoon air. Good-by and good riddance, he thought.

Mildred brought the crutches close to the bed. She stood there with them, looking fondly down at him.

"Put them away in the closet, Mildred," he said.

Not only did Cumberland have his own work to do, but he had most of Weatherby's too, for Babcock didn't try to fill the vacuum Weatherby had left. If a problem arose, Babcock sent word to Morganton to get Weatherby's decision; the trip to Morganton and back took several hours, and Weatherby preferred not to give a decision, anyway. So Cumberland began to take command, and Babcock assented, although he resented any decisions Cumberland made which reversed one Weatherby had made earlier.

Cumberland administered the Road with less urgency than had Weatherby. At the doctor's insistence, the workday was shortened; also, Cumberland permitted the doctor to begin construction of an infirmary, and agreed it could be at Babcock Station, which was the least rigidly administered of the three camps. He agreed that men who claimed to be ill were to be taken to Babcock Station for examination rather than be made to wait for the doctor to visit them in places where facilities for medical work were more primitive. He took several of the free workers off the Road and set them to hunting game, in an effort to improve the food supply. When the Babcock tree gang finished its work cutting bridge timbers, rather than assign them to work the tunnels as diggers or powder men, he had them begin to plant tunnel timbers, thus increasing the provisions for the safety of the men. These decisions and some others were made over a six- or eight-week period. None of them in itself was drastic; however, they represented finally a sizable change.

One afternoon when he visited Weatherby, Cumberland took with him a pack of reports on these and other matters, and sat in the room by the fire and sifted through them, relating what he had done.

There was the matter of Mud Cut. It seemed to be somewhat worsened under the impact of the recent thaw. While the ground had been frozen, the cut was controllable, but now the thawed clay was rising in the wound. Cumberland thought perhaps the Road should be rerouted, even if the degree of grade resulting was somewhat excessive, unless the condition improved by spring.

He reported on Long Bridge. The rock wall which had been built to contain the fill on the east embankment had been pushed over. A new wall was being constructed ten feet farther from the bottom of the embankment. Meanwhile, there had been minor damage to the bridge itself, caused by the creeping.

He reported on Lick Log tunnel. The men remained at work, but as the surface of the mountain thawed the water flowed more freely around the rocks, and it had got so misty in there the candles went out. On the damper days a large percentage of the men, up to one third of them, reported for sick call, and thus avoided work.

He told about the mammoth supply of medicine the doctor now required. All of this he told in detail, then waited for Weatherby's opinions.

"How is HenryAnna?" Weatherby said.

Cumberland was startled; the question seemed to him to be a distraction. "She's talkative as ever."

"Tell her I asked about her."

He hesitated. "Do you want her to come to see you?"

"No, no."

"It occurred to me that she might be suitable help for Mildred."

"Tell her I think about her and wish her well, and that I'm not as sick as she has heard."

"I'll tell her whatever you say. But what of my report? I realize some of the changes are working out poorly. We aren't getting the work done, not like we used to."

"Oh, you are doing very well. You are being humane about the thing, which is only right."

"But we aren't getting the work done."

"Yes, of course, that's the problem. I know. So what's the solution—to become inhumane?"

"No."

"No, indeed. Yet you must match them up, somehow."

Cumberland waited. "Match what up?"

"The men, the temper of the men, the iron and hardness in the men."

"Yes? Match that up with what?"

Weatherby's gaze snapped to him. "Her temper. I judge it's a vicious one. In my days as a boy, I never saw worse. She has no sense of mercy, I assure you."

Cumberland stared at him, astonished. "I suppose I understand," he said.

"You must look to her with care. And be careful yourself." He held out his hand to him and Cumberland rose at once. Weatherby squeezed his hand tightly. "Take care, take care," he said. His eyes watered as he looked up from the bed at the young man. "Will you?"

"Yes," Cumberland said, not able quite to focus on what he meant, but realizing it was a personal matter and contained respect and affection for him.

"She'll mark you now . . ." He faltered; the strength left him. "Do what you can about it."

Cumberland, before he left the house, went by to talk with Mildred. She insisted on fixing his dinner, so he sat down at the kitchen table and waited. He idly poured salt on the tabletop and with his finger traced the outline of the Road in it. "He appears to be better, Mildred, though he doesn't talk about the Road."

"You know, I've got too much buttermilk in this batter," she said. "I'll need to make muffins rather than biscuits."

"I like one as well as another," he said. He told her about his cottage and about the miller and the smith and the storekeeper. "I used to think I would always be an outlander to them, but they've halfway accepted me, and sometimes I think I'll settle down up there, Mildred."

"Why don't you?"

"I'm happier there than anywhere else. I can make a future in the village, particularly when you and Weatherby move there, too, as he once told me he hoped to."

She slipped the muffins into the oven and stirred the pot of beans with a spoon. "When we'll move up there I don't know. Everything is confusing now. He lies in there and talks sometimes in his sleep, and it's to the snakes, or it's to the mountain, as if the mountain has ears and can hear what he says, or it's to you."

"What does he say to me?"

"It's jarbled words is all. Sometimes he talks to others." She stopped her work at the stove. "May I ask you something?"

"Yes," he said.

"I don't know how to ask it."

"Please ask whatever you want to," he said simply.

She came close to him. "Who is HenryAnna?"

He tried not to show his surprise, but he couldn't hide it completely, and he didn't know what to say to her.

"He talks to her more than to anybody else," she said.

He stared at her, helpless to determine what he ought to say, trying to think of some way even to avoid knowing what she had told him, for his own life was trembling from the knowledge more than hers was.

She sank into her chair and laid clenched hands on her lap, composing herself. "I see that you won't tell me."

He had no idea what conclusion she drew from that, but it was so that he couldn't tell her who HenryAnna was in terms of her husband. "I'm sorry," he said.

When he had eaten, he went to Weatherby's door and saw that he was lying there staring at the wall. Cumberland said good-by to him. There was no response. Cumberland went out of the house and down the walk, the air of outdoors bathing over him, relieving him somewhat. He hurried down the road toward the railroad yard, his emotions reeling crazily.

Early in the fourth month, during the third week of March, lines of authority broke down. Cumberland tried to mend them by requiring that everything of consequence be written down, but this only resulted in long delays. Babcock and Cumberland began bickering over everything, and Dr. Chester assumed more discretion; not only was he now building an infirmary but he was requisitioning labor and wasn't reporting this to anybody. The infirmary, which everybody had assumed would be a modest affair, was a long structure with a stone foundation.

There was little being done on the Road itself. The men were sick or had been diverted to a task not central to the enterprise. The storms as a consequence were given free rein to erode and wash away; they did quite a lot of damage. Out of a sense of desperation, Cumberland tried to put the mechanism of the Road back as Weatherby had had it; he sent out new orders, but nothing came of them. Even Babcock was not attentive to what he said. He made schedules, but nobody met them. One night even the safety gang, which was putting timbers in the tunnel to protect the workers, came to Cumberland's office and said they would not work any more because the work was dangerous.

Fourteen men tried to escape during March, and four were shot and only two of the ten who got away were later found.

On March 30 Cumberland wrote Weatherby a letter, telling him of the failures, reminding him of the importance of the enterprise. "I have never presumed to believe I could run such a project; therefore, it isn't personally destructive to find out that I cannot. But no one else here can, either. We stand hopefully aside and wait for you."

CHAPTER FIFTEEN

MILDRED AWOKE and heard a noise in the house, a thumping sound. She got out of bed and hurried down the stairs to Weatherby's door. As soon as she got there, the sound stopped.

She started to open the door to see if he was all right, but she was so unnerved that she went back up to her own room, telling herself it had only been the March wind.

The thumping started again. This time when she went downstairs, she opened the door and there in the center of the room stood Weatherby. A candle was lighted on the mantel, and the light was flickering on him. He was in his nightgown and was firmly holding the crutches under his arms. "What in the world?" she said.

"We must not delay, Mildred," he said, "for it's spring."

On one of the first really warm days, Weatherby visited the Road. He had told nobody he was coming, so no preparation had been made to welcome him; he appeared at Henry Station, was simply there among the workmen. He had his left pants leg pulled down over the cast on his leg, so that there was not much visible evidence that he was injured at all, except for the crutches, and even these he handled deftly. He was smiling, seemed to be in fair spirits, but on leaving he stopped on the turnpike to look up sternly at the side of the mountain, toward the place of the cave in which he had lain, then his gaze scanned the range itself, and rested finally on the crest, which was white-topped, like the white hair of an old woman.

He did only one other thing before leaving Henry Station. He wrote a letter to the governor, explaining his illness and the consequent delay in the work. He asked for an extension of three months on the use of the convicts, and for the loan of 100 additional men.

With this addition in time and manpower, we can have the Road open by spring of next year. If we do not succeed by then, the future disposition of convicts or of myself will be of little consequence to this enterprise, anyway. We stand at the portal of the mountains, and at a portal to the West. I have only confidence in the importance of this mission and in our ultimate victory, but I have come to measure success realistically. We need more men and more time.

In a land where winter is barren and spring is everywhere lush and beautiful, the awakening of spring is most welcome. One responds to it personally, and no doubt Weatherby's return to the Road at this time was in accompaniment to this awakening. He visited the Road again soon and talked with the men, stopping the work long enough to reckon with them about the coming months. He talked hopefully to them about the Road and about the challenge that had been laid to them to build the Road here.

He did not assume administrative control, however. It seemed he was merely courting the idea of returning to work.

At the time of his second visit, the maple trees had budded at their tops. One could look down from the Tunnel Station, as he did, and see them spotted everywhere on the mountain, like dots of fire. The bloodroot flower, the eyebrights and trilliums had appeared too, and certain birds had returned: warblers and bluebirds and robins. A chickadee had built her nest near the office at the Tunnel Station and could be heard frequently complaining about something.

A letter arrived from the governor to Weatherby, one solicitous of his health.

I have managed to inveigle an additional three months for you, so you will have the convicts until the last day of March next. I can do no more, and I think no man can, now or later, for spring begins early in the East and they are most anxious to have convict labor begin their enterprise there by April first and are jealous already of our attention to the West.

I can find only 75 prisoners in excess, and those are being sent to you. We can supply additional ones over the months to replace such losses as you must inevitably suffer in this dangerous work. May God help you, heal you, and give you success.

The 75 convicts arrived and were housed temporarily in sheds at the Tunnel Station. There were no tools for the men to use, and no mule carts and no mules to be hired, especially now at plowing time.

Weatherby was more often to be seen on the Road, but he controlled his participation closely. The steady, rising tide of nature was matched by a gradual increase in his interest, and both were accompanied by the sound of the hammers falling more often, the carts rolling again, the foremen giving instructions. The men had more confidence now, in the Road and in themselves. The rate of the work increased slowly, steadily.

In his journal Cumberland noted the return of the black-and-white and the yellow-throated warblers, the black-throated green warblers, the rough-winged swallows, the brown thrashers, the rusty blackbirds, the cowbirds, the chipping sparrows, all of which were fussing and feuding over the space they found and the nests they made and the births they were getting ready for. Duck hawks were nesting on the cliffs and broad-winged hawks were staking their claims. The grouse was strutting with tail feathers spread and head held erect, his neck feathers ruffled and his body appearing larger than usual.

The forest on the lower ridges, then later at the Gap, then later on the wall of the higher reaches of the mountain, became green, as elms, sweet gums, ironwoods and sycamores put out their leaves, the tide of life moving upward to the forest of yellow birch and mountain ash. There was on the mountainside the lighter green of the pine trees, which had some new needles.

The grass also was a new-green on the hillsides. The dogwood broke into bloom, then the apple trees and the cherry trees began to scatter their blossoms.

HenryAnna came home with pollen in her hair and on her shoulders and clinging to the flax of her dress; she brought home armloads of laurel. She and Cumberland together studied the flowers and filled their cottage with them.

In June near Henry Station bushes of rhododendron fifteen feet high bloomed lilac, purple, and sometimes with a rose-red flower, and as these bushes stopped blooming, other rhododendron bushes, perhaps twice as large, bloomed in ravines and on the higher slopes.

Weatherby saw all this and received it into himself. He let himself be soothed and healed by it, by the same healing spirit which healed the mountain itself. No place on earth was more lovely, he thought, more likely to appear to invite one to come close to it. He let the place heal him.

Yet at night, if he was still at the Road, he could be seen going out into the yard and looking up at the mountain herself. He would sniff the scented air, but he would not breathe deeply of it. He would sniff it suspiciously, and he might talk to the mountain. "You have your net out now, don't you?" he would say. "You are getting yourself all decked out, are you, ma'am? You are acting like a young girl again. You are saying welcome to us all, are you, my lady? You are clothing yourself and perfuming yourself, but I think I see through it now. Your thorns are sharp and will grow longer. Your knife and fang are being sharpened all the while."

Ah, yes, lady, he would think, moving along the paths to the stockade. Ah, yes, lady, I see through all the paint on your face the years of wrinkled age.

"There comes a close to trying to figure it all out," Cumberland said to him one night at the Tunnel Station.

"Figure what out?" Weatherby said.

"Whether it can be done or not."

"Well, that's the point," Weatherby admitted to him. "I don't know what to make for a new schedule."

"Are you afraid of it?"

"I wouldn't admit it if I were."

"I waken at night and realize I'm in agony, and it's because I can't see a way out. We have brought a road onto a mountain that I'm not sure now we can climb."

"Yes, it's the mountain all right, she's the problem," Weatherby said.

"I've never thought nature had senses and could think, or out-think us."

"Haven't you? Hers might not be a mind like ours, or lend itself to our analysis. After all, our minds are beyond our own comprehension, but it appears they act on the basis of prior experiences, and these experiences accumulate, so that we do much automatically, without concentrating on it. We don't have to stop and think about picking up a poker and stirring the fire; we see the fire needs stirring and automatically we have the poker in our hands and stir it. I don't know that nature can think new thoughts, but she has a storehouse of old ones. When a man goes about changing nature he sets off her response, and a chain reaction is set in motion which defeats him, unless, of course, he is adequately prepared."

Cumberland realized that Weatherby's attitude could be related to that of the mountain boys who had found him in the cave. He was attentive to the ways of the creature he was trying to change; his purpose was to discover its purposes, then to defeat them.

"The question is: are we in combat with a force we can expect to conquer?" Weatherby said.

"Is that what you want to do?" Cumberland said.

"Want?" Weatherby said. "I want to be done with it. I want it over. I want to be free of it. If they were to say to me, 'Very well, don't build it,' then I would be relieved and free. But I can't desert it, even though I realize I'm engaging myself in a death challenge. The place and I will die somewhat, to some extent; death will track me down again, all right, try to get me back into its cave. And that cave comes in many forms."

"But do you want to continue?"

"No, of course not. But I will."

He referred to the matter later that night. He said suddenly, and without any bearing on the conversation of the moment, "There is no need to deliberate about what is inevitable. We've spent men and time and money, and we can't stop here."

Will Sanders and others on the crew began to whisper among themselves, saying that whenever Weatherby came near a tunnel, he would stand like a man possessed, a sweat appearing on his flesh, and his hands would grip ever more tightly the rungs of his crutch, as if his hands were closing in to break them.

Weatherby sensed that they were watching him and talking about him, and one afternoon he overheard one of the men say: "The old man won't go in there; he's afraid of it." The words struck him deeply, and he moved forthrightly to the entrance of Lick Log tunnel and started inside, to prove that such opinions were unfounded. He stepped over the bits of rubble at the portal and continued resolutely, but at the place where the light of the sun was shadowed by the overhanging rocks, he stopped. He stood there stern at first, then gradually weakening; his shoulders straight at first, then sagging; his head high, then bowed; his body tense, then limp; so that finally he who had held the crutches was held up by them. He stood there for a long while, nobody moving past him, either to go into the tunnel or to leave. He was unable to turn to face the men or to go forward.

He turned around slowly. At once the men acted as if they were busy with their work. He stood most humbly before them. He still held power over them, of course, even though at the moment he seemed not to be powerful himself. "It's only the cave," he said to a man standing there. He moved away from them, stopping once to turn on his crutches and look at the entrance, at that black spot in the rocks.

Three times in his adult life had he been afraid: first, at Mud Cut, when he awoke and the mountain was shifting; second, inside the cave; and third, here, when he realized he could not move into the tunnel he made other men enter.

He reasoned that his mind knew some things deeper than what he was himself aware of; his body had not responded to its own instruction because of the depth and strength of its own feeling. It was as if beyond himself was a secret world of his own being, as beyond the mountain and its representative processes were the secret being of itself, and maybe even the secret beings themselves, the ghosts and spirits which his mother and father had believed in.

He mentioned his worry to Cumberland, who said his fear would soon go away, that he had suffered a desperate experience and was not recovered fully, in terms of either his leg or his attitudes.

"The leg has bones to mend, but what can mend amid the attitudes?" Weatherby said.

"I don't know," Cumberland said. "Nobody knows."

"I find it easier to believe in ghosts than attitudes. I could believe my mother's ghost was standing at Lick Log tunnel and restrained me, for she knows by now that the mountain has identified me, that her first affront was to Bolton, but that she later came to realize that it wasn't the driver of the engine at all, but the chief maker of the Road who must be got rid of. I can imagine my mother's ghost standing at the entrance of the tunnel easier than I can imagine the knitting together of attitudes."

"Yes, of course, it's easier," Cumberland said, "but it's also less meaningful, for your mother's ghost wasn't there, and you were restrained by yourself."

"Much easier to believe in ghosts and miracles," Weatherby said.

"If your mother's ghost were moving at large today," Cumberland said, "she would have dragged you from the cave you were in."

Weatherby's gaze snapped to him. "A ghost has no hands to move me."

Cumberland thought about that. "Does it have hands to restrain you, then?"

"I didn't feel any hands on me."

"Did you feel restrained by attitudes?"

"I felt restrained by fear."

"Fear of what was safe. You mother's ghost would know the cave endangered you, and that the tunnel did not."

"But she might know the tunnel endangered me most of all."

"Men go and come in that tunnel every hour, they work there, and it doesn't hurt them."

Weatherby leaned far forward over the table. "But the mountain does not want them."

Cumberland stared at him, amazed at him. "Just as you say," he said finally, not wanting to argue about it or pursue the subject now, though he felt that if Weatherby persisted in giving personalities to unnatural as well as natural objects, it would be confusing to try to help him. Cumberland realized Weatherby had been born in the mountains, and that his people, like the mountain people around them, attributed personalities to beasts and brutes, to rivers and springs and mountains and trees, and also to ghosts and spirits, both kind and unkind. All of this was part of their thinking, and therefore could not be idly dismissed, not even by Weatherby. The animals in the woods had personalities, so had the tree by the spring, so had the spring itself. "I've talked sometimes with the mountain boys," Cumberland said, "and they have many superstitious cures for sickness."

Weatherby sat back, attentive.

"They carry all sorts of herbs, and trade them among themselves. For a chill they sometimes bore a deep hole in the sunny side of an oak tree and blow their breath into it, then plug the hole up. For hemorrhages they say to scrape an old felt hat. For shingles they bathe the irritated portion of the skin with fresh warm blood of a chicken."

"That cure might be as good as any other," Weatherby said defensively.

"It has to be, they told me, a black chicken."

Weatherby shrugged. "There's some superstition in what any-body does."

"For diphtheria they claim a toad ought to be split open and bound to the throat of the patient, quickly, while the toad's blood is warm. For treating warts they gather a pebble for each wart, put them in a bag and drop the bag in the road, and whoever picks it up will get their warts. For blood poisoning they put sugar in a yarn sock and set it afire, then cut the poisoned part of the body and hold it over the blaze, so that the bad blood can run out."

"The people depend more on herbs, I believe you'll find," Weatherby said. "My mother gathered herbs every spring and fall. My sisters helped her more than I, but when I was a little boy I went with her one spring, up on the mountain and also down into some valley places, and we gathered galax and ginseng and heart leaves and boneset and walnut bark. These were only part of her store of herbs, and with them she used hog lard, mutton, beef tallow, beeswax and God knows what. She was the family doctor. If my throat was sore, I got sweet gum tea; if the baby had hives, she got red alder tea; if we had boils, we got a poultice made of dock leaves."

"Yes, but when one says a chicken must be black rather than red, that is merely superstition."

"I don't doubt it one bit. You know cherry bark bitters and whisky will cure most anything, they tell me."

"Will it?" Cumberland said. "And Jimson root is good for palsy, I'm told."

"If you steep dogwood bark in whisky, it'll cure the shakes," Weatherby said. "That's all I need, maybe, you know it? Or a jug of apple brandy."

"It would help us both," Cumberland said, smiling. He pulled on his coat, for the nights were cool. "The mountain boys say one can cure foot troubles by placing one's shoes upside down before going to bed. You might see if that helps your leg." He went to the door and opened it, stood in the open doorway looking out.

"My leg's not what bothers me most," Weatherby said.

"You can get a bag of asafetida and tie it around your neck to ward off evil spirits." He went outside on the porch, then walked toward the guards' fire.

Weatherby got up and closed the door, then limped into the bedroom, where he took off his shirt. He pulled his pants off over his splinted leg.

Naked except for his underclothes, with his eyes closed, he sat on the bed remembering his Grandmother King, who was the most superstitious person in his family. He could see her squatted on the milk stool by the fireplace in her cabin, her mouth empty of teeth, her face kindly with lively eyes and clean, shiny skin pulled tightly over her bones. "The devil finished eating," she said, commencing a story. "He had a lamb for supper and laid the fiddle acrost his knees and sawed away a tune, and his hag wife went to the doorway and called to all the pretty women in the fields, and when they had come into the house she shet the door and the firelight burned on them. The devil played his fiddle a devil's tune while she opened up the waists of the nine pretty women and made a cross on each of their breasts with the pointed end of a turkey bone. Then the fiddle played louder and the nine women danced for the devil and his wife."

Had she believed it? She told it all so seriously she might have believed it. He had thought she believed it, and had never before tonight wondered if she did, because as a child he had accepted what was told him.

Did the devil play a fiddle and have a wife? he wondered.

He threw his pants into the corner of the room and stretched out on the mattress. He lifted his leg onto the bed and pulled a blanket over his body. He closed his eyes and thought of the tunnel and knew he would dream that night of the cave, and a shudder went through him. He always dreamed about the cave.

The Bible, he thought. He got up at once and with the help of one crutch made his way to the office desk and took out his Bible; he brought it back to the bed and put it under the pillow.

Oh, he thought, as he closed his eyes again, what good was that? What possible help could come from the paper and leather of that book to heal his dreams? Yet his mother had claimed for the Bible such powers.

He breathed deeply, forced his muscles to relax. He recalled his grandmother in her old age, when she had lost much of her powers of mind, going outside the back door of her house, pulling up her dress, squatting down and urinating on the ground. "Mama, you go into the woods or to the privy," Weatherby's mother would insist, but his grandmother only cackled in the free and broken way she had in those final years of her life.

"The hellcats began snooping around," she told Weatherby once, the firelight glowing on her and all her grandchildren listening intently to her in the nighttime before sleep. "And they was like any cats but was hellcats, and a woman I knowed throwed a kettleful of boiling water at them, but they bowed their backs and the water rolled off in steam. Her cabin room got so steamed she couldn't see, and the air was flavored of brimstone, so she couldn't fetch her breath. 'The devil's routed me,' she told herself, 'and fell to the floor and the hot tongues of the hellcats began to lick her clothes off her body until she was naked and was writhing on the floor boards with the cats licking her face and stomach and atween her legs, licking her—"

"Grandma, stop talking to them children that-a-way. My Lord, mama, stop it, you hear. You're getting worse."

"The lady crawled to the door and throwed it open."

"Mama, for God's sake—"

"And saw white chickens scratchin' on the doorstone, and she didn't keep a white chicken on the place."

"Mama, you got them little children trembling. You young'uns listen no more."

"Hit war a dark night, but down the side of the mountain, through bresh so thick it couldn't be opened by a bear, come the devil riding in a coal-black cart, driving a coal-black ox, and the cart come to the door and stopped, and the devil come to her at the doorway and the hellcats pulled way back in the corner. The woman looked up at him from the floor, and he said, 'I come fer your body first, and then fer your soul.' And the woman, writhing there, said, 'I'll give ye both if ye'll take me now.' "

"Mama, God knows. Come on here with me. Mama, come on to bed now. Here, let me take your arm."

"I don't want to go to bed."

"Come on."

"She give him body and soul, Martha."

"Yes, mama. Come to bed now, that's the way."

"And she was the prettiest woman to look at in the face, Martha, and no sooner had she give him her body but she turned so old, and her teeth come out and her skin got tight on her bones."

"Come on to your bed, mama."

"She ate them nine witch balls, Martha. Do you hear me, Martha?"

"Come to bed. Here, lie down. Let me shut the door. You children get out of here."

"Them balls was nothing but nine needles wrapped with fine

woman's hair. She give him herself and he rode her on the floor, then turned her into a horse and rode her up and down the valley until she fitified."

"Mama, please, for God's sake hush. Now, here, you children get out of this room this minute. And don't listen at the door, neither. Go, scat. . . . And now, mama, you listen to me—you can't keep telling those stories to my children. If you live in my house, you start using the privy and stop telling them about the devil."

"That yellow dog of your'n ain't no ordinary dog, Martha."

"Oh, God, mama."

"I seen it rise and run along in the air, going toward the mill."

"There's no ghost in that mill, mama."

"I followed down there full moon afore last—"

"You was in this bed—"

"It was dark as the closed mouth of a yellow dog. Your dog led me there, beckoning, and I crept inside and was in the corner when I heard the sound of his footsteps coming toward me out of the mountain and across the valley floor. He come to the door, and I heard it creak open and saw the moonlight fall on the floor, and he appeared, black-clothed and handsome, and he said, 'I come fer ye,' and I said 'I been waitin'.' He turned his face at once and I saw he was dripping water and blood from his side, and I saw his eyes was maggot-coated. The worms ate his eyes and his face rotted away before me, and his mouth was open and I saw his rotted teeth and his purple gums as he come to me, and I began to cry out— 'No, God, no, God, no!' "

He awoke. He lay on the bed, sweat dripping on him, and the open mouth of the devil was the cave in which he had lain, and the rotted teeth were the broken rocks, and the spittle was the water from the underground spring, and the purple gums were the wound on his leg, which throbbed now.

"God knows," he whispered, "God help me."

He took the Bible from under his pillow and clutched it firmly, pressed it close to his chest. He laid it against his face, knowing it did have, if any object on earth had, secret, magic powers to ward off evil, and he heard his own voice whisper out of his own mind of science and wonder: "Protect me, forgive me, I pray God."

The mountain boys told Cumberland that spirits could get into any person, and into any animal, and could even inhabit wood, as it did a cradle now and then, so that the cradle would rock every night, all night through. "You're 'fraid to chop it up and 'fraid to burn it, neither one," Dozen told him, "lest it scatter the spirit far and wide."

Dozen said a person could bewitch himself if he chose to. He said his sister Mary was once out washing clothes and suddenly he heard a queer sound and turned to see her standing on her head in the washtub. "I got her pulled out and held to the ground while she thrashed."

"How do you know she was bewitched? Might have been a stroke," Cumberland said.

"She was standing on her head in the wash water."

"Yes, but even so—"

"And when we took the snuff stick from her mouth, it was dry."

Cumberland stared at him, not a muscle moving in his face. He nodded simply. "Of course," he said.

Day by day Weatherby took more control of the Road, and the Road day by day discovered its functioning channels again. With a smile he would encourage an action or with a frown he would change one. Cumberland noticed that he never needed to take back the reins of command; it was as if they were his by natural right. The decisions he made were unchallengeable, yet rarely did he seem to decide.

CHAPTER SIXTEEN

WEATHERBY HAD HOPED to raise enough food for the men, and enough feed for the mules and oxen. As of August the corn had done well, but the oats and sorghum and the patch of rye along Mill Creek had been destroyed in a flood. Also, the hogs had been severely bothered by the wolves and bears. They were razorbacks and were shaped in front like a thin wedge and were armored with tough hide and bristles. They had long snouts which they used to uproot and overturn, they had long legs and thin flanks and pliant hoofs. They could run as fast as a horse and could climb as well as a goat and were born warriors and strategists, and had good memories for dangers and enemies, and even for indignities. They were fierce fighters and protectors, and it had been supposed that, back in the woods where they were permitted to root and graze, they would ward off their enemies, but now that the count had been made, their number was not advanced over last year's.

"We'll get back what we put in 'em," the foreman of the farm told Weatherby. "We'll get maybe half a dozen more than that. The rest are gone, as if they disappeared from sight. Last spring I put a few cattle out to graze on that there mountain pasture, and they're gone now. I went to salt them a week back and not a one was to be found. Seems like it all has happened here at the start of summer, for some reason. Even the chickens is halfway gone, as if the minks and foxes and weasels and snakes has just developed a taste fer 'em."

"Might be the cattle have strayed," Weatherby said.

"I sent two men out to cattle hunt and they was gone for three days and nights. I give 'em corn pone and sowbelly and a grain sack, but they found not a one."

"All of this in recent weeks, is it?" Weatherby said.

"All here lately, yes. That flood and these losses of stock is hard to bear."

Weatherby on crutches moved through the farm, nodding to the men and asking a spare question now and then, not showing the weight of worry he carried in his mind. The early cornfields, which were above floodwaters, already could be stripped of some of their ears; men were moving among them, pulling and shucking now. In the next field stubble was being turned under by a plowman. "What you planting there?"

"Oats, though I could put it in flax, if you'd permit, or make a pasture if you want to buy a flock of sheep. We ain't got nary one now."

"We have no time for sheep or flax either," Weatherby said.

"The men need blankets and clothes."

"The state supplies what they need."

"Don't appear to do well by them. Some of the men is nigh barefoot and most ain't got underclothes."

"We're making such improvements as we can, I assure you," Weatherby said, wishing he could walk across the newly plowed field and let the earth squish under his feet, as he used to. He smelled the odor of the torn ground, being reminded pleasantly of his youth. He stopped the plowman, who was sweating through his shirt and the hips of his pants, who was a white convict sent to the Road for thievery. They talked for a while about the way the sod was breaking. Then Weatherby walked with the foreman to the farm office and rested there.

They had planted potatoes in late May, and they were growing poorly. The stand of corn that had been planted in late April had been uprooted by a hard rain; it had been replanted in July and was growing well. The turnip seeds that had been started in late July never did vegetate. "It's not a typical situation here," the foreman said.

"I have no money to buy food with," Weatherby said. "I get money from Raleigh to feed the convicts, but I need that for the Road, for nitroglycerin mostly."

213

"Yes, sir. I understand. We can plant beans."

"All right. And cabbages?"

"We have a few. Enough for a taste now and then."

"But the main thing is corn and pork."

"There ye air, ye see, for I ain't got the pork, seems like, nor cattle neither."

Summer was the rainy season here. It rained about every afternoon, a shower to cool off the day and the trees, and every week there would be a big rain to fill the pores of the ground and make the tunnels soppy wet.

That and the heat made the work more strenuous and debilitating, but Weatherby insisted on holding to the dawn-to-dusk schedule, even though a summer day is longer than a spring day. The men were working fourteen hours at a stretch. Even so, Weatherby would tell the worried foremen, "We're not making more progress than we need to, as you see here on the schedule." The schedule he had made became the taskmaster. The pace was set not by what was convenient but by what had to be achieved if the Road was to be finished on time.

To relieve the situation somewhat, Weatherby tried to figure out a way to use the engines more efficiently, and thus help the men move more earth easier and faster. His chief problem here was that track had not yet been laid to the tunnels, so the engines couldn't reach them. The major obstacle remaining in the way, Bloody Ridge, was only a third cut through. The best hope of getting it completed in a short period of time was to cut its sides steep. This would admittedly offer a dangerous problem of falling rock, but in a year or so other men could take the time to widen and improve it.

All he wanted now was a cut through the ridge, so that he could get an engine to the first of the series of tunnels, where it was needed.

"How many days will you need to clear a path through there barely wide enough for a train?" he asked a gang foreman out of Babcock Station.

"Four months at least," the foreman said.

"If you work men from both sides?" Weatherby asked.

"It's dangerous that-a-way," the foreman said, "to blast from both sides."

"It's dangerous to work like the men at the tunnel have to. If you keep the sides steep and blast from both sides and move a work engine up on the downgrade side, can you finish in a month?"

"Sir?" the foreman said, stunned.

"We need it done," Weatherby said.

"Yes, sir, but—"

"You know what long hours these men are working."

"Yes, but my men are—"

"Can you do it?"

The foreman was wet with sweat. He turned to look at the ridge. "Might be dangerous to leave steep sides, Mr. Weatherby."

"It's dangerous either way," Weatherby said. "We're all in danger here."

"That cut will be a hundred feet deep at its center, and if its sides—"

"It's your decision, you're the foreman here," Weatherby said as he hobbled away, leaving the foreman to think about it.

The foreman's name was Rollin Marland, and he came to be called Fool Marland by the men. It was the pace he set that first surprised them about him; later it was the rocks. Then it was the nitroglycerin, blasting off from both sides of the same cut, shaking the ridge and tearing boulders free of their beds. Marland had the men at Bloody Cut by sunup. They worked each day until they couldn't see what they were working on, and, of course, no candles could be used out there in the open, or he might have kept going into the night. Now and then as they worked the cry would go out: "Falling rock!" The men would look up, and those in danger would try to get to safety. Sometimes a mule got hit by the falling rock, too.

These were not slides, but were merely rocks falling, some of them the size of a man's head, some of them as big as a bed. Sometimes it was one rock that fell, sometimes it was fifty or a hundred at a time. Sometimes they fell from low on the walls, more often they fell from up high. If they landed on clay, they plopped solidly and without bounding; if they landed on rock they smashed and sent splinters flying about. A man could be injured by them, either way.

If rock began to fall from above and a man was near the middle of the cut, he had well over 100 feet to run in order to reach either end. Of course, he couldn't run 100 feet while rock was falling 100 feet, so he had to do what he could, and he had to do what he could while other men were doing what they could, too. Protection was often dearly evaluated in Bloody Cut.

Two weeks after the work was started, the cut was not halfway done, and Marland, badly worried, sought out Weatherby to reason with him.

"You have two weeks yet to make up lost time," Weatherby told him.

"I can't go faster. My God, sir, they're bleeding from their hands now."

"Don't drive the men so hard. Use heavier charges of explosive."

"Those charges are shaking down rocks all over us now."

"Get more carts parked in the cut for the men to take cover under. Can't you do that?"

Marland was irritated, yet he was also impressed by the calmness with which Weatherby spoke of the dangers. "We've lost several men in that cut so far, Mr. Wright. I don't mind telling you I remember that of a night."

"I remember things of a night, too," Weatherby said.

"Others have been injured. There's been eighteen injured."

"I'll send you twenty men from Henry Station to take their places," Weatherby said. "You get those carts, so that you can protect your men," he said.

Five weeks after the work had started, Bloody Cut was open. Work track was laid and the engine rolled through the cut and to the place where the first tunnel was to be located.

For some time tunnel work had been under way at Lick Log, the third tunnel in the chain, but downhill of it two short tunnels had been left for the men of Babcock Station to do, once they broke through to them. Weatherby now told Mr. Marland to go ahead with that work. "It's not much different from making a cut," he told him.

"I've never done tunnels," Marland said.

"Keep the men blasting and clearing, and get the engine to help on the downgrade side. That first tunnel is a little one. It's not more than 125 feet long, and you can get the heading through in three weeks."

Marland was stunned. "One hundred twenty-five feet in three weeks?"

"It's not like a high cut. There's less earth to move."

By noon on the twenty-first day the convicts broke the heading through. In three weeks, with liberal amounts of nitroglycerin, an engine, and 150 convicts, Long Branch tunnel had been opened to light. An engine went all the way through it on Saturday afternoon, setting up such a cheer among the men and such joy and celebrating that there was danger the guards would lose control. Men of Babcock Station had finished the first of the tunnels.

Weatherby on crutches stood at the tunnel that evening and watched the men go home. "You did well, Mr. Marland," he said, turning to look again at what they had done, at this short but clean tunnel in the ridge. A few days before it had been a cave, but now it was an opening that a man could see his way through.

"You want to walk through it?" Marland asked him.

Weatherby stood quiet for a moment. Then the two men started through. But as soon as the walls closed in around him Weatherby began to hobble along faster, his crutches smacking hard on the tunnel floor. One of them struck a rock that was part of the rubble, and as he tried to recover his balance, his leg slipped on another rock and he went sprawling forward onto the track. He lay there holding to the track with his two hands, one hand on each of the rails, his face pressed against a tie.

Marland, terrified, bent over him. "Are you all right, sir?"

"Am I?" he said.

"Sir?"

"Am I all right?"

"It was nothing, Mr. Wright. You tripped over a rock."

Weatherby pushed himself to his feet, turned at once and, hobbling on one crutch, went back the way he had come.

Later the foreman found him sitting on a rock, looking off at the lowlands. His clasped hands were held between his legs, his face was calm, without worry on it. He was simply looking off at the valley below, much as if he had been there for a while and was thinking about something of little immediate consequence.

"I must say, Mr. Wright, you gave me a start," Marland said, laying the other crutch down. "I doubted you could run with a cast on your leg."

"Did you?" Weatherby said simply.

"The chances of a man running through there and not falling over a stone are slight, but you managed."

"A man can do what he has to," Weatherby said. He cleared his throat uneasily, got up, picked up the crutches, feeling of them as if weighing them, testing them. "You've done well here," he said, and hobbled up the trail toward the Tunnel Station.

The heading of Lick Log tunnel was 340 feet into the ground when one Saturday morning Moses noticed that the earth had begun to heave, as if in labor, and he heard a moaning sound, perhaps made by the creaking of the rocks and the sopping noises of the clay. The dangerous moment passed, and he started to work again, not fully convinced that he had noticed anything at all, for in the darkness of the cave, lost in his work, he did get dizzy often and lost his sense of balance. He was surrounded by darkness, deprived of air, and the work pressed his senses against the floor and walls and ceiling all around.

So he wasn't sure there had been a tremor, and the other men were doubtless of the same mind, but he did notice that the mules were nervous and were anxious to be out of the tunnel. They even had to be restrained.

The men cleaned out the blastings that lay about them. They

turned the last mule and started toward the dot of light in the distance.

Moses, who had been at the heading, was at the rear of the group, accompanying a candle boy from near Morganton, who was snuffing out the candles and laying them on his cart. "I'm going to leave the candles from here on out," he told Moses. "The blasting won't break them?"

"No, not at this distance," Moses said. "How come you work?" Moses asked him.

"Get money for the farm."

"What farm?"

"Papa's. He was to lose it."

He will lose it then, Moses thought. If something bad was about to happen to a man, it would most likely happen. The boy perhaps thought he could keep the world from beating in, he could plan and dicker and escape, but Moses had no confidence in planning. He had learned to endure what came. "You'll lose it," he said to the boy.

The boy turned to him with pain on his face. "No," he said.

They were near the entrance now and the boy could see Moses' smile reflected in the dim light. "You'll lose it," Moses said again.

No sooner had he spoken than the earth moaned. It was as if the earth had heard him and was commenting on what he said. The boy ran, but Moses turned to face the thing that challenged him. He saw the tunnel floor rise before him into the air, as if pushed up from below; then it leveled out again, but crackled with gunlike explosions. Bits of rock were flung around, and as he watched the collapse of the tunnel began a hundred feet or more away and moved toward him with a giant undulation.

Moses stood his ground, fearless of it because he was confident of himself to stand there and endure what was offered him. It moved toward him, burying the tunnel as it swept along, the sound reverberating and shockingly loud, yet he stood there, not evading the challenge put to him. The portal of the tunnel was only a few steps behind him. He could run and be free, but he stood there and watched as the tunnel collapsed in a mighty sweep, the collapse stopping perhaps forty feet in front of him, the stone from the last of the collapse bounding against his feet.

It was quiet then. There was no sound at all. There was much dust in the air, and a seam had opened above his head and water from a spring was trickling down on him. Before him was the closed-in, partially buried tunnel; behind him was the open air; around him, around his legs, pinning his feet to the tunnel floor, were the rocks from the cave-in.

He groaned a guttural, defiant sound and spat on the rocks. He wiped his arm across his face to get the grime out of his nostrils. His eyes were almost closed by the dust.

Other men freed him and he walked out of the tunnel. He saw the candle boy watching him and he grinned at the boy. "You'll lose it," he said to him. He saw anguish sweep across the boy's face, and he knew the boy couldn't stand to face it. "Do you see it coming?" he said.

The boy nodded.

"Stand and face it," Moses said.

That night as he lay on his pallet, he heard a man twenty feet away in the barracks talking to several others. The words seemed to come off the ceiling of the room and fall into Moses' ears.

"I went on a bear hunt once," the man said, "and we was running one heavy, the dogs marking the morning in this valley and then in that one and then some'ers else. We saw the bear one time; he was about as big as this building, seemed to me. Like a deer I saw once was head and shoulders above ary other deer I ever saw. They named a mountain atter him: Head and Shoulders Mountain is the name, and the people will tell you about that deer and the morning he was killed and the way the blood from his chest made all the streams run red, from the top of the mountain where he was shot, along the fingers of the branches to the creeks, and on down to the river, all red to the river.

"This bear was the biggest by head and shoulder over ary other bear I ever saw, and he was swift as a deer. We heard the dogs begin to yelp and we run to where they had him treed, but he come out of the tree when he saw us, and he stood there at the base looking at them dogs, not running, facing them and batting them aside one at a time, one atter another as they come at him, until there was dogs bleeding and licking theirselves all over the lot, and even so that bear was covered with dogs hanging to him by their jaws. He stood there batting dogs, and seeing us walking up toward him step by step. All morning he had been run by dogs, and now he was facing them, and he saw us and he was facing us, and he batted himself clean of dogs, opening the last one's belly afore he knocked him dead as hell agin a tree, and he could a run, but he stood there waiting. We walked up toward him like a tunnel collapsing in front of him, three of us with our guns loaded and ready, and he stood there slobbering onto his chest, his eyes red, his body bleeding, but he wouldn't run. Behind him was a drop he coulda leaped over and been gone, but he wouldn't undo what he'd spent his life doing. He faced us with all the slobbering, living fear of any beast, yet he faced us. I didn't want to shoot him, to tell you the truth. I've shot bears and deers and coons, which is the hardest thing for me to shoot, fer I like coons better'n ary other of them.

"I had a friend who had a coon call, and he could rouse 'em. It was a death-cry call of a coon, and it made any treed coon look down smartly. He would go into the woods with a lantern and begin to shake a bush, as if a dog was fighting a coon, then he'd make his call, and you'd sometimes see two eyes look down at you, and that was a coon. Sometimes he got so loud on his call and so desperate with his bush that he forgot to shoot, but one night he shot at them two eyes, and he heard a growl and heard tree limbs breaking as a major animal come down, and by damn, he'd shot a bear. The bear struck the ground mad as could be, and that there man run, left his lantern and dropped his coon death-cry call. He stopped finally by his house and sent his neighbor's boys to fetch his lantern and his call fer him, and they come home and said to him, 'Mr. Jasper, there was a bear dead on the ground up thar. You run from him?' 'I shot him and then forgot about hit,' the old liar said.

"But this big head and shoulder bear couldn't avoid us because he wouldn't run. We raised the guns and I said to one man, 'I don't want to shoot him,' and only old man Turpin said, 'Look what he done to my dog there.' And it was so, his dog was crawling on his belly trying to soothe his wounds. And I said, 'Well, I'll shoot him in the head.' And each man took a place to shoot him, and we aimed and shot him, all three at the same time, and even so he stood there looking at us fer a little while. The dogs come back, and he never lifted his paw to 'em now, and they covered him with themselves, even as he fell backwards over that there drop, the dogs with him, mind you, and they must a fell thirty feet to land in the ivy below, and we never went to get him. We sat there and called our dogs as best we could, and all come save one, so he was maybe under the bear dead. We never heard him make a sound, anyway, from nowheres. We had dead and wounded dogs all over. It was a bad time, and Sims said, 'Let's get that bear's liver and eat hit.' And I said, 'Sims, I hain't hongry.' Which was all I said, but what I meant was that a bear that dies that-a-way ought to be left to his own skin. Oh, I know the vultures will get him, them or the wolves or a cat, but let him be, fer he stood his ground. Like in a tunnel when it's coming toward you."

Weatherby moved Moses off Lick Log tunnel. Monday wasn't half gone when he took him aside and talked with him about the Swannanoa tunnel that was going to have to be started. It was going to be 2,000 feet long and the only hope of having it opened in time was for Weatherby to do a special surveying job and start a gang working at each end, and expect the two gangs to meet in the middle, on tangent and on grade.

Moses agreed to do work there, and the next day he and eighty men congregated at a spot near the turnpike where Weatherby had been making readings with his surveying instruments. Weatherby said the east portal would be where a big ledge now overhung a laurel stand.

There was more surveying and discussing. Then Esau, smiling and whistling, came forward with a hammer in one hand and a five-pound bucket of mash in the other.

Several farmers traveling the turnpike had heard there was going to be a blast, and had stopped to see it. Those who had stock turned them into the woods and set their boys to watching over them, but the boys were interested in the blast, too, so soon the woods and turnpike were full of sheep and hogs running all over the place.

Esau swung the hammer and the drill began chipping the stone. He poured water into the hole and set the hammer to ringing again. He laid the mash, set the caps and waved everybody back, but there was a problem moving the mountain people. "Will you go on back a ways now," Esau asked them. He knew full well they wouldn't do anything they were ordered to.

"Will you please get off them rocks afore they are blown up?" Babcock asked them.

Some of them would and some of them wouldn't.

Weatherby himself came forward and asked the people to get back. The delay was exasperating, and Babcock had lost his temper by the time the last of them, lazily stretching his arms above his head as if the whole event made him sleepy, walked out of the danger area.

Esau set fire to the fuse at once and directly the eastern face of the Swannanoa tunnel appeared on the rock wall beneath the ledge. Later that day the west portal also was started.

CHAPTER SEVENTEEN

SHE POURED WATER into the salt gourd and let that set; then she sat down in the back yard of her parents' house and let the summer sun fall on her face and told herself she enjoyed being here, that it was better to be here and off to herself than to spend the rest of the weekend with Cumberland, who was more suspicious of her than he was kind, who had that morning irritated her with his extraordinary claims about her and Weatherby.

Maybe if there had been justification for them, any act between them at all, she wouldn't have got so fierce about it, but she was innocent, and that made the charges all the more unreasonable and hurtful. It was true she had been visiting Weatherby often, but that was because he was so bruised of mind and was angry within himself.

Gourds were drying on a rock, and there was a coil of hickory bark nearby, which was partly unwound and led to the kitchen door, where bleeding heart flowers were paled in brush. Chickens were scratching the ground and pecking what they found, and there were three geese. They were her dowry, she guessed. She had been given seven goose eggs by her mother two years before, and she had hatched them. The goslings had been cute as could be and she had taken time to guard them against the foxes and snakes, but four of them wandered off and were lost to her, so she had only three geese now. She had tried to pick them a time or two, for goose feathers were the prize of all that country and she would want at least a feather pillow, if not a mattress, once she married, but all she had got for her efforts were three ounces of feathers and bruises all over her arms and chest where the geese had beat her with their wings.

She went into the cabin. There were coverlets on the earthen floor, most of them blue and white and raggedy. She snaked them and threw them on one of the beds. The room was so crowded with beds that she could scarcely move to the fireplace, and the fire there was small and meager-looking, like everything else. There was grease in the only pot. She put in two handfuls of wheat flour, dusted the dough with lye water her mother had drained through hickory ashes. She mixed this with her hand and poured in grease and salt brine from the gourd and made the dough into a ball.

She had no board to roll it on, so she broke off pieces of dough and kneaded them until they were smooth. She laid them in the bottom of the pot and set the pot in the fireplace near the fire. She put a thin flat rock on it and heaped hot coals on top of that.

Her brothers, Closet and Penny, came inside. Every time cooking started, they would appear, looking hungry. "What you doin', Anna?" Closet asked, squatting beside her at the fireplace.

"Leave that rock on that pot. Now you leave that be."

"When we going to eat?"

"We don't have meat to eat, unless papa brings something."

"I'm goin' hunting tomorry," Penny said.

"Where you get powder to shoot with?" she asked him.

Closet said, "I can steal some potatoes."

"Not nothing to cook them with," she said. "We could bake them naked, but there's no salt."

Closet moaned. "We'll get salt when we have the drive."

"The drive, the drive," she said. "I hear about the drive every year. What you plan to take on the drive?"

The boys stared at the fire and sniffled and moaned, as their mother often did. "A drove of hogs," Closet said.

"Huh," she said.

"You want the geese to go?"

"If I do I'll take them myself."

The boys stared disconsolately at the fire. "Might take some of the corn," Penny said.

"Not corn enough to eat, if you ask me," she said. "And when are you going to finish pulling the fodder? If you don't pull that fodder, there won't be feed for the horse to eat."

"We been busy gathering wild cherries," Closet said.

"Well, go eat wild cherries, then."

"I'm tired of eating them."

"Get your hand off that pot rock, Closet."

The smell of the biscuits made the boys' mouths water, and she kept elbowing them back from the front of the fireplace. She knew from long experience that if she lost her place at the fire she would lose her biscuits, too, before long. "I want you boys to figure out a way to make more money," she said.

Neither boy said a word.

She looked up at once, suspicious, but decided not to ask them if they had any money. She would have to try to find out when they went to sleep that night. They slept in their pants, but she had searched their pants pockets often before and guessed she could again. "What you boys do this evening?"

"Went into a tunnel," Closet said.

"Did ye?" she said. "Which tunnel?"

"Lick Log."

"Can't see through it yet, can you?"

"The foreman let us carry candles in there today," Penny said, "and we was inside when they laid the mash, and we went back after the blasting to light the candles."

"How much they pay?"

"Don't pay much," Penny said evasively.

"I'd like to go inside there," she said. She took the rock off the pot to see how the biscuits were doing. They were browning, so she knew they were about done. She set the rock back in place. "You boys go see if that horse is fed," she said.

Neither boy moved.

"Where's mama? Did she go to the river?" she asked.

Neither boy said anything. They were looking at the pot and their mouths were moving, as if they were chewing on something, and they were sniffing the air.

"Penny, how much money you goin' to pay me for a biscuit?"

"I ain't got none."

"Closet?" she said.

"I ain't got none," he said.

"Turn your pockets inside out."

Neither boy moved, except that their jaws kept chewing.

"You turn them pockets out," she said bluntly, "or you don't get a bite of my food."

They knew she was telling the truth. Penny stood and turned one pocket out but not the other, until she insisted. He had nothing inside at all, except a beat-up knife.

"Now hold both hands open," she said.

He put two little fists out and she grabbed one of them and wrenched it open and took the sack out of it, but he snatched it from her and went running toward the door with it. She grabbed his foot and tripped him and they rolled over on the floor, struggling for the sack. She was much stronger and she got it and brought it back to the fire and opened it, revealing seven cents. Closet was crying, his breath was choking him he was so angry. He crawled over to the fireplace and struck her on the arm, and tried to take his money back, but she held it tight.

"I'll give you a biscuit in a minute," she said removing the rock.

"You give me that there money." He struck her breast and she cried out, and she grabbed him and threw him to the floor and began to strike him, and Penny jumped on her back and began to strike her.

She kicked Penny away from the fireplace, where he had got two of the hot biscuits, one in each hand. "You let them biscuits go free," she shouted at him, but he ran to the corner, stuffing biscuits in his mouth. She went after him and Closet got a biscuit, so she came storming back and tried to retrieve that one, only to see Penny start out the door with the whole pot, even though it was hot and no doubt his hands were in pain.

"Drop that pot," she shouted, and went after him, but he was running across the yard, scattering the chickens and geese before him. She stumbled over a goose and lay on the ground, exasperated and furious. "You better not come back to this house," she yelled.

She saw one biscuit that had dropped from the pot, and she crawled on the ground to where it was and blew dust off it. She took a bite, spat specks of dust from her mouth.

She sat there munching bread and considering the sorry predicament of her life, the worn, lost fragment of her childhood hopes. Cumberland had irritated her so much that morning, she guessed she was through with him, and all men; yet she had nothing here in this place, either. She saw her mother come trudging up from the battling block, where she had been beating clothes. She was carrying a pail of water that sloshed out on her leg, and she was so tired that she didn't even notice. She was only forty-two years old, but she was lined of face and her teeth were gone. She had borne nine children, most of which had lived, and she had lost as many prior to birth, some naturally and some with a needle or with herbs. She had worked from sunup to sunset every day, and had slept in her filthy clothes, in the rags that she had made years ago. In a sudden moment of horror, HenryAnna saw herself in her mother's body, caught a glimpse of herself walking there twenty years or so later, up from her own battling block and her own spring, through her own yard to her own weary home, water sloshing unnoticed on her own leg. She closed her eyes tight and tried to do away with the vision, and when she opened her eyes again her mother was standing before her looking at her sharply.

"Why don't you go back down to your house, Anna?" she asked.

"He's there this weekend."

"You could spend the days with him, like you used to."

"I'll go down there Monday and spend the day when he's gone. I need to hoe the corn then, too."

The mother fanned her face with a piece of pine bark and belched. "My stomach's sour, Anna," she said.

"I'm sorry, mama."

"You'll have worse complaints. Your body gets to belching and objecting to might nigh everthing. Of course, if you marry that nice rich young man, you'll be able to have help around the house, which is a godsend. You can let somebody else do the diaper and cleaning work for you."

"He's not going to marry me, mama."

"Your pa says he's in love of you."

HenryAnna frowned up at her. "What's papa know about it?"

"He talked with him once or twice about you."

She was furious. "He better let me do my own life in my own way."

"Why ain't ye down there in the potter's house with him then?"

"We had an argument, that's all. He says I like Weatherby Wright."

The mother stood there fanning herself. "Has he a need to be jealous?"

"No, though I like Weatherby, and he needs me more now. He needs me more than anybody else."

"What's the matter with him that he needs you for?"

It was a fair question, she supposed. All she knew was that he was unhappy, not in a vague sense at all but deeply worried, that he was in need of being cheerful. "I help him laugh is all," she said.

"My, my. You'll lose your best chance over that?"

"Why not?" HenryAnna said, flaring up at her.

"Not much of a future in laughing, is there?"

"I don't want to talk any more, mama."

"He's got a wife to comfort him, ain't he?"

"I don't think of him in a husbandy way," she said.

The mother got to coughing and spitting and mopping at her brow. "You can't have two men at ary one time," she said. "You have to choose, and you have no choice, as I see it, for one's taken."

"I never said I had a choice."

"So you have to let the one man you can hope to get know he's the man you choose."

It seemed too simple. And too carefully planned. "Sounds like a game," she said bitterly.

"Does it?" the mother said. "It's not a game to me now, is it? It's not a game in that house, would you say? Or tramping back and forth for water six times a day. You listen to me, you figure out which man you can get and get him, if he's got money. I never had such a fine chance as you got."

"For God's sake, mama, you think it's a trap I'm to lay."

"You do what you need to do, damn ye," she said, and picked up the water pail and went on to the cabin, fussing to herself about having a daughter without good sense.

She stopped at the door and yelled to Penny to bring her cook pot back to the hearth.

That night the family assembled at dusk to go to bed. There was no fighting after her father got home, for he got nervous even if an argument developed. The children pinched each other, and they even struck one another when he wasn't looking, but they didn't fight.

HenryAnna helped her mother cook a fish stew. They put potatoes, onions and tomatoes in the pot with it. There were not enough bowls for everybody, so the boys used the same bowl, and HenryAnna and the baby ate out of the same bowl. They sat on the edge of the beds while they ate.

The father sang to them. He sang several songs, then lay back on his bed, curled up, and went to sleep in his clothes. He slept on the bed farthest from the fire, it being summertime; in wintertime he used the bed nearest the fire. The little children crawled onto other beds.

HenryAnna went outdoors and sat down near the spring, where she could let the air cool her for the night. The stars were clear and cluttered, like bits of ashes fallen into a dough. Penny came outside, yawning and stretching. He frowned at her and half apologetically said, "You want to go inside a tunnel tomorrow?"

"I do," she said.

"We was going to buy you and mama a present in Morganton with that money."

"You better use it for something more profitable," she said.

"We aim to get you a present."

"Yes, and eat it up afore I have a bite of it."

"I hope not, but when I get hungry I get spiced up," he said.

"I'll go in a tunnel, if it's safe. Do you think it is?"

"They go inside ever day," Penny said. "Except Mr. Weatherby is afraid to go."

She looked up sharply, but there was no sign of animosity on his face, so she let the remark slip by.

The owls were hooting, and now and then a wolf called. The wolves were the scourge of the earth, seemed like. They were everywhere abounding now. She got up and stretched, then knelt at the branch and splashed water on her face and arms. She stayed still while most of it dripped off, then she rose and went back to the cabin, stopping near Penny at the door. He stepped aside to let her enter, if she wanted to. "Good night," she said.

"Good night," he said.

She crawled onto a bed near her next oldest sister and lay there looking at the fire, which was bent low and was smoking. She could see her mother stretched out in the bed nearest the fire. That was her place in summer; in winter she was back next to the wall. Why she put up with such as that, HenryAnna didn't know, but maybe it was because there were traps in life that caught a person, like a trap in the woods would catch a fox or a beaver and hold it tight.

She knew she was trapped herself, trapped by her family and the need she had to leave home, and trapped by the love she had for Cumberland and the love she had for Weatherby. Her attitude toward them both was complicated by the Road, which daily became more and more dangerous to them and others, more and more demanding of them and others, so that both of them were tense all the time now and were less apt to be understanding.

It was all too complicated for her to develop a scheme, to make a plan. The three of them were like corks on a big sea. What she knew she really wanted was the house, and a man made up of qualities of both Weatherby and Cumberland. The closest she could come to that would be with Cumberland, and she did love him, but she didn't think he ought to boss her every action, or be jealous of her either, for she was a grown person. She knew well enough how to handle her relationship with Weatherby; there was nothing illicit about it, nor did she want anything illicit to come of it.

What she ought to do, she decided, was talk with Cumberland soon, and try to let him know she liked him better than anyone else, and wanted him more. And maybe try to want him more.

Next day the west portal foreman wouldn't let her go into Swannanoa tunnel. The idea of a woman going into the tunnel so perplexed him that he became upset. No woman had ever been in the tunnel, he said.

She sat down near the entrance and wouldn't go away. Mule carts were being pulled past her, and there were many stares from the men, but she sat there, anyway.

"You shouldn't ought to be here," the foreman told her. "These men get nervous when a woman comes about. It's bad luck fer 'em. A woman is problem enough fer a man even when he ain't in dangers."

The men did look at her strangely, she admitted to herself. They looked at her with squinted eyes and their teeth showing, even the Negro men. She guessed her dress was too thin, but there was not much she could do about that, and she knew her legs were long, but she couldn't shorten them, and the sunlight doubtless made her hair shimmer brightly, but there was no bonnet to hide it under.

"Be better if you was to go," the foreman said.

"Can I go inside?"

"Lord, no."

Soon she went on down to the Tunnel Station. She decided not to go into the office, for Weatherby always received her so cordially it would further estrange Cumberland. She waited outside in the yard, and after ten minutes or so Cumberland saw her and came outside, fumbling with papers and acting as if he was busy.

"Hello," she said.

He stopped and acted surprised, but he wasn't. They walked a ways together, and when she sat down on a log, he sat down beside her. She mentioned the weather kindly, and he said it was too warm except of an evening, and she told him the pool was full of cool water and had warm rocks for drying. "You might want to use that."

The suggestion did interest him. "Will you be there?" he said.

"Oh, I bathed this morning, and do most mornings," she said. She smiled as she glanced at him. "I haven't ever swam with you for long, though, have I?"

"How long you suppose we could swim before I started trying to make love?" he said.

"Till you caught me."

He looked at her sharply. "I'd catch you inside a minute."

"Not if I'm wet and slippery," she said. "Might take longer."

"I could get a hold of your ankle if I dove under the water."

"Law, what you going to do with my ankle?" she said.

"If I got your ankle I might get a hold of your leg."

"Yes? And what would that do for you?"

"If I follow your leg high enough, I'd get to the rest of you, wouldn't I?"

"Are you holding your breath underwater all this while?"

"I could."

"Wouldn't it be a sight if you got to where you was going only to drown?"

He laughed. He rocked back and forth on the log seat, laughing. "Anna, I don't know anybody else who can talk like you or look like you, who can get me so anxious. I've missed you, I admit it."

"Well, why did you? I only went home."

"I got to thinking such bitter thoughts, Anna."

"None of them so."

"Aren't they?"

"No," she said. "I told you they wasn't so."

"I'm—more ashamed than anything else. It would be the easiest thing in the world for me if I could forget you and, once the Road is finished, go back home. It's going to be complicated to change my life all around." He pressed her hand. "But I will. I will, do you know that? I can't help it."

"I can't either," she said.

He took her in his arms, even with the clerks watching from the office. He didn't care. But when he stopped kissing her and looked up again, standing in the office doorway was Weatherby, and the strangest look was on his face, an expression of pain and gladness mingled. Awkwardly Weatherby turned away, then impetuously he came out on the porch and waved to them and said, "I see you've found a proper way to spend the day." He went hurrying off toward a group of workers, not waiting for a reply.

HenryAnna wanted to go running after him; she would have

normally, for she sensed that he was hurt. But she knew now to stay with Cumberland. She closed her eyes tight and heard herself say, "I watched that path to my papa's house yesterday, and there was not a sign of you coming for me, and I spent time out working the garden at the cottage we rented, waiting for you, and you never come to walk the rows with me."

"I'm sorry, Anna."

"I missed you," she said.

"Yes," he said. "And I."

"Will you come have supper with me now, if I fix it?"

"Yes."

They walked toward the turnpike together, and only once did she look back in the direction Weatherby had taken, but Cumberland said nothing, and she didn't trust herself to say anything. When they reached the turnpike, he stopped her and slipped his arms around her and kissed her face and her nose and cheeks, then her lips, and he kissed her neck and she began to squirm, because she couldn't stand being kissed on the neck.

They reached the house in midafternoon. She had several kinds of apples in a bag, and they ate a few of those. She suggested they go out to the pool, so he agreed. Of course, once they got there, got acclimated to the cold water, he began to try to catch her and hold her, but she was able to escape him. Once he dove under the water, caught her ankle and turned her upside down in the water. He held her legs tightly, letting her up for air slowly, and he carried her out of the water and across the warm rocks to where moss grew on the warm ground. But even so and even there she scampered away, tantalizing him all the more.

Late that afternoon they walked through their garden, where she had planted cabbages, potatoes, onions, okra, corn and beans, and he helped her chop weeds from around the plants—even though she told him he ought not to do women's work. They talked with a farmer who was driving his wagon home from Old Fort, who said explosions on the mountainside had that day "deafened" his horse.

"The air has been so full of noise, it's deafened her, for she's not heard me since," he said, and to prove it he spoke to the horse and, indeed, she didn't move. "I'm agoin' to sue the Road," he said.

They walked to where the church stood back among the trees, serene in the late light, shaded and gray-colored from the aging of its wood. They went to the graveyard, where weeds grew among the stones, and they crossed a fence and went down to the river and walked along the river to where the millstream was, and came up that stream to the pond and went around the pond to their own house, arriving when it was so dark they had to help each other make out the path. "It's going to storm, I expect," she said.

"It didn't rain this afternoon."

"No, but it meant to."

"Can you see to build up the fire?"

There were warm coals left and she put new wood over them and blew on them, and he blew on them, until the fire licked at the logs and was burning well. They sat near it, and she said something about cooking supper, but she didn't move yet. "I missed you more'n I meant to," she said. "I suppose I told you."

"Yes," he said.

"We've got so much that hasn't been said that needs saying to one another. You want to visit me so's to make me happy, don't you?"

"Yes," he said.

"I don't want that," she said simply. "I don't want you to do what you do to make me happy. I hope someday you'll do it because of yourself."

"Yes, I am, Anna."

"Not because you want to, but because you have to, because of a need as fierce as any need can be."

He sat there not understanding, wondering about her, impressed with the calm maturity of her. "Anna, do you love me?" he said.

"Yes," she said simply.

"You have pretty blue eyes, Anna. I remember you down there in that pond today. You're pretty all over. Your legs were moving through the water like flashes of brown, and your thighs were white." He kissed her and picked her up in his arms carried her to the bed and looked down at her as his hand touched her face. "I love you," he said. His hand touched her breast. His hand moved to her stomach and her thigh, and she lay there watching him.

The fire burned brightly for a while, as if it knew them and wanted to see if they were loving each other. The fire was red and reflected on her skin as she lay in his arms, looking at his face and beyond his face, considering the thoughts she guessed he had which she wonderingly thought might be reflected in the light on the ceiling beyond his head. His hands were warm, as was the light on the wall beyond his shoulder, and she thought her feelings were as fine as a certain song she had composed and sung years ago when she had felt a pang of wonder so strong in her heart that her body had got as warm as a warming stone.

How gentle, she thought; how fine to find a man that wasn't all muscles and hurrying on with ever chance he got. How slow and gentle, she thought, as the fire grew warm and red and she heard her breathing grow faster. She clung to him as if she were fastened to the fire beyond his head, and she didn't want to scratch or bite him, but she guessed she did.

CHAPTER EIGHTEEN

TROY CAME UP to the mountains late that summer. He lived in the house with his father, but since Weatherby still had trouble sleeping, he asked Cumberland if a cot could be placed in his room for the boy, which was agreed to. Troy usually was in bed by eight o'clock anyway, and, of course, he was up at dawn, as was everybody else in the camp, so he was no problem.

He spent the days working at the nitroglycerin manufactory, which was not the job his father had chosen for him at all. He helped mix the mash and carried pails of it to the tunnels. There were five headings being worked on—two at Swannanoa, one at Lick Log, and two at the 220-foot tunnel down from Lick Log—so there were a lot of deliveries to tend to.

Troy came to know and like Esau pretty well, and he soon came to know Closet and Penny, too. One of their favorite habits was to gather fruit and nuts on the mountains and trade them to the guards and hired workers. Both boys could scamper up and down trees without even bothering to look where their feet were resting. Troy, of course, was jealous of their ability and felt self-conscious about his own ignorance of the mountain and of mountain ways, and of such swift tree climbing.

He was with them one evening outside Lick Log tunnel when Penny said, "We ought to go out on the mountain and gather new chestnuts in the morning."

"I expect we ought to," Closet said.

Troy noticed that neither of them looked toward him, and probably they weren't including him in the party at all, which hurt his feelings.

"Best way I ever saw to gather nuts was to blast the tree," he said, expecting at the very least to gain their attention.

Closet and Penny remained silent and studied that over. They looked off through the woods, letting the idea sink into their minds. "With what?" Closet said.

"Mash," Troy said.

The two mountain boys continued to speculate silently. Closet said, "You saw it done?"

Troy cleared his throat. "Yes," he said.

"You'd not be afeared to do it, would you?" Penny said.

"I aim to blast one tomorrow morning, close by," Troy said.

"You want to come in with us?" Closet said. "We could go in together, all three, and divide what profits we make."

"I'd best get back to camp right now," Troy said.

He started toward the station, but the two boys tagged along with him, mentioning the possibility of a partnership.

He was elated to know he could be accepted by them, but he was in a state of fever whenever he thought about the conditions. He was simply going to have to swipe a pailful of the mash and blast a tree, he supposed.

That evening he mentioned his general interest in blasting and nitroglycerin to his father, who discussed the subject in broad terms, saying little that Troy could apply to nut trees. Next morning, he told Esau "somebody had mentioned to him how they had used mash to blast nuts out of a tree."

"Don't think so," Esau said. "If anybody comes to you with a story like that, you ought to set him down for a fool. Nobody would use mash that-a-way."

"They shook the tree with a blast," he said.

"Don't think so," Esau said.

Dejectedly Troy went off to mix mash. He had no sooner climbed into the trough with the meal and started wading about than he saw Closet and Penny stick their heads up above a nearby rock. They whistled for him and held up a basket they had brought with them. He acted as if he didn't hear them. They began tossing pebbles at him, and he acted as if he didn't see them. So directly they came down to the edge of the trough and said, "When are you going to blast a tree?"

"Have to mix this mash afore I can blast with it."

"We're ready to commence," Closet said.

"Maybe you'd better go without me."

"We aimed to have a tree blasted sometime afore noon," Closet said. "You want to be in partners with us, don't ye?"

Troy looked at them frankly and had to admit to himself that he did want to be one with them and to be accepted by them. "All right, I'll blast one tree and that's all," he said.

They found a tree far off on the mountain, one which had been gaining its size for centuries. It had a fortune in nuts on it. "Law, look at them up there," Penny said, impressed.

Troy said, "Might be better to go higher on the ridge."

Penny caught his arm and detained him. "We've gone far enough," he said bluntly.

Troy sat down near the tree trunk and stared dejectedly at the pail of mash he had brought along.

"What you groanin' for?" Closet asked him suspiciously.

"Was I groaning?" Troy said. He crawled over to the trunk and examined it. There were many holes under its bigger roots. "No need to drill, I reckon."

"We ain't got a drill," Penny said.

"I'll pack the mash under these roots," Troy said, expecting them to object if what he said was wrong. All they did was back away and look solemn. "I'll pack it in now," Troy said, shoving his hand down into the pail, lifting a handful of mash and plopping it under the biggest root of all.

"You need enough to shake all the nuts free," Closet advised him. "Have you got enough mash in one pail?"

"Ought to be enough," Troy said. Lord, he didn't know how much it took to shake a tree. "I don't aim to do this ever day," he said. He laid a cap in place. "You want to bring me some dry leaves?" he said.

Closet and Penny gathered a supply of leaves, then retreated to a more distant place.

"What you running around so for?" Troy asked them. He laid the leaves in series, putting one dried leaf halfway under another, working his way down the bank from the cap until he had a five-foot length of fuse. He took out a match, gritting his teeth to keep them from chattering, and struck it.

Closet and Penny turned and fled. Troy was so astonished he dropped the match on the ground. "What's the matter?" he called after them, but they were hurtling down the side of the mountain as fast as they could run. "Hey?" Troy called. He saw that his fuse had taken light from the match, and his legs began trembling under him; panic got control of him and he thought he couldn't move, but suddenly he turned and ran for all he was worth. He clapped his hands over his ears, as he had seen Esau do, and braced himself for the explosion.

"WhaaaaaaaaaaaaaaaaaaaaaaaaaaaaaaaaaaaaaAAAAAAAMMMMMM!"

The explosion rolled across him. He was lifted from the ground and sent through the air. After him came a wall of loose earth which seemed to be enveloping him, even as he went sailing along. He was caught in the earth and cushioned by it as he fell.

He was dizzy and dazed by the fall, but he could see through the haze that where the chestnut tree had been standing was a hole in the ground big enough for a five-room house. There were no nuts on the tree because there was no tree. His own legs and chest were buried in dirt; only his head was free. He could breathe very well, he could yell, too, but he couldn't move and he sort of hoped he wouldn't ever be found.

It seemed like a long time went by before he saw Closet and Penny approaching about a hundred yards away.

"How you adoing?" Penny called. "Troy?"

Troy guessed they didn't see him.

"Where was that there tree standing at, Closet?" Penny said.

"Beyond that rock," Closet said.

"There ain't a tree there," Penny said.

The two boys stood in what had been the shadow of the chestnut tree. They looked up into the clear blue sky above, and stared around them vacantly, curiously waiting to be surprised by the tree.

"Where's the trunk?" Closet said.

"Must be down the mountain some'ers," Penny said.

"Where's Troy at?"

"Musta gone on home," Penny said, his voice trembling.

"Musta went on down the mountain with the tree," Closet said, "but I didn't see a sign of him passing by, did you?"

"No, that's the truth," Penny said. Turning in one direction and another, he began to whisper, "Troy? Hey, Troy?"

"He ain't anywheres about," Closet said softly.

"Him or his ghost is here for certain," Penny said. "Hey, Troy?"

"Musta gone down the mountain," Penny said hopefully. "Where you reckon them nuts are?"

"Hey, Troy, where are you, boy?" Penny said desperately.

Troy, who was only thirty feet away, spoke to them. "I'm behind you," he said.

Both boys turned slowly, reverently to look in his direction. Neither of them saw him. "Where?" Closet whispered.

Troy's arms and legs were paining him from being cramped in the earth. "Do you have a shovel?" he asked.

"No," Penny said, bewildered. He said to Closet, "Where is he? Can ye see him?"

"His ghost is atalking to us," Closet whispered.

"No, I'm not a ghost," Troy said.

The two boys began to scout along, keeping their eyes open for the telltale sign of ghost-wisps, walking softly, pushing bushes aside. Penny saw the head and he stopped and his teeth began to chatter. Closet told him to hush making strange noises, then he saw the head. It was nothing in the world but Troy's head on the ground.

"Ain't ye got a shovel?" the head said, and both boys turned and fled.

By late in the day Troy had chewed and spit out enough dirt to free one arm. It was easy after that to get out of the hole. He trudged to the station and stood under the creek spout for a while, then he went to supper. He saw Penny and Closet eating molasses and corn bread, and he stopped near them, considering them critically, realizing that they were not as courageous and daring as he had been, for all their boastfulness and signs of prowess. He heard Penny say, "He said he wouldn't do it ever day."

Closet nodded gravely and sopped more bread into his mouth. "It's just as well, for all the nuts it gained us."

CHAPTER NINETEEN

"IT GETS STUFFY in here, not going to be air to breathe," the Negro named Adam said. He was in the chain gang for murdering a man in a fight over money. "It gets ye by the throat and chokes ye," he said, breathing through his mouth. He held the drill for a minute, then stood back, gasping. "It's got my chest. It's like a man's got his arm around my chest, pulling close and tightening on me."

"Adam, we all go through it, same as you," a hammer man told him. "So hush your damn complaining." The men didn't like to listen to him talk about choking to death.

"How do you breathe in here?" Adam asked.

"Leave it be," somebody said. "If we don't work hard, we won't choke much."

The men were having a tightness in their chests, too, and a drowsiness in their heads. They drilled into the rock and gasped for breath, deep in the ground now, in the second little tunnel the Babcock gangs had to build.

It was getting late in the day when they hit a bed of shale through which water seeped steadily. Before long they were standing waist-deep in water, and a stream was flowing the length of the tunnel. The men waded outside, but the foreman came up to them. "You get back on the job," he said.

"We ain't got no job left," Adam said, inhaling deeply of the fresh air. "It's all water in there."

"Mister, we ain't fish," another convict told the foreman.

"Get back in there and drill," the foreman said. "We got a schedule to keep."

There was a lot of grumbling. It was nighttime, anyway.

"You goin' back in there?" Adam said to the other convicts. "You'll die in there."

"I know it," one man said. But they all went back in there, anyway.

At noon of the following day the men reported that the water had slackened. By nightfall it was merely a trickle. The foreman told the men to pump out the tunnel, which they did.

"When they going to have us carry our caskets in, Adam?" a convict asked him.

"We got a stone coffin this time," Adam said.

"When that judge said four year, did he know I never meant to do no harm?"

"Never mind, never mind."

"If he'd said two year, I'd be free by now."

"Man, feel your chest. Can't you feel the tightening?" Adam said. He had a headache, too, from the smell of the unexploded mash. And he was sleepy. Seemed like there was no air in there.

Esau came along with a pail of mash, crimping the cap with his teeth even as he smiled. He packed mash into the drilled holes and set the cap. "You men want to stay or leave?" he asked, and laughed as they started running.

The fuse was lighted, and he came running down the tunnel, along the rock-strewn floor, in the darkness, yelling. "Fall down and die, damn ye, Adam."

"I ain't planning to fall this time," Adam said, gasping for breath.

"She's going to blow in one second more," Esau said. They all yelled as they neared the exit. "Fire in the heading!"

They reached the portal as the blast came. They fell to the ground and rolled over seeking safety, Esau laughing all the while. That was the blast that opened up the heading of Number 2 tunnel.

Esau laughed easily, even about danger, but he could see what lay ahead for them, and certainly for himself. If he stayed a while longer, he might be given his freedom, but he might not, for

Raleigh wouldn't assure him of a pardon, and even worse, he might not be alive to enjoy it. He decided he ought to get away from this place where everything was all the time exploding. It was cool here in the summer, he would admit, but he would accept lowland heat if he could get home again and see his wife.

All he needed was a plan of escape, some way to avoid a trail those dogs could track.

Something fast and ready.

Like a train, he thought.

He would like to see those dogs try to trail a train. A train left no scent, and a train moved fast, and there was train track laid from Henry up to the Tunnel Station now—two boxcars had just been brought up for the women to live in. The work track was downhill all the way, so he wouldn't need the engine, which was up at Lick Log. The track went downward through little Tunnels 1 and 2 and through Bloody Cut, and went past Babcock Station and over Long Bridge, and through Mud Cut to Henry Station, and beyond. It was rough track but it was open all the way, and assuming he had luck he could ride a car down, maybe even to Old Fort, for it would be rolling so fast by the time it came to the bottom of the mountain it wouldn't want to stop soon.

It might take him to the first big river. There would be no finding him if it did.

He could take a boxcar of women with him, take them to freedom, too. That would serve his soul well. He could maybe take Lola with him.

No, he couldn't for she was in the uphill boxcar, and he would need to escape in the other one. That was the way life had of foxing a man, he thought, and foxing a woman, too, for if she had been in the other boxcar, she could ride to freedom in a train and, if she was caught, nobody could even say she had tried to escape.

He wished he could take her, if only to get even with Moses, who thought she was his own property. That irritated Esau, for he liked the woman very well and had wanted to spend time with her now and then on Saturday night. He had mentioned this to her at the serving line, but she had always been true to Moses, even though she claimed to be afraid of him.

Want to take a train ride, Esau? he asked himself. Want to go to ride? Want to see those mountain boys and dogs try to trail a train?

One day he cut a length of vine and wrapped it around his body, and that evening, the moon being bright, he took off his shoes and looped them by their straps around his neck. He crept out of the barracks to the wall of the stockade.

The vine was about twelve feet long. He held an end of it in each hand and pushed the looped end up the side of a post until it came to the top. He dropped it around the top of the post. He twisted the two strands of the vine together, then easily climbed the side of the stockade.

When he could see over the top of it, he saw that the guards were talking. The two guards for this stockade were supposed to stay at opposite corners, so each one could see two walls, but they wandered about keeping company with each other and the other guards. They had started a fire, they and the guards from the other stockades and the guard who watched the women's boxcars. The fire was downhill from the boxcars and the stockades. The guards were there talking and drinking coffee, and one of them jokingly said he wished the woman-convict guard would produce company for them. One of the men remembered a time he had slept with a woman convict in the East, and they listened to him, nodding and laughing and contemplating what he had to say.

Esau climbed over the top of the stockade wall and dropped quietly to the ground. A dog lifted its head and began to sniff the air; it barked a time or two, but it was only an unsure bark, as if the dog were asking something rather than reporting danger.

"I better get on back," the guard of the women convicts was saying. "My maids'll miss me."

"Miss who? You got any miss in there?"

"Not a miss among 'em any more," the guard said. "They been put to the ground so often here lately it's a wonder they don't sprout."

"You know for a fact that some of them don't?"

"No, not fer a fact yet." He got up and brushed his pants off, and one of the guards said he wished the judges would send more white women to the chain gang. "I get so tired going all the way to Morganton for so short a time," he said.

"Phil, they ain't going to send no pretty woman here."

"Don't they murder?"

"Yes."

"Then where air they?"

"The judge probably keeps them for his ownself."

Phil laughed. "No, no," he said and went on up the hill toward the stockades. He hadn't walked far when he saw the boxcar move. At least it flitted across his mind that the boxcar was moving toward him down the hill, and he blinked and looked again, and sure enough, there it was, rolling toward him. "Hell, look at that," he said to the others. "Hey, that damn thing is rolling, ain't it?"

The other guards could hear and see it now, too. It was coming toward them out of the dark, and one of them said, "Well, how you goin' to stop it?"

"Throw rocks on the track," somebody said, but there were no rocks at hand. There was nothing there but the logs on the fire, so they began throwing them onto the track. "It'll stop on that," somebody said, as the boxcar rumbled nearer, going faster. "Better take care it don't hit us," one guard said, and they ran to one side as the boxcar came sweeping through the logs, scattering the fire. Two of the logs got caught, and the car dragged them with a big thumping sound, and the fire on them was whipped higher by the wind as the boxcar rolled on.

"Come here, damn ye!" a guard yelled after it.

There it went, on down the track, gaining speed, dragging two lighted logs. At the curve the logs fell to the wayside, but they had caught the corner of the boxcar on fire. It wasn't much of a blaze, but it got bigger as it caught breath.

"Somebody stop it!"

"Get them dogs. Escape! Escape!"

Escape? Phil thought. Why, they stole the prison, as well as the inmates. He had to laugh. It was funny as could be to see a prison rolling away. "I wonder if them women is awake yet?" he said.

Down the mountain went the boxcar, a fire fluttering at its tail. It went through little Tunnel 2, and went faster through the other little tunnel, and went through Bloody Cut with a roar, scattering the loose rock that had fallen there.

Esau climbed to the top of the boxcar and held on desperately. The car was rocking and pitching, seemed like, and fire was swirling behind him. He forced his way into the wind until he could reach down and touch the boxcar door, and he leaned far over the boxcar and tried to catch the latch. He could see the latch, but he couldn't quite touch it, so he caught hold of a roof board with both hands and tried to knock open the latch with his feet.

He could hear the women inside screaming, and he saw the fire and smoke billowing up from the back of the car. The car would explode, he thought; it would explode like a puffball on a summer's day.

He caught the latch with his foot, but the train entered the curve that led down the hill to Babcock Station. He dug his fingers into the crack between two roof boards, and let the momentum of the car lift his body into the air.

Fire was licking at the front of the car now, as the car straightened into the tangent that led into Babcock Station. The fire was flashing at him. He kicked at the latch with his foot, but it wouldn't open. The fire was swirling around him, just as the cries of the women were around him. He pulled himself onto the roof of the car as the flames swept over him. An immense, smothering pain engulfed him as he lay there, and he heard himself laugh. He stood up. The women were screaming with the sound that was the color of the fire around him, enveloping him and coming from him, consuming him as he stood and saw the Road unwind before him.

The Babcock Station guards looked up, puzzled to see a lighted boxcar roll past. It was a ball of fire appearing out of the darkness, coming with a loud wail, a woman's wail sounded like. It rolled through the station and entered onto Long Bridge, trailing smoke and fire for a hundred feet, dropping lighted pieces of itself now; it tilted and jerked on the track and almost threw itself into the river. A guard later said it looked to him to be "a ball of fire with a big nigger standing on top of it burning like a torch."

"Fire, fire!" a guard called, but the words were lost in the confusion of the place, and the screaming of women—God knows where they were, but they sounded like women.

Down through Mud Cut, the white clay glistening red as the fireball rolled over it, going so fast now its wheels were almost coming from its axles, and the sound was a rumble and a wail as loud as wheels and fire and human voices could make it. Now and then a hurtling body, all afire, would appear to be shot from the back of the car, setting the forest ablaze along the Road, but most of all there was this sound the car made of crying and roaring and burning. The smoke rose from it and from the path it made, the car going faster, passing through Henry Station with a sound like thunder cracking that awakened and terrified everybody and brought Cumberland and the clerks to the porch of the office building, where they were working books. They saw a fireball go past, lighting its own path before it, burning a trail as it went, leaving a trail of fire, and shooting even now behind it a torch aflame which cried in a shrill voice, AHEeeeeeeeeeeeeeeeeeeEEE!

It went rocking on the rails across the big field toward Old Fort, leaving stunned men watching as smoke rose from the track where it had passed—ghost-wisps, they said, or brimstone smoke, Satan's signs of evil. Nobody knew what it had been, and Cumberland went to find it if he could. He had seen it, so it had been there, and it was not the devil, he concluded. Only one guard and one clerk dared come with him.

When they got to the curve at the far end of the field, they saw that a torch had been left on the track, and they ran to it, but the odor was stifling and the men drew back. "It's flesh," a man said.

"How's that?" Cumberland said, knowing what it must be but not accepting it, for he couldn't put it all together in any sensible way. "Is it a man?"

"Or woman."

"Why would he be afire?" Cumberland asked.

"It was the whitest blaze," the clerk said. "It was white as a piece of parchment."

Cumberland led the way past the burning figure on the track, moving upwind of it. They followed along by the light of the burning bushes near the track. The forest was burning, too, over beyond the station, in the places the ball of fire had passed. The forest and the roadbed had been seared into a blaze.

"There's a wheel," Cumberland said. A metal wheel was propped against a tree, as if somebody had left it there. It was sizzling and frying of its own heat. The scent of burning flesh nauseated them. They came to pieces of steaming metal, then to another wheel which was hot and was caught in a crotch of a maple tree. "Now how did it get there?" Cumberland said.

There was, of course, no explanation for it. The three men stared at the wheel, then moved on and walked for perhaps half a mile, until the smoke and odor were gone, and there were no other burning bushes or burning wheels, or anything else burning. Behind them they could see fire and smoke up on the mountain, twisting about on the side of the ridge, following the course of the Road, but there was no sign here of the projectile itself which had hurtled past. It had disappeared. It had burned itself to its own last cinder. It was left as nothing in the world but steaming iron rods and wheels.

CHAPTER TWENTY

RED TUTTLE, the engineer of the Mud-Digger, found a farm woman at Swannanoa, a Mrs. Nettie Davis, who didn't seem to have much to do; nothing, in fact, that would interfere with her fixing meals for him now and then, and sitting by the fire with him. He called this "keeping fire" with him, and nobody knew quite what he meant by that. He knew the woman was lonely, and he was often lonely for being with a woman, and he liked the way she cooked and the way she left silence alone and didn't try to fill every pause with a word or two.

She had married when she was eighteen, and had borne four children to that man. He died, and she married again "spanking soon," as she said, for with four children she had to do something to provide for them. This second husband had not been well chosen; he had been so mean "his own meanness killed him afore his years did," she said. By him she had four children, so she had eight, and they were grown now and, with their families, were scattered up and down one of the coves. From their many cabins they watched Red Tuttle come and go with a suspicious eye.

She was a red-haired woman, though it was partly gray now, and had bright eyes and a pleasant smile, and Red liked her. He explained the railroad to her. One night he talked an hour about how an engine gathered steam and how the steam was fed through pistons to turn its wheels. He told how the wheels held to the track even in wet weather, and maybe held to the track better in wet weather than dry. He told about the time this past winter when the fireman hadn't got the fire made in time and he had started the engine anyway, with much difficulty, and on the first grade he had been incautious about opening the throttle valves and had broken the key of the main connection of the crank axle.

The rod of the pump, which was halfway frozen, broke, and he bent the piston rod, and before an hour was up found he had water in his cylinders. He told it all, with the vexation and excitement of a man experiencing a vital experience, and she went on rocking and sewing and maybe listening.

He liked her; he liked quiet in a woman. What he wanted was to be able to talk himself. In an engine, with all the roar and clanking, he had precious little opportunity for it, or even to do much thinking.

He assumed she was interested in what interested him. "Come that boxcar down the track on fire, not that anybody knows it was that for nobody ever saw such a sight before, but we know there was a place where there was a boxcar parked, and it's not there now. Cumberland found wheels in the lowlands parked in trees, and any number of men remember seeing this rolling ball of fire that seared the countryside. I think it was a fired-up boxcar, but nobody knows what it was that did it."

She nodded while she darned, marveling to herself about his erratic way of breathing, like a nervous man using a chopping block.

"Cumberland says Esau must have started it and escaped in the confusion, but Weatherby says Esau wouldn't burn all those women. He says it was a tremor that started it."

She looked up at that. "Tremor?"

"Yes, tremor. He says there was a tremor. Did you ever have one?"

"I don't recall," she said.

"He says the earth moved, and that jarred the car loose."

"A tremor?"

"Yes," He didn't know what one was either and hoped she would tell him.

She went back to her darning.

"First one since I was in Pennsylvania," he said. "It burned down everything at Babcock except the infirmary. Babcock Station is nothing now but a hospital set in a burned-off field that is halfway a cemetery, overlooking a burned-down bridge trestle. Cumberland says it looks so bleak over there that a man sent there for sickness is bound to die. Weatherby don't visit the place now, even to go moaning over; he give it to that quare Dr. Chester for his own, and that's where the dead and dying crawl off to. Henry Station come out better. Those men go out of a morning to help repair what was done, and they haul in timbers for building Long Bridge back. To get enough dry timbers they're replacing two little bridges with culverts and a fill. All this is being done in hopes of having the Road open by spring, mind you, and 130 men are working out of Henry every day, dawn to dusk."

She was darning a pair of wool pants that her first husband, for the last three years of his life, had used in wintertime, whenever he wasn't hunting. Whenever he went hunting he put on cotton pants. He said a beast "could hear wool acoming," and he wouldn't have it about him on a hunt. He put on three or four layers of cotton and claimed he was warm enough. After he died, her second husband wore the pants until he got so big there was danger he would break them. He had worn the pants for about four months; that was all the time he had been both married and thin. Later, her youngest son had spent about two winters in the pants, growing large enough for them, but he had kept growing, not in fat but in bone and muscle. All in all, the pants hadn't been used much thus far, even counting all three men, so she was repairing the breaks in them and would see if Mr. Tuttle wanted to wear them when he came in from the train. She had heard so much about the train she felt like she knew what it was, all right, even without ever having seen one.

"Henry Station has about as many men as it was meant to hold, and they're also farming all we got to eat, which is corn meal, and now and then somebody shoots a deer or a bear. When the bears go into hibernation next month, we'll probably starve. Weatherby has ten mountain boys doing nothing but hunting game, but there's more'n 700 men and women down there with yawning mouths to fill, and you can't fill them with game. Weatherby trapped five wolves with bait the other night in a chicken coop, and the women must have cooked them, for I never tasted such a stew as we got the next day—not many men and not one cook would eat it. I picked out what I could recognize and ate that, the cabbage and beans parts of it. If I didn't come here to eat on Sundays, I'd be a long backbone with little pieces of skin fastened to it."

She had to laugh at that. And baggy pants, she thought, when he puts this pair on. These were tough pants, her first husband had said, and he swore by them for anything except hunting. She had made them of black wool. That was back when she had a fine flock of little black sheep. Her second husband had done away with the flock by driving all of them to market one October, for no reason except he knew she and her first husband had given special care to them and loved them so much. He finished that flock off in one drive. One season she had sheared them and had enough wool for pants and a blanket. She had never dyed them. They were natural and limber, as if they had just recently been carded and spun. The threads were strong and woven loose; they held well, and she had used new thread on the seams.

"So one camp is decent and one camp is a hospital now, and the big tunnel camp at the top is so crowded with men and women that it's like fair day in Reading. They had to move 150 men and women from Babcock up there, when Babcock Station burned. Weatherby said the men could sleep in shifts, one night and one day. He first had 300 on the day shift and 225 on the night, but he's about got it evened out now. There's men getting up as other men goes to bed, men picking up hammers as one gang goes home; we wash pots while we're cooking new meals in them. Most all the mules at Babcock was burned up or was maimed, and eight mules at Henry run and never was found. We're short of mules, so the men on the day shift usually don't have mules; they pull their own carts. Six men do the work of one mule. But you take sixty such men pulling carts, they don't do what my engine does. I can back two flats into a tunnel, and men can stand along either side and at the back of the flats, and load on rock as long as rock will stay, then ride it out and unload it. That beats anything you can do with mules. The mules are in the way and the carts are small and one man fills up his cart and the other eight or nine men ain't finished yet, so he has to wait, and they turn the mules, and there's always somebody getting kicked by one of them, or run over by a cart that one of them drags scared. But the only locomotive we got is mine and it's working at the downhill end of the tunnels, you see, working out of Tunnel Station like everybody else, like the mules and the men who work in the place of mules, but my engine beats all the rest put together, makes more progress in a day than any two gangs do without my engine. That's what I mean, it takes an engine to make a road."

Buttons were the worst of it. Years before she had put only two buttons on the pants. Her first husband had said they no more than closed up the gap partway, but she said there was nobody around the house to see in there, anyway, except her, and she had the washing to do of a daytime.

"Weatherby said if the men had to sleep in two shifts in order to have shelter, then they could work in two shifts. We had lost the Babcock tools, too, for they burned and melted, and the smith shop at Henry Station burned to the ground. He said that the day and night shifts would use the same tools. He solved the bedding and tool problems by putting men to work all night long. "It's dark in a tunnel, anyway," he told them, and they had to admit it. But one of them jumped up at the night-shift meeting and complained about the night's being so cold; and Weatherby said Lick Log tunnel, of a day and night, at the depth the men were working, was all the same temperature. Another man jumped up and said that when they came out to unload, the air was colder, and Weatherby said the men could warm up again when they went back into the tunnel. So they hushed, for they saw they couldn't outtalk him. We got to talking poor-mouth about how he wouldn't order them to do it, but how he was down to his last cent, with only enough to buy nitroglycerin with, and how there were thirty-one men on the sick call at that moment, some ill and some pretending to be ill, and how there were only five to six more months before a train had to roll from Old Fort to the Gap, either that or the Road wouldn't get finished in his lifetime and tens of thousands of people would be maimed for their lifetimes and poverty would continue to stalk God's mountains and a new way to the West wouldn't be opened up. He told them all that big news, and how they were a link in the chain that had started at Salisbury twenty years ago, before the thieving of the officers set in, and before the war. He told how the forest fire had cost them dearly of some of their timbers and tools, and he told how the rains had got in after the fire to erode the fills and undermine some of the little trestles. He said he wouldn't stop and they mustn't stop, either. 'Everything fails now and then before it succeeds,' he told them. 'This is your big chance to make your lives into a monument,' he told them. He said that to them big niggers and white convicts, and they believed him, and then he said, 'Are you willing to do this extra duty?' And by God about half of them shouted out all in a voice that they would, and the other half got ashamed of their reluctance and tried to be the first ones to get the mules hitched, for they were all part of the night crew and did at least get the best use of whatever mules we have left. They're a pitiful sight of mules, for they've not had much grain and God knows they're shy of tunnels. They've been driven and beat and prodded into them till they're red-eyed and mean; you'd think they'd get accustomed to it, even if it is misery, and go ahead. I take my train into tunnels ten times a day and it don't bother me, and now I'll start taking it in at night and sleep in between the trips, either that or Weatherby will find a new engineer at night. He's a driver. He's like a person that's possessed with a single idea, and not slides nor injury nor fire will deter him. He's got that look in his eye that Jesus musta had when they were beating him with their whips in the Temple, as if to say, 'All right, I'll forgive you what you're doing to me but I won't stop doing what I've been doing to you.' He's like that with her."

"With her?" Nettie said, looking up. "With her?" she said.

"With the mountain," he said.

It made no sense at all, so she went back to darning. She had guessed he had HenryAnna in mind, for she had seen Weatherby and HenryAnna together often. Not that anything went on between them, necessarily. And on weekends that college man come there and HenryAnna was with him, and maybe nothing went on with him either, but she guessed something had to go on with somebody now and then, even if by accident, for no woman stayed in a warm house with a man and nothing ever happened. If that HenryAnna wasn't pregnant by now, she would be, and which man it was done it to her would be a question fairly asked, and maybe the hair and eye coloring of the child itself would, years later, be the only answer given.

She tied the thread, bit it off and held out the pants to Tuttle, who glared at them. She had interrupted him in talking about how somebody named Moses could haul a mule cart by himself. She tossed the pants onto his lap. "I fixed them for you," she said.

"For me?" he said. "Why, I got pants."

"I want you to have them," she said.

"Why?" he said blankly, baldly. "Why, Nettie?"

"Well, you come to eat my meals and set by my fire, and I thought you might as well wear pants I'd made, too."

"Then I'd be hog-tied for sure, huh?" he said, grinning.

"You're going to be struck with a poker," she said. She folded her arms tightly on her breast and glared at the fire.

"You want me to wear them?"

She said nothing.

He got up right then, went behind her chair and put them on. He appeared before her again, looking down at himself, feeling the pants to see how they fitted across the hip. "I'd rather have them big," he told her, showing her how they sagged on him. "I have to clamber up and down in that there Road so much—"

"You're not to wear them on the Road," she said.

"Huh?" he said, startled. "I allus wear my pants on the Road, in my work."

"No," she said. "When you come to see me, you can take off your Road pants and put on these. You can have one pair for work, and one pair for comfort."

He could understand the sense in it, though he would never have thought of such an arrangement himself.

"Them other pants smell like they been inside a firebox," she said.

"You and me planning to go to church sometime?" he asked, winking.

"We can go any Sunday you want to," she said.

"You ain't planning to get married, are ye?" he said, brushing the pants down smooth, feeling the good cloth they were made of.

"Not likely," she said.

"I'd marry ye, Nettie," he said.

She pressed her arms more tightly against herself, but she didn't say a word to him.

"You come with me some afternoon and we'll get together. What do you say?"

She said nothing.

"Huh?"

"I say you don't love me."

He sat down on the rocking chair and stared at her bleakly. "You know how often I come here."

"You like to be here, I know."

"Because of you. Why, you often surprise me pleasantly, Nettie. And whenever I'm not here, I think about you and wish I was here."

She rocked and said nothing, but after a long time she said, "I once knew a young woman that was courted by a young handsome man, and he come to her house ever week and said the prettiest things to her, and he did like her ever so much and liked to be with her, for she was a pleasant, smiling person, and they could walk together and have a considerable time. And there was another man, much older, who come to her place; he was a farmer and chair-maker, and he was lonely, and he seemed to find meaning to himself only when he was with her. It wasn't only pleasure with him. And she married him."

"She did?" Tuttle said.

"A woman won't marry the man who offers the most or even is the most handsome, not if somebody else needs her the most."

Her pretty voice spun out the meaning, and Red Tuttle sat in the rocker and tried to figure it out. "Well, I don't know," he said finally.

"Of course, one can marry for pleasure, and soon a baby comes and binds all three together. The couple comes to needing each other in that-a-way, so love can grow that-a-way with the young, but it can't go that-a-way with me."

"No," Red Tuttle murmured. She never had said all that before, and he wasn't sure he liked it. He had thought he understood her, that she was comforted by his being with her and wanted him to be there, and here she had given him a pair of pants and had let him talk about trains, yet she wouldn't marry him. Hell, he would marry her; might as well, for he had nothing else on the boards. But she wouldn't marry him, and her refusal would have hurt his feelings, if she hadn't just given him the pants. "I'll get on back to the Road," he said. It was early evening and he could stay longer, but he was anxious to go think for a while. "Nettie, you're complicated," he said.

"Listen to that," she said.

"You are."

"Is there a woman who's not?" she said.

"I thought you was one."

"No, no. We all have to be needed, not in passing but needed, even if we know it's only for a little while."

"Uh-huh," he said uneasily. He went behind her rocker and changed pants. He came back into view, feeling awkward in the work pants he had on. "I'll be going, Nettie," he said. She said nothing, and he leaned over and pecked her fondly on the cheek. She had rosy cheeks, even though she was in her fifties. "Good-by, Nettie."

"You come back soon," she said. "I'll make a chicken dumpling pie Sunday morning."

"I'll think about all you told me," he said. "Where you want me to hang up these new pants?"

She took them from him and laid them on her lap. "I'll hang them," she said.

"Nettie, I like what you said," he said gently. He went to the door and fiddled with the handle, wondering if there was something he had forgot to say. "Was he your first husband, that older man?"

"Yes, he was," she said.

He went out, and she sat there, listening to his footsteps on the porch and on the steps that went down to the walk. She thought she could hear his footsteps on the walk, just as she sometimes had thought as a young woman she could hear her first husband's footsteps.

She sat there rocking and felt fondly of the cloth from the black flock, and even put a bit of it against her cheek where he had kissed her.

Night and day now the Tunnel Station was a hive for labor. At dawn corn meal was mixed with water in the kettles, and it was served without ceremony, slopped onto the men's plates. There was a time to eat: one ate quickly. There was a time to go to the Road: one moved quickly. There was a time for work, twelve hours each day for each man, and the new schedule permitted only half an hour each day for the noon and midnight meals.

When, finally, it was time for one gang to return to the camp, they passed the other gang on the trail. "We got the tunnel warmed up for you," they told them.

There was a time for getting into the barracks: If you don't get the same bed as last time, get another, but try to get an untorn one, and maybe even a clean one.

There was a time for sleep, if you could sleep with men around you moaning and arguing and fighting.

But on weekends there were the parties at the fields and in the woods, with singers and women—Saturday night for the day shifts and Sunday afternoon for the night.

Weatherby had hoped to construct a road that would be stabilized and finished, with tunnels at least 10 feet wide and 12 feet high, with broadly based fills and wide cuts, with steady bridges that would last for decades, with good ballast on the roadbed and closely spaced ties and the best grade of iron.

Now he was willing as a temporary measure to settle for anything he could get, provided he could have it operable by spring. A train must leave Henry Station and climb to the Gap unhindered. Maybe the ballast wouldn't be deep, maybe the iron wouldn't be heavy, maybe the roadbed wouldn't be even, maybe the benching in the tunnels wouldn't be finished or the full height wouldn't have been blasted out yet, but it would be open, and so it would prove that a road could be opened. Later, men would simply have to finish it, spend a year or two putting it in proper shape for comfort and permanence. What he was willing to settle for was the basic Road itself, the lifeline which would let trade start moving between the two worlds. The Road could be improved month by month, out of the profits from the traffic on it.

The part of the Road in the lowlands, which he was also responsible for, needed repairs. Thousand of its ties were rotted, and its iron had proved to be too light a weight for the loads it had carried. Later, later, he thought, he would have to worry about all that, too.

He told Red Tuttle he would open the mountain Road by spring. "But if your engine breaks down, we'll have to repair it on the spot," he said. "With Long Bridge out there's no way to get it back to Henry Station. We'll move a forge in there, when it breaks down." His schedule had all sorts of contingencies in it like that; the schedule would work out, provided there was no breakdown anywhere, and provided the men did as much work as he required of them. This schedule for work was devised simply:

1. There were 1,600 feet of tunnel heading yet to be broken through.
2. There were 100 days, working six days a week.
3. This meant the men must open 16 feet of heading a day.

The schedule was set so that the gang at the west portal of the Swannanoa tunnel did 4 feet of heading a day, the east portal gang did 5, and the gangs that worked on Lick Log tunnel, with the Mud-Digger and Red Tuttle, did 7. If the gangs could hold to this schedule, the last load of rock would be taken from the Swannanoa tunnel on the last day the convicts were to remain.

It was a simple figure: 16 feet of heading a day, 96 feet a week. The figure was the critical one for the Road. Beyond that,

Weatherby needed to know how the benching was going, how well the fills were being made, how progress was going on the work track and on Long Bridge. All these reports were due each Thursday night. Also, a report was due from Babcock Station concerning the number of men on sick call and their condition. Also, a report was due from Henry Station on the progress of repairing the erosion, on the condition of Mud Cut, on repairs being made to existing fills and bridges, and on the finances of the Road. In addition, each Friday night Weatherby would receive a report on the condition of the remainder of the Road.

For the first week in October the report stood at 88 feet of heading, eight short of what was needed. He urged the men to make even greater effort, and he urged the explosives men to take more chances. The second week in October the report was 92 feet of heading, only four short of what was needed. He urged the men on, and he talked with Tuttle and urged him to take even more risks with the Mud-Digger. At the end of that week the report was 90 feet of heading—that was all.

He bought wounded stock from the drovers at low prices, and the food on the Road improved. He told the convicts he was doing this in hopes of better work, and the fourth week in October the report was 100 feet of heading.

So they could do it; they had done 100 feet in one week, but for the month they had done less than enough to meet the schedule.

He bought all the wounded stock he could, signing notes payable in a year. He had a smoker built near the turnpike, had hickory wood brought there, and four convicts butchered stock, peppered and smoked it; they made jerky out of it and put the jerky in meal sacks. They worked the smoker night and day for two weeks, and cured enough meat to give a taste, anyway, to the stews for a month or more.

When Weatherby got to Morganton on Friday night, he would usually go over to the engine house and shake hands with the men and ask them how they were getting along, and he would climb the steps to his old office. Every time he went into that room, he stopped at the window and looked off at the mountain, but he didn't have much affection for it now. The mountain wasn't any longer a kindly creature; it was vicious and dangerous. Yet beyond it lay the mountain world, and he remained idealistic about that; he longed to help the people there and to free himself from a sense of obligation to them. He was idealistic not about the Road, which was a muddy problem, and not about the mountain, which was antagonistic, but about them, the cause and motive of his labor. He was in the yoke, pulling at the hard load, because of them, and to help free them. So he told himself, and justified even the excesses, the illnesses and deaths—almost every week at least one man was dead, and sometimes there were two or three men died of the croup, died of a blast, died of old age, died in a slide, died when struck by a hammer . . . The graveyard there on the hill above the infirmary was a festering sore that wouldn't heal until the labor had finally ended, with success or failure.

When he left the office, he crossed the yard and climbed the hill to the square. He noticed that Mildred didn't rush to meet him now, and he understood why. Once he had come home gladly and had brought with him a feeling of health and warmth; of late he had been gloomy.

He opened the door quietly and felt in his pocket for his matchbox, took out a match and lighted the lantern; he heard Troy and Mildred. "He's home," Troy said, and ran to greet him, and Mildred came hurrying downstairs. He embraced her and went with the boy upstairs and put him to bed and talked with him. When he came downstairs, Mildred fixed hot cider for him, then gave him a report for the week. She told him what the boy had done, and how the grocery had overcharged her one day, and how the roof leaked over the back bedroom and how much cordwood had arrived.

So in the course of a few days he got reports from just about everybody, and made decisions about just about everything from cordwood to the lives of workmen, and the desperateness of some of it made all of it desperate to him and tinged all his conversations with grimness, made his attitude toward the kindliest family concerns tense and exaggerated. He realized this and regretted it, but he couldn't seem to do anything about it.

If he were confident of winning, he would be more relaxed, but even the Morganton newspaper, which had supported the Road all along, now wrote in a piece, one Mildred showed him when he got home in late October, that the Road obviously could not be done by spring, and maybe could not be done at all. "There are rumors of a possible investigation of negligence," the paper said.

"Negligence?" he said. "Were you worried about this?"

"Yes," she said.

"You believe this?"

"I don't know," she said simply.

He went to her and tilted her chin up in his hand. "Mildred, trust me—"

"We all trust you. But I'm worried about you, too."

"Mildred, don't worry—"

"What would happen to you," she said, "if ever you were to fail?"

"We won't fail. The men are capable of it, Mildred."

"Even convicts?"

"Yes," he said. "Thieves, murderers, rapists, vagrants. We'll open up the Road."

PART III

Swannanoa tunnel, all caved in,
Head it out, boys, head it out;
   Pull the mule lines,
   Sledge the drill,
   Lay the mash
   And blow it to hell,
My girl is waitin' on the other side.

CHAPTER TWENTY-ONE

THE COTTAGE OF Cumberland and HenryAnna was only half a mile from the west entrance to the Swannanoa tunnel; she could walk to it in less than ten minutes. The men were always blasting over there, and the mule carts were unloading rock, so it was worth the effort to get to, and the variety of activity was such that she never tired of it.

She could even hear some of the work from the house.

One of the nearby farmers said the noise had made his cows stop giving milk. The miller was disgruntled, even though the clanking of his millwheel had pestered the community for a generation or so. The storekeeper said the noise and earth-shaking explosions had caused his stove chimney to stop drawing smoke. But HenryAnna enjoyed the spectacle, and the smith also was happy and spent most of every day at the more distant Lick Log tunnel, hoping Tuttle's engine would need repair.

Penny and Closet had got themselves assigned to the Swannanoa tunnel, to this west portal, which was near their own house, and sometimes of an afternoon HenryAnna would walk over there and wait for them to get off work. They would often come home with her to supper. If Cumberland got to the cottage, he could eat with them, too.

She was at the tunnel on a Wednesday in the second week of November when she heard a rumble, as if the earth itself were clearing its throat. She felt the rock under her tremble. Men near the entrance looked up questioningly but they weren't startled or afraid, and she wasn't either. There had been no loud report, there was no shocking sound at all, nothing to indicate danger.

A big man came running out of the tunnel, and Closet came close behind him. Both of them were dust-covered, and the man suddenly stopped and put his hands to his mouth and shouted "Cave-in!" There was terror in his voice, which so surprised HenryAnna that it lifted her to her feet and she began to walk along the Road, away from the tunnel entrance, seeking a place for protection. "Where's Penny?" she asked Closet, who had fallen to the ground; he was lying there trembling. "Where is he?" she said, shaking him.

"I don't know nothing," he said, tears running down his face.

"Did it bury them?"

"Anna, I don't know," he said.

Dust was pouring out of the tunnel now. It gushed out and rose far into the air. Men started coming toward the tunnel from the direction of the Tunnel Station, but they had to stop outside, where HenryAnna was. She asked one of them if he was going to save her brother Penny. The man grimly stared at the tunnel. She moved past him and went through the cloud of dust and on inside. A man ordered her to come back out of there, but she went on anyway.

She couldn't see, so she groped along, feeling her way. A man grabbed her. He held her around the waist tightly, even when she beat on him; she realized finally that he wasn't harming her. "You can see better if you hold a candle," he said.

He went on, other men following. They were black shadows around her. A few of them had lanterns. She heard a man at the tunnel entrance say, "Move those mule carts in, if we call fer 'em."

They stumbled over loose stone, and then they stumbled over a man's body. One of the men turned him over and held a light close to his face. "Ain't that Fletcher?" he said.

"Leave him there," a man said, and went on, the others following. Nobody else paid attention to the dead man until HenryAnna knelt beside him. He was a young white man. She pulled him to one side, so people wouldn't have to step over him, and she held him for a moment.

She could see dimly the dusty tunnel entrance. Several men were standing there; beyond them a few mules, their carts hitched behind, were waiting.

When she went deeper into the tunnel she came to the wall of rock which had fallen to block the passage. None of the men standing there seemed to know what to do. "Can you hear them?" she whispered.

"No," a man said.

"Have you called to them?"

"No," he said.

After a while a man knelt at the wall and used a stone to tap on another stone. He tapped a number of times, then listened. There as no answer.

"We ought to dig them out," a man said.

"Has it stopped yet?"

"What?"

"The cave-in. Has it stopped?"

The men slowly turned to look at the walls around them, and at the ceiling above them, moving the lanterns through the dusty air.

"Here's a shovel to start with now," a man said.

"When you reckon they'll tell us to dig them out," a man said.

The mules were driven into the tunnel. Other workers went inside. Weatherby arrived. He stood outside the tunnel and listened to the men tell him part of the tunnel had fallen in and only two men had got out. Another forty men were inside, and there were mules in there, too, maybe four mules. "It was the day shift and they didn't have many mules, or it'd be worse," the gang foreman said.

"The carts were in there. Maybe some of the men got under the carts," Weatherby said. He was pale and agitated.

"Maybe they had time fer it."

"Nobody knows how far it fell in," a man said. "They might not a got under it."

"The night shift is due," Weatherby said.

"Yes, there'll be another seventy men here afore long."

"How long will they live and not smother?" a worker said.

"How far to the start of the cave-in?" Weatherby said.

"Eighty to a hundred feet."

"How far into the ground were they working?"

"Five hundred feet. Wasn't they that far, Jim?"

"Take thirty of the night-shift men and start digging in from above on the ridge," Weatherby told the foreman.

"Can we free them that way?" he asked.

"I don't know," Weatherby said. "The rest of you men ought to start to work in the tunnel here."

When the night shift arrived and were busy, Weatherby had time to stop near the fire HenryAnna was sitting by. He sat down near her.

"My brother name of Penny is in there," she said.

"No," he said. "Is he?"

"I saw him go in."

"What was he doing in there?"

"Candlelighting."

"I'm sorry, Anna." His hand trembled as he reached out to touch her arm.

"Are they dead?" she asked.

"If we can get air to them, they won't die. We're doing that now."

"I saw papa here a minute ago. There he is, standing over there." She called to him and he came over to her and embraced her. "Don't you worry none yet," he said. "That boy is a lucky one. I named him for his strange way of always turning up bright."

Closet sat down across the fire from them.

"How much of it caved in?" the father asked.

"Maybe only a short way," Weatherby said.

"It's not got you worried yet?"

"Yes, it has."

"Not enough to stop building a road, though?"

"No."

"Change the face of the world, will ye? One man's custom is

another man's change, they tell me. I lose a son and the community maybe ends up with a new machine to ride pigs on." He dusted his pants off and went stumbling toward the tunnel entrance.

HenryAnna said, "Don't worry about what he says to you. He's so worried about Penny is all."

"I know."

"You look so tired."

"Oh, I am tired, Anna."

"You're more than tired. You're troubled."

"Yes. The pressure's not great, except when you're losing. You feel the full weight on you then."

She took his hand in her own and held it. He looked at her and she kindly smiled at him, then she leaned over and kissed his hand and released it, as if it pained her to hold it any longer. She sat there looking into the fire, and all the while he watched her.

"You're beautiful," he said quietly.

"Am I?"

"Even more beautiful than you were when I first saw you many months ago. You're more mature."

"I'm not as brash as I used to be, but I'm more confused now."

"About yourself? About what you want?"

"Oh, I can't say what I want, except I know I want to leave that little rotten cabin of my papa's and have a place of my own. That isn't what I want either, though."

"What else?"

"I don't know how to say it."

"Try to say it."

"I want to love somebody."

"Cumberland doesn't love you so deeply, does he?"

"Can he love deeply, when he's not known a need in his life?" She smiled briefly. "I'm sorry to be so personal," she said.

The men in the tunnel found a body, one crushed by the rocks and cut by the picks and shovels of the workers digging him free. The corpse was laid in one of the mule carts and was brought out, two men leading the mule, which was shying as if it knew it carted a dead man.

"What does the mule care? It's a lighter load than stone," a convict said.

A dead mule was uncovered, too, so the men hitched another mule to it and dragged the body out. The live mule must have guessed what was bumping along the stone floor, and it began to pull faster, then faster still, and was running as it came out of the tunnel's mouth, two men holding to it, trying to hold it back. The mule came swiftly into the open, kicking defiantly.

"Get her stopped, damn her," but there was no stopping it now, and the mule went running down the valley, pulling the dead mule, fleeing from the thing it dragged behind.

Closet stood nearby, looking at HenryAnna, trying to decide what he ought to say. He was mournful, and he kept saying, "Anna, you want to go home? I do, Anna."

"Not yet."

"I want to lie down."

She made him lie down close to her and put his head in her lap.

The workmen were hauling rock out. The carts continuously creaked on the stone floor. The men wanted to hurry, but they were working around death, so they moved cautiously. The mule carts rolled slowly into the tunnel, and after a while they came out loaded. Men solemnly came with them and unloaded them. It was all part of a dream, or so it seemed to HenryAnna, and there was no sense of emergency to any of it. The men sometimes sang; they made up a song they repeated back and forth to each other.

> Rocks fall, a man can't hold them.
> Rocks fall; a mule can't hold them.
> Rocks fall; a prayer can't hold them.
> Rocks fall, rocks fall on me.

Other men were working on the hill, trying to break through from above.

Closet lay with his head in HenryAnna's lap, now and then sleeping, moaning when he slept. Cumberland came up to the fire and sat down. He tried to comfort her; he was confident Penny would be all right, he said. "A boy is agile and quick, and that brother of yours takes care of himself. They'll probably find him nestled in some cranny or other, as healthy as ever."

She wanted to believe it. "He always was one to come up bright, papa says."

"He'll be safe."

The diggers found another body and carted it out. Cumberland said, "The men must have been on their way outside when it caved in."

"What could have made the tunnel fall?" she said.

"The mountain takes a contrary notion," he said, and he realized he had answered like Weatherby would, and even had used words Weatherby might have used.

At dawn she and Cumberland walked over to the cottage and made coffee. Closet came over soon and went to sleep on the bed. Cumberland said he would go back to the tunnel, but HenryAnna lay down on the bed and rested for an hour or so. When she returned to the tunnel, the work was proceeding and workers said Cumberland had gone to the office with Weatherby. "Could Penny still be alive?" she asked a foreman.

"Yes," he said, "for there's plenty of tunnel in there and maybe not all of it collapsed at the one time." He grumbled disheartenedly. "Though it all will someday, no doubt."

"Shouldn't you prop it up with logs?" she asked.

"We could do something like that if we had time."

"Maybe better take the time," she said.

"We'll get the Road open first. We're in a combat with this old woman here, Mr. Weatherby says." He looked up respectfully at the dome of the mountain. This was his third autumn on the Road; he had joined the Road when it was laying iron out of Morganton toward the west. "If we can meet the dangers for another three months, we can worry then about how to prop it up."

"Boys shouldn't be worked in there," she said.

"I agree with that," he said, "but those brothers of yours are as eager as can be."

A few of the night gang stayed on to help the day gang, and ten or twelve mountain boys were standing around, leaning on rifles and sitting on rocks near their hound dogs. Farmers on the turnpike, hearing about the cave-in, came over to be near what was happening. They stood about the tunnel entrance, or near where the crews were trying to get through from above, and squinted at the eastern sun and hummed old tunes. The two dead men who had been found were in carts, covered with boughs to keep the sun off them, and to keep the swarms of flies away, too.

Weatherby came across the field toward the tunnel, his crutches catching on briers. He came on to where HenryAnna sat. She felt the sense of sympathy he had for her, one deeper than anybody else's, and she instinctively held out her hand to him and he took it. Another cart rolled noisily out of the tunnel entrance. The mule shied from it and had to be restrained. A man called to Weatherby, "It's the third 'un," and the mountain boys drew back, suspicions chilling them. They didn't want even the sight of a dead man to contaminate them.

Weatherby walked to where the gang on the ridge had blasted out a hole about eight feet deep. It was such a small heading that only one man could work in there at a time. "We're depending on the mash to open it up big for us," the foreman told him.

Weatherby reached inside with a crutch and tapped on the far end of the hole. There was no answering tap at all. The foreman dropped into the hole and tapped on the wall with a rock.

There was no answer.

Two men approached with a drill and two hammers. Weatherby and the guard got out of their way, and they crawled in and began to work. Most of the workmen were merely standing about.

Weatherby walked to the Gap, then back to the west portal, where men were gathered around a mule cart that the mule was shying from. "We keep finding them, Mr. Weatherby," a foreman said.

Later that morning everybody ate corn bread and some kind of stew, maybe a lamb stew. HenryAnna ate along with the others.

Cumberland came up to see what progress had been made, and he went into the tunnel and walked with the men to where the cave-in had been. While he was inside HenryAnna was beside herself with worry for him, and so was Weatherby. When he came back outside, both of them embraced him, and Weatherby emphatically told him not to go in there again. "What if we lost you?"

"The Road would make out," Cumberland said.

"The Road might not," Weatherby said. "And we might not. What about Anna here?"

Cumberland was embarrassed to hear such sentiments expressed, and was unable to reply. "I'll be all right," he said.

By now a large group of mountain men and boys were camped there in the field, patiently waiting to find out what the cave-in outcome would be. "I wouldn't want to miss out on something that might matter to somebody," one of them explained to Cumberland. Most of them were on their way home, but a few even had their stock around them; by dusk the field had twenty fires burning, and several flocks and herds and droves, penned and unpenned. Cumberland could distinguish the different calls for geese and sheep and cattle and hogs and horses and dogs.

The night gangs came on. The day gangs went to supper, except for Moses and a few workers who didn't want to leave yet, who were willing to work at night, too. Weatherby told the sled boy to bring food for ten such men.

Moses, as Weatherby walked past, spoke to him. Weatherby turned to him.

"You'll lose it," Moses said.

"You and me?" Weatherby said at once.

"You can't build it now," Moses said.

"You can't, Moses?" Weatherby said.

Moses frowned at him, his eyes squinting. "I'm not the one."

Weatherby stared at the tunnel entrance, and when he looked again at Moses he saw the most perplexed look on his face, as Moses tried to study it through.

"You'll lose it all," Moses said.

Weatherby walked off from him, shaking his head.

If the rest of the men were alive, as he believed they were, he could expect to make up all this lost time, but if the forty men were dead, he would be deeply in debt, indeed. If the cave-in was fifty feet long, he would be able to clear it within a week or so; if it was a hundred feet or two hundred feet long, he would have a near-hopeless amount of heading to do, beyond what he had scheduled.

He felt he could win out if his losses were no greater than he now knew them to be: four men dead and a day and a half of work lost for three gangs. He might overcome such a loss as that.

Another cart rolled out, a dead man in it. So there were five men dead.

Another mule was dragged out, two convicts holding to the harness to keep the pull-mule from shying.

Weatherby saw Moses watching him from across the fire. He saw HenryAnna's father watching him accusingly, and he turned from him and went over to where HenryAnna was. Cumberland came up to him and said he was dead-tired and would go down to the office and wait for telegrams. "We're beginning to get inquiries from newspapers," he said.

Weatherby nodded. "You know what to tell them better than I do."

HenryAnna's father had heard the word "telegram" and had come closer. "They want to know, do they?" he said. "Tell them the Road is through, and by that I mean it's finished. Tell them at this place, on this night, the Road to the West came still."

Cumberland ignored him. "You going to sleep?" he said to Weatherby.

"No, not yet."

"Anna, you better get some sleep," Cumberland said gently.

"I'm not sleepy."

"Tell them anything done beyond now is wasted effort," Henry-Anna's father said, moving along beside Cumberland.

Weatherby stayed with HenryAnna. When she became conscious of his watching her, he moved from her and went to the tunnel's entrance and stood there in the hollow, black pit and listened to the echoing sounds of the men working in the distance, picking up the rubble that had fallen, dumping it into the wooden carts. A mule appeared, blacking out the line of candles. Slowly it came toward him, a convict leading it. Weatherby stepped aside as it came past and he saw, even though he meant not to look, the body of a dead man in the cart, one crushed and broken, a white convict named Kraft whom he had often talked with on the Road. The convict had been reared in the mountains and had believed in the importance of the Road, had wanted it to go, as he had said, "right up to my front door and circle the house afore it passes on into Tennessee."

Weatherby stood there for an hour or so, and in that time maybe twenty mule carts came out loaded with stone, and two came out carrying one dead man each.

Dinner was corn bread and cabbage stew, and the men ate as much as they wanted. There was coffee, steaming hot and, because of the rye, "bitter as sin." The dinner sleds went back toward the Tunnel Station, and the carts began to roll again. Weatherby remained there at the western portal. The sun was beaming down on him from the south, and he let it warm his back and shoulders. He counted the carts of dead men: eight carts, nine carts, and by the time the sun had moved to the southwest, ten carts. He listened in agony to a guard tell two Negroes to stack the corpses in three carts. "We can't spare ten carts," he said. The Negroes said the dead men were "crushed and bleedy." They didn't want to touch them. The guard said the men inside the tunnel needed the carts. The Negroes shied away; they began to moan and complain.

Weatherby approached the first cart himself and looked down at the mashed, broken body. He reached inside and lifted the body in his hands; even on one crutch he moved with it to the second cart and laid it there on top of the corpse that was already there. The two Negroes moaned deeply and one said, "We'll do it, we'll do it." Weatherby hobbled to the third cart and lifted the bloody body of that man and laid it on the other two. He was breathing deeply from the exertion of the lifting, and also from the emotional pain he felt, lifting the dead who had died inside the tunnels, where he had sent them, where he couldn't go himself. The fourth cart's corpse he put on top of the fifth cart's, and on top of both of those he put the body from the sixth cart. When he could do no more he stumbled away, conscious that Moses was watching him, and HenryAnna's father, and HenryAnna too. He saw her through the blur of his vision, anxiously watching as he came toward her and sat down next to her, as her two cool hands came to clasp themselves on his face.

When he went to the portal of the tunnel again, he was told that twelve men had thus far been found dead. "They've got it cleared back maybe ninety feet, Mr. Weatherby. The rock that fell is mostly loose, and they don't have to bench, so the work goes fast."

Dr. Chester sent word by messenger that the dead should be brought to Babcock Station, but Weatherby said to leave them here for now. "We'll break through the cave-in soon, then we'll know how many dead there are."

"The doctor said to bring them now," the messenger said. "He has a hole dug that's big enough for all of them."

"We'll wait a while longer," Weatherby said.

The messenger went back to say so, and about suppertime Dr. Chester arrived. "Somebody at least has to say officially they're dead," he said, complaining bitterly. "You could have sent down what you have." He looked into one of the carts and backed away, murmuring, "They're dead, well enough. I can see that."

"You expect us to send you bodies all that way, if they might be alive?"

The doctor looked into another cart. "My God," he said.

"She's cruel, doctor. She's got a bite on her. She's mean. It's no challenge to see that men are dead, once she kills them."

"How many have you?" Chester said.

"Twelve."

"You ought to have put in tunnel timbers."

"Yes, yes," Weatherby said, "we ought to have done a lot of things."

"It's unchristian what you've done."

"Twelve men is unchristian, doctor?" Weatherby said, and walked away.

There came the sound of a blast up on the ridge. Weatherby waited expectantly, anxious to hear a report that the blast had opened a way into the tunnel itself, but there was no report at all.

Dr. Chester approached him. "The sun is good to warm with."

Weatherby laid a few more boughs over the dead men's carts. "I want each one put in his own grave," he said simply, "with a headstone or cross of his own."

"We always bury them in their own grave when they die one at a time," Dr. Chester said.

"That's the way these man ought to be buried, not all in a hole, not as if they never mattered."

"You talk about their mattering when you had them sent in there?"

"You talk about them mattering when you intend to put them in a common hole?"

"You put them in that common hole," the doctor said, pointing to the tunnel.

Weatherby angrily turned from him, even as he told him, "Put each in his own grave." He went to the portal of the tunnel, where he stood off to himself.

Workmen approached him and told him they had dug a shaft "into the fallings and we ain't come to a clear place. Dug a shaft thirty feet in, and no relief yet."

"Another five feet, and you might come upon them waiting for you," Weatherby said.

"They don't answer our knocks."

"They might be unconscious by now, for lack of air. But once they get air, they'll revive. You keep digging. Another five feet might be all it takes."

"We've found four carts, and one man was under one of them and wasn't crushed, but he must have smothered to death."

"You'll come upon the ones that aren't dead soon," Weatherby said.

The dead, numbered thirteen and fourteen, were brought out in the same cart. By suppertime the fifteenth was brought out.

Weatherby ate nothing, nor did HenryAnna. Her father ate as much as usual. "It brings us up short agin the wall, don't it?" he said, chewing on the food greedily. "We go through life not thinking about it, and suddenly we're up agin it, and it gives me heartburn. Don't death give you heartburn, Weatherby?"

"Yes," he said.

"Gas on your stomach?" He belched loud. "All preachers has gas on their stomachs. It's because they see so much death. They get bloated with the thought of it, and they get to hanging so desperate to Jesus' garment that their own legs wobble. If they didn't see so much death they might come to know life better. Or at least be tolerant of it."

"I have gas on my stomach, all right," Weatherby said simply.

"Belch and it'll help," he said, belching. "A cow is a better instrument. A cow don't belch so much. She's a kindly creature and has a vegetable diet. A man would come to be like Jesus better if he ate only grass and herbs, what do you think?"

"I think he might," Weatherby said, not wanting to discuss it with him now.

"Or grass and whisky," he said, belching again. "A man eats meat and he comes to be like a beast. He gnaws at every bone that passes, he lusts for every piece of flesh, to make it part of himself. Oh, God knows, a man lusts through life." He belched loud again. "Drinking whisky to forget his woes, either to help him forget or to prepare him to do some further awful thing he really wants to do and lacks the courage for and later will need to forget, and will do again. I've drunk for that reason. Once a woman up North Cove seemed to fancy me and, oh, she shouldn't have been that-a-way for she had a husband and I knowed it, and when I went to meet her that night I wished to God I coulda stayed away, and I could have, too, except for whisky, and I could have left that alone, too, except I needed it so's I could go to her." He wiped his mouth with the back of his hand. "To make her flesh part of my own."

He saw that HenryAnna was studying him suspiciously. He glared at her sternly. "Don't you believe what I say, not a word, daughter. Strike me dead if what I say is so. That's another thing whisky does for a man: makes a liar out of him."

The sixteenth and seventeenth men had died near carts loaded with stone, so bring an empty cart to load their corpses in, then haul the stone-loaded carts out of the tunnel and dump them. If there is no empty cart, next time put the dead man on top of a loaded cart, lay him on the stones, and roll him over the stones to where the fires are and the farmers are standing. Lay the man there, the eighteenth, on top of the stones in the loaded cart he filled.

The night gang came on, and the day gang went limping off, weary and coughing. Moses went to the stockade now, too. A blast went off up on the ridge, and everybody waited to hear if the blast had broken through, and when no shout was heard, they knew it had not.

The nineteenth body was rolled out.

The twentieth body was rolled out.

There was no moon at all that night. There were only the fires, there at the tunnel and out over the field, where the farmers were. "No hurry to get home," they said. "Might as well take the news with us, whatever it turns out to be," a farmer told his son.

"It'll be some'ers between twenty and forty, won't it?" the son said.

"We need to know, don't we? What kind of news is it when you say 'some'ers between twenty and forty'?"

"The news is that there was a cave-in, seems to me," the boy said.

"That's one news, but the number is the other news, and whether or not there's to be a road is the last news."

"Who knows that?" the boy said.

"You ask so many questions you ought to be a schoolteacher."

"But who decides?"

"That tall man over there on the crutches. He's supposed to have a mind fer figures. His pa was a preacher. Seems like I heard him preach once, but there's been so many, I can't keep it all straight."

"What's he on crutches fer?"

"I don't know, mister schoolteacher. Why don't you ask him?"

"Something bite him on the leg?"

"I don't know, mister schoolteacher."

"Broke his leg in a fall, maybe."

"Maybe, mister schoolteacher, he broke his leg."

"If there's no road, what'll we do?"

"Do? Do? Why, make do, like we've always done. Time was when there was free land out west. A man could go out there, could leave such a desperate place as this'n, but that's all been picked through and bankered into debts. A poor man can't do nothing, except vote agin the government doing anything more than it has to, for everything it's done to help us has more'n benefited the banks. I'm agin government."

"Ain't government building the Road?"

"God damn, hush and listen. You got a question a minute. I'm going to take that spare corncrib to home and turn it into a schoolroom and get you a gang of children to ask of. You can pin their ears back for not telling you what you want to know. I'll get you a piece of slate and a chalk and set you up in it, and then maybe, if you have to teach, you'll learn something."

"There comes a cart with a man on it," the boy said.

"Twenty-one," the father said, making a mark in the dirt. "Twenty-one. That there tunnel has come of age, hain't it?"

Soon it was twenty-two, and a Negro said to Weatherby, "We seem to find them more often now. It's going fast, for whenever we come to a cart we can pull it out and that gives us five feet of space to work out of. We're going deep into it now."

"You'll come to the end of the cave-in directly," Weatherby said.

"We're well into it."

Workmen brought out numbers twenty-three and twenty-four on the same cart.

Cumberland brought a telegram for Weatherby to read. It was from the Raleigh newspaper and asked what the situation was. Weatherby dictated a reply, saying twenty-two men were dead, and that the hope was that the other eighteen men would be rescued that night. He added the words, "The damage to the tunnel appears to be slight. The Road will be completed by spring."

Cumberland said there were people stopping by the office, asking what the cave-in would mean. "Two workers have quit and gone home. They said the Road was lost now."

"No, don't let them leave," Weatherby said. "Hold them."

"They say it can't be done."

"No, no. The first need is to free the men in there, then somehow we'll make out an emergency schedule."

"But if it can't be done by any schedule—"

"No, no," Weatherby said, "it has to be done. Don't you understand that?" He moved off to himself and stared at the portal of the tunnel, where a fire burned to light the way of the workmen and the mules coming out.

"I wish we had moonlight to keep us company," he told a guard.

"You afraid men will escape in the dark?"

"I was thinking how much better I'd feel if I could see a presence up there. The moon is eternal and considerate. I can hold to something, if it's eternal and considerate."

"Yes, sir," the guard said.

"The sun shows every flaw in a surface; the moon shows none. I'd rather have the moon than the sun."

"Not for work, surely?"

"Not to grow crops by, no. You might say, I'd rather live by the sun than the moon, though I like the moon better."

The guard laughed. "Yes, sir," he said.

A convict came out of the tunnel and stopped at the portal. He was dusty all over. He stood there, wearily gazing at the fire, then at Weatherby. At last he said, "I think they've broke through."

Weatherby looked up sharply.

The convict said, "I'm afraid to know yet."

Directly they heard a man running inside the tunnel, running toward them. He appeared, grinning broadly. "They done it," he said.

"Are they alive?" Weatherby said.

"They ain't all dead," the man said.

Weatherby hurried to the tunnel, but stopped at the entrance. Dr. Chester moved past him and went into the tunnel, followed by four convicts. They had scarcely got inside when men were heard approaching from the distance, talking and laughing. Farmers came closer to the portal and men from up on the ridge came to see the survivors appear.

The first two survivors were Negroes, and both were too sick and tired to show pleasure, but their helpers were smiling. "These two is alive," one of the men said jubilantly.

Another survivor appeared, helped by a friend. He was a white man named Ed. Then came a series of men lying in carts, all of them alive, all of them reviving as the air swept over them.

Dr. Chester came out of the tunnel. "That makes all but four," he said.

"Where's Penny?" Weatherby said.

A mule appeared, and behind it was a cart with two bodies in it. Chester examined them and said they were dead. The cart moved away, creaking. A man was heard approaching from inside the tunnel. He reached the portal, dust-coated. Only his eyes were clear and shiny. He pulled himself to the portal and stood there, holding himself erect with one hand on the stone, and he looked out with those two bright eyes, which were firelighted now. His gaze rested finally on Weatherby. He began to murmur, to speak in an unknown tongue. He slobbered at the mouth.

"Harry, is that you?" a convict called to him.

"Harry?" another man said.

But the man named Harry only glared at Weatherby. "Come on," he said finally.

"Come where?" Weatherby said.

"Come inside."

"Inside where?" Weatherby said.

"I'll show you where I was." He turned back into the tunnel and stood waiting.

"I've been in there. I was in there long before you," Weatherby said.

"I'll show you where my coffin was," the man said.

"No, not now, not now," Weatherby said.

The man glared at Weatherby. He smiled grimly, and his gaze swept over the silent, watching congregation of workers and mountain people. "He won't," he said. "I can but he won't."

A mule came up behind him. The mule nudged him and he got out of the way, stumbled down into the midst of the group of men, laughing now crazily. The mule came on out, a Negro convict leading it; a cart was behind it and in the cart, propped up, was a body, and it was Penny. He was lying there, and his eyes were open and a big grin was on his face.

He waved at Weatherby. "How you adoing?" he said. He saw his father and waved to him. "I been inside," he said. "I got a plenty of pay coming to me for all that time." He saw HenryAnna and laughed out loud. "I don't aim to do that agin," he said.

"I runned," Closet said, hurrying along beside him.

"No need," Penny said, grinning at him. "If you'd laid there long enough, they'd a come to fetch you with a carriage."

CHAPTER TWENTY-TWO

THE HUSKS ON THE CHESTNUTS were thick, so were the husks on the corn, and the mountain people said this meant a hard winter was ahead. There were other signs, too. "The fur on the bears is so thick they can't hardly carry it, I expect. Winter's going to come in cold, this'n is." The mountain people predicted this even in the warm days of Indian summer, dreamy, misty days that splintered off and were left over from summer.

The light was brighter than in summer. It was strange about that, because the days were misty, too. The reason was that the leaves had fallen from the hardwood trees, and now the sun beamed down more freely than usually. The leaves had started falling one evening, and that night a high wind had come and had shaken the limbs. When morning came the places that had been dark woods were sunlighted, and one could walk along the same path one had walked yesterday and could see the earth differently, see details in the leaves and rocks missed before, see small insects and bugs and other creatures that one hadn't noticed.

Of course, the place the Road ran had been cleared all along; it was a gash in the forest covering. The big fields burned by the fire also had dried out earlier. But in the forest the late-autumn sunlight fell gently on moist earth, sparkled on the damp moss and the colored fallen leaves.

Violets bloomed at Henry Station. "It's a beautiful day," men were heard to say. Yet the winter wrens left their nests high on the mountain and moved to new ones at its base. In many places on the mountain, streamers of gossamer waved from bushes and low limbs of trees, left by spiders that had used them to float to a place safer for winter sleep. Squirrels busily stuffed hollow logs with nuts; even the flying squirrels, which didn't hibernate, selected places to live together and keep each other warm—as many as forty volunteering for a hollow chestnut trunk near Mud Cut.

Cumberland walked on the side of the mountain with Henry-Anna, and they lay together on the warm ferns and talked about buying a farm sometime, tending to the seasons and to a family in a two-story farmhouse with a fireplace in each room. By this time of year logs for the fires would be stacked head-high along the edge of the porch, and apples would be in bins and potatoes in baskets under the kitchen floor. They visited all the places they had gone to in the summer. The pines, hemlocks and laurel glistened in the sunlight, lending to the hillsides bright patches of green. They walked along paths soft with fallen leaves and made their plans. "When the Road is open, we could buy a farm," he said. "I'd like to buy a piece of land that borders on the river, that has enough valley in it to make grain crops, and that extends high on the mountain. We could see the seasons change on the length of our own place."

"A farm costs money," she said.

"I have money that was left me. Enough," he said. "And I'll make money on the Road, when we get paid."

"Weatherby owns most all the mountain below the Gap."

"But not much of the river valley or above the valley. Where would you put your house, if you could put it anywhere you pleased."

"I would hide it deep in a cove, so the fireplaces would warm the rooms."

"I would expose it to a view, let it look out at the whole world, so that I could get up in the morning and see the sun come out of the lowlands way off."

"You'd freeze in the northeastern winds, too," she said. "The house would rock and shudder and the floor boards would creak and the dust would fly."

"I'd put it there anyway," he said.

"I'd hide it in a cove," she said, "and plant apple trees around it."

They looked for a place that would suit them both, but they

never could agree, until one morning they went to swim below the waterfall. Since the leaves were off the trees, he could see a long way through the naked forest, and just below them he saw a cup-shaped plateau that would hold fields and a house. It was a compact, level piece of land with water washing down from the waterfall's pool, and it extended to the western cliffs, so that one could look far to the east. He said they might think of buying that waterfall and pool, and those flatlands. "We could put a house near those rocks," he said, "beside the pool."

"That's where snakes spend the winter," she said. "You wouldn't want to build there."

"We could set it on the hillside then, and sit in the house and look down on the pool."

"It'd be too damp and cold here," she said. "You ever been up here in a cold winter, when your hearth freezes the fire out?"

"Anna, we can build a tight house; we don't have to build a log place that leaves holes big enough for cats to come through."

He paced the plateau he had found, measuring it. He spent half a day out there in the sun, returning to the pool now and then, reporting on what he had seen. "This place can be made into a great estate," he told her. "I estimate there are twelve acres of flatland, and on the hillside we could put a pasture. There's water flowing down most everywhere. We can have our own place back in here."

"I've always liked this place," she admitted. "This place and the potter's house."

"We could buy the potter's house and move it here. It comes apart, like every other log house. In one day our friends could move it. What do you say to that?"

She began to like the idea very well, and got to pacing and counting, too, studying the way the clearing ought to lie. "The trees is so big it'll take year to get rid of them."

"Look off there, Anna. You can see a hundred miles."

"You can see farther than that, if you look straight up," she said, and she had to laugh at the startled expression that came on his face.

She liked a view very well, but she had grown up in the mountains and had seen thousands of them.

"If we set the house close under the cliff—" he said.

"Where the rocks can fall on it?"

"Well, Anna, where would you put it?"

She walked about, studying the matter, and at last found a place about a hundred yards from the pool, which looked at the waterfall and the fields they planned to clear and plant, yet was protected on three sides. Cumberland wouldn't get to see the sun rise out of the east, but he could see it once it got into the sky a ways.

They laid rocks on the ground where foundation posts would need to go. "The barn can go back there, and the crib there, and that spring will do for water," she said.

"We'll make a wooden trough to bring water into the house."

"Won't leaves clog it?"

"We'll tend to that."

"Won't it freeze in the winter? Sometimes a hard freeze freezes all the streams," she said.

"We'll make the trough of half-logs, then a freeze can't break it. Once the Road is finished, Anna—"

"If the Road is finished," she said.

He stopped where he was, standing in what was, in their Indian-summer dream, the place their parlor was to be. "Wouldn't you want to stay up here, if the Road isn't finished?" he said.

"To see you try to make a drive each autumn, and sell your stock in Old Fort for what you can get for it, and see your sons grow up poor?"

"Would you?" he said.

She tossed a stick into the pool. "You wouldn't stay," she said.

"Then we'll go to the lowlands and have a place."

"I wouldn't know how to do that kind of life."

"Oh, I don't think so. Look at all you know, all about the land and the trees and the animals and the stock and crops and cooking and canning and clothmaking. No school teaches as much as you know."

"I know it here," she said, "but I don't know it off somewheres else." She walked to the spring's branch and sat down, disconsolate, conscious that she and Cumberland were from two worlds, each rich in its own way, knowing neither of them could belong to the world of the other, unless one world changed. "I saw Weatherby yesterday," she said, "hobbling along in the woods, studying the mountain as if tearing secrets out of her, and I asked him how the Road was doing now, and he said, 'Not so well, Anna.' Usually he has said it was doing awfully well, and I wondered what to make of it. I saw the sadness on him again."

"The losses of the men in the tunnel affected him," Cumberland said. "That convict, Harry, at the mouth of the tunnel, telling him to come inside, that affected him, too. And next day the survivors refused to work, so he sent them to Henry Station to work in Mud Cut. I told him he ought to send them back to Raleigh, but he said he couldn't have them spreading dissent in Raleigh. They are bitter about him."

"Yet he's the kindest, most considerate man."

"Oh, yes, a great man." He smiled at her warmly and took her hand. "You love him, don't you?"

"Yes," she said.

"And you love me?"

"Yes."

"How does one differ from the other?"

"I love him more deeply," she said simply.

Cumberland was hurt, yet he had been prepared for her reply.

He sat down in what was someday to be the kitchen and rested back on a deep bed of leaves, cushioning his head with his hands. "I know you do; I sensed that," he said.

"The love I have for him won't ever grow," she said. "It's not something I can do anything more about. I love him, meaning I wouldn't want him hurt, and would try to soothe him, if I could, and would tend him if he was ill and make his food and care for him, if he needed someone to, and I like to be with him. But the love I have for you grows. It grows ever time I see you. It was such a little sprig at first, and maybe wasn't love so much as interest. I found you so stiff and filled with ideas and words and money that you were nothing so much as a spectacle to me. But time by time we've walked up here, and up there, and we've talked together often, and each time I've come to know you better. The attraction has become a love I have now, and it grows day by day. If we had a house of our own that was really our own, the love would grow another bound. If we had a child, it would grow another bound. If you get sick and I can tend to you, it will grow another bound. The love I have for you is different from the love I have for anybody else, because it has no bounds that I know of."

He put his arms around her and held her close to him for a long while, wondering if she were not more mature now than he. For a long while they lay there together, and he kissed her and loved her and let the warm day come to rest this way.

"You smell like flowers, Anna," he said, getting up and stretching.

"I washed my dress yesterday."

"How did you make it smell like flowers?"

"Last spring I put flower petals in soap and set it in the sun."

He laughed. "Does your mother do that, too?"

"Oh, she has no time for flowering soap."

He looked down kindly at her, knowing she would be his wife, knowing he might someday think of the world he had left and regret having married her, yet believing that if he didn't marry her he would regret that all his life, too. "I could hear your heartbeat," he said. "I can almost hear it from here."

"Does it beat strong?"

"It beats strong."

"It beats for you."

"Will you marry me?" he said.

"Yes," she said, stretching languidly as she lay on the bright leaves before him.

"Road or no Road, house or no house?" he said.

"Yes," she said.

"I love you the way you love me," he said. He looked down

calmly at her body, the dress just above her knees, her blouse held tightly about her breasts, one button still unbuttoned. He leaned over and took her hand and kissed it, and pulled her gently to her feet. "Did I ever tell you I like the way you talk."

"You said you did."

"It's like a song. A sad song, Anna. Why is it a sad song?"

"I've got so much to be pleased about it burdens me."

There was much activity on the mountain farms now, and many of the hired laborers had left the Road to go home to see the work get done, and to enjoy the harvest and the food their women made, and to hunt. Many of the cornfields had been stripped of their blades, and the bare stalks stood holding individual ears, which were tightly wrapped, heavy packages, yet they were carried lightly by the slender stalks. In other cornfields the families moved among the stalks, even now, pulling the fodder and bundling it, women and children and men working leisurely together. Stubble fields were turned under and grain was sown. The sheep were sheared: sheep sometimes were sheared twice a year in the mountains; and the wool was tromped clean, then laid on the roofs of the cabins and sheds to dry. The homesteads as a consequence took on a clean and festive look. The new turnip plants were growing nicely, although in HenryAnna's father's patch they hadn't germinated. Potatoes were ready for digging and burying, and other holes were being made ready for burying beets.

The apples had made a fine crop. There were winter Johns, Sheepnose, Lewis greens, Baldwins, and other kinds, and those farmers who were successful grafters had two or three kinds growing on the tree nearest their house, where they could go to pick an apple of their choice over a period of weeks, for the different kinds matured at different times. Neighbors freely bargained about what grafts they would exchange.

Those who had put cattle on the balds of the mountains went to bring them home. Men and boys went with a supply of bacon and cornpone and salt; sometimes they found them, sometimes they found most of them, and in the area of the new Road they found none. Some farmers blamed it on the Road and others said the wolves had got them.

"Wolves don't pack on the summer. How could they fell cattle? No, I tell you, it's the Road, it's that cantankerous Road. It's something to do with all that blasting."

Weatherby tried to get the hired men to come back to work, and some of them did come back in mid-November, but the word had got around that the Road couldn't be finished, and even if it were finished, that the work for them would be over come spring, when only a few men would be retained permanently. Weatherby said all the men could be retained, for there would be shoring-up labor to do for months to come, but the hired men weren't convinced. Also, they said they saw too much risk in it, anyway. "I'll not shore up what might cave in on me," one of them told Babcock. "You want me to do convict work, after they're gone?"

The farmers wanted the Road, but they were farmers who wanted the Road so they could get a crop out to market; they weren't roadmakers by trade, and they were tired of the vagaries of it. Their women said not to go back and get killed, and they had children to think about caring for. If a man got killed on the Road, who would watch out for his family? Of course, if he had brothers, they were obligated by the Bible to do so, but some farmers had brothers who didn't follow Bible teachings unless they wanted to.

More than half the mountain boys went home to hunt, and by mid-November only a few of them had come back.

By all statistical measurements, Weatherby was waging a losing struggle now, but he refused to admit it. Not only had he lost experienced labor but the convicts were downcast; they were frightened of the tunnels and did less work than before. He talked with them individually and in small groups on the Road, and they listened attentively; the Road mattered to them, was the biggest challenge ever to come to them, but they had no confidence left in their ability to see the work through. Only at Lick Log tunnel, where the engine and Red Tuttle were, was the work being done on schedule. At the Swannanoa tunnel, neither the east nor the west portal was doing well.

On the third Thursday in November, a warm night with a mild wind from the south, Weatherby was sitting in his office with Cumberland, Babcock and Tuttle. The night gangs had left the station for the tunnels, and Tuttle was, as he put it, "resting his supper" before going out on the Road again. He had trained a mountain boy to run the engine for the hour or so each night that he was away.

Weatherby was only half listening to him talk about how incredible it was to him that an engine could have been buried by mud, and how impossible that it could have been righted and pulled out of such a grave by the power of men and oxen. "The idea that an engine can be moved, except by its own power, is hard to own up to for an engineer," he said.

Weatherby thought back on the experience at Mud Cut. He had used 6 oxen, 20 mules, and almost 150 men to pull the engine out.

"An engine is its own power and wheels," Tuttle said. "It's the thing itself and the thing that moves itself. Long ago when engines were new, men said to station the power on the ground and pull the train with a cable, but other men put the power inside the train itself, and that's what an engine is. It's not something to push and pull."

"It couldn't be fired up under mud," Cumberland said, teasing him.

"That's what I say," Tuttle said seriously. "But it strikes me as strange as giving a cow milk to drink, taking power to an engine."

Cumberland laughed, and Babcock said he had heard of giving milk to a calf.

"I wish I had an engine at the Swannanoa tunnel," Weatherby said.

"That's what we're trying for, all right," Tuttle said, "to reach the Gap come spring."

"We need one there now, to help make the tunnel, the way you help with Lick Log. If we had an engine at the west portal of the long tunnel, where the cave-in was, we'd get back on schedule there."

"If the world tips and that area lies downhill of here, you can do it," Babcock said, winking at him.

"I wish for it, but I know it can't be. We have Long Bridge out, and even if we had it back in we can't ride rails farther than Lick Log's heading. Even beyond that lies the last little tunnel."

"No way to get it up there," Tuttle said. He lighted his pipe and puffed at it until he had a screen of smoke around him. He felt more secure and at home with smoke around him, because of his years working the trains.

Cumberland said, "You might take one apart and haul the parts and have blacksmiths put them together for you."

Weatherby considered that. "It would take six months."

"How far is it from Henry Station to the Gap?" Cumberland asked.

"Nine miles or more, by track," Weatherby said.

How far is it up the turnpike?" Cumberland said.

"Three, four miles."

"Could you haul it up the turnpike?" Cumberland said.

Babcock laughed, and Tuttle snorted, but Weatherby said, "Could the men and mules pull one up there?"

Tuttle stared warily from out the depths of the tobacco smoke, looking from one man to the other to be certain they weren't serious. He winked at Babcock and shrugged, dismissing all of it. "It can't be done," he said. "An engine does its own pulling. I tell you, it's got its own personality, too, and if you humiliate an engine, it won't work for you any more."

Next morning Weatherby went to Babcock Station, as usual, to talk with the doctor and the sick. There were forty-two men who claimed to be sick, but when he arrived many of them were joking and laughing. Dr. Chester didn't care if he had men who were well; he was disgruntled with Weatherby and the Road, anyway. He even had a dozen patients working on the infirmary grounds and tending to the graveyard, which had burned over in the fire and was eroding; some of the graves had opened, he said, and the headstones stood in disarray.

Chester was putting in a gravity water system. He was proud of this. He had no authorization from anybody to make it, or to use laborers at all, and the men were using timbers, at a time when Long Bridge needed all the timbers that could be found or purchased anywhere around. Weatherby thought maybe he would lose his temper with this doctor before long, but he held his temper now and talked most pleasantly with him. They had dinner there, had beef stew, the first beef Weatherby had had on the Road in a month. He didn't ask where Chester got money to buy beef with; he guessed it came out of the medicine account.

"Can you get the Road open?" Chester said.

"Oh, yes," Weatherby said confidently. He wanted to tell him he would have to open it in spite of the likes of him, but he didn't.

"You're behind your own schedule by three weeks."

"Am I?" Weatherby said simply.

"As I read it, and receive reports."

"Do you receive reports?"

"I have men who tell me how much heading is done a week. You're three weeks behind schedule."

Weatherby went on eating. It was good beef stew, he would say that for the doctor.

That afternoon he went down to Henry Station and on the way noticed that the workers were sloppy in what they were doing. It seemed the spirit had gone out of everybody on the Road. One couldn't keep a spark going all the time, he knew; one had to let it linger sometimes, and expect it to burn brightly at others. "Those men up at the Gap need that big locomotive you're working with," he told the men at Mud Cut. "Only way to get it there is to pull it up the turnpike, but they tell me Henry Station men can't do it."

The convicts squinted their eyes and watched him critically. "Can't do what?" a big Negro said.

"They tell me the men at the Tunnel Station can pull it up there in three days, and Henry men can't do it at all." He was calm and gentle while talking about it; he appeared to be unconcerned, one way or another.

"How you roll it up there?" a man said. "Lay work track?"

"We haven't got the track," Weatherby said.

"Roll it on the ground?"

"It would mud up too much that way and break its wheels," Weatherby said.

"How then?" a white convict said.

Weatherby picked up a rock and idly tossed it toward a stack of timbers, and he said something about the weather being warm today.

"Roll it on planks, how about that?" a convict said.

"Would it skid?" a man said.

"It might roll on planks," a man said.

"You mean put planks on the road and pull the engine over them?" Weatherby said.

Two or three convicts got to talking at once. "If we had mules enough and used the logging chains," one said. "If we got the oxen," another said. They went on talking, and soon Weatherby wandered on down the Road toward Henry Station, leaving them to worry over it.

When he got home he told Mildred and Troy he was anxious to try this idea out. She could tell he had special hopes for it, even gained strength from thinking about it. "I tell you," he told her, "we're down now to scraping bottom on anything we do." He told her and Troy that when he got back to Henry Station he expected the men would offer to try to do the work. "They'll have it planned," he said.

It was so. On Monday he had no sooner walked onto the Henry Station lot than the men began to call to him, and one of them, a white convict named Tom Burlington, seemed to be the spokesman for them all. He was from near Wilmington, far off down east. He wasn't big, but he was feisty and alert.

"Yes, I'll see that you get the use of mules and oxen," Weatherby assured him, "though I can't lend any more men."

"We're going to do it ourselves," Tom said.

"And you can use such rope and chains as you round up. But you wouldn't want to start work like this and not finish it, for the other camps will know what you do."

"We'll finish it," Tom said.

"That locomotive is a heavy one."

"We'll get it up there," Tom said. "And later take its tender, too."

"What you going to do about the turnpike bridges?"

Tom thought about that. "We'll shore them. Are they weak?"

"Oh, they're only stagecoach spans. They run five to twenty feet, and they're old and risky."

"We can borrow timbers and return them later."

"And there are many uneven places," Weatherby said.

"We got shovels and picks; we'll fix them all right."

All the men standing there were anxious to do it, except the men who had been in the tunnel cave-in. They remained disgruntled, particularly Harry, the man who had accosted Weatherby at the west portal. "You ship me back to Raleigh, mister?" he asked Weatherby. "I want to go on back to Raleigh."

"Oh, they're going to start making roads again down east before long," Weatherby said.

"Not underground," Harry said.

"Not blasting and all that noise," another sullen man said. "There's nothing there but sand and water. You can make a road down there without giving your life to it."

"You can't breathe in a tunnel, and then you get trapped in there," Harry said. "My God, my God, when I recall—"

"Yes, I know," Weatherby said, moving on, anxious to be away from him, trying to close his mind to him, even as Harry called, "I'll take you into a tunnel, any time you want to go."

Sweat was on Weatherby's face, but they didn't know that, and anger and fear were flushing through him, though he gave no sign of it. Other convicts, working at an eroded fill, stood by respectfully as he walked past, his crutches finding solid footing for him.

CHAPTER TWENTY-THREE

THE PLANKS WERE THREE inches thick, two feet wide, and ten feet long. The idea was to lay the planks across the road; by this means the wheels wouldn't slip off a plank, and the planks could be laid to round the curves.

The road bent and twisted so much it was going to take care to get the train around some of the places, and the road wasn't wide either. It was wide enough for a stagecoach; if the stagecoach came upon a wagon or another coach, the uphill vehicle was, by custom, supposed to pull off the road to one side. There were such places for passing. But there were no places for a locomotive to pull off, of course, and no easy way to get through the narrower places where trees were shouldering the road with their trunks and roots. At several places streams washed across the road. They were easy for a wagon to ford; whether a locomotive could ford them or not, nobody had experience enough to know.

"You say ye don't have track enough?" Babcock asked Weatherby.

"We don't have track to ruin," Weatherby said. "We have iron enough to reach the Gap, and we can't buy more."

"I suppose a train couldn't make a sharp curve on iron anyways." Babcock offered to help with the experiment, but Weatherby told him it was important for him to urge the tunnel men on to harder efforts.

"I've done all I can, short of a whip. They don't get enough to eat, if you want my opinion."

"I'll move this engine up there," Weatherby said. "Tell the workers an engine is on its way."

"Don't you think you'd better wait until you find out if you can do it?"

"We can't make a secret out of moving a train," Weatherby said.

"You going to tell the mountain people?"

"I can't move a train on the turnpike without letting people know."

"If it can't be got up there, how you going to explain it?"

"We won't explain it very well."

Weatherby talked with Tom Burlington, and they agreed on a route from the track to the turnpike, across a cornfield. The distance was 110 yards. "What day you want to start moving the locomotive, Tom?" Weatherby asked. It was a Wednesday.

"I'll go get my tin plate and be ready," Tom said. "I don't have much packing to do."

"You want to try to do it this week? You've got Thursday, Friday and Saturday. You have to have it there by Saturday night."

"Three days is time enough for four miles."

Weatherby agreed, and next morning 125 men gathered at the Henry Station office and walked together to where the engine was parked. Tom told them how to lay the planks, and they laid out a thickness of them. There was no way to get the engine off the tracks, except to lift it, so the men wedged poles and iron pipe under it and, on signal, lifted the front part a few inches and nudged the wheels onto the boards. The boards held all right. The men got to the back wheels, lifted them off the track and onto the wood, too. They worked the front and then the back until the engine was straddling the track and was headed in the direction of the turnpike.

The mules and oxen were brought forward. There were sixteen mules and six oxen. Weatherby said only the oxen ought to be used, here on level ground, so logging chains were fastened to the boiler of the engine, one on each side, and the oxen were yoked. "See if they can pull it over the planks," Weatherby said.

The oxen pulled and the engine rolled along to the edge of the planks, and more planks were laid. Whenever the engine faltered, the men gave a hand to it. Planks were taken up as the engine passed over them and were moved to the front.

Tuttle came down from the Tunnel Station and began to complain. He said an engine shouldn't be treated this way. He wrung his hands and berated Weatherby, even before the men.

Weatherby got to laughing at him. "You go on home," he told him, but Tuttle didn't see anything humorous about it.

The men laid the planks onto the turnpike, and up the turnpike forty feet. The logging chain was fifty feet long, and if they went past forty feet the oxen had to pull from the planks, and their hoofs would slip. They couldn't very well do it.

Tuttle argued with Weatherby all the while the engine was being pulled onto the turnpike itself. Tuttle said they would wreck it for certain. They didn't, though. The engine scraped its bottom on a little ridge in the turnpike, but the men kept it erect and pushed it along. The engine rested level on the planks by noon, and half an hour later, after their bellies were filled, the men got it turned so that its lantern was aimed up the mountain. It was ready to start its climb.

A farmer in a wagon happened to come down the turnpike. He saw the locomotive sitting there. "Air ye daft?" he shouted. He was sitting stiffly on the edge of the wagon seat, staring at the men, mules, oxen, and the engine blocking the turnpike. "Air ye daft?" he shouted, and his horse shied all the more. "Ye can't block a public road," he said, beating his whip in the air toward them as if to tell them to be gone.

Eight convicts approached his wagon, picked it up, hauled it around the engine and set it down on the turnpike, well on the other side. The horse had been pushed along, too, and now started on toward Old Fort, trotting nervously, then galloping at full speed. The farmer turned on his seat, looking back at the black apparition on the turnpike road, and at the laughing men. "Air ye daft?" he called, striking his whip defiantly toward them.

Weatherby had the chains lengthened and he harnessed sixteen mules to four of them. He had two more chains run from the sides of the engine, and he hitched the six oxen to those. So he had twenty-two head hitched. Other shorter chains and ropes were bolted to the engine, and the men themselves were told to use those, and other men were to turn the wheels. On signal from Weatherby, the whips cracked over the lead mules, men shouted as they strained at the ropes, and the engine began slowly, with groans on the lumber, to roll up the hill. It was a monstrously heavy weight to pull.

Tuttle predicted catastrophe. He climbed into the engine cabin, poked his head out the window and shouted at the men, demanding they stop their labor, but nobody paid any attention to him. The engine moved on, slowly, over one dangerous place and another, while sixty of the men hauled planks from the rear, carried them around the locomotive, and laid them in the front.

Mountain boys were yelling at the mules and oxen all the while, and beating on them.

At sundown the work stopped, and the men parked the locomotive to one side of the road, as far to the side as they could get it. They built big fires in the turnpike to warn approaching traffic, while other men unhitched the mules, which were lathered and fretful, and took them to Henry Station for the night. Tuttle said he would stay with the locomotive. He also said it was an awful thing that was being done.

At dawn the procession began again. Weatherby had divided the remaining three miles into two days of work, with less distance for the last day because the turnpike was steeper as it neared the Gap. He went ahead of the men to inspect the bridges and he assigned fifteen men to the bridge detail. Another fifteen were made to fill in pits in the road and level off the rougher places. There were 95 men left to work the boards and pull the engine.

The first really trying test was a bridge on a curve. The morning stage was waiting, anxious for a chance to get by, but the driver was more curious than angry about this delay. "I've had everything else happen at least once, except this," he told Weatherby. "I've had sick horses and sick passengers; I've had women bear babies; I've broke wheels; I've had runaways; I've had one tornado, a fellow said it was. But this is the first time I've had a locomotive."

In two hours' time the men worked the engine around the curve and let the stage go by. They pulled the engine on up the straight tangent, men going ahead to prop up the next bridge. Everybody was pleased with the progress being made, except for the fretful survivors of the cave-in. Weatherby had purposefully assigned them to the leveling and bridge gangs, where they couldn't interfere with the hauling, which was the complicated part because of the long chains.

As the engine approached the next sharp curve, the teams were so far out in front that they rounded the curve before the locomotive reached it, so they couldn't do much direct pulling. The oxen had to be brought back closer to the locomotive and the mules had to be unhitched. The oxen and the men got the locomotive turned, but it took another two hours.

The engine often scraped the branches of overhanging trees. Sometimes it broke them; sometimes Tuttle would push the limbs back out of the way, or snap them off. Yard by yard, curve by curve, the locomotive moved, until by nightfall the men could see far down into the valley, could see Henry Station's lanterns and fires. They knew they were doing well, that they had made every bit as much distance as anybody had expected them to make that day.

A few of the men slept on the turnpike that night. They said they had rather stay there, and Weatherby permitted the trusties to do so. He stayed there, too. Most of the guards went home, however, so eighty convicts and Weatherby, and one or two guards and Tuttle, stayed together.

Tuttle was hoarse from complaining. "I like that locomotive," he told Weatherby. "She's well balanced. But this will ruin her."

"She doesn't complain," Weatherby said.

"Not many creaks in her," Tuttle said. "I'd like to work her myself if she is not destroyed by this move."

"She won't be," Weatherby said.

"Which tunnel are you going to run her in?"

"The west portal of the Swannanoa."

"The one that caved in?" Tuttle thought that over. "I'd like to work her, anyway."

"I'd like to work with you," Tom Burlington said. "I always wanted to run machinery." He sat down beside him on the turnpike. "Can I work with you?"

"You can learn, can you?" Tuttle said.

"I can learn anything that don't require memory. I can do most anything and learn by doing it, so that I can do it might nigh any time I take a notion to, but thinking about something trips me up. A man was trying to teach me something in the way of milling once, and he wasn't doing nothing in the world but talking, and my hands got so anxious to do something, to touch that machinery and do what this fellow was saying, that I couldn't stop myself."

"Stop yourself from what?" Tuttle said.

"I hit him."

"Hit who?"

"The teacher."

Tuttle laughed. "Ay, God, there's a way to improve teaching in this country."

"I can't remember or think about a thing, but I can do. My mind simply ain't a machine," Tom said.

"The hell it ain't!" Tuttle said. "We're all machinery. But what God made is quieter than what's made in Philadelphia."

"A machine don't feel things, though," Tom Burlington said.

"Oh, yes, it does, too," Tuttle said. "A machine can't be mistreated and not respond. That engine there senses the way she's treated. If she's poked with poles and if we jerk the lines, she knows; if we keep her clean and oiled, she knows. I don't understand just how."

"You ever see an engine weep?" Tom said.

"No, not precisely," Tuttle said.

"I thought maybe oil come out of its lantern, or something like that."

"You're joking with me, are you?"

"No offense," Tom said quickly.

"Why don't you teach Tom how to run one?" Weatherby said to Tuttle. "You two could work the west portal."

"He might hit me," Tuttle said.

"No, I wouldn't," Tom said.

"Then come along and I'll teach you. But when you roll to a heading deep in the ground, and that engine noise smothers you, and when the smoke is misting your eyes, and the candlelight is so dim you can't see what's going on, and the shovels are banging on the rocks and the men are cursing, and you turn and look back and way off, way, way off you see a dot of light and know that's daylight, that's safety—then, by God, you stay where you are until the cars are loaded, you hear?"

Their eyes met and each man drew instinctively into his own sense of dignity, then both relaxed and went back to studying the fire, and after a long while Tom said, "I'd like to be there when the tunnel breaks through, and you can see the spot of light each way you look."

They slept under the engine; they crawled in under it to keep from being dew-wet in the morning. When the night stage came by the driver saw this encampment and claimed it reminded him of "a gypsy band that's stole a train."

Weatherby slept soundly. He didn't awaken the entire night, even though he slept on the ground, and even though about 3 A.M. the rain began gently falling, nothing more than a damp spray that settled the dust and splotched the engine. It didn't even put out the fires.

About 5 A.M. the rain got to falling stronger, however, coming down more directly and sharply, and it made a racket on the engine's cab. The turnpike got slick and, in soft places, became

sloppy. "Time to move her on," Tom Burlington told the Henry
Station men, and they crawled out onto the turnpike. They began
to move about, going down to the creek to wash and to stare at the
white water. They came back up to the engine and sleepily stared at
it, and directly they heard the mules and oxen coming, and they saw
the chow cart, too. By now the rain was swishing down persistently
on them, and somebody said the creeks were likely to rise by
afternoon.

"Move her on soon," Tom Burlington told the men, and Tuttle
walked about, saying they had best delay the enterprise. Weatherby
would have, if the announcement hadn't already been made to the
Tunnel Station men that the engine would be at the Gap that night.
Even as important to him as having the engine up there was having
the benefit of a victory, something to lift their spirits.

So he said to go on. The oxen were yoked and sixteen mules were
hitched. The men got handholds on the ropes or on the body of the
engine. The signal was given to start the pull. The planks groaned
and crackled as the locomotive rolled again, and the chains clanged
against the boiler. Mountain boys beat at the oxen in the lead, all of
this while the rain came down, pelting brutes and men and the metal
sides of the locomotive, washing down along the boards, men
slipping on the boards and in the mud of the turnpike.

Two mounted riders stopped; they were on their way down, and
they saw this procession and turned without a word and rode back
up the mountain. They no doubt had remembered from stories told
them many years before not to question what they were suspicious
of. They didn't even talk about seeing it until they got to the Gap,
where they reined in under a pine tree and each silently considered
whether he had seen it or not, and what his opinion was of it.

Tuttle again rode in the cab. Somebody ought to, he felt; the
engine expected that sort of company. He could sight along the
chains, drawn taut for eighty feet in front of the engine, six logging
chains. A web of other chains and ropes were at the sides. He
looked down at the shoulders of Negroes and whites pushing at the

boiler and at the wheels; below them were the creaking, unsettling planks, splinters breaking off as the wheels cut into them.

A Negro began to sing:

> First train I ever saw that rolls
> And rolls and rolls
> And leaves no track behind.

Weatherby went ahead with the bridge crew and studied what was needed at the creek crossing at the next curve. The rainwater was moss-held yet, but it would soon be released to come washing down in steep torrents. He was wet to his skin, of course; there was no way to protect oneself from the rain, and it was cold rain, too.

There was a rotting wooden bridge over the creek, nothing stout enough to do. There was only a four-foot clearance under the bridge, but he got down in the creek to see what might be done to support the structure. When he crawled out he told the men to lay two eight-inch beams lengthwise under the bridge, one on top of the other, and to slide planks on the beams until the boards of the old bridge were supported. Then they were to lay boards lengthwise over the floor of the bridge.

As the procession approached the bridge, the oxen were driven straight ahead onto the mountainside, for this was the only way the oxen's pulling would do much good. The mules were driven onto the mountain, too, but the chains got twisted in among the trees. The work was stopped. The locomotive was seven feet from the bridge.

The oxen were brought in close to the locomotive now. A few mules were hooked to the side chains, and men got firm holds. The order was given, and men and oxen pulled and pushed, and the engine rolled onto the bridge. The front and middle wheels rolled over it, but the right power wheel, a big one, broke through both the planks and the bridge boards and went into the creek bed.

The engine threatened to topple over, and any number of different orders were given by almost everybody with a voice, including Tuttle, who screamed warnings and instructions in a series; it was all confusion. Two men were pinned under the engine, and all the oxen and mules and men were trying to pull forward and sideways and every other way. "Pull it on out," Tom Burlington shouted, as if they could pull it out now.

It took twenty minutes to get the two injured men free of the locomotive and the doctor sent for. Meanwhile, Weatherby got down again into the creek to see what had happened. The lodged wheel was five feet in diameter; it was now tightly fitted into the rotting bridge; resting on the wheel was the weight of the engine. Some way must be found to lift the wheel straight up for two and a half feet, so that it could be rolled off the bridge.

Weatherby saw that the support hadn't been put under the bridge in the way he had directed; this end of the bridge hadn't been supported at all. He came up out of the creek and, when he turned, he saw before him two members of the bridge crew. One of them was Harry, the man who had accosted him at the portal after the cave-in. Harry met his gaze only for a second. "You can't look at me now, can you?" Weatherby said.

Harry looked up at him again.

"You could look at me so strongly up at the Gap, I recall. And you could yesterday. Can you look at me now?"

Harry looked away and mumbled something.

"What say?" Weatherby said.

Harry mumbled something.

A convict said, "Did he cause all this?"

"No," Weatherby said. "The creek washed the underpinning to one side, that's all."

Harry didn't look up.

"If he done it, we'll string him up fer you," a voice back in the crowd said.

Harry still didn't look up.

"You'll need to string up something heavier," Weatherby said. "Put a scaffold over that engine wheel and lift it."

They had timbers and planks enough to make a scaffold, and several of the convicts jokingly said they had studied scaffolds for years. They had no carriage bolts, but they cut wooden pegs and used some of the ropes and had lashed together a scaffold by noon dinnertime.

They got their food at the chow sleds and retreated under laurel bushes, out of the rain, which was gushing from the sky and down along the creek bed, washing it to overflowing, for the wheel dammed much of it now. The men ate in gulps and threw the tin plates toward the chow sleds, and went back to work.

They hooked a chain onto the wheel's axle, and ran the other end through the top of the scaffold, then they yoked the oxen. The mountain boys beat the oxen to move them, and they pulled heavily, deep in the mud of the turnpike, but they couldn't lift the wheel. Men got hold of the chains and pulled, but the wheel wouldn't lift, and there wasn't room for the mules to help, so the men stopped trying and Weatherby went up on the mountainside above it all and looked down at it and tried to decide what else could be done.

He saw two wagons coming up the turnpike. They wouldn't be able to get by, and he knew by nightfall there might be a procession of them waiting on both sides.

When he came back to the turnpike he showed Tom Burlington two limbs that overhung the creek. He had the men lash ropes together, and Tom himself climbed the tree with one end of one rope and dropped it over the first of the two limbs, then he did the same with the other rope, dropping it over the other limb.

"Put four mules on a rope," Weatherby said. The more mules that were used the more power; he didn't want to see the wheel lifted six feet into the air. With a machine, one could measure power, use it evenly, as needed, but with mules one took the power the mule had, so one had to estimate the number of mules one needed.

Six oxen and eight mules were hitched, and poles were set in under the boiler of the train, so that leverage could be exerted there. "Gentle with the poles, you hear?" Weatherby told the men. "Don't let the locomotive rest its full weight on the boiler. If one of the limbs breaks, lower the poles."

He had other men ready to push, once the wheel was lifted, and he had six men whose job it was to slip ends of planks under the wheel as it was raised.

Tom Burlington climbed a rock above the turnpike and counted out an order. The brutes put their strength into the yokes, and the men pried and pulled and lifted, and the engine began to rise. "Get planks in under there," Weatherby said, watching the wheel. Also he was watching the tree limbs high overhead, which were bending threateningly. He saw one of them bend suddenly and the rope snapped and four mules were released to their own power and went sprawling forward. "Hold the other four mules in place," Weatherby said, but it was too late, for the men moved to help control the fallen mules. The result was that the oven were pulled backward through the mud as the wheel settled onto the two planks that had been inserted under it.

The effort had raised the wheel six inches.

The mountain boys got the mules quieted down, and men started piecing together a new rope.

Weatherby let the rain wash the mud off his feet and crutches. Tuttle came over to him, stationed himself beside him, and said not a word in criticism, though he was worried and disgruntled. Weatherby said, "It takes a strong stomach if a man's to build a road."

Tuttle nodded. "Always has."

"Put only two mules on that rope this time," Weatherby said, for the rope looked none too strong. He saw Harry, the convict who had caused the bridge to break; the man had a smirk on his face, even now. "You take the ropes up the tree," Weatherby said to him. "I don't want to lose Tom Burlington."

"I don't climb trees so well," Harry said.

"Nobody wants to climb it," Weatherby said.

"Why don't you?" Harry said, his voice trembling now.

Weatherby threw him the ends of the ropes. "Take them up there," he said.

Harry sullenly went to the tree. He studied the trunk, then began to climb. He was strong, all right. He climbed to the first limb and started to get one rope free from his belt, but Tom shouted, "It's the next limb," and Harry went on up the tree, everybody watching him, and he got to the next limb and looped the rope.

"You can come down now," Tom Burlington called to him, but Harry sat in the crotch of the tree. "Come on down," Tom said.

Harry didn't move.

"For God's sake," Tom said, "we got a cat up a tree."

"Leave him alone for now," Weatherby said.

"I hope he stays up there," Tom said.

It was midafternoon when the order was given to try a second time, and this time there were two fewer mules. The pull began, and almost at once the hickory limb broke, split off not more than a foot from where Harry sat. He reached out for it, as if to hold to it, and lost his balance and fell forty feet, landed flat on his back on the muddy road with a plop.

The engine wheel had fallen back through the bridge again, with two more boards under it—that was all.

Weatherby looked up at the broken limb and asked what had happened to the convict, and he saw four men bending over him on the turnpike.

At dusk the wheel was lifted again, this time at last to turnpike level, and was rolled across the bridge. New planks were put on the bridge and the dammed-up wagon traffic began to roll past the engine and the place where the doctor was working over the injured men. The creek was now up to bridge level.

The food sleds brought supper to the men here. The men ate quickly, then got the ropes unknotted and separated and rolled up. Tom Burlington asked Weatherby what they ought to do to secure the engine for the night.

"We'll take it on up the mountain tonight," Weatherby said.

Tom had never known a tireder group of men, and the rain had dampened everybody's spirits.

"On up to the Gap," Weatherby insisted. He talked softly, but nobody who heard him doubted that he meant it.

When Tom gave the order, the men set up a cry of protest. They said they wanted to get out of this mud and Tom could go to hell. He could shoot them if he wanted to, they said, but when Weatherby, crippled as he was, climbed to the engine's cab, they grew quiet. Weatherby said, "You'll work, by God, tonight, to take this engine to the Gap, and we'll all stay here to see it done. Now, get the ropes and chains fastened."

They were as stunned as if he had struck them. They had never heard him talk angrily before. Without a word, in darkness, they moved the oxen to the front and hitched the chains. They drove the mules into place, and more than 120 men came to take their places as Weatherby climbed down to the turnpike again, wishing he had not berated them, sensing in his show of force a sign of his own weakness. He knew he was on the edge of his own limits of endurance. "Lay the planks up to the ox hoofs," he told Tom Burlington. "Is that man all right, the one who fell?"

"Who knows?" Tom said, not caring.

Weatherby couldn't see well through the darkness and the rain. "Old woman," he murmured, "you're doing all you can, aren't you?" He slipped and slid in the mud and made his way to where Harry was lying. He was unconscious and was talking aloud about being "let out," and Weatherby guessed he thought he was in the tunnel again.

Let out, let out, Weatherby thought. Yes, let us all out. Let us get free of this soon. Three months more. Ninety days.

"You men ready up there?" Tom Burlington called.

From far ahead on the turnpike men shouted that they were. "But the stage is coming," they said.

"Flag it down," Tom yelled.

They couldn't, apparently. The driver knew about the engine and was watching for it, but in the dark his horses came suddenly upon the oxen and panicked. They swerved and came down toward the engine, fleeing the oxen, and dashed the stagecoach into the engine, scattering goods on the turnpike. There was plenty of cursing from both drivers and convicts, while the horses tried to go on, dragging the coach. The convicts stopped them, held them, calmed them, cursing them all the while.

What was left of the stagecoach was lifted to one side of the turnpike, and the driver said he would have to sue the Road. He wanted to talk with Weatherby about it right then, but Weatherby ignored him. "I can't do anything for you now, if at all," he said. He walked forward, his crutch slipping and his boots sliding, the rain slashing in his face. He got to where the oxen were, and he heard Tom Burlington call, asking if everything was all right, and the word went back that it was. He heard the order to pull forward. The men urged the oxen on and the chains lifted from the mud; he heard them free themselves all down along the turnpike, and he heard the snap of the chains as they tightened around the body of the engine. The oxen moved forward in the mud, and the great locomotive moved up the hill. Men came hurrying forward, carrying planks, and they slid them into place in the mud, one after another, as the oxen moved forward.

The Negroes began to sing:

> Mud on the iron wheels,
> Mud on the planks and mules,
> Mud on the ox and your slippy feet,
> Mud on the chains and your weary feet.

The locomotive tilted at one bad place, but men held her up. At a steep incline the locomotive stopped, and chocks had to be put under the wheels to keep them from rolling back. The rain washed in on her; water ran in rivulets in the ruts of the road under the planks, unseating the planks. Men too tired to think, working the night too long to wonder how they were doing all of it, sleeping as they worked, as they pulled on the ropes or held to the cold wheels, listening to the men sing.

> Nighttime come,
> Nighttime and rain,
> Cain killed Abel,
> Now we kill Cain,
> Building this Road.

Slip and slide. It was cold up here at night. "Wish I was back at Henry, don't you?" a convict said.

"Ain't never going to see Henry. We'll be holding to the rope when this thing goes in that Gap tunnel."

"Not me."

"Can't let go."

"I can let go this wheel."

"I can't let go this rope, even if I wanted to. My hands and this rope are the same."

They moved on up the mountain, foot by foot, plank by plank. Move the planks forward to the oxen hooves, slide them down into the mud. Pull and push, turn and slip upward toward the Gap.

They stopped at a deep curve and had to figure out a way to get around it. They ran two chains around a hickory tree and brought them back to the road and had the oxen pull that way. They put two other chains around an oak and had the mules pull on them. They pulled that way, and one mule fell and couldn't get up, or wouldn't get up, so they cut it out of the harness and dragged it aside, and three convicts took its place.

Pull and push, push and slip and slide toward the Gap.

"Not never going to get there, do you hear?"

"We'll be there afore we're old."

"I'm old now."

"No, you're just gray."

"I'm not pushing. I'm only holding on."

Hold on and turn, too, and slip and slide toward the Gap, all up-hill, all the way.

They got to a straight stretch and adjusted the mules and oxen and ropes and chains and men, and went on.

"Ain't we up there yet?"

"You'll know when you get there. It levels off."

"Seems like I'm going all the way up to heaven tonight. Are these chains made of gold?"

"They feel like they's made of lead."

Weatherby wants the Road
Going to have to put it in.
Never doubted it'd be done all right,
But didn't know it had to be done tonight.

Creeks gushed across the turnpike. At one ford the water was two feet deep and powerful in its flow. It was black as the night and came roaring from off the mountain. Even the mountain boys lost their footing in the stream.

"Take it on through," Weatherby said.

Nobody could keep a footing.

"Bring up the timbers," he called. "Span it with timbers."

Men came dragging timbers through the mud, toward what they didn't know, for nobody could see anything.

"Here, lay them lengthwise."

They spanned the branch, then laid the boards over the sills.

"Pull it on over," Weatherby said.

Creaking, clanking, cursing, over the threatening cascades and creeks, over the mud pits and slippery rutted places, falling on the wet boards, but going uphill, the oxen pulling and the mules deep in the mud, and the men shoving and pulling. Black as pitch in a pail, feeling their way, seeing enough ahead to know the turnpike went this way, going this way with it, hauling the locomotive up the mountain.

They heard an explosion at the Gap tunnel. It was close. Probably from the east portal. They were close to the east portal, but Weatherby said the west portal was where they were going.

They bent against the rain. They had to bend to pull, anyway, to pull or push, either, so it beat at their backs and shoulders. A man fell and couldn't get up and he was rolled to one side, and one of the mules fell and had to be cut out of its harness; they were dragging it along and they cut it free rather than stop the little momentum they had, the slow rolling wheels toward the Gap.

Blood got on the rope and wheels. The gravelly mud cut at their hands, but the men held to the rope and wheels, anyway. The chain was cold from the rain, but they held to the chain. They dug their feet into the mud, a hundred men, some asleep as they walked, some fretful and sighing and moaning, and a few praying, and quite a few cursing the Road.

Mountain boys beating at the mules. The mules sensed they were approaching the end. Beat the mules on.

The oxen had their heads low, moving step by step, setting the slow, heavy pace up the turnpike.

Step by step.

Tuttle in the cab, looking out, the rain washing down his face. This was no ignominious use of a locomotive, after all, but was a heroic one, he decided; it caused his heart to beat faster even to think of it, men and brutes moving a machine to where they needed it most, taking a locomotive onto the mountain to help make its own road. "You're coming closer ever' step," he called down to the men. "We're slipping but we're slipping up the mountain. God help us, you're going to do it!"

They were part of the machinery of the turning wheels and the chains and the ropes and the mules; they were part of the slippery turning and the moving of the planks.

Abruptly they were above the rain. They had come to a misty place where there was no rain, and soon they were out of the mist. They could see the place on the mountain where the Gap was, they could see it just above them, steeply up there, the turnpike rising to it.

"Haul, there!" Tuttle shouted. "Ay, can you see it?"

They were leaning forward, pulling, pushing, and they couldn't see it.

"It's there before you," Tuttle shouted.

They were part of the chains and the rope and the wheels, and they didn't see it.

The oxen, heads bent low, didn't see it.

"Keep it moving," Tuttle shouted. He saw Weatherby hobbling along before the engine, and he shouted out at him to keep it moving. He saw a man appear at the Gap and take off his hat and wave it in the air. Other people appeared at the Gap, and the Swannanoa tunnel workers started down the turnpike, shouting them on. The mules and oxen sensed that they were almost there, that just above them was the place the wheels could stop turning.

Tuttle shouted out at the top of his voice, yelling, as the Gap workers gathered at each side of the turnpike. The oxen plodded on. The Gap men didn't help at all—it was for these Henry men to take the locomotive up there; they stood to either side and shouted them on as in the moonlight the mules plodded upward, men's blood on the chains and the ropes and the wheels, a Negro on each of the wheels turning them, their shoulders bleeding against the cold steel, turning them.

"Get on up there, man," a Gap convict called, tears in his eyes to see such a sight. "Get that up there, man!"

It was arriving. The great iron locomotive had come to make the tunnel and build the Road. It was almost there, where it could never be, its black shiny body gleaming in the dim moonlight. Men shouted out to see it. "Get it up there, man, get it up there!"

It had been their hope all along to build this road.

All the Gap men began to shout. The locomotive rolled board by board. People standing beyond the Gap saw oxen appear and mules; then the black lantern of the locomotive appeared, and then the top of its black boiler appeared, and then appeared the face of the engine and the bent men turning the wheels and pulling at the chains which spanned out from its sides, and the men pushing at it from the sides, and Tuttle standing in the cab looking out and down and forward. There was no power in the black boiler, but he was the engineer going to the Gap, and he was weeping from excitement as the call went out from Weatherby:

"Lash her there!"

It was done.

Men were lying on the Road back for a ways, but it was done.

Seven oxen and mules lay on the Road back there, but it was done.

It was lashed there, faced to look west into the Swannanoa valley.

Behind it were the lowlands. It was at the Gap. It had arrived now, and the men could rest, the men and oxen and mules. The ropes and chains could be coiled now.

It was there where almost nobody had thought it would ever be. It had come up through the rain and mud. And people came forward reverently to touch its black shiny body.

A day later the locomotive was moved to the tunnel's west portal, where a stretch of track was laid for it, so it occupied its own territory. The boxcars that the women used at the Tunnel Station were unbolted and set on logs—each being given a small porch and made to look like a house—and the wheels from the boxcars were rolled cross-country to the tunnel, where timbers were bolted to them and they were made into flatcars. Part of one of them served as a tender. The smith at the Gap community helped Tuttle and Tom Burlington clean the locomotive and oil it, each man learning from the others, the smith beside himself with pleasure to be at last so productively engaged.

The three of them fired the boiler and backed the engine slowly to the tunnel's mouth, pushing the two flatcars, convicts with lanterns sitting on the first flatcar, reflecting light on the rails. Convicts pressed themselves close to the tunnel walls to let the locomotive and cars pass. "You going to help us now?" they asked Tuttle. "We been waiting for you," one of them said.

"We're here," Tuttle said, his voice hollow in the rock tunnel. He sounded jubilant, as if being here were an idea he had favored all along.

He did favor it now. The workers were claiming victory for the Road, acting as if victory were imminent. The mountain people also were affected deeply by the appearance of the locomotive in their own valley. They came in droves to see it. The locomotive was theirs, whether there was to be a road or not. Those men who had once worked on the Road and had gone home considered coming back, wondered if they might be hired again. "I put time in when it was in doubt; I might as well help open it," they said.

Weatherby hired those who returned, writing into their contracts that pay could be delayed month by month, subject to the profits made by the Road.

News of the success went to newspapers, and reporters wrote several stories about "the road that refuses to die."

That first week the schedule's quota was met, and in each succeeding week a few feet of headings were made up from the languid months and the cave-in week. Weatherby became more friendly and relaxed. He told Cumberland that the Road would surely be open now, and he asked him to make plans for the men's Christmas and for a celebration in the spring to welcome the first engine and cars up the Road. He slept well. His dreams were not so ragged and painful to him. He chided Cumberland, even in HenryAnna's presence, for having, a few weeks before, given up on the enterprise. "Everything fails a time or two before it succeeds," he said. And he praised him for suggesting the way to get the engine to the Gap. "Except for a few convicts, you and I were the only ones who believed it could be done."

CHAPTER TWENTY-FOUR

THE MEN WOULD SIT in the stores and lean back in their chairs and talk big. The men did a good deal more talking than did the women; the women did more work. The men planned and evaluated. "I figure my cattle strayed to another bald some'ers, and that I could stand down on the road when drovers next are passing and find my cattle sooner or later," HenryAnna's Uncle Charlie said.

"Everbody found his cattle 'cept here near the Road," the old man said. "Seems like the wolves congregated here, like at camp meetings."

"Wolves don't congregate at ary camp meeting I ever was at," Uncle Charlie said.

"Oh, I didn't mean it so strict."

"You mean the animals come together fer a service of their own?"

"I was speaking at random, didn't mean to get your ears lifted off your head."

"I ain't never heard it said that way afore."

"I sprout new ways of talk. People that talk the same way all the time get to sounding alike."

"What you two men arguing about? I forgot what you said," Old Whitaker, the storekeeper, said.

"He was saying the animals had a meeting and got saved," Charlie said.

"Hell, I said nothing about being saved," the old man said.

"They got saved when they saw that new locomotive," a tall, lean man said. "I ain't heard a wolf howl more'n a dozen nights since that contraption come up here."

"Them wolves left this country entirely. That engine was the finest idea ever thought of for scaring wolves. They never saw nothing belch fire and smoke afore."

"It cost us our cattle," Charlie said.

"On that one bald, ain't that all? On the mountain here. And they might turn up any time now in your barrel of cider, Charlie. You might be making a kind of beef cider that this country ain't seen afore now."

"Ain't that the cutest idea you ever heard spoke by a man?" Charlie said.

"When you goin' back to the Road, Charlie? Your two candle-bearing nephews is working it yet."

"I ought to have done it, but there's no point in a man working on a pretty day, for all he's doing is trying to get money enough stored by so he can enjoy his time, and there he is out there working to get time to enjoy, when he's using the best time he's ever goin' to have by working. Now, damn it, does that make sense to anyone?"

"Not the way you say it."

"I said it straight. I got an allotment of time; that's about all God give me, and my pa give me a horse and a few pigs and some seed, and that plot of land I call my farm. Now that's my fortune, right there. And I went courting one night too many and got myself in deep with this here woman, and if I don't lose her to pneumonia or meanness, I'll live with her till she dies. And she's bred a flock of kids until I'm weary countin'."

"What's your point, Charlie?"

"Huh? What I said is the point, damn ye. Ain't ye listening?"

"Would you mind saying it agin, in case it's important enough to remember?"

"I said I've got nothing but time that's give me, and I use it on the Road to make some money ahead, so that I can afford to use my time like I want to. Well, sir, what I'm saying beyond that—if you'll lean your ear this way just a mite more so the sounds won't spill out of it—is that I don't see why I don't go on and use the time I got and not try to save fer it, fer I'm losing what I got now trying to get ahead to use my time. What the hell kind of nonsense is that?"

"Don't get so angry you hurl yourself out of your chair, Charlie."

"Working them damn convicts, working like a convict myself. I spent all summer adoing it and missed my chances to fish and lay low, and what the hell did I get fer it but some damn money that my wife's going to get the use of fer cloth and candles and other fashions that we could do without."

"You can't do without everthing."

"Why, she don't need much cloth. We make some cloth ourselves there at the place. She could get them girls to spinning more. We'd have enough cloth, if they'd put in a bigger flax patch and do right by it. She don't like to weave as much as most women do."

"Mine don't, neither. No woman does."

"My old mama—bless her heart, she was a good one," Charlie said, "she told me what she liked the best of all in life was carding and spinning. She said she liked it best of all."

"Best of all what, Charlie?"

"She liked that best of all she done."

"Don't say much for your pa, does it?"

"Oh, shet your mouth. I'm atalking about my ma, for God's sake."

"Charlie, you reckon that hunt done away with the bears, too?"

"No, fer I seen bears coming through bresh the other day."

"I'd hate to miss out on getting a bear this year. I hain't missed one year since I started hunting."

"How old was ye when ye started, Jamie?"

"Oh, how do I know? I ain't going to set here by the fire atrying to remember numbers."

"Well, was ye fifteen, sixteen?"

"I don't know, figuring it that-a-way. I recall the other day I come across the piece of rope I'd used fer a belt when I was first strappling, and I tried to put it around my waist and, Lord knows, it weren't anywhere nigh meeting. It didn't touch at the ends at all."

"You ain't fat, Jamie."

"No, but I appear to have settled."

"Anybody can get a bear that wants to. But they'll hibernate soon this month."

"Well, I worked the Road all summer and I don't know what I done. Now what did I do? A drop in the bucket. It's too big for a man to do anything much."

"Charlie, you're disgruntled by nature, seems like."

"My people has been here fer generations without no railroad, I'll say that."

"Your people has been moving on fer generations, too," Old Whitaker said. "Where's your oldest brother at?"

"Oh, he's in California now."

"When you come down to it, Charlie, ain't nobody here but has thought of leaving, and nobody here but has brothers who has gone, and sisters, and has maybe even parents who left, and sons."

"Well, I ain't left yet and I'm living, that's what I'm saying, and I'm happier setting by this fire than I'd be down there making tunnels. So let somebody else build the Road. They even got my brother-in-law working at last, setting telegraph cable. I'll let him support me if I get pressed."

"You'll get lean as ary rail in your own pasture, doing that, Charlie."

"They'll stop work agin in a few weeks now, anyway, 'cause it's going to be a cold winter."

"How you know?"

"It's been a warm fall, ain't it? Ain't that a sign?"

"I tell ye how I know—the mast is more'n I ever saw afore, and that's a shore sign. When them nuts and acorns is scattering everywhere like they are, you can tell to get ready, fer it's about to burn you with winds, ain't that so?"

"I remember four year ago it was a cornhusky year, and it come a cold winter that froze this countryside and cut the feet off the chickens," Charlie said.

"Weren't that six year ago, not four?"

"Huh? Oh, I don't know numbers."

"I think so."

"More likely seven, if you're goin' to talk numbers. Seven is the number I read in the Bible to be God's number. It's all in there in the Revelation about seven. And I have no doubt if a man was able to read straight he could find in that book all the prophecies he ever needed to make his winter plans. I have no doubt you could read that book clear and plain and find out what the winter would be like."

"We just told ye what it was going to be like, Charlie."

"Ohhhh, my God, I hate to think of the coldness of it all. And to think you want me to be out there making the Road. I think I'll stay home and play with my children."

"You ain't going to play with yer wife?"

"I might. Or somebody else's."

"Yeah, God. Listen at him talk."

"I'm old enough to get safely into trouble."

"You'll be having young'uns named after ye in ever valley, too."

"I don't much care. My pa had that happen four time, and he was so much a gentleman he never denied any child its ma claimed was his'n."

"You say he was a gentleman?"

"One of the women told him once that she laid awake the night her baby was born and sweated drops of sweat on her face, thinking, thinking, trying to figure out which man had fathered her new child 'because one thing I'm particular about is my honor.' "

"Listen at him talk. He-haw! Damn ye fer making me laugh when I'm leaning back in a chair."

"They say they's a preacher up Swannanoa River that has been so active in so many coves, tending to his flock, that when he looked down one Sunday morning and said in his sermon, 'Now, my little chillun,' a man stood up at the back and said to him, 'I knowed one of these mornings you'd own up to hit!' "

"*He-haw, he-haw!*"

"Listen at Harry laugh. Don't it sound like a mule?"

"Harry, you goin' to break that chair. I ain't aimin' to make nary 'nother chair this year."

"I wish I'd done more'n I done when I was young. It's a shame to think back on all the chances I missed."

"Missed? Lord, hear him now. You ain't missed many, Charlie, if I can judge."

"No, I used to let 'em all go by."

"You mean, walking on the road and you setting on the porch."

"You could get to be a convict, Charlie. They have a comfortable woods down there with no charges for the use of it, and it's done more or less like the cattle or the hogs, one to another."

"Oh, I heard all that, but I don't prefer the ground."

"No wonder you let your chances slip by. Nothing in that world gives better comfort and support, and has more throwback to it than a laurel limb."

"You put your woman on a limb?"

"Huh? Yeh. Put the limb down to the ground, hold it thar with your foot, lay her down on it, and—listen to what I say—it has a drive to it that's jest nice."

"I'll take a feather bed fer mine," Charlie said. "I expect a laurel limb would feed too fast fer me."

"There ain't no drive to a feather at all, that I ever felt."

"I'll get in a feather mattress with her, and take my time. I don't like to rush ary meal that ain't got but one course."

"He-haw, he-haw, he-haw!"

"I'm going home and sort my pumpkins. Anybody want to help me?"

"Not me, Charlie."

"Huh? Nobody? Well, I say that Road's done ruined you all, fer you're so damn rich with cash pay that you don't want to work in the old ways at all."

"If that Road ever pays me my pay, I'll be rich."

"They won't pay up unless it gets finished and starts to profit."

"You ain't even worked fer the Road, have ye, Harry?" Charlie said.

"No. I hain't got to it yet."

"Well, it'll be finished afore ye do then."

"They hain't goin' to finish it ary time soon, in my mind."

"Is that HenryAnna out there?" a man said.

"Where?" Harry said.

"Don't push me back from the winder. You can see her as well as you need to from there."

"Lord knows, she's got nice hips on her, ain't she?" Harry said.

"They been fitted, all right."

"Fer what?"

"A laurel limb."

"She's going to that pott'ry house agin, ain't she?"

"She used to go up on the mountain alone. I'd see her up there, but she's about stopped them walks, except with him, that teacher fellow that works books for the Road."

Charlie went to the door and stood there looking out at the bare-branched trees. "They got Smith doing work for the Road now, have they?"

"He works keeping the engine in repair."

"I know he's pleased by that."

"He'll be wealthy, too, if they ever get that Road through."

"I can stand here and feel like I'm a rich man," Charlie said. "I can stand here at this here open door and see the whole world. There it is, and I can't see why we want to change it any, for it's got all the offerings a man needs fer happiness. Why, you can't tell me there's ary thing in life we need that we don't have right here, now. Can you men think of ary thing?"

"No, Charlie, I can't. But my woman can."

"Life needs to be enjoyed, don't it?" Charlie said. "It don't need to be worked out entirely, for it gets lean that way. I bet you them men down on the Road don't even know the trees have fallen, except that the leaves get in the way of their cleaning up the Road. Oh my, what a waste, what a waste, for life ain't an engine. It ain't to be forged nor bolted. Life ain't a farm, neither, that needs clearing and planting, for all one needs to do is harvest. What else is there? That's the gist of it. You take them men on the Road, they're clearers and planters, but they don't know how to harvest; they spend all their time clearing and planting, but where is the harvest? While all about them is the harvest, wanting to fill them up with good things, and they miss it, for their eyes is on the harvest away off which they won't never have." He stood there staring out, nodding, and turned with a wry smile and looked at the other men and nodded, a single bob of his head, and he winked at the storekeeper and said, "You got a warm place here. I hope someday I need to buy something you stock." He went out, stopping at the trail to breathe in deeply of the fresh air, then going on up toward the turnpike, but stopping when he got to the potter's house and moving toward it.

He stopped on the path and stood there a minute, listening to the birds and staring off at the farmed mountains, speculating in his mind about the outland places of the earth and wondering how men there could know themselves if they had no mountains to judge themselves by.

"HenryAnna," he called.

She came to the door of the house and looked at him kindly. "Uncle Charlie, is that you?"

"HenryAnna, you better watch yourself if you go into the woods alone any more."

She smiled at him, with eyes like a friendly doe, and nodded. "Are they talking about me?"

"No more'n they ought to. It's just natural that you've filled out nigh perfect and also have let yourself be marked, and I don't blame anybody for anything that happens in life, but that railroad bookman marks you when he housekeeps with you."

"We're planning to marry soon."

"Well, that's all right, once you do. All of us comes to it." He stood looking off at the mountaintop. "I went to work for the Road, and I figured it'd be a big thing, and while I was there I got tied up in my gut worrying lest it don't work out. But when I got backed up here to home and saw my woman and boys and them little tattered girls of mine, and saw the hills as lonely and secure as the day we was born, I got a new view, and what the hell does it matter about the Road?"

"I expect it matters a lot to them that cares," she said.

"It drives them crazy, is all."

"Who's crazy?"

He looked up. "Oh, I didn't mean any person. I didn't mean to suggest any one person." He smiled briefly and seemed to be preparing himself to leave, yet he stood there kindly staring at her. "I wish I was a young man and had a cabin built and was ready to start my family, and you was free. I'd court you, HenryAnna."

"Would ye?"

"Would I? Oh my, girl, I'd be wherever you was. I'd shadow your steps and get myself to where all I wanted was you. I guess I could fall in love yet, fer I'm not so old I've forgot how to do it, but it's not my time of life. My wife'd cut my head off with an ax and bury me in a pool. But I do sometimes think about love again."

"You don't love Aunt Matily?"

"Oh, I do and I don't. It's give-and-take with her. She comes and goes, for she's been there so long it's sort of like trying to fall in love with the gatepost."

"That's not true, Uncle Charlie, and you know it."

He laughed gently, kindly. "You know I love her. What it is, though, ain't bondage, like it used to be. Falling in love ought to be a fever, and I'd feel foolish having a fever over Matily, fer I've knowed her so much and so long. If I was to have a stone fer ever time I've crawled in bed with Matily, I'd be able to fence my property."

HenryAnna laughed.

"You got a few chickens, I notice," he said. "Your garden didn't do well, though, did it?"

"Nothing last season growed well for me."

"You farm about as well as your papa. You know, Anna, he was a fair man at the start, but seems like he caved in under the weight of it all, though I never knowed what weight it was, did you?"

"No," she said.

"He come nigh being a friend to me, then one day we was up in the mountain hunting, and he stayed with me right close, so that finally I said to him to go on away, and when I said that, it appeared to crush him. Later when we come into camp, he was hurt and he never said much to me after that, not that day and not since. Seemed like he wanted to be close to me, Anna."

"What you mean?"

"Well, we're talking honest, ain't we?"

"I don't know what ye mean by what ye say."

"Well, then it don't mean nothing, fer I was wondering, is all, about what crushed him."

"You think what you said to him crushed him?"

"No. I don't think it did." He stood there for a moment, watching Cumberland who was away off on the field, coming toward them. "I wonder what makes the trees shed their leaves, ever one and ever year."

"God does it," she said.

"Think o' that, will ye?" He watched Cumberland for a while. "Does God do it all, Anna?"

"I reckon he uses what help he can get."

"He judges all of us by the same rod. And what will he do to those who friction what he's made, who grate agin it, who anvil it, who tear it, who blast it?"

She studied him thoughtfully.

"I worry about them men, Weatherby and your man both, fer someday they're going to come close to the nerves; one more time they'll come nigh the nerves and the nerves will grab them, the exposed nerves of the thing will grab them, and it's awful to think about. I said to Weatherby once, I said, 'Ain't ye afeared fer yourself in all this that ye do?' And he said to me, 'Charlie, I knowed when I come back up here last spring what the story would be.' Ain't that something, that he knowed and come back, and ain't it something that I know and I'll go back, and leave this view and leave you and my wife and young'uns. Why in tarnation am I going to do it?" He stared at the water of the pond, his face frowning and his brow knitted and his lips tightly pressed together.

"You sound like the Road is going to kill you," she said softly. "You shouldn't talk so loud about what you fear."

"I don't fear at all," he said calmly, "and that's part of it, too. I ain't afeared one bit."

"Them men in the store are looking over this way."

"I ain't afeared to see it through, but it'll kill those it wants to. It's like bear hunting, once the bear is wounded and knows he can't run away any more, and he stands on his hind legs to meet you, and he's fighting dogs and stands there, unable to flee and trying to meet you on his own terms. That's the way it is now with us, as all the power of this place rises to meet us and there we are with picks and shovels and engines, like toys before them mountains, new toys newly made. And is it God that'll strike us down or our own audacity?"

"Law, I don't know who'll do it," she said.

"Fer there's not going to be any more running soon."

"You sound like you miss being where it's all going on."

"It's strange to say, but I do. I'll go back to it now, though I don't want to." He smiled grimly, then kindly at her, and he put his arm around her and hugged her. "You want to help me hide pumpkins, Anna?"

"Yes. If you'll let Cumberland help, too."

"Come on, we'll meet him on the path; he's coming along."

"I'll get a shawl."

"Get a bonnet, too, if one's in there."

They started out swiftly. She was anxious to see Cumberland, and she called ahead for him to wait. "We're going to Uncle Charlie's for work and supper," she said. She swung back to Charlie. "I'll cook it."

"All right, all right, see that you do, but let Matily think she done most of it."

The woodchucks and jumping mice were asleep by now; so were the bats and chipmunks. The snakes and lizards and frogs and toads and salamanders were asleep. The bears were grumpy with weight and were settling in now, under heavy blankets of boughs, or in caves.

A cold wind snapped in from the north and Weatherby awoke one morning to see that snow had fallen on top of the mountain. "The woman is white-haired now," he told Cumberland.

"Women sometimes get mean when they get old."

"Do they?" Weatherby pulled on a thick pair of socks that Mildred had recently knitted for him. "She was mean enough already."

"When you going to put those crutches away?"

"When the Road is through."

"Not till then?"

"I'm afraid to make a change, while our luck is good." He put on his boots and laced them. "I don't need them now, in my opinion."

"You might ask the doctor if they're needed?"

"I don't plan to ask him anything I don't have to. He's a stranger to me, even after a year or so of working with him. He's honest, but I wouldn't trust him."

Cumberland laughed. "I agree."

"There's something off-tangent with him."

"I made out a death report on the man that fell from the tree."

"Did he die?" Weatherby said, looking up sharply. "Did he die?"

"I'm afraid so. And another tubercular man died."

"Did the doctor report any others?"

"No, only those two for this week, and several injuries, but I don't report injuries to Raleigh."

"It's dangerous work; it's as dangerous as a war." He put on two shirts, put on his leather coat. He carried a sheathed kitchen knife with him now, and he fastened it to his belt.

As he and Cumberland walked to the kitchen area, they saw that a light snow had fallen at the uphill edge of their camp. "She's warning us," Weatherby said.

"She warned us last year, seems to me," Cumberland said.

"You have the men's Christmas planned?"

"I asked Anna's father to preach a sermon."

"Oh, he can't preach well. He's too confused to preach."

"I couldn't get a real preacher, and he wanted to do it. He's preparing night and day for it, 'turning the pages,' as he says."

"Pages of what?"

"His Bible. He says this Road is a journey between life and death."

"Oh, Lord. I wish he'd sing songs and not preach."

"And I've bought four pigs to barbecue for dinner."

"We have that kind of money?"

"I paid it."

"You personally? Where did you get it?"

"That big salary you pay me."

Weatherby laughed. "How far behind are we on your salary?"

"Five months. And yours is seven."

He stopped on the trail and looked off at the night gang coming from Lick Log tunnel. The men were tired but gleeful, pushing at each other and yelling about "come Saturday night" and swearing at the "powder man," who was, they claimed, losing his mind completely. "He's going to take the top off this whole hill if he don't take care," one man said, and they were all laughing. They saw Weatherby and Cumberland and waved to them, and a guard called out, "We're almost broke through on Lick Log, ain't we?"

"Ought to break through the heading soon," Weatherby replied.

"We gone about eighteen mile into the ground," a white convict said.

"It's a good tunnel," Weatherby said.

"We'll take care of Swannanoa when we get done with this," the guard said. They passed on by, a happy crew, sweated down from the work, lean men, for they had to live on what food they got.

"Someday the history books will say something about this Road," Weatherby said, "and they'll say you and I built it, Cumberland."

"Not I," Cumberland said.

"Without you, I couldn't do it."

"They won't mention me, except they'll say you got some help from a fellow recently out of college."

"They'll say what they please. But they won't say it was the niggers who built the railroad."

"No, they won't say that," Cumberland agreed. "But those niggers couldn't build a tobacco barn without directions from you."

"I don't know about that. You consider those men, who have been slaves, and so were their people, yet they've just now come out of a tunnel that's over 700 feet deep. It's awful to think about being under the ground like that, with mash exploding close by, and that engine coming at you from the portal, a big black unfeeling thing, smoking, its wheels grinding as they swirl by you while you press against the benching. Consider that."

Cumberland nodded. "I've been in there," he said quietly.

"You ought not to go in there again," Weatherby said. "We can't afford to lose you. I can't lose you. Don't you know the situation I'm in now?"

"I'm not hurt by it."

"You stay out, damn you," Weatherby said. "I need you and Babcock. With you two I can finish the Road. You two and convicts like Moses and Tom Burlington. But if anything happens to any one of us, I don't know how we'll manage. We're on the very end of the string now."

Cumberland noticed the excitement of Weatherby, and the tension, too. He had about fourteen weeks to go, and everything was working smoothly. The bridge was being assembled and would be complete in time; the iron was on hand, the ties had been cut and dried, the ballast could be broken from the rocks along the way, the fills were not creeping, the trestles were secure, the tunnels were being lengthened every day, steadily, predictably.

"It has to keep going this way for a little while longer," Weatherby said, facing into the wind as if testing it for secrets it might know, as if watching for a telltale sign of trouble. But there was none, and even the snow had not fallen on the Road. "Does she sleep in the winter?" he said, looking above him at the shoulders of the mountain.

"Last winter you were away, weren't you?" Cumberland said.

"I've tried to recall how it was up here when I was a boy, in the winter, and I can recall warm winters when we didn't even have to wear a coat to the fields, not on most days. My father might wear a jacket, but he would take it off and put it on a bush. That was in January, February."

"Can you remember winters that froze the cattle in the fields?" Cumberland asked. "Anna says the old folks can."

Weatherby thought about it. "No, I don't recall anything like that."

The day gang came past, going toward Lick Log tunnel. The men were yelling at each other about today being the one that Lick Log would come through. "Where's the man with the mash pails?" a convict shouted. "Blow the damn thing open by dinner." That was how they felt.

Weatherby and Cumberland went on down to the kitchen. The

convict women seemed to be more tired than usual. They had been up working since well before dawn, and they would work until midafternoon, when the other woman-gang would be roused from their house cars. They sleepily poured the coffee into cups and served up heaping plates of mush. "Where's that jerky?" Weatherby asked one of them, an elderly white woman who was superintendent of the kitchen.

"It's all gone," she said.

"Well, not many weeks to go now, anyway," Weatherby said, eating the hot mush, not liking it any better than he had as a boy, but eating it, anyway. "We'll all have milk and honey and bacon and beefsteak come spring."

CHAPTER TWENTY-FIVE

Most of the preparations for the Christmas service were developed by HenryAnna's father, who called himself Rev. Plover now, but since the service was to be held at Babcock Station, the doctor sought to influence him. The doctor occasionally even felt he had made his point, only to realize later that Plover had veered sharply off on his own again, most unpredictably.

He would show up at the infirmary at any hour, day or night, prepared to discuss a theological device or point he had conceived, that might do for his sermon, and he would talk for an hour or two about it. He fretted constantly, designing and redesigning. He would drop by to talk with Cumberland, too, and he confided to him, "I ain't spoke in so long I'm nigh afeared of it."

"You'll do well," Cumberland said, though none too sure of it himself. "How long will your sermon be?"

"I don't know that I'll use any of it that's ready," he said mournfully. He trembled in throes of frustration. "It's not too late to start afresh, is it?"

He had persuaded several of the convicts to take part in certain scenes he planned to use to dramatize the Christmas story. The woman originally cast to play Mary turned out to be six months pregnant—the first advanced pregnancy among the convicts—so he looked about at all three stations for the most suitable replacement and persuaded Dr. Chester to accept the new player into the infirmary as a patient. "I can't rehearse unless the cast is all in the one place," he said.

Cumberland fussed at him over such breaches of the Road's rules, but Plover was so worried and besieged that fresh criticism splashed as ineffectively as stones in a big pool.

Chester told Cumberland that the man was disrupting everything at the infirmary. "For example, he sent a group of my patients to gather lightwood. He said he needed firewood for his scenes that would flare up when lighted."

"And railroad ties," Rev. Plover had said. "I want railroad ties." For what purpose he wanted them nobody was able to say. "And I want three trestle timbers," he had insisted. They were brought to him. These arrangements he made, Cumberland and Chester conceding to him always, while they tried to guess what he was doing.

As Christmas Day approached, the doctor and the preacher became more aggravated with each other, and the preacher became more secretive about what his plans were, even refusing to tell Chester what the hymns were to be. He insisted that he was in charge of the entire affair; he had merely come to the doctor for advice. He said now the doctor was trying to take charge of everything.

By Christmas morning the two men were not speaking to each other, and there was a great deal of worry lest the performance not be held at all, but Cumberland helped soothe both men's tempers. Weatherby arrived, speaking to the convicts, who were also arriving, shaking hands with them, and wishing each person he encountered a merry Christmas. He went over to the barbecue pit, which Cumberland had had dug into the ground. Inside the pit were hickory coals; on the iron grill were four pigs, halved and split and steaming. "We'll have the world's best barbecue," Cumberland told Weatherby.

When the pork was about done, the women set to baking cornbread and cooking salet greens—watercress and rape and turniptops mixed together. They had big pots and were cooking the greens with fatback, stirring the mass of greens now and then with a long wooden paddle.

HenryAnna arrived, more nervous than Cumberland had ever seen her. She was scared to death that her father would have a heart attack or do something silly. "I don't think he's going to be able to say a word when he gets up there to speak," she said.

Cumberland had told the free workers they could invite their wives to dinner if they wanted to. Several mountain women were already present, and for the convenience of the lowland women a small excursion train was to be run in from Morganton. Weatherby didn't like to have special privileges shown employees of the Road, but Cumberland signed the authorization for it and said he would stand responsible, which, of course, he would have to.

To Weatherby's surprise, when the excursion train arrived at the other side of Long Bridge, Mildred got out of the car. This was a Christmas surprise that she and Cumberland had arranged for him. He had not thought to see her here at all, and he greeted her gratefully and enthusiastically, though he wished in a way she hadn't come to this convict place.

Everybody ate what he wanted. There was plenty of food. And the remainder of the afternoon was spent in games, the men being modest in their language and efforts, since so many wives were present.

By dusk about 800 men, women and mountain boys settled down on a plot of slanted land where they could hear the service. They looked down at the infirmary and across at the cemetery on the hill above it. Over to their right was the Road as it wound about the building and went on up the mountain.

As the sun began to set there was a stir of anticipation from the congregation, and soon appeared Beulah, the big Negro singer, carrying a lantern and singing a Negro carol about the baby Jesus. Behind her came the Convict Quartet, and behind them came two mountain men playing fiddles, holding them against their chests and sawing away rapidly.

Behind the fiddlers appeared a choir of the sick. They were quite sick, too, and Dr. Chester jumped up from his place in the audience and began to shout for them to get back to bed.

Cumberland pulled him down to his seat again.

"My God, some of those people are dying," Chester said.

"It's too late to interfere now," Cumberland said. The singers were so weak that they tottered and weaved as they walked, and they didn't sing very loud.

"He'll kill them," Chester murmured over and over, astounded.

Rev. Plover appeared, dressed in one of the doctor's white robes.

"He's got on my clothes," Dr. Chester moaned.

Plover stood trembling before them and lifted his hand for silence. The choir on his signal began a hymn, the two fiddle players accompanying them diligently. As they did so, fire started in the valley, and Mary and Joseph appeared, Mary seated on a tunnel mule which Joseph led. They came out of a laurel slick and approached a stable made of bridge lumber. They went into its dark interior and the choir got hushed and began to sing "Holy Birth, the pain is easily borne, the son of God is born," the fiddles playing softly. As they sang, a fire started high on the hill near the Road, to one side of the cemetery, and lighted a group of shepherds who were watching their flocks. They got up lazily from the ground and walked about among a flock of sheep. One of the shepherds noticed a star and pointed at it; the other shepherds gathered together to view it. They appeared to be much impressed with it and began gesturing wildly, then began gathering up their things. They got their ram and started down the hill toward the star.

As the music ended, Joseph started a fire in the stable, revealing two oxen and two mules in stalls, all of them looking at the holy scene, with Mary sitting near the fire rock, a quilt over her legs and stomach. Joseph was a big convict named Zeb Larson. As the choir began singing joyously, the shepherds arrived, driving their sheep before them, and the sheep were baaing and were anxious to be back on the hill and be done with showmanship. They did as they had to, though, for the ram was on a rope and was being led.

The shepherds shoved him into a pen, where he could butt wood if he wanted to, and came to the manger and knelt reverently as the choir sang: "Holy is the Lamb, God's Son; Holy is the Lamb of God."

The preacher, Rev. Plover, said, "So he was born lowly. He didn't have even a cabin to sleep in. He had a stable without a door to it, nothing even to keep the wolves away. He wasn't a rich outlander, with all his needs supplied. He was as poor as any other mountain man, and Joseph weren't nothing but a chairmaker, who used as good a wood as he could cut for himself from the sorry forests right around Nazareth. His mama weren't a wealthy land-owner, neither, but she could cook and spin, and the baby growed up, working the foot pedal of the lathe and weaving seats out of oak splints. He loved music better'n anything in this world, and growed up knowing plain truths. When he got to be old enough to stand the shock of it, he went into the world."

He had said it well, and HenryAnna relaxed. "Thank you, God," she whispered.

Up on the hill out of a laurel thicket appeared a man of about thirty, dressed in another long white robe of the doctor's. He carried a shepherd's crook in his hand, and he walked staunchly down the hill, walking like he knew where he was going, and behind him appeared from out of the thicket his following, fifteen men and women convicts, dressed in sheets, all of them shivering in the wind. Jesus, who was played by a convict named Sam Goddard, stopped, held up his hand, and the multitude stopped. He spoke, shouted more than anything, for he was a long way off:

"Blessed is the poor in spirit, for theirs is the kingdom of heaven.

"Blessed is they that mourn, for they'll be comforted.

"Blessed is the meek, for they'll inherit the earth."

He was preaching an old sermon, but it took on a new quality, being shouted this way. When Sam shouted out that the meek would inherit the earth, the words had strength and challenge, especially to men subjugated by life and the state. He went on to say that his followers were not to murder or commit adultery, and were not to be angry with their brother, and were to be friendly with their adversaries. He said they were not to swear. They were to love their neighbors and their enemies.

"Bless them that curse you, do good to them that hate you, and pray for them which despitefully use you, and persecute you, that ye may be the children of your Father which is in heaven, for he maketh his sun to rise on the evil and on the good, and sendeth rain on the just and the unjust."

He let the words float off in the wind before he moved from there; then he came on down the hill, stopping along the way to cure a man or woman who appeared out of the laurel bushes. These were patients in the infirmary, too, and every time one appeared Dr. Chester gasped. As they were healed, they joined the multitude, and Dr. Chester sat there moaning, holding his head in his hands, as nervous as was Anna, who was clenching and unclenching her hands and clutching Cumberland's hand and arm, so anxious she was that it all go right.

It was, of course, going wonderfully well.

Again the preacher came forward. The choir began softly to sing, and Jesus went on off along a path behind the infirmary. The preacher said: " 'To whom shall we liken God?' Isaiah asked a long time ago. Ask yerself that and see where you arrive in your own thinking. Is God revealed in the petal of the flower, or the sharp tooth of the lion? In the lamb or in the wolf?"

Mildred drew her shawl closer around her shoulders and glanced contentedly at Weatherby, who was puffing at his pipe, enthralled.

"We heard what Jesus said and we've heard what all Jesus done, how he went about strewing good and telling people to forgive and be humble and not fight all the time and cut one another. Jesus was a forgiving man, and he come here, according to Paul and others, from God's own throne to reveal God. Now you think of that. So he's the one we have to liken to God, wouldn't you say?

"But I have to put in a word or two from the Old Testament, too, for Isaiah said the sword of God is filled with blood. In the Old Testament is where justice is found so stark and real, and justice is like the lion and maybe like the wolf, and it's more like this mountain here. Justice ain't forgiving. Mercy is what made Jesus, that there kindly man, to go about teaching and healing, spending a three-year hitch at hit, and what he said was right and needed, and what he done was to solve and cure. But what did Justice do to him? Isaiah said the sword of the Lord is made fat with fatness and with the blood of lambs, and the Bible says it was Jesus' own Father, it was God who had Jesus killed as a human sacrifice. So think on that and then come around again and ask to whom we can liken God."

There was a silence in that big field. Everybody was hushed. Even the doctor was leaning forward, catching every word.

"You're here to build a road, air ye? You're going to do this noble thing fer the world. Naturally you assume that you're going to be favored with kindness, since all you're trying to do is take medicine to the sick and food to the hungry and teachers to the ignorant. You expect courtesy from God."

Small fires were being lighted on the cemetery hill, and the tombstones began appearing, shining.

"Jesus had a large following, and they were marchers together, they were workers alongside. But they come to their reward, some slaughtered by outlanders, some ate by lions. The road of Galilee is a symbol to us all, for Jesus was himself killed there, and ye who build a road will need to reckon with that, for you are here on this hill overlooking them crosses for that purpose. Isaiah said to us: They shall be gathered together, as prisoners are gathered in the pit. And Isaiah also said: Their slain also shall be cast out, and their stink shall come up out of their carcases, and the mountains shall be melted with their blood. Knowing what Jesus did and how it ended for him, and knowing God, which of you can doubt the way it must end here for us, for you on this hillside, beside the new Road, on the new mountain, with the new crosses hung heavy with the newly dead?"

High at the top of the cemetery a big fire suddenly flared up. A gasp went through the congregation, and Dr. Chester and Cumberland stood up, struck dumb, and both started forward, but the preacher held up his hand and detained them. "See what Justice is," he said. "Do you see? Do you see what awaits the man of God?"

The fire lighted the top of cemetery knoll where, made out of bridge timbers and ties, were three great crosses, and on each dangled the body of a man.

Somebody said, his voice shaking, "That's not Sam Goddard hanging there, that's Marland, ain't it, him that died of t.b.?"

Another convict in horror said, "That man on the left is the one that used to bunk at the back wall of number three."

The firelighted, terrible sight struck fear and confusion into the men. The preacher tried to continue, but the convicts began yelling protests. Guards ran forward. The women were terrified.

Cumberland ran to the stage, arriving there a few steps ahead of Chester, and he held up his hands for quiet, but there was no quieting the men now. He took a gun from a guard and fired into the air. There was quiet almost at once; everybody turned to see what had happened, and he said, "It's only a play. It's not real."

The men stared at him, startled to hear such a thought, to be brought out of the world of their fears and back into the real world of their bondage.

"It's only a play," he told them. "It's all over. Let's sing a song here. Somebody line out a song."

The fiddle players obediently started in, playing "Barbara Allen" at a fast clip, and two of the guards began to clap their hands to the tune. Cumberland called several white convicts forward to begin a dance. Others came to dance, white and Negro, and soon fifty or more men and women were dancing, the others watching, some of them clapping, the twanging music and the dance caller's voice going out against the mountain wall.

Standing off to one side, his head low, was Rev. Plover, and on the mountain the fires still burned. The fields were empty where the shepherds had been. The multitude had gone again into the thickets. But the three crosses were heavy-laden, and the hollow eyes of the corpses looked down on the swirling scene.

Cumberland helped Dr. Chester get his patients back to bed, and he had convicts take down the three corpses and bury them properly. Then he and HenryAnna took the dejected preacher to their house and made hot soup for him. They told him he had done well; they had been thrilled to see the shepherds, they said, and to see Mary on the mule, and to see Jesus curing the sick.

At last the preacher raised his head and said, "I had to put that crucifixion in there, for it's part of the Christmas story, ain't it?"

Cumberland said, "The way you staged the manger scene was ingenius—"

"The crucifixion is the message, don't you agree? It's not in the manger."

"And in the Sermon on the Mount was one truth after another—"

"It's in the crucifixion." He would not be distracted from it. "That's the secret of it, that's where the Old and the New Testament come together, in the final justice, God sacrificing the best of all for the worst of us, and that's where the Road and the Cross converge, for it was by the Road that the Cross was stationed, and he died a common death, as he was born and growed, and there he was in public on the Road, deserted by God, his father. And it's the cross we're moving toward on this Road, not the manger. So I had to put it all in there."

On January 5 a snow came. It started flaking down that morning, and by evening it lightly covered the ground. As night came on, the flakes became larger and fell more slowly and heavily. Each flake fell individually, retaining its identity to the end.

When morning of the next day came the mountain was covered deeply. Snow fell all that day, too, and the men slipped and slid as they worked the carts. It stopped on the afternoon of the second day, and that night the temperature dropped lower. The wind grew gusty, and soon the turnpike was ice-coated, as was the Road. When the day gangs came from their barracks, they had a rough time making their way to breakfast. The wind was noisy and shrill, and when the men went along to the tunnels they were chilled through to their bones, and they moaned, and their ears and noses were pained, as if they were being bit by an animal. They had rather be inside the tunnels than out on the Road now, for the tunnels were warmer.

That night the temperature dropped still lower.

The next day the sun came out, and the mountain world was fashioned in whiteness and new shapes, where bushes huddled under shiny blankets. Here and there the prints of deer and rabbits were seen, trailing off along the paths, and the men cuffed each other and hurled snowballs at the barracks' walls and joked boisterously with the women. They worked hard that day.

The snow began to melt, and the trickling water sloshed across the ground where they worked, and seeped into their shoes. They cared little about that, for the sun was what they liked, the sun was warm and was warm on them; they could feel its health.

As soon as the snow had melted off the ground, men began to lay work track south from Lick Log tunnel, even though the tunnel had more benching to be done before the engine could get all the way through. They laid the track for a quarter of a mile to the portal of the new tunnel, which was to be only 150 feet long. It was the only tunnel yet remaining to begin.

The other major works uncompleted were the Swannanoa tunnel and Long Bridge. The lower level of the bridge was assembled and the timbers for the remainder of it were being notched. Work on the Swannanoa tunnel was going ahead on schedule, too, now that the engine was stationed at its western portal. The west gangs were 690 feet into the ground. The east gangs, in which Moses worked, had only mules to help and were 620 into the ground. In all, about 1,600 feet were done, and only 400 feet were left to dig out.

Putting the two tunnels together, there were about 850 feet of heading to do, and 10 weeks to do them in. Before the men got the new engine to the Gap, they had been doing about 80 feet of heading a week; now, with the engine, they were doing almost 100. Of course they were dead-tired and their mules were tired. "They's most dead," Ham told Babcock. "We's going to come out just about even with the mules." The oxen were about done. It was going to be a race for the finish line with the stock, but Weatherby had never been more confident of anything than he was of the Road being opened by the end of March.

Later in the week he got a bagpipe player from one of the many Scottish families in the mountains to play as the Mud-Digger rolled through Lick Log tunnel. The young mountaineer whom Tuttle had trained in engineering drove her through, waving at the men and laughing. He waved at Tuttle, too. "When you going to drive your train all the way through the Swannanoa?" he shouted.

"Oh, not till Monday," Tuttle said.

The bagpipe player played Scottish airs, and the Mud-Digger dragged its flatcars toward the next portal, which was "drilled and powdered." The engine stopped back a ways, and everybody got behind it while the blast took place.

Then the bagpipe began playing again, and the men moved on up to the wall; the engine backed its cars up there, and the work started on the new tunnel. "It's only a baby one," a Negro convict said. "You men go work some'ers else, and I'll do this one."

Beyond the new tunnel lay the turnpike, and beyond that lay the Swannanoa tunnel.

"We're standing in sight of a new day for this whole territory," Weatherby told Cumberland, and he had to say it again and say it louder, because of the bagpipe playing.

CHAPTER TWENTY-SIX

On February 4 an old Negro convict named Harley came out the east portal of the Swannanoa tunnel, complaining about a tightening in his chest. He had complained often before about sickness.

"We all have a pain in our chest," another convict told him. "What do you expect working 600 feet in the ground?"

But Harley said it was different with him now, and he said his head ached.

"All our heads ache," the man said to him. "Oh, no need to complain about what's always so and is almost ended, anyway."

But Harley said he felt different, he felt weak, he said.

"We all do," he was told.

But he said it was different and he had to lie down.

"Don't lie down here, where the blastings have to be carried out."

"Harley, you can't lie down; you're in the chain gang."

"Have to finish this here road, Harley."

But even their voices were far-off sounding. "It's different," he told them.

"Hell, you go tell the foreman it's different," a man said, "and see what he says."

But even their warning sounded different to him.

A chill came over him as he walked back toward the mouth of the tunnel. At the portal he stopped. A trickle of water was coming out of the wall, and he acted like he wanted a drink of it, but really he had to rest. He couldn't walk into the tunnel, seemed like, and all the sounds of mules and men were hollow in his head. He felt of his forehead and it seemed hot to him. "God, you help me," he whispered, for he often prayed. He knew God cared about him. "Oh my," he murmured, realizing an illness had come upon him.

He managed to avoid the foreman. He crept behind a mule cart and sat down, but the cart soon moved and he had to crawl behind another. He got to coughing, a raspy cough that worried him all the more. He spit but didn't see any blood.

A guard came up to him. "You sick?" he said.

"Yes, suh," Harley said.

"What you got?"

"It's inside."

"You quit working?"

"Suh, I'm dying out here," he said, tears forming in his eyes. He felt sorry for himself, for his own poor weak body. "I'm going to die, I'm fraid."

The guard went over to the fire and stood there warming. It was cold, though not as wintry as it had been for a few days. The winter weather had kept changing from time to time. "That nigger's sick," he told the foreman, once he came nigh.

"You say he is?"

"I think he's telling the truth. Look at him laying there."

"I got five men says they're sick, and that doctor will take them and more to his hospital if he gets a chance. What the hell does he think this is—a medical camp for experimenting?"

"Does he experiment?" the guard asked.

"He has enough notes to fill a ten-gallon crock. He uses more paper than medicine, examining every breath a man breathes. He believes everybody who says he's sick."

"That man over there is sick, I believe."

"You can't tell till you try to make him admit he's lying."

"Look at him, shivering. He's sick all right."

"Hey, you," the foreman said to Harley, "it's not fair to have a schedule to meet and you not help. It's not fair." He kicked him to make him turn over on his back and look up. "What you doing down there?"

Harley coughed deeply and wiped his mouth with his dirty hand. Tears welled to his eyes. "I sorry," he said.

"You ought to be. You get on in there and haul."

"Suh, I can't talk about it no more," Harley said slowly.

The foreman had to kick him until he got to his feet, but even then Harley wouldn't move on. "Damn ye, do ye have to be pushed?" the foreman said. But when he pushed him, Harley fell down. His hand fell in the fire and he didn't seem to know it. "Good God, get him out of the fire. He's addled for some reason."

"I think he's sick," the guard said.

"Well, he can work till the end of the day at least," the foreman said, "then we'll turn him in to the doctor if he still complains."

The foreman went into the tunnel and the guard told Harley to get up and help turn the mules. Harley crawled to his feet and held to the mules more than anything else.

"You got to stay on your feet," the guard told him, "or that foreman will beat hell out of ye."

"I got a pain in my side."

"Maybe you got hit with a rock or something. It'll go away."

"It's inside."

"Stay on your feet now. It's only two hours till sundown."

By the time darkness came Harley was delirious; he was talking such nonsense that the guard got to laughing at him. The guard couldn't help it, for the man was a fool and was stumbling around on his shaky legs, holding to the mules, trying to stay on his feet. It was as if the earth were appealing to him to fall down, were trying to pull him down, as if the ground were a magnet and his body were made of metal and his legs of stuffed cloth. He held to the mule's harness, or grasped the sides of a cart, and his eyes got big and the white part of them got red, and he said his side hurt and his head was bursting. He would cough and try not to let go of the mule when he coughed.

"You stay working, like the foreman said," the guard said, enjoying the show in spite of his pity for the man.

At last it was dark and the foreman called into the tunnel that it was quitting time; his words were passed from one worker to another, and each time an echo wrapped and hardened them. The foreman moved past the unloaders and through a corridor of mules to lead the way to the camp, and once more he noticed Harley, standing now in the middle of the Road, his eyes big and his mouth open, standing bent partway forward, not knowing where he was and not holding to anything at all.

"Help," Harley said, or something like that; the word was garbled and deep in his chest, where his cough was.

He was a poor pitiful sight, all right, and the guard asked the foreman, "You want to let him ride in a cart?"

"Help," Harley said, or something like that.

"Put him in a cart and let him ride," the foreman said.

"Can I ride, too, mister?" another convict said. "I got a chest pain, too."

"Put that sick man in the cart," the foreman said.

"Help," Harley said, even as they put him in the cart and were helping him all they could.

Dr. Chester was furious and wrote a blistering note to the foreman, telling him that when a man complained of illness he was to be sent to the infirmary, not held turning mules. He signed the note with his full name and sent a mountain boy with it, and the foreman found another mountain boy who could read and had it read to him.

He got flushed in the face as he listened and his fist clenched threateningly. "Can you write?" he asked the boy.

"Not too well."

"No, I'll bet not."

It had taken the boy several minutes to read the note, and he probably wrote even slower than he read. "I never have much to say that needs to be written down," the boy admitted.

"I wish I could write a note to that doctor and tell him to go to hell in a gourd. How can I believe every damn nigger convict that complains?"

"I'd write it if I could, just to see his face when I read it to him."

"Get on away and find a few words to read." He sought out Weatherby, who was at the far side of the long tunnel, and told him what had happened. "This nigger was lying out on the ground avoiding work, and all we had him do was turn mules, and then I have to take a cursing from that son of a bitch you hired to heal, and he ain't going to heal nothing for he's too busy awriting down what he's doing."

"I don't get along well with him, either," Weatherby admitted.

"God knows, I do what I can for any man, but we have a schedule."

"You follow the schedule," Weatherby said.

"I've got eight men on the sick call now."

"I'll try to pull them out of the infirmary for you."

"I'd rather have eight new men—"

"We get new men to replace those who are lost, that's all."

"Raleigh sends new'uns for sick or dead?"

"For dead."

"Well, if mine'd die, I could get another'n, but if they lay there under that doctor's care, I'm out a hand, is that it?"

"Yes," Weatherby said. "It's unfair, and I know you need hands."

"Also mules."

"I can't find more mules, and we need them bad."

"We do, we do," the foreman said. "I worry about that there schedule."

"So do I," Weatherby said. "But hold on tight, for we're coming in a few days early, as of now."

The foreman was lost in his own thoughts. "I'll say this, that nigger did appear to be sick, it's true."

Two of the women convicts at the Gap Station got sick, and Dr. Chester wrote a letter to the guard, officially criticizing him for dereliction in reporting the illnesses "to the proper authority." This didn't set well with the guard; he said he had been particularly careful about the welfare of his women. These two women had come down with colds, and the colds had got worse; they had complained of chills, so he hadn't made them wash clothes while they were sick, not after the chill started. "I tell you," he told Weatherby, "a nigger will get a chest cold, if you give him half a chance to, and there's nothing a body can do about it."

"Even so, we better take more care," Weatherby said cautiously. "I'm afraid of a winter sickness. God knows, we don't want more people dying here."

The next morning a telegram came over the line from Babcock Station, asking Weatherby to visit the hospital there. The infirmary was called a "hospital" now, by Dr. Chester. Of course, Weatherby visited it regularly, but this was a request for special help.

Weatherby telegraphed, asking for the reason. He had planned to be at the new tunnel that day and get some of the men working on the fill beyond it, so that, once the tunnel was opened, iron could at once be laid to the turnpike. He believed blasting out some of the hillside above the new fill would be the best method here. He would get two oxen working with scoops, arranging the fallen earth and rock after each blast, and keep the men on the tunnel and bridge work.

The telegraph started clicking. The clerk said the doctor wanted to see him. That was the reason, and no doubt the doctor thought that was reason enough.

Weatherby decided he wouldn't go. He told the clerk he had work to do on the Road. "I'm no doctor. Telegraph him that."

The clerk gladly started telegraphing that message. He didn't like Dr. Chester either. But Weatherby stopped him. "Tell him I'll be down this afternoon."

That morning Weatherby on crutches went to the new fill and started blasting on the cliff. He had the explosive mixed and set the way he wanted it, and he found he could direct the fall of the rock, so that he could make the fill without much hauling at all.

"It's an expensive use of mash," Babcock said.

"But we won't need but ten men on this fill, ten men and two oxen. What do you think of that?"

"You'll save plenty of time," Babcock admitted.

"That's what we most need to save. We can use even those men on the tunnels, once the iron is laid."

He asked the trainman to drive him to the infirmary and back. It would take only a few minutes to get there that way, and he could return all the sooner. He rode down in fine style, and when he arrived a white-cloaked Negro woman came to meet him, to say Dr. Chester was inside. She showed him the way past the medicine room and the operating room, which was the only painted room on the Road, and into a hallway off of which were two private rooms. In one of the private rooms two Negro women were lying on cots; in the other the doctor was standing at the foot of a narrow bed, and the old convict, Harley, was lying there talking.

Weatherby stood outside the door and listened as the old man talked about turning mules. Harley was delirious, of course. Suddenly he fell into a fit of coughing, and the Negro woman jumped forward with a towel. The old man coughed up something that she wiped off his face, and he tried to sit up, but she held him back on the mattress and said, "No, no," to him, and Dr. Chester said not to let him move except to turn him on the bed every half hour or so. "Don't let him even try to turn himself," he said. "Much less turn mules," he murmured.

Harley started talking about a fellow named Abe, and he said he was going to kill him. He held up one hand before his face as if to see it, but he didn't see it for some reason, even though it was before his very eyes, and he said he had killed him and was pleased to have done it so well. He then told how he had done it, and that he had blamed it on his brother, and he told how his brother had been sent to prison for it. He was talking as if explaining this to a confessor, as if his hand were somebody listening, and, of course, it was only the hand that must have killed this man named Abe. Harley said he had got so sorry for his brother and for Abe that he had gone out and done another awful thing so that he could be punished for it himself.

Then he got to talking to his hand, calling to his father, and a look of the deepest pain came at once over Weatherby's face.

"His fever is intense," Dr. Chester said. "His body is cooking with it, as well as his mind. I'll have to bleed him again." He stepped into the hall and told the nurse to watch Harley every minute. He opened the door across the hall and had Weatherby look at the two women in two cots inside there. One of them was the pretty girl named Lola, whom Moses liked. "They came in yesterday," Chester said. "They're cooking, too."

"What's the matter with them?" Weatherby said.

Dr. Chester closed the door. "Pneumonia," he said.

There they were standing in this little hallway, and Weatherby from that little spot could sense his whole world trembling, shaken from its roots, for the word carried meaning for him from a long time back.

Dr. Chester moved to the end of the hallway and opened a third door, and inside were many pallets on the floor, two lines of them, and men were lying on them. Two male orderlies were working with the patients. It was a nightmarish spectacle. "A few of them are sick with influenza or colds," he said. "When flu finds a patient that's weakened by poor food and who works in the open, it often sinks into his chest and pneumonia sets in." He closed the door and leaned his back against it and looked at Weatherby with weary eyes. His voice was soft and tired, too. "I saw it start like this in the war, in a prisoner-of-war camp. Some men had colds, some had influenza, some men had pneumonia of the type the man in the room there has, the type that takes several days to reach a crisis, and some men had pneumonia of the type those two Negro women have, which can kill a person in a day or two, or can linger for a long while. I don't know how many kinds there are, but I saw them all in the war and it became an epidemic that racked that camp and felled almost all the men in it, and killed one in four of them, and all

I knew to do was bleed the men. The more I bled them the more they seemed to weaken and die. But what else could I do? Did you ever see anything like that?"

"No," Weatherby said.

"Did you ever see men falling like flies, some with one sickness and some with another, some of it contagious, some of it not, but all of it inside the camp, like a plague?"

"I don't know what you mean," Weatherby said.

"You don't know what a plague is?" Chester said. He closed his eyes and an appearance of helplessness came over him. "I only know to bleed them, to bleed and purge them. Some doctors stand them up and bleed them until they fall down, but my records don't reveal any special benefit from that extreme."

"My father died of it, of pneumonia," Weatherby said.

"The type with a crisis, was it?"

"Yes."

"That's what Harley has. It doesn't spread, not as the other types, if I can judge."

"How many types are there?"

"Every day a new one," Chester said. He straightened and rubbed the back of his neck with his hand. "If I hadn't seen it in a prisoner camp in the war I wouldn't be so worried."

"Will it interfere with the work?" Weatherby asked.

"Will it?" Chester said sharply. "I'll draw you up a paper to say about that."

Weatherby waited there in the hallway, and the young trainman came to the door and looked in. "You 'bout ready?" he said.

Weatherby asked him to wait outside. "There's sickness inside here," he said. He went to shut the door and saw Moses in the yard. Moses came toward him, walking like a big cat, without a sound even though he walked on gravel. His face was drawn, but his body was relaxed, and he was part way crouched, as if prepared to spring. He stopped near the door and looked at Weatherby with the deepest sort of misery.

Weatherby was so engrossed in his own concerns that he scarcely could give attention to him. He told him to wait there until the doctor came.

Dr. Chester brought a note. Weatherby saw that he retained a copy of it; in case Raleigh ever asked, the doctor would be able to say what information he had given him. Weatherby also saw that a hired worker was standing in the hallway, watching, and no doubt he was Chester's witness. It was angering to be served like this by a subordinate, but Weatherby held his temper.

He read the note. It said that several cases of influenza and three cases of pneumonia had been reported in one day, and that both diseases struck most often when men and women got chilled and damp, and that it struck older people more often than young, and that it struck Negroes more often than whites. These cases could be the first signs of an epidemic or they might be only a warning.

In either case, the humane action to take is to do as follows:
(1) Improve the diet of the workers and convicts. Their diet has been deficient in quality and amount.
(2) Space the men no closer than 8 feet in the barracks.
(3) Cease all work in the damp tunnels, and other work on the colder days.
(4) Send men who complain of headaches or of pains in their chest or sides immediately to the infirmary.

The note was signed with the full name of the doctor.

Weatherby folded it and put it in his jacket. "There's a man here to see Lola," he said simply.

The doctor was stunned by the casualness of his reply. He and the witness had been watching for the reaction, expecting defiance and anger.

"He's outside there," Weatherby said.

The doctor saw Moses, but he didn't care about Moses just now. "What is your answer?" he said to Weatherby.

"I'll go home and talk it over with Cumberland and the others," Weatherby said. "I want to thank you for getting me down here and giving me this advice, because . . ." He looked out the door at the haggard big man, and his own sorrow for himself and for Moses welled up. "I'll talk with the men, ask them if they want to quit just now."

"The men can't judge a matter like this. You can get the men to say what you want them to."

"It's a matter of their lives; they'll have an opinion about the importance of that."

"You've got them dedicated to the Road."

"I have no way to space them eight feet apart, seems to me. We'll have to figure on such matters. Even before the fire, we were tighter for space than that."

"Unless you want a death camp on this mountain . . ."

"I understand," Weatherby said. He opened the door wider. "Now, if you'll let Moses see her for a minute, I'll wait and ride him back with me."

"Why, he can't go inside there," Chester said. "Go on away," he said to Moses.

"I wouldn't talk like that to him," Weatherby said softly. "He can look at her from the doorway, can't he?"

Chester turned impetuously into his office and slammed the door.

Moses came on inside the hall. The witness silently studied him, leery of him; there was a desperateness about him that boded no good.

"It's the first door on that side," Weatherby said to him. "Don't go into the room, though."

Moses went to the door and nudged it open. Weatherby, even from where he was standing, noticed a wave of tenderness come over him. Moses stood there, helpless, moaning.

Weatherby went quietly to him and touched his arm. "Come on now," he said. "She won't hear you, if you speak, nor know you."

Moses didn't move.

Weatherby took his arm and said, "We can talk outside about her."

Moses followed to the outdoors, which was sunlighted brightly in the clearing. He mopped his eyes dry.

"She's getting the best help that can be provided anywhere," Weatherby said.

Moses nodded. He stared off at the engine, not seeing it really.

"She's a pretty woman," Weatherby said simply. "She's young and will get well. I suspect she's only got a croup in her chest. You come with me now." Weatherby moved to the engine and climbed up into the cab. When he looked back, he saw Moses walk to a big rock near the door of the infirmary and sit down, stationing himself there.

Weatherby said to the engineer, "Back her up home," and the engineer opened the throttle and the engine started backing up, and even when they were well above Babcock Station, turning around one of the curves that overlooked the station, they could see the doorway and see Moses sitting on the big rock.

Weatherby got off the engine at the new tunnel. He said nothing to any of the workers. A man had crushed a thumb and was standing beside the Road, not knowing what to do, and Weatherby asked a mountain boy to go with him to the infirmary.

He walked to his office, trying to avoid thinking about the decision facing him. He asked Cumberland to come in and shut the door, and he gave him the doctor's letter.

Cumberland sat down and read it through before he looked up. "You're not going to do it, are you?"

"I once said I'd take medicine to the mountains; it seems I'll take it to them in a coffin."

"You can't move the men off the Road."

"It's a wave so disturbing I can't see the crest of it."

Cumberland folded the letter. "Will he send a copy of it to the prison people in Raleigh?"

"I don't know what he'll do, damn him."

"How would you house or feed the men any better?"

"Send half of them back to Raleigh, then we'd have room enough, and maybe food enough, and money enough."

"You'd have only half as many men working, though."

"Might as well send them all back in that case."

"Write the governor. You can get more time."

"I've written the governor three times of late, did you know that? I've sat here and written him, explaining how far along we are, asking him to send a man to see for himself, explaining the impossibility of rescheduling, but he's not helpful. I think he's up against a wall, the state has poured money and men into this mountain project so long now."

"Well, I think this sickness will pass over," Cumberland said.

"Do you?" Weatherby said. "Do you?"

"I think so."

"With all we know about the way things go on this mountain? Do you think it'll pass over? Didn't you hear that preacher tell us God is a hard one for justice?"

"Be like him then," Cumberland said.

Weatherby stared at the young man, then slowly sat back in his chair. "You used to be softer, more generous than that."

"I listened to this doctor, too, while you were away last winter, and we lost months of time."

"I knew what Babcock would advise me to do," Weatherby said. "I knew he wouldn't quit, even if the mountain herself told him to get down off here. He'd spit and tell her to go to hell and leave him be."

"You can't leave the Road now, when we're on top of it," Cumberland said.

"Well, we are on top of it. We're saving more time at that new fill, too. When that's done, we'll sweep right on over the turnpike above that whispery creek and skirt the ridge to the east portal of the Swannanoa tunnel. There's not but four hundred fifty feet of heading to open inside her. So it's easy to see it all now, even though there's some wilderness yet to go through. What's left is nothing compared to what we've done. It's nothing. It looks formidable, but it's nothing now. Why, I don't know how we can stop when we have only six weeks of work left to do. But take the men off it, and the Road will falter by spring, and we'll have not enough men to finish it, for these mountain men won't build it. They don't hold to anything they think is faltering."

"Except their own ways," Cumberland said dryly.

"Oh, yes. They'll prop up their own barn, even if it's twenty degrees slanted, and they'll repair a rotting fence, but they won't build a new barn, or a new fence, or a new road. Not like them convicts will." He walked to the window and looked out toward the wild country yet to be gone through. "That sick old man, Harley, was talking about sending his brother to prison for a crime he did himself. Write to Raleigh and ask them if he has a brother in prison."

"The prison department's records aren't dependable, you know."

"Harley said he killed a man named Abe, apparently with his hands."

"Was he talking rationally?"

"That's what I want to know. See if their records show anything at all. And put that doctor's letter away in a private place. Don't mention it around, if you don't mind. I know what Babcock will say, so no need to mention it to him, or mention influenza or pneumonia at all."

"You won't let the Road go, will you?" Cumberland said.

"Well, it's like standing at the forks of a trail, and I see punishment if I travel that way and punishment if I travel the other, so I'll go wrong either way. I don't know that it's going to be clear to me, even when I'm old, what I ought to do now."

"Don't let the Road go."

"All those mountain people will be better off if it's built, yet all these men are endangered if it's built."

"They're endangered, anyway."

"And they're criminals, anyway, and they've all done crimes, anyway, and maybe that's part of it." He took his crutches and went out of doors and passed Babcock, who told him the work was going well. He went along the rails to where the steam engine was, and went past that to the new fill, and on to the east portal of the long tunnel. He asked if Moses had come back. He hadn't. "Anybody sick?" he said.

The foreman shook his head. "Not that I know of."

"Anybody complaining about being sick?"

"No."

He walked to the other portal of the tunnel and asked Tuttle how the work was going. "Is the engine holding up all right?"

"That smith oils it day and night. He works on it whenever it's stopped."

"No sickness reported?"

"Nothing, except a man got his foot hurt."

"Is it broken?"

"No, it's just bruised. He says it feels like it felt on the third day after he last tried to break in a new pair of shoes."

Weatherby laughed and went on, wondering how there could be an epidemic if nobody was reporting sickness. Maybe the doctor was wrong.

He saw that the cottage over at the millpond had smoke coming out of its chimney, so he went over there. "You come on," he said to HenryAnna. "I want you to come with me." He told her to get a coat, and she put on one Cumberland kept in the house.

They walked around the pond, and along the path to the waterfall. "Does that trail lead to the bald?" he said.

"That path is one way," she said.

"You know, Anna, I saw you taking a bath in that pool once."

"You did?" she said, aghast. "You looked?"

"Oh, yes, I looked," he said, amused by her discomfort. "You're made pretty all over."

"You ought'n to have looked."

"Oh, I've never harmed you, have I?"

"No," she said.

"Is the end of that path through a laurel slick?"

"Not if you know how to go." She led the way, and they went up the steep path and around the roots of a big oak tree, following the path that wound steeply through woods and rhododendron. They walked until below them they could see the Gap and the west portal of the tunnel. They went farther up the mountain and reached an overlook where they could see Cemetery Hill and the infirmary. They could even make out the tombstones there. "All those dead, and in addition the ones that burned in the boxcar. Almost a hundred dead, Anna," he said.

"Have there been that many?" she said.

"Some were shot. Some died of age or natural sickness. But fifty-one died of rocks falling and cave-ins and the like, and that boxcar fire."

"How many men did you think the Road would cost?"

"I knew it would take aplenty. Any road does. It's like a battle. You use explosives, the same as in a war. You're engaged in danger all the time. I never tried to estimate what it would cost. I was willing to give my own life for it; it's the only work I ever felt that way about. And if you feel that way about something you can risk the lives of others, too, don't you see, and not feel guilty."

"Yes, I see that."

"But the time comes when you have to measure more carefully." He looked up at the dome of the mountain, which was quite near. "You stay here, Anna," he said.

He walked alone on his crutches along the path to the heathland, and made his way until he stood finally on the crest of the dome, where the wind was a continuous, rushing stream. A light snow was falling on the far valley. He stood there in the great field and looked about in every direction. There was no peak here, no one site of rock or trees that represented the pinnacle. He stood where he was in the wind, with snow falling nearby, saying over to himself the words of promise and of death, in anguish saying the same words he had said at the burial thirty years ago of his father.

CHAPTER TWENTY-SEVEN

THE NEXT DAY Harley's fever remained high, as did the two women's. Moses stayed at the hospital. A mountain boy told Weatherby the doctor wouldn't let Moses come inside, so he made a shelter under Long Bridge, about a hundred yards from the infirmary. The mountain boy said Moses stayed out most of the night in the snow and didn't seem to mind it. "He sneezes like an old bear and eats what food he can scrounge and stays near the building," he said.

That night Harley's fever relaxed, and Lola's did, too, but the other woman's increased and she had to be bled again.

All this while Weatherby wrestled with the decision, but on the third morning he called in Cumberland and confided in him that he was going on with the Road. "It's the only choice I can make; I'm powerless to go the other way," he said. Later that day he told Babcock to send convicts who had colds and other minor illnesses to Henry Station. "Trade Henry Station man for man," he said. "Don't send minor ailments to the infirmary, for they're lost to us when we need them most."

Cumberland assured him that the proper decision had been reached.

"Well, I don't know, I don't know," Weatherby said. "But we can only go one way or the other, and this way at least offers hope."

That same day Harley's fever started falling. That night his temperature went on down to almost normal. Cumberland predicted that Dr. Chester had diagnosed his illness wrong in the first place. But when morning came the infirmary reported that the fever was increasing, and that night Harley was delirious again.

Weatherby was tortured by every report, yet he kept asking how Harley and the women were, and if other illnesses had been reported.

On the fifth day Harley's temperature remained high. On the sixth day it increased again, so that the old man had to be strapped to his bed. Weatherby sent word to Mildred that he wouldn't be home that weekend at all; he stayed in the office, waiting for new signs. On the sixth day the temperature remained intense, and on the seventh day it dropped to normal. The next morning it was below normal. At noon on the ninth day Harley died.

Dr. Chester came to the Gap station that afternoon and sat in Weatherby's office. He drank coffee and talked philosophically about Harley's death. Even as he sat there, a blast went off at the new fill, then a muffled blast at the new tunnel; there wasn't a critical gaze or word from him. He didn't mention the pneumonia, except to say that Lola had survived the illness and the other woman might do so.

It was a relief to Weatherby to have the doctor more satisfied than he had been.

About four o'clock Dr. Chester got up to go, and casually, as if he only now remembered it, he said, "They brought in three men from Henry complaining of colds, and I've examined them."

Weatherby knew the doctor was going to criticize him for not sending the men directly to him.

"One has influenza. The other two have pneumonia," he said.

The words were quietly put. The doctor set his coffee cup down and went out, leaving the office door open, leaving Weatherby sitting there at the desk staring before him. Weatherby heard the front door close, heard Cumberland's chair scrape as he got up, heard his footsteps approach the desk.

"He seemed to be in good spirits." Cumberland said.

"Yes," Weatherby said. "He's a pleasant fellow."

"No troubles?"

"He mentioned two or three matters, on leaving." Snow was falling, he noticed. He got up and went to the window. "Sometimes she has a bite like a wolf, and at other times she smothers you to death. She's going to smother me to death this time, Cumberland." There was a drawn, haggard look about him, and his face was sallow and his cheeks were hollow. "That's what pneumonia is, smothering to death."

Cumberland didn't know what to say to him. "It's all right now, isn't it?" he said.

"Oh, yes," Weatherby said. "We have our part to play, and we'll play it out. This time the walls of the cave are soft, not rock at all, but I'm just as powerless to escape as I was before."

"What in the world is the matter?"

Weatherby went out the door, forgetting his crutches, not stopping even when Cumberland called to him, not even putting a coat on. He went out into the snow, slipping on it, and made his way toward where the blasting was being done.

Cumberland found him at the new fill, up on the rocks helping to put mash in the drilled holes. "Why is he doing that work?" Cumberland said to Babcock, unnerved by the erratic actions of the man.

"I don't know," Babcock said. "He moved in there and took charge."

"He'll blow himself up."

"No, he's careful." They watched as, high up, he lighted a fuse and made his way on his weakened leg over snow-covered rocks.

"My God," Cumberland murmured.

He reached safety as the explosion rang out.

When Weatherby came off the cliff, he took his coat, which Cumberland had brought him, but he didn't put it on. His lips were blue and he was pale of face. His teeth were chattering. He refused to take the crutches. "I'll not be hurt anymore, not in such a way. I won't need them any more."

"You'll catch cold, or worse," Cumberland said.

"No, no. She's got me where she wants me already. She's going to take care of me another way."

He wouldn't explain what he meant.

He and Cumberland walked together over the snow-packed trail to the office. "I'm through with crutches. She won't let anything happen to me," Weatherby said.

A mountain boy brought hot water and filled a tub. Weatherby bathed and went to bed, without bothering to wait for supper, but Cumberland got a bowl of stew and brought it to him.

"You're a kind man," Weatherby said to him gratefully. "You stay with me now, you hear?"

"You mean tonight?"

"No, no. I mean a longer and harder time than that. You stay with me."

"You know I will."

"Unless I have to leave, and in that case you stay with what's left of me here. Every man has a birthright, did you know it? Some are born with a birthright, money or position or power. And some who don't have one born to them have one left to them."

"That's so," Cumberland said, though he had never thought of it that way before.

"I'm giving you one," Weatherby said. He closed his eyes and seemed to want to be alone, but as Cumberland started to leave, Weatherby said, "I thought the cave was the jaws of the mountain, but this new trap is more like the womb of the mountain, taking me into herself, sucking me in, closing in on me, smothering me, taking me back into herself so she can devour me that way. There's nothing unnatural about it. It's the most gentle, inevitable, natural thing in the world to be taken into death this way."

Next morning Weatherby got word that Dr. Chester was building a new addition onto the infirmary. He had fifty men working on it, men who had been working on Long Bridge the day before. It was more than Weatherby could bring himself to do to go down there, and he knew Babcock would get angry with him, so he asked Cumberland to go. At noon Cumberland came back, looking tired. He sank down at a desk. "I put them back to work on the bridge," he said.

"What was his attitude?" Weatherby said.

"He wouldn't come out of his office. He sat in there behind a big desk he has had made for himself. He has a slate on the wall behind it, with a few words written on it. He sat in there with a wry smile on his face, as if somehow we were torturing him and he was superior to us all, and he mentioned you a time or two, with the most intense hatred."

"What's written on the slate?" Weatherby said.

"Nine pneumonia; twenty-three influenza! That's all it said."

"Nine, you say?" Weatherby said, stunned.

"He sat there behind that desk that's got nothing on it, not a book nor paper nor piece of chalk, and he smiled in that bitter way he's got, and he kept saying something under his breath over and over."

"Saying what?"

"It's murder."

"Uh-huh. Maybe it is. Do you think it is?"

"I didn't even know there were new cases down there."

"Well, I don't know where it stops. I don't know what to say except I'm going on. If I didn't go through with this it'd be unnatural. I'm going to play my part, and no doubt he'll play his."

"He's bound to have sent a report to Raleigh."

"Nine, you say? Think of that."

"But I put the workers back on Long Bridge. The foreman said they ought to finish it inside of two weeks. He told me the doctor had ordered them to build a new hospital, had them use bridge timbers for the addition, timbers already notched for the bridge. Is he crazy?"

"You might say he's crazy. Either that or he's the only sane man here. It's a judgment I won't try to make. Nine, you say?"

A blast was heard from far off, and the ink in the well rippled for a moment and the lantern trembled. "That's the east portal, I think," Cumberland said.

"No, we don't hear the Swannanoa blasts here, now that they've gone so deep. It's at the new tunnel." He stared at Cumberland for a moment, then calmly said, "I feel all right about it. I had to decide something, and I did, and it's done now. You were right to put the men back on the bridge. Send word to the foreman at Henry and tell him to keep them there, regardless of what the doctor or anybody else tells him. Tell him to move ahead expeditiously while he can, for a tide's coming. No, don't tell him a tide's coming, but tell him the rest of it. And you might stay away from the men yourself, and keep Anna out of the stations and away from the tunnels. You better tell her that today. Tell her to stay away from her brothers, too, and her father. You hear?"

"Yes."

Weatherby pulled on his coat. "I'll go watch the blasting at the tunnels." He stopped at the door. "You ought to be friendly to that doctor next time you see him."

"Why?"

"You might need him soon."

On February 21 the report from Babcock Station was 19 cases of pneumonia, 35 of influenza, and 3 new deaths.

On February 25 there were 25 cases of pneumonia, 62 of influenza, and another 5 deaths.

On February 28 Dr. Chester, tense and desperate, came to the Tunnel Station office and asked Weatherby to cease all operations in construction of the Road and "turn all facilities into rest camps for the workers in order to heal the sick and save those who are yet well."

Weatherby told him he was unable to stop the construction of the Road. "I'm as unable to do that as you would be unable to take a surgeon's knife and destroy the life of a patient who trusted you."

Chester was on the verge of exhaustion. Tears welled up into his eyes. "I have no beds even for the desperately sick. My God, it's inhuman!"

"Don't expect me to do what it's humanly impossible for me to do," Weatherby said. "We'll use one barracks at Henry if you need more room."

"It's the tunnels that are choking them. It's the blasting and candle fumes in there, and the cold. It's the exhausting work and the lack of food. The flu and pneumonia are going from one man to another. It's murder. What you do here is murder. I can't cure them."

"I can't save them either."

"I bleed them and purge them, but it doesn't cure them. I don't know how to cure them."

"I don't know how to stop the work," Weatherby said.

"I have to watch them die again, but you're killing them!"

"Yes, very well," Weatherby said in anguish. "And you're letting them die."

On March 4 two officials from Raleigh, one of them of the Prison Department, arrived at Henry Station. They questioned foremen and a few convicts there, then walked to Babcock Station, where they talked for an hour with Dr. Chester. That afternoon, accompanied by Chester, they walked to the Tunnel Station and waited in the office. Weatherby was setting off nitroglycerin at the new fill, and Cumberland went to get him. They walked together back to the office.

"We moved forty cubic yards of rock today," Weatherby said. "We've learned how to blast rock accurately into the fills."

"You're making fast progress, I know."

"No, I think not, not any more," Weatherby said.

He stopped to get a cup of coffee, but his hand was trembling so much he couldn't hold it. He set the cup on a log. The convict women, Lola among them, were watching him. "You feeling all right, Lola?" he said.

"Yes, sir. I almost died, Mr. Weatherby. I never went so low."

"Moses was watching over you," he said. "He wouldn't let you die."

"I knowed he was out there," she said.

Weatherby went on, and Cumberland said, "Your leg doesn't limp."

"No, I won't limp going home," Weatherby said. When he got to the steps of the office house, he stopped. "Don't come in," he said.

"Sir?" Cumberland said, surprised.

"No, you stay out here."

"Babcock and the doctor are in there."

"I don't want you to see this. You go on up to your house and see Anna. You marry her and be done with roads, you hear me? I never should have started a road that's nothing but a rope around my neck. I should have seen it months ago, coiling at me. I don't mind dangling, but you go on now and see her, and I'll see you tonight sometime."

He went inside and firmly shut the door. Cumberland heard him say something to a clerk about keeping people out. Then there was quiet from that small building where the fate of the Road was to be worked out, and there was quiet on the Road except, way off at the new tunnel, an explosion was heard that rocked the earth slightly even where Cumberland stood.

Weatherby saw that the doctor was sitting near the door inside his own office. Three other men were in there, one of whom was Babcock, who had his head down dejectedly, his hands pressed tightly together and hung between his legs. Weatherby stopped at the door and looked at the other two men. He knew one of them, a Prison Department official, and said hello to him and called his name. The other man was a Mr. Principal, and he worked with the governor.

There was an awkwardness in the room which Weatherby didn't attempt at once to dispel. He sat down and laid his hands on his lap. He began talking, and he told the officials about the Road and the need for the Road, and they listened politely, though it was clear that their thoughts were elsewhere. "When the Road is open, I suppose it'll be of political consequence," Weatherby said. The Raleigh men showed some interest in that. "The time will come when those who supported the Road will be heroes to the voters in the mountains." He had their attention now, so he talked about that point for a few minutes, closing with the quiet admission that "We've had some sickness come in here lately, and it's hampered the work, but even so we've kept at our final schedule. Not to do so would have caused distress up here."

Nobody said anything. The doctor stood near the door, waiting. Finally, Mr. Principal said, "Do you know how many patients are sick this morning? Thirty-five came in to Babcock Hospital last night, another twenty-two have come in so far today, and we found at Henry Station thirty or forty men who were too sick to get to Babcock at all."

The figures overshadowed the arguments Weatherby had given. There was no explanation that would any longer suffice, he realized.

"At both places men are being kept waiting in carts. There's a terrible epidemic here, Mr. Weatherby. We wouldn't be surprised if almost everybody in all three camps comes down with flu or pneumonia before it's over. God knows how many will die. We came up here today to make a few decisions, and we hope to do this without an official investigation."

"What sort of investigation?" Weatherby said.

"Well, you take the agreement about food. The convicts are to have half a pound of bacon apiece each day, and this has not been done."

"You're going to investigate the bacon scarcity, are you?"

"Well, there are other things," Principal said defensively. "There are all these men sick and dying. My God, you talk about political implications!"

"Do you say I made them sick?"

"No, of course not, not directly."

"Do you say I've made them die?"

"No, I don't." he said.

Weatherby was aware of weaknesses in the official. At the same time he knew about a weakness in himself: he didn't want the officials to falter. He wanted to be relieved of responsibility here. The number of men who were now sick was beyond his mind's power to comprehend; he couldn't be the one to stop the work but he couldn't endure further the suffering the work caused him. "I think there's no need for an investigation, that's all I'm saying."

The two men from Raleigh nodded, pleased to accept that, and finally Mr. Principal said, "We would like to bring in such doctors as we can hire in Old Fort and Morganton."

"Yes, of course," Weatherby said.

"We'd like for all work to stop on the Road."

"Yes, it will need to stop now. I agree," Weatherby said.

"We will as soon as practicable move the convicts back to Raleigh."

"Yes. Well, they are due to go back soon."

"In the meantime it would help matters if you would cooperate in one more decision," Principal said.

"I'll do whatever I can."

"We want you to resign."

"Yes, I'll do that," Weatherby said, relief sweeping over him. "I will," he said. Babcock started to make an objection, but Weatherby interrupted him. "It's all right," he said.

The two officials looked to the doctor for comment, but he was too surprised by the ready agreement, too startled to get his thoughts in order.

"My resignation will be submitted to the Road's Board of Directors, appointed by the governor, and I will assume their acceptance of it, for practical purposes. Mr. Cumberland, of course, is the next official in line and is a good man to straighten out the complications. He is a bookkeeper by trade, an office manager sort of fellow, and he can represent the interests of the Road very well. He will be in charge."

The two officials from Raleigh looked at Dr. Chester, who was flushed and unsettled.

Weatherby continued. "Mr. Cumberland has the loyalty of the men and the foremen, and knows all of them, and he has been fair in his dealings with everybody, and so far as I know he has not been involved in policy decisions concerning the sick people. He has only done what I directed him to do. He is the one who, as an officer appointed by the Board, will be legally responsible."

Chester said nothing, and the men from Raleigh finally said that would be all right with them.

"Then you deliver this." Weatherby took an envelope from his desk. "It's my resignation. I give pressures of illness as my reason. It's an apt reason, I'm sure you will agree." He handed it to Mr. Principal. "Now I'll pack my things and go home."

Cumberland walked with him. It was afternoon now. They walked along the Road to Babcock Station, past the graveyard, where four men were working with shovels to dig the graves for the newly dead whose bodies were laid out nearby. They walked to the infirmary, and Weatherby wouldn't stop there, or even look at the place, or the crowd of men and women, some standing at the door and some sitting and lying on the ground. They walked unnoticed down the path to Babcock Fish Creek, and crossed it near the place they had camped two and a half years before. Above them were the poles of Long Bridge, and Weatherby stopped under them and looked up at them. "You ever think you'd see a structure like that here? Why, those men can do anything. But it's wasted work, I fear." He climbed the opposite bank and stood for a moment looking back at the bridge, and beyond the bridge at the way the Road twisted as it gained elevation above the station and the grave-yard, and entered Bloody Cut. That was the last sight they had of it, until it appeared out of the trees again higher up, near where the tunnels started. "You see that little creek washing down far up there? You see that waterfall it makes?"

"Yes, I see it."

"We could have captured that creek and brought it down to this valley, to Babcock Station, and made a fountain out of it. I suspect that creek would send a spout fifty or more feet into the air. Oh my, yes, it would be a sight."

They walked along the iron track to Mud Cut, and Weatherby stopped in the middle of that and looked up at the sluice canal, which now was diverted, which wasn't needed today. "How much rock have we put in here?"

"Maybe twenty carloads."

"Seems solid now. She's tricky as can be, though, all of this is. But I tell you, the time would have come when the Road was accepted as part of the mountain's way of life, and then anything which tried to change the Road would be the enemy. Nature would accept the changes we've made; creeks we've diverted would have developed their new channels, and the plants and bushes would grow to protect the fills, and the trestles would settle into their holds, and the tunnels would be safe enough by then. It could have turned out that way."

When they came near Henry Station they saw that an engine waited there to take Weatherby to Morganton. They entered the station grounds and only then did the sounds of the sick reach them, the babble of men in delirium, recounting in groans and words the guilt of their deranged minds. There were any number of carts there, and men lying in the carts, blankets and even mattresses over them. On the ground near the carts other men were lying, and convict women were coming to them, bringing them dippers of watery soup. Everywhere was the smell of sickness and the hideous aspect of dead and dying men.

A convict saw Weatherby and called to him. "Make them help me," he said. He said he knew Weatherby would help him. Other convicts started calling to him for help. Eight or ten men, sitting in carts and on the ground, began calling to him desperately. Somebody called from the stockade to him. "Is he out there?"

Another voice called, "Come help me; God, come help me."

"He's come to help us at last," a man said.

He stood there in the midst of the sound, and Cumberland sensed how cruel their confidence was to him, how close he was to lashing out desperately to free himself from it, from the frustration of the death sounds and the fact of his guilt and inadequacy. Cumberland called for the engineer to back the engine up to him. "It's ready to take you home," he told Weatherby, his voice almost lost in the sounds of the men and women calling for help, sick, smothering people, desperate, lying on the ground and in the carts and at the stockade doors, the dying shadows of his dying father and his dying lifework. "Get aboard, go now," Cumberland said. He had to lead him to the engine and help him into the cab.

Weatherby stood stiff and silent, and Cumberland told the engineer to take him to the door of his home. The engineer let the throttle out, calling ahead for the sick to clear the tracks. Weatherby stood in the open cab, looking down at the crowd of pleading men and women on both sides of him who were reaching up to him for help, as the engine moved through them, its bell all the while ringing, the sound bounding back from the face of the mountain.

CHAPTER TWENTY-EIGHT

THE CORPSES WERE TAKEN from Henry to Long Bridge, and were carried across the bridge to the burial ground, where six men were working now, burying, and where Henry-Anna's father preached the services, recalling what he could about each man he buried. "No, let me see him afore you put him in the hole. Let me see his face. Ay, I knew you'd be here afore long. Ay, I tried to tell you and save you a trip you'd regret. Ah, he was a fine man for work. Well, lay him in, and be careful not to bruise him needlessly. I knew him when he breathed as well as you. I told him then he'd be here afore spring."

Sometimes he would play a tune on the dulcimer, which he said was the best instrument for burials. "I'd a used it for my Christmas service, but it's got no span to it. It won't carry out into the air like a fiddle will, or even like a guitar. But here at the grave it sounds loud enough for the dead to hear us."

Whenever snow fell the men had to dig through the soft crust. They dug the graves none too deep, even though Plover complained if they were shallow. One night the wolves came down to the graveyard and dug up seven new graves, and the next morning, when he saw what had been done, he began to weep aloud and to berate the men, and he told them they would dig deeper holes or perish. "Think of yourself being buried in a place for wolves to get to. Now go fetch an ox and drag stones and mound them over ever grave, a foot deep of stones. It's a weight they've carried afore. Ay, God, we'll protect the dead even if we didn't know how to protect the living."

Red Tuttle told Nettie about the chaos on the Road. He came up to her place and bathed in the woodshed before he would approach the house; she had to haul hot water out there and put it in a tub, then he locked the shed door and undressed and washed. He put on the pair of pants her first husband had once worn and a clean shirt and clean socks. When he got to dinner—this was on a Sunday—he told her and one of her grown sons, who was there to eat with them, that he felt like he had come out of the grave. "There are people falling over in the camps the worst I ever saw. There are people walking from the barracks to get their food, and they suddenly stop on the Road and can't go any farther, so a mule cart comes along and they get in it and pull the blankets over themselves and are taken to Henry, or to Babcock. It's got so diseased, I wouldn't ride a car of the Western North Carolina Railroad for a year."

"Are you yet blasting?" Nettie asked. "I ain't heard ye."

"No, we don't blast now. We don't dig, don't haul. That last snow melted and the water started washing and damming up, and nobody even lifted a hand to free it, so it carried off a piece of fill at Holly Ridge. I said to Cumberland, 'Look, that fill's going to slip,' and he said he guessed it would, but he don't have time or men to undam anything. The free workers have fled away from there, except for Babcock and me, and the mountain boys are gone, too, or they hang back a long way from camp and come to the edges of it sometimes. They try to hold their jobs that way, in order not to lose out on their back pay."

Nettie's son ate even faster than Tuttle. He shoveled the food into his mouth. He got his head down close to his plate and slid the food into his mouth and swallowed, all in one motion. The food didn't stop moving from the time the spoon touched it to the time it landed in his stomach, so far as Tuttle could tell. There was precious little chewing connected with it. The son was a big, handsome man, who claimed to be a sheep farmer.

"That doctor, who interferes with more than he fixes, and did in Pennsylvania, too, is going to and fro," Tuttle said, "riding the trains back and forth, telling everybody what to do, but since everybody is leaving it scarcely matters what he says, for there's nobody to talk to now except the patients, and they're dying or getting ready to leave. Two train cars of them left this morning, with signs on the door saying: 'Epidemic—Western North Carolina Railroad—Do Not Open This Door.' "

"You better stay here with us and not go back," Mrs. Davis said.

"I'm one to throttle engines; I can't stay away from it."

"It's not worth your life to work for a sick company."

"Oh, I know that, but I took the place of a dead man, so I feel protected."

"I wouldn't feel safe with all that suffering going on." She was worried about him, that was plain. "You can stay here and use that front parlor room; it's got the best bed in it."

Her son stopped shoveling food and looked up, startled by the suggestion. He had food in his mouth but he wasn't chewing it. He glared from his mother to Tuttle and back again, not quite sure he believed what he wasn't quite sure he had heard amid his swallowing.

Tuttle said he wouldn't be able to stay in the house overnight.

The son swallowed.

"And that preacher, or music man, or whatever he is, claims to have predicted it all. Well, I was there Christmas night and heard him preach and couldn't make any more sense out of it than if a woman was talking, but he claims now to be a prophet. He stands up there in the graveyard and preaches to the six men that dig graves, and he has fires burning out on the hillside every night, whether to keep the dead warm or warn the wolves I don't know, but the wolves come to the field anyway. You can see their eyes reflected in the firelight, and there's not a mountain boy left to shoot them, and not a guard cares about them or the dead, for they're so concerned with the living and themselves. The preacher sleeps there, but he gets little sleep, even though all day he preaches. He's got so wobbly from weariness that he has to prop himself up with Weatherby's old crutches. Sometimes even in the middle of his sermons he'll start dozing. The doctor cares nothing about the graveyard, and Cumberland stays in the office, making out forms, reporting everything to

Raleigh, trying to explain what went with the bacon money the Prison Department sent to the Road. Cumberland is as calm as you please, burying records in a box in a hole in the ground and stuffing other records in the stove. He keeps warm at night by burning records."

"It's awful to hear it told about," she said, shivering. "And I'd hoped sometime to see a train run."

"I'd a given you a whistle whenever I passed your lane."

"Would you?" she said, pleased.

"I'd a pulled the bell, too, you know that."

"I guess you would have."

"Lord, yes."

He ate chicken and dressing and salet greens and what was left of a jug of molasses, which he poured on corn bread, and he drank cider, for she had no coffee. He liked cider, anyway.

"I been meaning to buy coffee," she said, "but it's so dear."

"We've none left at the camp, either."

"I've got so I like warm milk about as well as anything. And I drink buttermilk. Mostly my own suppers is buttermilk with corn bread crumbled up in it."

"It's good."

"Mr. Thomas Coleman killed a beef, and he brought me a roast, and I cooked it four hours and ate it last Sunday. I was expecting you to come by."

"Well, I couldn't leave the Road, there was so much damage being done on every side."

"It was fresh and tender. Didn't you think it was tender, Hiram?"

"Uh-huh," he grunted.

"And I had gravy and potatoes and made a cherry pie. I have might nigh twenty jugs of cherries sugared and set back, some of them a year and a half old, and they have a brandied taste to them."

"Were they sealed tight?"

"I thought they was, but they must a broke the seals loose."

"They might have fermented. Where are they?"

She brought a jug of them and he removed the cork. He poured out some of the cherries on his plate. The smell of cherry wine came up to his nose. He sniffed and got to chuckling. He tasted a cherry and it was good, so he started eating them, and Hiram got the jug and poured out a major quantity of them. Mrs. Davis watched them eat, pleased that they liked the food. "It made a rich pie, I'll say that for it," she said.

"It's a wonder it didn't vinegar," her son said. It was the first and last comment he made that evening, but he stayed the whole time Tuttle was in the house, and even walked down the turnpike part way with him.

Hiram's brothers and sisters had arranged for him to be at his mother's house, to be certain all went well, so next day he had to report to them. There had been, he said, no talk of marriage or of the sale of land, the two matters which had concerned them most.

The one thing that Hiram couldn't satisfactorily explain was the matter of clothing. He said Mr. Tuttle changed his pants when he arrived and when he left. Hiram was not a discerning fellow, he was not acutely observant, and these bare facts were all he was certain of about the matter.

He received instructions from his brothers and sisters to watch next time to see what the reason might be.

"There's nothing I saw wrong with it," Hiram said. "He done it both times in the woodshed."

In that entire, painful month of March Weatherby didn't visit the Road. At the end of the month, when the epidemic of influenza and pneumonia had about run its course, Cumberland and Tuttle went to Morganton to call on him. Mildred was obviously glad to see them, and she took them to Weatherby, who was seated in the parlor before the fire, reading in the Bible. He closed the book as they came in and welcomed them to the house.

He listened to them report about what had taken place, listening tensely as if waiting to be touched with pain, now and then closing his eyes tightly. "How many were sick in all?" he asked. "Somebody said two boxcars come through, marked on the doors."

"There were over 250 taken sick," Cumberland said.

"And died? How many died—fifty?" He said that hoping it would be enough, that the weight wouldn't need to be heavier than that.

"More than that, I'm afraid," Cumberland said.

"Ah? More? How many more? Sixty?"

"Seventy-eight," Cumberland said.

Weatherby's breathing, which was raspy and deep, was heard for moment, then he said, "Seventy-eight. Of course, there were inadequate facilities to care for them, and no food to help with. No doubt that added to the total. Are others going to die?"

"We hope not," Cumberland said.

"Of course you do, but what is your prediction?"

Cumberland glanced at Tuttle. "There's sixty now in the throes of flu or worse, and some of them will die. We don't know how many yet."

"Say fifteen of them?"

"Weatherby, we don't know."

"Seventy-eight and fifteen, that's ninety-three. Say ninety-three in all before it's run its course. Or will you say an even hundred?"

"I'd rather say ninety-three, if that's what it adds up to. But we might get by well under that."

"A hundred, more or less. Bloody ground, bloody ground. And what of Moses?"

"He never took sick," Tuttle said.

"What about that white man from Durham, name of Soforth?"

"He's dead," Tuttle said.

"Ah my. And what about that little woman that was so fat, that Ruth?"

"She's well of it."

"What about that white man from Durham, name of Tom Burlington, who helped move the locomotive?"

"He got it but recovered," Tuttle said.

"Uh-huh. What about that singer woman, name of Beulah?"

"She's dead," Cumberland said.

"Oh my. My, my. She could sing, too."

So it went, on and on, as Weatherby remembered first one and then another and asked about them, and heard the news, which sometimes fell like a knife piercing into him. Whenever he heard good news, he moved on quickly to the next name he remembered, anxious to use good news to breed more good news if he could. Bad news brought him up short each time, and he would hesitate, not sure he would go on.

Tuttle began talking about the locomotives and how they were being cared for. "Don't worry about them," he said. "You can relieve your mind of them."

Cumberland began talking about the financial and other records, and he said that everything was in sound shape. He talked about the condition of the Road; there had been storm damage, he said, and no way to repair any of it, and no man left to repair it except convicts who couldn't be worked on the Road now. He said Babcock had measured what tunnel work was left at Swannanoa and had figured 220 feet of heading remained to be done, and there was about a mile of track to lay from the new tunnel, which was not finished, to the east portal of the Swannanoa tunnel. "I met with the superintendent of the Road between Salisbury and Old Fort and asked him to finish repairs on Long Bridge."

"Did you? That's not a bad idea," Weatherby said. "What did he tell you?"

"Oh, he had a list of forty items which need repair on his own stretch of line. He says he can't keep running on the old rails, and that he was promised special consideration come the end of March."

"That's so. He's telling the truth. I promised him that."

"Then we'll have to cooperate with him," Cumberland said.

"Wouldn't you think ties would last more than two, three years?" Weatherby said. "They're rotting out in five areas between here and Henry Station. A tie costs twenty cents to buy. Think of that and multiply it by 2,600 to the mile, and then by 90 miles and see what the expense is, and that's only for ties, mind you, not iron, and doesn't include the cost of laying them. Of course, you can cut your own ties, but now you have to pay labor to cut them and you have to buy the wood from landowners. You have no free labor now."

"Not a minute of it," Cumberland said, "Except from Tuttle and Babcock and me."

"And the doctor? Is he paid regularly?"

"Yes, and the Prison Department has two other doctors helping him."

"He's a deceptive fellow. I don't like him personally, and that has been allowed to cloud my judgment of him more than it should. Even so, if he had been Gabriel himself, I wouldn't have stopped work on the Road. We gambled and we lost, but I had to play my own hand out. I smothered, the same as those ninety or a hundred others. You'd be surprised how I've smothered."

Mildred called them to dinner. Weatherby kept his chair and waved them on. "I'll be there directly," he said. They took seats at the round oak table in the dining room and began eating the good food she had made, but Weatherby didn't join them. She went to ask him to come in. They heard her talking with him but couldn't make out what was said; he didn't return to the room with her, though, and she said he felt sick and didn't want to look at food just now.

When they had finished eating they went to the parlor to say good-by to him, but the door was shut. Cumberland asked Mildred if he ought to go in, anyway, and she said she didn't know. He knocked. There was no answer. He knocked again, then opened the door enough to let himself in. He closed the door and stood there with his back to it.

Weatherby was lying on the bed, his eyes closed, the Bible laid on his forehead, held there with one hand, and his lips were moving, as if he were praying.

"We're leaving now," Cumberland said.

Weatherby's lips stopped moving, but there was no reply.

"We'll be going on back to the mountain now," Cumberland said.

"Oh, yes, will ye?" Weatherby said. A while later he said, "You do what you need to do and don't refer to me. My mind is sore. I'm lame in my mind now."

"Yes, sir," Cumberland said. It was as it had been fourteen months before, the time before, Cumberland thought.

"One hundred dead, ye say? And there was already a hundred dead, might nigh." He had his eyes closed, had the Bible resting on his forehead yet. "Say a hundred eighty dead." He lay there, his lips moving, as if seeking other words to add emphasis to what he had said, then he seemed to rest back on the bed, and his hand took the Bible away and held it to his chest, but his eyes remained closed. "You go on away now," he said. "Tell Anna I'm all right, not to listen to any reports to the contrary."

Cumberland glanced back as the door closed and saw the pale-faced man, an old old man lying on the bed still as death.

Next day Cumberland moved his papers into Weatherby's office and started making out another report to the Prison Department. He had found that the records sent earlier to the Road by the Raleigh officials were in error; there were prisoners in the camps who were not listed by the Raleigh office at all, and there were other prisoners' names on the lists who had not been sent to the Road. He did as best he could with it all, and began to confer with the prisoners themselves. He got from them their own full names and tried to find out the names of those who had died.

While talking with them, he asked them if they would like to keep working on the Road, should a way be found to retain them. There were some who would, and many who wouldn't. "I like the flatlands, Mr. Cumbersome," one man said, getting Cumberland's name a bit wrong, but being more accurate than he knew, Cumberland told himself. "I'm a level-water man, Mr. Cumbersome. I don't like rushing streams and height. I don't rest easy unless I rest straight out."

"So you'd rather go down east and build roads?"

"East?"

"To the lowlands?"

"Oh, I'd a heap rather."

The older the convict the more likely it was he wanted to go east. Many of the younger ones, however, preferred the challenge of the mountain Road. "If I ever get free of the chain gang, I'd like to come back up here to work, if they'd let me," one Negro said. "Once you get used to the air and the water, it's a fair place to live."

Moses said he would rather work in the mountains. "It's rock work here, and sand work there." But he said he didn't know where Lola was to be sent.

Cumberland talked with some of the women and made notes on what they preferred, and on the fourth day of April, when he was trying to make a final reckoning with Raleigh, he made out three lists:

First was a list of convict men and women who were well and were ready now to go back to Raleigh; at the bottom of this list he appended the names of those who had already been returned.

Second was a list of those who were in the hospital and would need to stay there until they could be sent to Raleigh.

The third was a list of the dead, and to the bottom of this one he appended the names of sixteen convict men and three convict women who preferred to stay on the Road and who were not being sent back to Raleigh at this time.

He wrote a cover letter, saying that the convicts mentioned on list one were being dispatched in a few days, on April 6, and the convicts on list two would be dispatched by April 15. He said nothing about the convicts on list three at all.

He showed the letter and the lists to Babcock, who read the letter and glanced at the lists, seeing nothing unusual about them. He showed the letter and the lists to Tuttle, who didn't see anything amiss either. He showed the letter and the lists to a clerk at Henry Station, and the clerk said everything seemed to him to be in order. So Cumberland mailed in the report.

Then, before he dispatched the trainload of convicts to Raleigh on April 6, he sent sixteen convict men, one of whom was Moses, and three women, one of whom was Lola, to work at Swannanoa Gap, milling corn. He told HenryAnna to let them sleep on the floor in their cottage and in the smith's forge. They were to keep to themselves, Cumberland said, until he had time to prepare instructions for them.

Next day Dr. Chester, unannounced, visited the Tunnel Station. He went in all the barracks; there was nothing in any of them except torn ticks and blankets. He looked into the boxcars that had been made into women's houses; nobody was there. He went to the mule pen; nobody was left even to feed them. Only then did he come into the office.

He gave Cumberland a report on the patients under his care. There were 53 patients remaining, of whom 9 had pneumonia and 30 had influenza. There hadn't been a new case reported for three days.

"So you can take your patients to Raleigh, as planned, on the fifteenth," Cumberland said.

"Send them there if you will," Chester said. "I have my old job back, working for the railroad in Pennsylvania, and I'll want to go directly there soon."

Cumberland said nothing about that, except to wish him well.

"I suppose you'll be closing up shop here," Chester said.

"Yes, though officially it's up to the Board of Directors in August. They're going to meet," Cumberland said.

"Do you think Weatherby ever could have got this Road open, even if it hadn't been for the diseases?" Chester said.

"I don't know," Cumberland said simply. He was critical of himself for being so civil; he was as conciliatory as Weatherby would be.

"And could he have kept it in repair year by year?" Chester said. "You take that line of track at Henry Station; it's already rusty and decaying from the wet."

"I noticed that."

"And Bloody Cut is impassable, until men spend time cleaning out the fallen rock. And any one of these tunnels can cave in most any day."

"Oh, there's no predicting a thing like that."

"I'll confide in you this much; there are those of us who never were convinced the Road could be built."

Cumberland murmured something about he supposed so, and Chester held out his hand, and Cumberland shook hands with him, smiling at him, much as Weatherby would have, and Cumberland stood there watching him walk ever so proudly, like a fighting bantam rooster, out of the building and toward his Hospital Number One, as he now called the infirmary at Babcock Station.

On the 15th day of April, Dr. Chester left, he and the other doctors and the last of the patients. So all the convicts were gone now except, of course, for the sixteen men and three women who were on the special milling detail. Cumberland wrote the Prison Department, saying he would be pleased "to receive and dutifully execute any further order about financial or personnel matters."

The sixteen men and three women convicts returned to the Tunnel Station. Babcock, Tuttle and Cumberland lived there, too. HenryAnna and her father and brothers were about the only others who ever came to the camp, so twenty-three was now the number of the Road's company.

Whenever he was asked by anybody why nineteen convicts were left, Cumberland said there had been no order to send them along.

He and the men made an inventory of what possessions remained the property of the Road. There were twenty-one large bags of corn and six bags of meal. There were 30 gallon jugs of molasses. There were 40 bushels of potatoes, 2 of onions and 2 of cabbages. There was iron enough to finish the Road. There were 3,000 eight-foot ties and 22 cords of firewood. There was a large supply of liquid nitroglycerin.

"If they don't call for them convicts soon, why don't we use them for something?" Babcock asked. The three women convicts were already doing the cooking for everybody. "We could at least all keep busy," Babcock said.

Tuttle said he and the smith and Tom Burlington could operate one or both of the locomotives. "We might as well keep the Road from slipping on down the mountain," he said.

"You think we could finish the long tunnel?" Cumberland asked.

The suggestion brought both men up short. They both said no. Nobody wanted to go back into the belly of the ground. Cumberland said there was only 220 feet of heading to do. "We have the nitroglycerin on hand. We have a powder man. Moses is a heading man. We have an engine at the west portal. And we'll be blasting so deep underground nobody will know what we're doing in there." He talked gently about it, casually, saying there was no way to get the engines back down to the lowlands, anyway, until Long Bridge was finished, and even then the engine at Swannanoa tunnel couldn't be got down there. He talked about how the supply of ties and iron couldn't be taken away either until Long Bridge was finished. All of this he talked about as if it might happen, not as if it would. It was something to think about.

The other men thought about it and discussed it. They knew it wouldn't happen, any more than anything on the Road had ever happened the way it was planned. They said there were enough crosses now in that graveyard hill above the death camp. Yet they couldn't stop wondering about it, and they sought Cumberland out to ask about it, and patiently he kept wondering with them about the hope that someday the Road would be built. "It's a big challenge to think about," he said.

He said maybe they could all go out to the tunnel to see if they wanted to go back to work in it or not. Spring was coming, he said, and it would be warmer to work out in the open now. Most farmers were plowing their fields; he said maybe the men would want to do something, to do what they did best.

So on the 24th day of April, as matters came about, the men found themselves gathered outside the west portal of the Swannanoa tunnel, from which now a trickle of water flowed from some innard spring. The powder man had spent the previous day mixing mash; he stood there with a pail of mash in his hand, and Cumberland asked him if he wanted a drill team to go back in there with him. The man said he wouldn't mind, and he would need a candle.

When a candle was supplied and lighted, he picked out two caps and a length of fuse, a long length, since he would need to run 800 feet to reach safety before the blast. "You reckon there's snakes in there by now?" he said.

"Nothing in there for snakes to go in there for," Tuttle said.

The powder man led the way inside, three men carrying drills and hammers going with him, and Tuttle and Burlington went to fire the engine. The other men stood around, talking idly, and watching HenryAnna walking across the field toward them.

An hour later they heard the heading men running. The men came outside panting from their run and sank down to rest. A minute later they heard the blast, a grumble which made the earth tremble. The powder man looked up and grinned. "Won't be any snakes in there soon, anyway," he said.

Tuttle and Burlington backed the flats up to the tunnel's mouth and waited, and the men stood around wondering how it would be inside there. Moses, who had been sitting at one side, walked to the tunnel's mouth and looked around for the candle boys. "It's time now," he said.

Penny and Closet pushed the candle cart up to the mouth of the tunnel.

"It's time, don't you know that?" Moses said to them, and he nodded to the other convicts. Some of them said they would walk in and some said they would ride the flats in. Moses walked ahead with the two boys, and he stayed with them for a while, but soon he took a candle and lighted it; cupping it with his hand, he walked on ahead of them, to see what the blast had opened up inside the ground.

CHAPTER TWENTY-NINE

THE "SARVACE" TREES, as the mountain people called them, which Tuttle said was a shadbush, were in bloom at the Tunnel Station. They were always the first blooms seen, and were the first used in the church "sarvaces," as a consequence.

In May magnolias bloomed, and the dogwoods. There was a field of flame azaleas, an orange flower, which HenryAnna called a honeysuckle bush.

It was spring, so the old women mixed tonic for the families. The old women also aired the quilts and coverlets and set about beating the hooked rugs, and the curtains were boiled and were ironed with the smoothing irons that were lined up to heat before the hearth fire.

HenryAnna captured her geese and took them down to her place and tried to pluck them, and she got herself beat by the wings so fierce she swore she would give up all hope of having a feather bed, "unless it was a gift from a stranger."

"We'll get married, now that your geese are here," Cumberland said, laughing gently at her complaints, "if you'll find the preacher you want."

"Later," she said.

"You're waiting for the rhododendron to bloom, are you?" he said. It would bloom in about a month, in June.

There was no hurry to get married, she said.

Every day except Sunday he worked on the Road. He did the office work and he spent perhaps half of each day standing at the west portal. The workers made steady progress, but one afternoon, as Tuttle backed the flatcars into place, the convicts saw water start to gush down; they ran to safety, but they couldn't shout loud enough for Tuttle to hear them over the tunnel-contained sound of the engine. The rock ceiling at this place gave way all in a big tumble, and piled itself into and around the flatcars.

Tuttle, once he realized what had happened, let the throttle out and tried to pull the cars to the tunnel's mouth. By moving forward, then backward, then forward—doing this until the cars were free— he was able to pull them out all right. "Look there," he said, joking about it, trying to hide the scare he had had. "Look how the mountain loaded the cars for us!"

HenryAnna wanted to invite Weatherby to come to see them, so Cumberland wrote the letter for her. She knew little about writing letters herself. They suggested that Weatherby and Mildred spend a weekend or longer with them at the late-June time when rhododendron was in bloom. The letter didn't mention the Road or that work was being done on the Road. Mildred wrote a reply, accepting, and on the last weekend in June, on Saturday evening, Weatherby and Mildred came to Swannanoa Gap on the stage. They arrived in the afternoon, and as they made their way to the house, HenryAnna saw them and ran across the fields, and greeted them, almost bursting with pleasure. It was wonderful to see that he looked so well, she told him—though he had a languid look about his eyes, even yet. They walked back to the house, HenryAnna bubbling along with one idea and then another, pointing out her crops and claiming this was the most beautiful spring she had ever seen and she was more happy than she had ever been.

She fixed supper and Cumberland got out a supply of brandy that her Uncle Charlie had made. There was a burgeoning reunion, a time of gladness which was marred only when Weatherby somewhat abruptly refused Cumberland's request that he walk with him over to the Road. Later, whenever the Road was mentioned, even casually, Weatherby made no effort to conceal his irritation.

His chief interest was in talking with HenryAnna. If she was walking the rows of her garden, he would go there to walk with her; if she was going to the spring, he would go to the spring with her. And on Sunday morning he invited her to come to walk with him.

They walked to the falls and sat near the pool, and she told him about the plans for a house and plantation which she and Cumberland had evolved and refined over the months. It was a most idyllic morning, with late-spring flowers blooming almost everywhere, and she, radiant with beauty, talking the romantic notions she and Cumberland had agreed upon. "Of course," she said finally, "it won't ever be."

The comment was so unexpected that it took Weatherby's breath away. "You're not going to do what you were saying?"

"No, no," she said.

"Are you going to marry him, Anna?"

"No," she said.

"You aren't?"

She smiled in the plaintively sweet way she had. "He's no mountain farmer, and there are no such things as plantations up here. It's only a springtime notion."

"But it's a beautiful one," Weatherby said critically.

"A laurel slick is the prettiest thing in the world, but it traps a person," she said.

He sought some way around the problem, an evasion of it. "What about you, Anna? What's fair to you?"

"I don't want to be thought of as a laurel slick for a man," she said.

"Well, no, but how will you live?"

"I'm not doing this for him, like a person sacrificing herself on an altar in Jerusalem. I've got that little cottage over near the pond."

"Who'll pay the rent?"

"We've paid so much rent now, it's a shame. I was told to try to get four dollars a month rent, so I asked for eight dollars, and he agreed. I never was so surprised in my life as when he pulled out that roll of bills. I never heard of anybody getting what he asked for any time in my life afore, and I almost chewed my tongue in two trying to keep quiet. So I saved six dollars a month of that, myself."

"You mean you saved four dollars a month, don't you?"

"Law, no. I never give Uncle Charlie what he asked for it. I allus figure about half of an asking price is what a man can afford to accept. So I've got rent enough left over, and the place is owned by Uncle Charlie anyway, and he wouldn't evict me unless he was starving."

Weatherby had to smile, for there was something mystical and marvelous about her, and about the way she talked, with each sentence getting more and more somber as she pronounced it, then rising at the close to a minor chant; she almost sang as she talked.

"Since a little girl I've wanted to live in that potter's house, but I never thought I'd get it for my own, and now it's mine, for a few years anyway. It'll do well enough for me. Of course maybe it would continue to do well for him, too. I don't think so, though, for his challenges up here are about gone now, and he comes from way off. He's enamored of this place, just as once he was enamored of a vision of making a road up a mountainside. It was going to be so nice a thing to spend a year or two adoing. But it got bloody and smelly and like life, and it was a trap, like life is a trap."

"Yes, I know it is," he said. "But you're young, and he's young, and you have this vision for yourselves and this spot of—"

"Listen to you," she said, smiling at him.

He stared at her, studying her, wondering if she was strong enough to go her own way. "How long have you known you wouldn't marry him?"

"A month or two I've knowed it, though I've knowed it in my heart from the moment I first met him down on that weeping rock that overlooks the lowlands."

"You've lived with him, knowing you wouldn't marry him?"

"At first I thought I would, but I've grown older inside myself and know he has to be set free and go away to make his way. When he does I know that this place will only be a dream he had once; that's what he'll say to himself. I know he will. And I'd rather have it done now than after years of being married and trying to make everyday into a dream world that it can't be." She was somber and miserable for a brief while, but she suddenly brightened. "I hope there's somebody to take care of him and not let him do much trading, for he allus pays what anybody asks for anything. I recall my cousin come in with curtains for his windows and said she wanted three dollars for them. Why, you coulda bought gold dust for that, but he had his hand dug down in his pocket to get his money and I had to kick him in the shins to keep him from saying yes. I knowed my cousin didn't aim to get more than a dollar for them, so we argued and she agreed to a dollar and a half, and later she give me fifty cents of it."

Weatherby laughed out loud; he couldn't help but laugh at such a marvelously forthright attitude.

"And he paid that potter thirty dollars to repair the kiln, and when the potter wanted to use it for his own baking, he charged him nothing for it, though the potter's own kiln is tumbling down so bad that when he builds a fire the wind blows it out. He woulda paid something, even if only in bowls. I'd like to see him ever get a pot inside that kiln again without talking terms about the use of it. He's not to be trusted far, anyway, for they tell me he has a mirror in his bedroom."

Weatherby tried to figure that out. "I have one in mine, too," he said.

"Not like his'n, one about four feet wide and two feet deep, tilted so he can lie in bed and look into it."

"Well, what's wrong with that?"

"It's claimed he's got it aimed so he can lie there and look at himself when he's with his wife, or so she can look, I don't know which it is. I never heard of anything so vulgar in my life. It's likely to addle his children, those born in such a bed. A child born of them will look exactly like its ugliest parent."

"Oh, you think so, do you?" Weatherby said.

When they went back to the house she cooked dinner for the four of them, making corn bread in the hearth oven, and even as they sat around and ate their dinner, Weatherby couldn't stop looking at her and wondering about her, realizing he had many images in his mind of her—some of them not of her at all, so much as of the little Plover girls he had courted in his youth. HenryAnna was one of those girls, and was as naïve as they; she was also the girl he had seen at the overlook over two years ago, and was the naked girl swimming in the pool who raked her fingernails down the back of the man she now lived with; she was also a mature woman, and it was this image of her that was most appealing to him, and most difficult for him. This morning at the pool she seemed to him to have accepted the roundness and wholeness and goodness and independence of her life, without compromising it or seeking to anchor it to the body of another person.

After dinner he suggested to Cumberland that they go to walk, and as they started out along the path, he sought ways to bring up such personal matters, but Cumberland avoided them. Weatherby didn't feel he could bluntly talk with Cumberland about the confidences HenryAnna had shared with him, so he bided his time, contenting himself with talking in general terms about the individuality of the mountain people, their pride, which was their most striking characteristic. He became so engrossed in talking about this that he was scarcely aware that they were now crossing the field, going away from the pond and toward the turnpike. When they were opposite the west portal of the tunnel, though perhaps a hundred yards away from it, Cumberland interrupted Weatherby's monologue by suddenly commenting that he thought he saw two boys playing around the engine. "Come help me chase them home," he said, hurrying that way.

Weatherby went along to be of whatever help he could.

Cumberland found nobody there at all, but he noticed that there was a bridge timber left awkwardly placed at the portal of the tunnel. He said he would secure it, and he went to do so. When he reached the portal and turned back again he saw that Weatherby was staring most intently, not at him but at the portal itself. He watched as Weatherby moved forward toward the portal, acknowledging no distractions, until he was within fifty feet of it.

"My mind is often drugged with strange thoughts," Weatherby said. "I imagine experiences that never were. I suffer a lack of sharpness between what actually was and what I once believed would be, so that I can't always distinguish." He looked at Cumberland, asking for assurance. "Will you tell me what it is?"

"Do you see it?" Cumberland said.

"I have seen it so often, I— Do I see it?"

"Yes."

Weatherby studied his expression, to be certain there was honesty in it. He turned to look again at the spot of light at the far end of the Swannanoa tunnel, 2,000 feet away. Yes, he saw it clearly; it was there. He tried to suppress his feelings, but abruptly his energy broke free and he took his hat off and threw it on the ground and leaped on it and stomped the earth. "Ay, God, it's headed through! It's headed through! It's headed through!"

Exhausted, he sank down on the ground and stared at the dot of light. "It justifies us all," he said.

They walked around the tunnel to the east portal, neither man speaking, neither suggesting they go through the tunnel itself. They reached the other portal and looked into its dark depths and at the small light in it, away off. Weatherby said, "I can see it beckoning." He was so overcome that he wept.

In a way, it was a weak man weeping, Cumberland thought, and in a way it was a strong man weeping. "You should have been here day before yesterday when it was broken through," he said. He told him about the convicts he was using and how he had got them. "The Raleigh men found out we were blasting. An official came to see, and they found nineteen convicts, so they said to send them back. This was last Tuesday. I said I would, come next Tuesday. They said to send them that day, but I told them we had about broken the heading through and told them what it meant to the men to work in a tunnel and at last to achieve something with their labor. So the official stayed here, too, and he was here Saturday when the powder crew came out of the tunnel. We were using plenty of mash, I assure you. After the blast, when we looked inside, there was no spot of light at all. 'Well, tomorrow,' we said. 'Maybe tomorrow.' And Moses shook his big head, as if to say it wouldn't be tomorrow. Then Tuttle said, 'Is it a piece of light in there?' We looked again and said no. There was dust inside, because of the blast. We stood there watching and nobody spoke. All of us, including the Raleigh man, were grouped there at the west portal. The dust settled and there did seem to be a dim light, a dot of light, like a piece of life out of the dust slowly appearing. I turned and saw some of the men were weeping, and that was when I was sure the light was there."

They walked to the lookout nearby, where they had first surveyed the east portal, and sat at the place they had camped months ago, and Weatherby said he should have known that the Road would be finished. "Once a thing is born, it's the devil's own time to kill it. I've seen grass break a creek rock. Think of that. Plover said death was coming if we continued; he said that failure trapped the good man every time. But what he didn't say is that it's through failures that we make progress. I'm part now of the failure."

"No, no," Cumberland said softly.

"Oh, yes, I know I'm a casualty along the way. I can't even bring myself to ride on a train, Cumberland—think of that, will you? I won't ride one of them, the Road broke me so bad. But look at the light off there at the heading, with nothing remaining except benching and shoring. Look at how you managed to persevere, the idea taking hold in you, and in Tuttle, and in Moses and Babcock, an idea I had years ago when I was young, too. So it lives here yet, even though I'm an outlander now and always will be. I live in you, in you and Anna—"

He stopped abruptly, remembering her and the talk he had had with her. He saw Cumberland look over at him questioningly. "You'll be leaving here soon, I suppose," Weatherby said simply.

Cumberland closed his eyes tightly. When he looked up again, he said, "I love her very much."

"Oh, yes. As a companion. But would you give up everything out there for her?"

"Yes."

"Sacrifice it, would you?"

"Yes."

"Cut yourself off permanently from your work and your class, your kin and others who have your manner?"

"Yes."

"Even if it made a husk of you in ten or twenty years?"

"I would."

"And you think she would love you for that?"

Cumberland came against the steel-like question and he hesitated. "How can I know that?"

"But that's what you have to reckon with."

Cumberland considered it for a while, staring off to the east. "What should I do?" he said.

"If you can ask, then you can go," Weatherby said calmly.

"Should I go?"

"If you can, you should go."

"And how will she live?"

"Oh, my, she'll make do; she asks no pity from you."

When they got back to the turnpike, the afternoon stage was waiting. Weatherby told Mildred to go along home and see after Troy. "I'll stay here till the late stage," he said. He seemed to want her to go and he helped her aboard, not accepting her protestations about leaving him.

"You know you've not been well," she said.

He closed the coach door and reached through the window and touched her face gently. "I'll not be long, Mildred," he said. "I want to say good-by to several friends I didn't know were here."

"Let me stay with you."

"No," he said. "They're convicts, Mildred." He waved the stage on and stood in the turnpike and waved at her, and she at him, until the stage disappeared. "Go along with you two, he said to Henry-Anna and Cumberland. "I'll walk down to the camp and see the men and take the evening stage." He stood, awkward, before them, and suddenly he closed his eyes and murmured something about being all right. Then he smiled, the kindest sort of smile, and said good-by as he turned and went down the turnpike toward the Tunnel Station.

They watched him go. "Is he all right?" Cumberland said.

She took his hand. "Yes," she said. They walked toward their cottage together, and the sun was kind to them and warmed them, and Cumberland said something about planting another few rows of late corn in the garden soon, and she said, yes, that would do well. The geese waddled out to meet them, and she scolded them for being so noisy. She asked Cumberland if he wanted to come swimming with her, "now that the weather is so warm and lifey."

They walked past the store, the mill, the forge, past the fishing place her father had used almost every day before he became a telegraph man and a preacher; they went down the path to the waterfall. "Over there we were going to put the house," he said. "See how the blossoms would have hung around the front of it."

"It would have been as pretty as colored rocks laid in a spring," she said.

She undressed, and so did he, and they splashed down into the cold water. "What if I catch you?" he said.

"Why, I thought that's what you would try to do," she said.

In the lapse of the day they went home to the cottage, and she cooked what was left of a piece of deer meat her Uncle Charlie had brought her. She took all the fat off it, worked it out of the meat, for she said deer fat tasted awful. She put the roast in the oven, with a big blob of butter on top of it and onions around it. Then she went out on the front stoop and sat down, and he came out there, too, and they looked at the pond and the mill wheel, which didn't turn on a Sunday. "We were always going to fire the kiln," he said.

"Yes, I remember."

"We never did get around to it, Anna."

"No. And we were living in a potter's house, too."

It was late afternoon when Weatherby stood at the east portal. "You want me, old woman?" he said. His hand touched the cold stone; it was sweaty and moist, like the palm of his hand. Far off was the light. The hard flesh of the mountain led to it but did not encompass it; the flesh limited it but did not contain it.

He moved into the mouth of the tunnel and stood there, his muscles taut like a tightened rope, his breathing deep. "Old lady," he said, whispering, "you want me?"

He placed his right palm on the rock and ran his fingers over the surface of it, as if touching a face, as if touching Mildred's face. "You've killed me already, old woman," he said.

He had once seen three sprigs of grass break a rock. Isn't it strange it had proved to be so memorable? he thought. There was a strength to life that wouldn't admit to dying, that even as it died wanted to reaffirm itself. In the midst of life death came; why couldn't it be that in the midst of death some life would come? A sprig of life like a sprig of grass, he thought.

He moved a few steps into the tunnel. Around him was the echo, the hollowness of his own breathing, and before him was the distant light, dim now, for the sun was setting.

No, he thought, it doesn't matter now. What does it matter whether you personally are dead completely or dead only in part? You have no work to do here, and the memories of this place will rust your spirit. Walk around by the path; there is light enough to walk around that way to the turnpike. You can find the trail that leads to the stage, and you can go home in time for a night's sleep. Why go this way home? What do you prove by going this way home?

Turn around and let the old woman be.

A step at a time, sweat on his face, he moved into the tunnel.

His palm slipped on the damp rock. His foot stumbled slightly. His eyes were on the ragged bit of light ahead; everything else was black now, even the stream of water that trickled along the floor; he could hear it and the sound magnified itself among his fears and seemed to cascade and roar. "Old woman, old woman," he murmured, his foot touching a piece of rubble on the floor or a snake on the floor, his hand touching a stone on the wall or a snake on the wall, his eyes focused on the light ahead, the failing dot of evening light.

He stopped. Sweat on his face, dripping into his eyes. He stood in an agony of life, his breathing caught in his throat and chest, his hands wet at his sides. He moved forward a step, another step.

He stood there staring at the dot of light until the light was gone, then he turned and stumbled back to the entrance of the tunnel, and went beyond it and slumped down on the trail that led to the turnpike, where the stage had not yet passed.

CHAPTER THIRTY

THE MEN CAME UP Monday from the station to work their last day on the Road. Moses sat down near the west portal, choosing a place in the warm early-morning sun, and waited for the powder man to go inside and lay the charge.

The powder man went inside, but he came out soon and stood awkward at the portal, unsure of himself for some reason. Babcock saw him, and the powder man, who was a white convict from down near Wilmington, said, "There's something in there."

"Oh, hell," Babcock said. "We got no time for such notions as that."

"It's breathing."

"Chase it out," Babcock said.

"There ain't nothing big in there," Tuttle said, "for you can see straight through the tunnel."

Babcock sent the powder man back in there to light the fuse in the benchings, but the man came back a while later and said there was something in there, standing against the wall near the heading hole.

"For God's sake," Babcock said, disgusted with him. He started inside himself, but he saw Cumberland approaching across the field, so he waited for him and told him what the powder man had said. "Here on a day when we got more to do than we can hope to get done!" he said.

There was no reason for a person to be inside there, or an animal either, though it was not impossible that a bear or a big cat had strayed into the tunnel overnight. "Hey, in there!" Cumberland shouted, his voice reverberating and echoing. "You in there!" he shouted, watching the dot of light but seeing no signs of a moving body. "Well, go on and blast," he told the powder man.

"A ghost of something is in there, if not something itself," the powder man said.

"I'll do it," Babcock said. He was anxious not to lose more time. But as he started inside he saw something move in there, he saw the blob of light blotted out for an instant. "Well, I'll be damned," he murmured.

"Hey you, get out," Cumberland shouted, but there was no response and nothing scurried away.

The powder man sat down near the portal, his shoulders trembling. "It breathes heavy; I could hear it breathing."

The other men were gathered around. Behind them the engine was smoking and throbbing, ready to begin work for the day. "We've got benching to do," Babcock said.

"I saw it move again," Cumberland said.

"It breathes heavy," the powder man said.

"Couldn't be a man," Cumberland said.

"It held close to the wall as it moved," the powder man said. "You see it now?"

"Way inside there?" Cumberland said.

"It must be deaf, not to answer."

"Hey, in there!" Cumberland said. "Hey, in there, damn you!"

"Might be a bear," Tuttle said.

"It's a man. I can see him," Babcock said.

"Can't be a man," Tuttle said.

"I can see him," Babcock insisted. "See him, Tuttle?"

"Holding to the wall, yes, I see him," Cumberland said.

"Must be crippled, to move so slow," Tuttle said.

"Crippled like Weatherby was a while ago," Babcock said.

"Holding to the wall," the powder man said.

"Hey in there!" Cumberland called. "Come on out of there!"

"Maybe it's Weatherby," Tuttle said, and there was a long silence.

Cumberland turned to stare at him. "Where is Weatherby?"

"It's not Weatherby," Babcock said. "Weatherby went home."

"That's what I know," Cumberland said.

"Don't yell at him again," Babcock said softly. "No telling who it is."

"It's not Weatherby," Cumberland said, wanting it not to be Weatherby, wanting not to go through the pain of Weatherby making that long walk through the open sinew of Sow Mountain, dimly lighted, moving slowly, his hands against the wet rocks, his hands feeling his way as if he couldn't see the way to walk, holding on as if he had no strength to stand on his own, for every foot he walked was dreaded and full of fire. . . .

"My God, no," Cumberland said softly.

"What say?" Babcock said.

"No, no."

"It's not Weatherby," Babcock said.

"No," Cumberland said.

Four hundred feet. One tortured step along the side of that tunnel at a time. In the dark, blinded by the dark.

"I'll go in there and get him," Moses said.

"Don't," Cumberland said.

"Who is it, do you know?" Moses said.

Babcock said, "It has Weatherby's shoulders. It's the way he was once."

"It's too deep to see who it is," Cumberland said.

Three hundred feet. The men were standing there watching, nobody moving away, watching the tiny sights they could see of the man as he now and then moved toward them, his silhouette breaking the spot of light far off there, until Babcock said suddenly, deeply, hoarsely, whispering to Cumberland, "Tell him to come on out now, for God's sake."

Cumberland shook his head. "Let him be."

"It can't be him," Babcock said.

"Let him be."

Two hundred feet away.

"Can you see the light?" Cumberland called into the tunnel, speaking a word at a time.

The man stopped, stood there listening.

"Can you see the light?" Cumberland called again.

The man stood there listening.

"We're here," Cumberland said.

The man stood deep in the tunnel. For a long while he stood there, and Moses said again he would go get him, but Cumberland said no, not to. "We're here," he called again into the tunnel.

The man moved toward them. Cumberland could see him now, moving toward them, appearing much as the dot of light had appeared, gradually, moving a step at a time, not holding to the side of the tunnel now, moving toward the opening, which must appear strangely large and bright to him now, walking toward where the light was large, larger than the men who stood inside it and the engine behind them. Moving toward them until he was blotting out the light at the far end of the tunnel, moving into the light that blinded him and shone on his shoes and legs and then on his chest and finally on his face, which was tortured and was wet as he came toward them.

"I'll go get him," Moses said, his voice trembling.

"Let him be," Cumberland whispered.

Weatherby stopped at the portal of the tunnel. His mouth was open, as if to cry out, his hands were bloody from where he had gripped the rocks along the way. He touched the side of the tunnel. He whispered some word which nobody could hear, and Cumberland went close to him. "Yes?" he said.

The old, dead-man's eyes focused on him again and Cumberland heard him say: "Your time will come."

In mid-October, as the leaves were changing color on the trees and the farmers were marking on their clay hearths the number of hogs and sheep they would take on the drive, the first train made its way from Henry Station to Swannanoa Gap, Penny riding in the cab with Tuttle and yanking on the bell rope all the way.

The trip was unannounced, but there was a big celebration, anyway, at the end of the day, and any number of telegrams were sent out, so many that Plover expressed the fear that his lines would catch on fire from an overload.

A week later there was a hundred-foot cave-in inside the Swannanoa tunnel, which buried four hired workmen who had been shoring up a weakened place. Moses was brought back from the Raleigh prison to help dig it out, and Babcock and Tuttle left their work at the river, there beyond the Gap community, where they were building a bridge for the Road's westward passage which had been authorized by the Board of Directors.

In November the Road was open again and was dedicated in an impressive ceremony at the place where once had stood the Praying Rock. Cumberland took the train from Chapel Hill and stopped by Morganton, where he found Weatherby in fair spirits but unwilling to go with him to the Road.

At the ceremony were many officials from Raleigh, and there was talk about how the Road had been made by the men who, three years before, had had vision enough to pass the bill in the North Carolina legislature. Reporters made notes on all this and wrote feature stories about the unusual manners and ways of the Appalachian mountain people.

One of the reporters on the way home noticed the graveyard above Babcock Station, and while the train was stopped at the station house, he asked a workman who were buried there. The workman said probably they were bodies of workmen who had died. The reporter saw another railroad man working a small gang in the vale below the cemetery, and he approached him. The man said he worked for the Road, but was a preacher, actually. "I'm constructing a fountain here," he said.

"Where's the water for it?" the reporter asked.

"You see that stream high on the mountain? We'll capture it in a pipe or trough and bring it down here and turn it up into the sky. It's an idea for a memorial passed on to me by a friend who sometimes visits my daughter from the college."

"You're making a fountain as a memorial to whom?"

"To them. To all them," he said, waving his hand at Cemetery Hill. "And to them that lived in the buildings and are gone. To all them. It's to have seven sides, for that's God's number, and on each side we'll put a reference to some action that took place. On this side we'll put the boxcar fire, for it needs to be remembered."

"What was that?"

"And here we'll put Mud Cut. And here we'll put Beulah's name, for she was the best singer of them all. And here we'll put Weatherby, for it was all a dream he had, and here we'll put Long Bridge, for men fought to build it, and here we'll put the Swannanoa, for that recalls the cave-ins and the deaths and the light that finally dawned in the stone."

"But what does all that mean?" the reporter asked, interrupting.

"Mean? Mean? Why, once at this very place I put on the doctor's robes and preached on that. I warned them, didn't I? Oh, you don't know, you don't recall. How can I tell you what it means, when you weren't here while the hammers were ringing? Ay, but I'm going to make this fountain and capture that stream up there and bring it down in a trough or a pipe, I don't know just how, and turn it upward at this very place. It'll be here near the graveyard, and doubtless it'll be here after all the tomb markers fall over, and maybe after the wolves has got what's left of the corpses, for this is a bad mountain for wolves. I'll capture the stream somehow and bring it here and point it upward, and let it go as high as it wants to into the sky."

AUTHOR'S NOTE

Research for *The Road* was done in the North Carolina State Library in Raleigh, the University of North Carolina Library in Chapel Hill, and the Pack Memorial Library in Asheville. I am indebted to all three places for their help. Changes made in incident, terrain and time are of my own doing, for reasons of the story itself, but my commitment has been to make the whole of the story true, even if parts of it and the characters are imagined.

The Road is a companion novel to two published earlier, *The Land Breakers* and *Lion on the Hearth*. The three books form a pattern whose design will be developed from time to time in other writings.

JOHN EHLE

Winston-Salem, N.C.
June 19, 1966

Format by Sidney Feinberg
Set in Linotype Janson
Composed, printed and bound by American Book–Stratford Press, Inc.
HARPER & ROW, PUBLISHERS, INCORPORATED